THE GRAVE RAVEN

THE BOOKS OF CONJURY, VOLUME TWO

KEVAN DALE

KEVAN **DALE** FICTION

INFERNAL VOX

I paused in my work, cringing, shoulders hunched. A moment passed. I opened my eye. No, nothing hurtled across the barn at me—it'd only been a long icicle fallen from the roof to shatter below the window behind me. I relaxed. The week before, one of Mr. Robert Twelves's hammers had flipped end over end from his workbench, the claw embedding into the wall a foot from my head. Just the afternoon before, another (or the same) demon had snapped a broom from its normal resting place as I'd passed it by, bashing me across my shin. The violet bruise still rose a good half inch from the rest of my skin, throbbing in time with my heartbeat. I questioned my fate for the five hundredth time.

We only spent three or four days (and never nights) each week back in Salem, the rest of our time in Andover. Although glamours crisscrossed the workspace, triple-strengthened in some cases, the demonic infestation still found ways around our best efforts.

"I'm the King of the Abyss, and I will devour you."

I glanced one last time at the window, beyond which the

nearby hemlocks wore late winter light, and turned to the source of the raspy voice. Propped in an elegant construction of stained wood and polished brass piping, an armless and legless torso hung in a series of leather straps, the thick neck and squat head of the corpse pinned in place within an iron cradle that surrounded it like the halo of a medieval saint. Behind it, piping extended across a stretch of floor and connected with a bellows compressed and expanded by a flywheel. A metallic squeak cycled every few seconds behind me, accompanying the heaving sound of lifeless lungs. Seated before the squeaking pedal that drove the flywheel was a revenant, pumping the pedal and staring ahead into space. The revenant, in life, had been a heavyset older man, bald on top, with a ring of mousy hair below, and dark circles beneath his black eyes. His considerable jowls jiggled with each press of the pedal. I associated the squeal and clank of the contraption with annoyance.

"Where did you come from?" I asked.

"I will drink your marrow, witch."

The voice came from the body in the device, a rather disturbing collaboration between my master, August Swaine, and Twelves dubbed the *infernal vox expander*. Designed to allow for the interrogation of demons caught in the planar clocks Twelves produced each week, the machinery allowed for a connection between the trapped demon and the corpse. The corpse was magicked to a state nearing—but not quite fully—revenated. The demons' words required breath, thus the bellows powered by the heavyset revenant. The voice emerging from the corpse was somewhere between a dry whisper and two pieces of slate grinding together. It had fallen to me to sit before the infernal vox expander and interrogate the demons, sorting them, and bringing the promising ones to the attention of my master.

Most of them weren't worth his time, say what you will about mine.

"Speak your true name."

A crude approximation of laughter shook the limbless corpse. The eyes remained rolled back into the head and the mouth quivered. "The very sound of it would shatter your ears and ignite every thought in your small mind. You do not understand—"

"Thank you." I leaned forward and blew out the flame on the candle. As a safety mechanism, while the incantation was invoked, a heavily magicked candle was lit that would seal off this new planar channel within one minute, through a series of spells imbued within the wick. I rarely needed a quarter of that time. The mouth of the corpse slackened.

Most demons proclaimed themselves to be the *King of the Abyss* or a *Lord of Hell* or the *Prince of Pain* or the *Queen of Damnation*, as if I might sit up straight, widen my eyes, and recognize what a special moment it was for me. They were sometimes more specific than that, coming from realms or planes with names that contained more consonants than vowels, and likely interspersed with strange apostrophes: *A'rrynithichre Yllongma* or *Thakathrullych Ta'imposhthrega* or some similar nonsense that sounded like someone trying to clear something thick from their throat.

Furthermore, I may tell you with great confidence that no demon took kindly to being questioned by a witch. Oh, the threats and promises. I needn't bore you with the specifics, but I'll say I've had every part of my body—from the ghastly to the inappropriate to the comical—singled out for chewing, clawing, gnashing, tearing, breaking, grinding, flaying, scorching, shredding, filling, filing, bruising, gouging, pounding, rending, stabbing, bursting, and a few more I shan't mention out of decency.

I pointed to the revenant at the bellows. "Stop." I rubbed my temples, each squeak of the pedal having made my headache worse. I stood and disconnected the planar clock and put it in the "not worth pursuing" stack. Swaine had hinted at plans for even those lesser entities, though he'd not elaborated. I looked over the remaining stack of devices. Now that we had our own clockmaker, we were working around the clock—I appreciated the irony. I selected another planar clock. I knew the incantation so well that if flowed out as one long phrase. As I lit the wick of the candle and spoke the final words, the light from the window dimmed. A fall of dust spiraled from the loft above.

Before I commanded the revenant to pump the bellow, the corpse within the vox expander trembled, then shook, then careened forward, taking the entire framework of the device with it.

"Wonderful," I said. The same thing had happened the week prior, leaving me guessing why. No feral demon ought to touch the contraption. The demon being questioned was still—in theory—safely within the planar clock, yet some combination of entities or planar instability was at play.

Ever since Swaine and I had passed into the demonmere, such puzzling incidents had plagued us.

As I heaved the jig back up to its proper place—the body was still weighty despite the missing limbs, forcing me to grab the back of its collar, my fingers brushing the cold skin—I glanced at the face. The eyes rolled forward. I'd seen them jiggle before, or flit about, but never anything such as that. The effect was disquieting, as they appeared to be watching me. Satisfying myself it was stable again, I returned to my seat and motioned to the revenant by the bellows.

"Begin." He leaned forward and pumped the foot pedal, starting the bellows to wheeze. *Squeak, squeak, squeak.* The sound of hissing air and hollow breathing followed. I didn't like the sensation that washed over me—a nervousness, a heightened awareness. The eyes of the corpse followed me and continued to stare. I allowed my witchcraft to rise around me for protection.

"Where did you come from?" I said.

The corpse stared at me. I repeated my question. The pedal

squeaked, the bellows heaved, the breath from the corpse wheezed. A look of terror twisted the corpse's face.

"Help me, help me, help me." The voice shifted into a timbre I hadn't heard before. "I see you—help, I beg you." The torso shook as though trying to break free.

"Where did you come from?" I repeated.

"It's me—Clara. God, please help me. I apologize for all I ever did to you, Miss Finch. Just help me. Get me out!"

I straightened. Clara?

I remained wary. In the first place, I was dealing with a demon. Lies, guile, and more lies.

In the second, since the lady Rattlesnake had disappeared into the demonmere after the death of General John Whitelocke, neither Swaine nor I had found as much of a hint of that strange realm since we'd fled it at the beginning of the winter, despite our best efforts. We'd searched every inch of the house in Andover. Nothing. As much of Salem as we'd dared. Also, nothing. All signs had vanished. The demonmere had eluded us, for reasons unknown. Swaine thought of little else, leading to more searches and even more elaborate experiments, enough to fill a good portion of every week. Only my master could spend days lost in the most dire peril only to brush aside the fear and consume himself with getting back to it.

I'd promised Francis that I'd try to rescue Clara (despite my less-than-admiring opinion of her), so my efforts with Swaine—and on my own—had been sincere.

I glanced over my shoulder toward the barn door. No one was near, Swaine and Twelves off testing yet another device designed to locate the demonmere.

I turned back to the corpse. "What did you say?"

Even with such a simple question, I veered from the script Swaine insisted upon. The deceit of demons demanded a fixed discipline of communication, even under the relative safety involved with the infernal vox expander and the various protections around it.

Tears spilled from the dull eyes of the corpse. "Can you get me out? Please don't let this be nothing."

"Where are you?"

"Hell. But I see you in this mirror. You're—it's a barn. Benches. You're wearing a blue dress. Black eye patch." The words spilled out.

She was correct. Was she seeing me? I inhaled, reminding myself: the *demon* could see me. It wasn't Clara, merely a trick.

The corpse's eyes blinked away the tears. "They said Hell was a fiery pit. It's not. It's room, after room, after room, after room. Bridges. Courtyards. Hallways that go on forever. Tiny doors. Windows that open out into dead worlds. Twists and turns and trapdoors. Teakettles. Music boxes. Footsteps. Forever. And it never changes. And time doesn't pass—only it does. Sometimes day. Sometimes night. Pass through one door, and you can see both at the same time."

A chagrined smile crossed the corpse's mouth. "At first—well. At first, I thought you'd put a spell on me. Dragged me off with magic. Because I'd pointed the gun at you—and we—you, or both of us—didn't trust each other. It seems so—so *petty* now, and I'm sorry for it. So deeply sorry. Down and down I was dragged, deeper and deeper, bruising me, cracking my ribs down stairs. And when I stopped, I was afraid. I don't think I moved for half an hour. Just lay there. Shaking. The soldier—well, he went farther. I heard him calling out. Moving around. I think he wandered off. I never saw him again. Though I thought I heard terrible screaming once. Later—but I'm not sure how much later."

"Where?"

"Not the house. It took time to realize. It wasn't the house any longer. I was somewhere else. Somewhere terrible. Alone—

except for strange footsteps I heard in the distance. Doors closing. Things dropping. Smashing. Shadows. Laughter. Crying. But never anyone else, just me." The eyes closed, then opened again, pitiful sadness and terror in them. "Then I thought: Clara, you've died. That horrible one-eyed wench killed you. And this is Hell. For all I'd done. Murder, especially. Murder a murderer and you're still a murderer, I decided. Or realized. I prayed. I prayed all day. All night. All I did was a prayer. None of it seemed to work. Or matter. So I moved, worrying more and more that I'm already—"

The magicked candle flared and then extinguished itself, one minute having passed. The planar channel shut, and the corpse went limp. I sat there staring at the doughy face, my limbs tingling with shock. Had I heard it correctly? I had. Behind me, the pedal for the bellows scraped and screeched its metal whine. I bent and picked up the tinderbox next to the magicked candle. After taking a moment to center myself, I again spoke the words of the incantation and lit the candle. A faint tremor passed underfoot and the beams and boards overhead groaned. Again, the light from outside appeared to grow muted for a moment. I walked around to the front of the vox expander and found the corpse staring at me.

"—dead," it said, as though not noticing the interruption. "But then I kept going. Because I said Clara, look—maybe it's not Hell. Maybe it's—something else. A test of the Lord. Do your time in it, keep moving, find a way out. Maybe it ends. Maybe it ends. Sins paid in full and then leave."

As the corpse spoke, my mind whirled, trying to see how a demon might have known about Clara, trying to make any sense out of it. I couldn't.

"But I doubted, again and again. Fearing it will go on forever and ever and ever. I still have my soul, but Judgment has been written on it. Ink that never leaves. Just like me, I thought—I'll never leave this Hell. I ran. I crawled. I hid. I circled back. And still the shadows followed me. Always following. Tormenting. But I smelled the air, just now—or, just hours ago. Fresh air. I followed it. Up. Taking stairs, hundreds of them. In a tower. And now I'm in a room, here at the top. Books and books and books. Out the windows on all sides, I see trees. Dawn. And this mirror flared with a beautiful light when I saw you. Have I paid the price of murder? And all else? Do I still have my soul? Please—say yes, Miss Finch. Please say I still have it—it's all I've ever had."

"What else do you see?"

"Nothing. Books. Trees. Don't make me go down those stairs again. I can't. Please—please—*please*—get me out. Get me out and I'll never do anything wrong, ever again. I promise on my soul."

"How do I know it's you?" I said.

The wail that burst from the corpse's lips went straight to my heart. "It's *me*. Who else would it be? I pointed a gun at you. You cast a spell on me. Francis, you set his clothes afire. Willie and Alfred—them, as well. You snuck us into the ball at the governor's, with magic. Help me, please—I'm begging. Get me out. It's been days."

"Days?" The bulk of winter had passed since she'd vanished. "That's not possible."

"Everything is possible in Hell. But surely you caaaaaaaaaah-hhh..." The words dissolved into a long vowel that sent a shiver across my skin. The corpse's eyes closed, the mouth went slack. I glanced at the candle, but it was still lit. When I looked back at the corpse, its eyes had opened again, the irises rolled back into the head. It spoke. "Did you enjoy her pleading, witch?"

The voice filled more than just the corpse's mouth; I also sensed it in the corners of the room, flitting about in the shadows.

"Where is she?" I said.

"Come and find her."

"How?"

"You know—all you need to do is look." The corpse smacked its pale lips in a fashion that repulsed me. It closed its mouth and appeared to choke, a glottal growl coming from its throat. After a moment it opened its mouth and stuck out its dead tongue, discolored and splotchy. A ring sat upon it. The corpse flicked its tongue, and the ring fell, bouncing off the lower bar of the infernal vox expander and landing on the floor with a delicate *clink*. "Have a key, won't you?"

"You're a liar," I said. I shouldn't have, especially as I felt anger rise inside me. It wasn't a way to talk to a demon—they lied. That's all they ever did.

"She's all alone."

"Liar."

"Say it again and I'll shove her down a score of stairs."

"Liar."

"One hundred stairs, witch."

I spared a glance at the ring. "What's your true name, demon?"

"Katherine Gertrude Finch," the corpse whispered, a smile wriggling its lips. It licked the air.

"You're not getting out of there, you know." I shouldn't have said anything, but fear, anger, and confusion rattled my poise. "We have you."

"In. Out. It's a thoughtless way to think. Planes are nothing. I'm everywhere. All your little friends. All your little family. Delicious—until I get what I'm after."

With that, the temperature plummeted in the barn and I saw my breath bloom out in a rolling steam. Something moved in the corner of my eye and I flinched, jerking forward. A handful of finger-long nails from a pail next to one of Twelves's benches slammed into the wooden beam behind me. The inside of the glamoured circle lit up with brilliant sparks. I went to blow out the candle, terrified that the demon was strong enough to manipulate objects beyond the protective glamour. The candle flame reared up, a snapping tongue of fire a foot long. I pulled back.

The corpse winked at me. "I get what I'm promised. Sorcerers. Witches. I devour them all. I've already had one. I have my eye on another, the sinister one. We must see what's left. And after that, you. I'll sing you soft lullabies below your window as though the glass wasn't even there. I know a beautiful song."

Before I could say another ill-considered word, the candle puffed out, a thin strand of smoke rising from the glowing tip of the wick. No further sounds came from the corpse, whose jaw dropped and whose eyes rolled back behind the lids. The atmosphere shifted, but left behind the unmistakable wake of a powerful demon. Next to me, the revenant continued to pump the bellows. I raised my hand without looking. "Stop."

The barn fell silent as the last of the air wheezed out of the corpse with a final hiss. I reached out my senses, making sure that no sign of the presence remained. Out of an abundance of care, I stepped into one of the glamoured stations and spoke the Twenty-Seventh Ward from Hume's *Srávobhiśśravasíyas*, a potent defense against the most subtle of planar currents, a ward that had taken months of daily practice to master. Thin lines of deepest indigo extended out from my hands and traced the contours of beam, post, board, bench, device, revenant, corpse, ring, up and across like the whorled lines of finger-prints. After a few moments, the light faded, indicating that the glamours held, and the barn was safe. A slight nausea from the planar energies that had occupied the glamoured circle gripped me.

I approached the device, searching the floor. The ring shone dully against the packed earth. I made no move to touch it for several moments. Uncertain, I reached to Twelves's workbench and grabbed a thin rasp by the maple handle. Kneeling by the ring, I poked it with the rasp, flipping it over. With a gasp, I saw the engraved *W* on its face—John Whitelocke's ring, which I'd seen twice before. Once on his hand, just before he was killed, and once in the demonmere. Or so it appeared.

From outside, I heard Swaine's voice. Not knowing what else to do, I slipped the ring from the rasp and dropped it into the pocket of my work dress. The metal was frigid to the touch. I lunged forward into the glamoured circle and retrieved the planar clock, yanking out the chains that connected it to the vox expander. With the length of the rasp, I scraped a coarse groove into the narrow end of the planar clock and replaced the tool. Hurrying back to the stack of planar clocks not worth pursuing, I lifted several from the stack and slid the now-marked planar clock into place.

Swaine and Twelves approached the barn, the gravel in the lane in front crunching beneath their shoes. I looked about the barn for any signs that might betray what I'd just heard and done. I forced myself to relax, and only at that moment realized that I still had my witchcraft up—I'd done it with nary a thought. I lowered it, the energy releasing back into my body.

Swaine entered the barn, followed by Twelves. My master looked at me. "Ah, Finch. Any luck?"

I brushed a stray lock of hair behind my ear and shook my head. "No, sir. Nothing worth your time."

"One sometimes wonders what all the fuss was about," Swaine said. He was already fishing around with his left hand in one of his pockets for what appeared to be a note. A shard of flying glass had sliced open the back of his right hand the week before, the bandaging still bulky. "Too many mackerel, not enough sharks."

"As you say, sir." I made sure not to so much as glance at the scratched planar clock just a foot from his elbow. "And you, sir? Anything?"

"Our intrepid Mr. Twelves here is on the verge of a breakthrough, aren't you, Mr. Twelves?"

Twelves nodded. He carried a pair of what looked to be

lanterns, each of which held complex gearing behind the glass. Lifting the glass from one lantern, he looked over the mechanism within. "I might be. Breakthrough being closer to *I have a thought*."

"Thoughts are breakthroughs waiting to take flight, Mr. Twelves."

"I've had plenty plop to the floor. Dead birds, sir. Still—if I can get these to synchronize. And add a third, also synchronized. We may be onto something."

"Triangulation," Swaine said. "Of course."

"But they're detecting the subtle planar readings?" I said.

Swaine pulled a piece of paper out and unfolded it with a snap. He handed it to me. "Indeed. You may start logging them. I'd like a bigger map. Something with pins corresponding to the readings. Coded by color, something reasonable. For a start."

"Yes, sir," I said, taking the paper and looking it over. Swaine's scrawl had become a second language, of sorts; one which I'd grown adept at decoding. The page was filled with numbers arranged in rough columns. Still, I mostly thought about the cold ring in my pocket. *Have a key, won't you?*

"We'll need more glassware," Swaine continued. He removed his coat and hung it on a peg by his bench. "I trust Mr. Keefe's work has proven acceptable, Mr. Twelves?"

"Fair enough. Maybe I'm more judgmental since he stopped speaking with me. But it'll do," Twelves said.

"One mustn't let one's emotions color the clarity of observation or analysis." Swaine pulled out a journal and scratched further notes. "A self-imposed disadvantage."

Twelves and I exchanged a quick glance, having both seen Swaine declare a small error to be nothing short of an epic blunder with all the storm-height rage of Lear, or slam a book shut with the declaration that no one with more than half a wit would seek an answer in a book, all when under the shadow of his more volcanic moods. I smiled.

"You have a comment, Finch?" Swaine said, continuing to write.

"Of course not, sir. I shall endeavor to keep my emotions at bay whenever possible."

Swaine sniffed. "Indeed. So might we all. Now that we've had our fun, onward. Work never waits."

I looked back at the stack of planar clocks.

Everything is possible in Hell.

A CRUEL TASKMASTER

Springtime in Boston. One is hard put to capture the delight that courses through the spirit when the sweet, soft air mingles with the first touch of the sun. On such days, a vital part of one's own awareness, a part gone dark for the winter months, stirs again to life. Thoughts grow crisp. Confidence sharper, as though encouraged by the new green of buds on the towering oaks that border the grazing commons or the slender shoots rising between cobblestones. Turned earth. Sweetspire, juniper, savin—such scents beguiled. Colors shine brighter, washed clear of the stains of winter and the slush and mud. Yet for me, it became a cruel reminder that while I walked in the warming sunshine, Clara was at that moment lost within the sunless depths of the demonmere.

Boston, at least, showed no signs of the demons that had turned Salem and, to a lesser extent, our house in Andover into something of a war zone. I encountered no tales of the infernal. In my errands for Swaine, I stopped by various taverns and inns, listening for talk of spirits, quietly asking after such tales as though it were a mere fascination. Owners and patrons seemed happy to indulge the curiosity of a young woman, though most of the tales were of the traditional variety, nothing that raised any suspicions that the increase in demonic activity we'd seen in Salem was spreading much farther.

As I neared the corner on Ann Street, I slowed. In the third-floor window of the narrow brick house across from me, a lantern burned—the signal. I crossed over to the narrow gap between that house and the wrought-iron fence that separated it from its neighbor. I didn't knock on the servants' door, but pushed it open and stepped inside. The house belonged to one Elsbeth Brewer, a spinster great-aunt of Mary Whitelocke. Elsbeth had been born in that house, and had lived each of her ninety-three years under its roof, never having married, nor even been courted, to hear Mary tell it. The dark rooms, while neat and ordered, held a peculiar mustiness—of old furnishings, old dresses, decades of meals for one, cramped cabinets that held who knew what. Even the dust smelled old.

As I passed through the dim kitchen to the stairs that ran to the second story, I hoped for more from this secret tryst than I'd seen on earlier occasions—and yet I found the prospect unlikely. I reminded myself that my satisfaction wasn't the focus. A sigh escaped me as I turned up one landing, then another. At the top, the door to the western bedroom stood open.

"Don't tell me that even on such a fine day as this, there's somewhere else you'd rather be, Miss Finch," came the voice from within. I put a smile on my face before stepping into the room. Mary Whitelocke reclined on the faded settee by the window, immaculate as usual. She wore a dress of deep blue silk that danced with the light coming in through the window. It had an immodest neckline in the Parisian style that showed the crest of her bosom. Her skin was flawless, her hair tumbled free over her slender shoulders. Below her hem, she crossed her bare ankles.

"Of course not, Mary." I reached to unclasp the light riding cape I wore.

"Stop. Turn around—all the way. Let's take a look at you."

Still smiling, I performed a quick twirl. Mary nodded.

"Didn't I tell you? Mr. Goodman is a wunderkind. Have you ever experienced such tailoring?" She sat up, running her hands along her waist, smoothing her dress. "It's as though he sees the form beneath with an unearthly precision. And still he's never misplaced a finger, or a glance, nor displayed either the infatuation or the lust so common to young men. This is one of his." She stood and showed me her dress, circling around much more elegantly than I had.

"It's lovely."

"I should hope so—my father paid a small fortune for it." She sauntered over to the table that extended out from the corner beneath another set of windows. Three silver coins lay on the varnished wood.

"You've been practicing?" I said.

"Not as much as I'd like."

"I see."

"Now, now—don't say it like that. One moment my day is firmly in hand, a dandelion. Then, puff—it flies off in all directions, leaving me chasing after each delightful little parasol."

I tried to imagine what Swaine would say if I ever made such an answer when asked about my studies. I gave Mary a soft tut. She glanced at me.

"I know. I'm terrible," she said. "And it's so—difficult."

I took my cape off and hung it over the back of a dark-stained cherry chair. "There's no secret, only—"

"Only practice, yes," she finished for me. "A clever little retort I very much feel to be a lie."

"It's no lie."

"Oh, but it is. It implies that there's no secret at all, which there very much is."

"Which practice will reveal."

"Yes, but if the secret could be communicated to begin with, all that practice wouldn't be necessary, now would it?"

"If magic were that easy, then everyone would do it, wouldn't they?"

"Easy for you to say—you're a witch, darling."

Whatever else Mary Whitelocke was, she was no fool. When the witch-pole outside the governor's manse had pushed back the winter dark with its silvery light on the night of John Whitelocke's murder—minutes after I'd excused myself from her presence—she'd guessed at the truth, confronting me with it during our first lesson. She'd found my denials insufferable, an affront to our newly minted alliance, and—knowing she had enough of my secrets to see me jailed—I relented, extracting yet further promises from her to never as much as hint at the word *witch* anywhere near my name or presence. She'd agreed with a quick, disarming smile. If the existence of a witch in the colony troubled her in any way, she didn't show it. As far as I could tell, she saw little distinction between magicians and witches; a difference in style, perhaps, akin to the fashions of Paris versus those of London. I didn't attempt to correct her misunderstanding—trusting instead that her lack of curiosity on the matter would somehow protect me.

"You promised not to use that word," I scolded.

"It's just the two of us." When I didn't lower my stare, she raised her hands. "Fine. My mistake. Still—you have quite an advantage, don't you?"

"Magic can be done by anyone with enough determination. Take comfort in that. You're a determined woman." To teach Mary Whitelocke rudimentary magic was somewhat less practical than dressing up dogs in frocks and shoes. Still, whatever she lacked in discipline toward her studies, Mary Whitelocke had the will of a terrier, and a nose for sniffing out the truth.

"Let's see how far you've gotten," I suggested.

"Not very far, I'm afraid. They bobble about. Mocking me."

"That's a start."

"A poor one."

"Not at all. Think back three months ago. You'd have been amazed."

She swatted me with one hand. "Enough of your logic. You're making me feel silly."

I thought her silly indeed, but held my tongue. What frustrated me was that she possessed a keen mind, which was the foundation of the unseen arts. It wasn't as though she couldn't grasp what I explained. No, the problem, at base, was that she was lazy. She resisted the truth that the proper development of magical skills required extreme diligence of effort, hours and hours and hours—hundreds of hours, thousands of them, tens of thousands—of practicing the basics before any glimmer of true understanding would develop. Mistakes weren't the enemy. Frustration wasn't a reason to give up. Hard work wasn't an unfortunate side effect of poor instruction or ill-thought planning. No, those were the fires within which progress was forged.

What Mary Whitelocke wanted—or expected—was for me to put a wand in her hand, and for magic to flow forth with the ease of imagination. As simple and as satisfying as buying a new dress. Skip the difficult parts, straight to the mastery. Well, that was fine, but it wasn't how it worked. Still, I didn't want her discouragement to tempt her to give up—with her on my side, possibilities for access in Boston remained. Were she to discard me, like one of her drifting dandelion parasols, I wasn't sure my secrets would remain secret for long.

"You remember the phrases?" I said.

"Of course."

"Then let's see."

"I thought we were going to work on the candle? I brought some."

"Let's do this first."

She narrowed her eyes. "You are a cruel taskmaster."

"I'm only here to help."

"Fine. As you say." She let out a dramatic sigh and twisted the signet ring off her finger as I'd advised when first showing her magic. Designed by Doctor Rush to protect the families of the colony's governors, the rings would counter most subtle magic. She left the ring on the settee.

"Did your brother John have one of those?" I said.

"For all the good it did him. If only it could have stopped a bullet."

"Was he—was he buried with it?"

"Why is that the most interesting thing about his interment?"

"Sorry?"

"Father harangued poor Doctor Rush on that very topic. The doctor himself had the household servants search, re-search, and search again the entirety of the manse for John's ring. I believe the old gentleman himself crawled into every corner of the cellar looking for it. The discussion devolved into raised voices. I hardly saw what the fuss was about—one would assume the ring had outlived its usefulness in any event. Why, darling?"

"No reason. The thought just crossed my mind seeing your ring." I cleared my throat. "Now—proper focus."

"Exactly how practical is magic if every time you want to use it, you must close your eyes, draw your attention down to your breath, and stand there like a statue for a full minute or more?"

"Once you get better at it, you don't."

"I don't believe you."

I turned to the trio of coins and lifted my hand toward them. They rose above the table by a foot and rotated clockwise. I had them spiral to the table, settling down with soft clinks.

"That's not fair at all," Mary said. "You didn't even say the words."

"Phrases. And I've practiced."

"I'm quite sure there's a secret to it. Just give me a hint."

"I just did."

"Obstinate." She closed her eyes and slowed her breathing. I swear that if she applied half the effort she spent complaining about practicing to practicing, she'd have already been able to do respectable magic. Still, everyone's mind is a different landscape. I was at least impressed that she didn't blurt out the incantation as she'd been wont to earlier. I felt her energy shift. That was progress. After more than a minute, she lifted both hands and held them above the coins.

"*Surgere, surgere de terra. Deficient in vinculis, et chorum mihi,*" she whispered.

A pulse of magic sputtered into the space between us. It wasn't strong—nor focused—but it was something. The coins shifted along the grain of the wood.

"Stay relaxed," I whispered.

"*Sicut stellas roto, te iubeo,*" she finished. One coin stood up on its thin side and the other two rattled. Besides being a simple incantation—though two months ought to have been more than enough time to master it, given I'd done so in less than a week— I'd chosen that magic for its property of connection. Some spells were a bomb: the incantation lights the fuse. Others, including the one that Mary was casting, were active: the effect required the sustained energies of the magician, as a puppet on strings. To experience the active flow of magic was instructive—or could be, if one wasn't used to shortcuts in every facet of life.

"Sense the lift," I said. "Rivers of energy flowing from your palms, gathering beneath the coins. Lifting."

"I'm trying."

"Relax more."

To her credit, she held her tongue, and dropped her shoulders. The two trembling coins rose onto their ends. I found that interesting. Mary shifted her stance. "Why aren't they floating?"

"They're doing something. Say the final phrases again."

She frowned. "*Sicut stellas roto, te iubeo.*" All three coins lifted into the air, vibrating. "It's working, they're—"

The coins dropped to the table, free of the magic.

"You broke your focus," I said.

"But you saw. They lifted, right up. I did it. I could feel it."

"Remember that feeling."

She looked at her palms, wonderment on her face, then up at me. "I want to try a candle."

"You've memorized the incantation?"

"*Ignis iussu—*"

I held up my hand. "Not until we're ready."

"Oh. Of course. Wouldn't want to set your dress on fire."

"Let's try the candle first."

"Brilliant."

I gathered up one of the thick candles she'd brought along and placed it on the far end of the table. "Distance will help you narrow the effects, and should help."

Mary straightened out her dress and moved her hair back over her shoulder. Her mild success with the coins had given her a boost. That said, I was dubious that the fire spell would work properly, so I'd put the candle far away, to lessen the chance she might accidentally set her—or my—dress on fire. To go from a simple levitation to a fire conjuring was a leap, but she'd harangued me for months, and I thought there was at least a small chance she might have made enough progress to try it.

"Now," I said. "This requires not just concentration, but visualization."

Mary nodded, raising her hand toward the candle.

"Feel it," I said. "The heat. It's all around you, like a burning stream—and you need to dip your mind into it."

Mary nodded again.

"Now picture the fire," I continued. "The heart of it. How it flutters and grabs. Its appetite. Heat that wants to burn up everything it touches. Hunger. Once you speak the incantation, throw it out—throw it forward. Through the center of your palms, straight to the wick."

For a few moments, Mary was still. She spoke. "*Ignis iussu meo fecerit, hoc est ad vitam fumigans.*"

The air in front of us shifted and grew warm. Mary leaned forward as though wanting to close the gap. Orange points of light appeared on her palms. After several long moments, the wick remained unlit.

"Almost," I said. I was half-tempted to give the incantation help of my own, to have a flame spring to life on the candle—but, no. Magic was an inner art, and if it couldn't be mastered as such, there was no point. She was doing something, however. I allowed my own sensitivities to extend outward to the current of her magic, as unstable and floppy as it was.

"There," she said.

I glanced at the candle, wondering if she'd sensed my own subtle magic, and then stepped back as a coil of blue flames erupted in the air before me with a whoosh. The fire darted about in zigs and zags, skirting along the surface of the table, climbing the front of the candle. Several licks of flame danced before my face, forcing me to step back. I raised my hands and recited the words to the most effective extinguishing incantations I knew. The air pressure in the room shifted, curtains, bedspreads, and the skirts of our dresses billowing out for half a moment as the flames snuffed. More of them bloomed before me, wisps and curls in blue and yellow. I twisted my hand downward and swept it up in a graceful arc. A freezing wind fell from the ceiling and the flames vanished. An acrid scent filled the room.

Mary stepped back, waving her hands. "Hot."

"Hold still," I said.

"What's happening?" Her voice rose.

"Mary—hold still." I used the sharp tone of my master and stepped toward her. I took both of her hands in mine. "*Swylt þrowade nihtgerimes.*" With that, I blew a cool breath over her fingers. After a moment of panic, I felt her fingers relax, and her chest shuddered. When I was certain that the magic dissipated, I rubbed her hands and then let them go.

"Was that supposed to happen?" she said. She examined her hands. I noticed that the porcelain skin of her face had gone a shade more pale.

"Not quite," I said. I let out my awareness and walked around the room.

"Great-Aunt Elsbeth would forgive me a lot—though possibly not burning down the family house."

"We're fine. Now."

She turned. "But I had it. The fire."

"Of course you did."

"Let me try it again."

"Once is enough."

"But it was amazing. I could cast it all day."

I searched the corners of the room for stray magic or flames. "Actually, you couldn't. Spells come with a cost."

"Since when has a cost slowed me down?"

"It's not in money. The source of the magic—the energy—is tricky. It comes from the energies of the boundaries between planes. Each instance of a spell increasingly limits access to those energies due to the ripples it causes. More casting, more ripples, less energy to be drawn upon."

There was some evidence that the dynamic differed for witches, to which Swaine attributed, among other things, my precocious facility with all he'd shown me. I glanced at Mary and saw she was barely listening. Her enthusiasm for magic was good —her temperament bad. She could barely focus for more than a few minutes, it seemed.

"Perhaps you should show me some water magic, just in case."

"Water magic is more difficult."

"A poor arrangement. Still, I did it. That's something."

"It is. But I think...that more practice is in order."

She tossed her hair back. "In other words, don't get too carried away with myself." She looked pleased, nonetheless.

No stray magic remained—and no other entity lay quiet in any of the corners, or just on the other side of the nearest planes, a problem that bedeviled my and my master's work of late. I turned to her. "Yes. Exactly."

Downstairs, Mary peppered me with questions as to why Swaine hadn't been to call on her, despite her invitations for him to go with her to any of the various plays, concerts, waxworks, and puppet shows she prowled. I'd urged him, more than once, to at least write to her, if not arrange for a visit. But, no. Everything revolved around the sorcerium and the preparations for Salem. For his masterwork. Fair enough, I understood that as well as anybody—but because he hadn't made the simplest efforts to explain away his absence from the social circles of Boston, I was left cleaning up after him. Again.

"Trust me," I told her, "when he's deep in his book, all else falls away. I'm lucky if I can keep him fed and in fresh clothing."

"Well, do let him know I shall brook no excuse for him not to attend my recital on the last Sunday of the month. Everyone of influence shall be there. I will sing Pergolesi's aria *Lieto Cosi Tal Volta*,' the 'imprisoned nightingale' from his opera *Adriano*. Men will weep. Maybe I'll even add a fiery flourish of magic to the ending. It would wake up Doctor Rush, who nods off after four bars of any music that doesn't involve him clanging away on the spinet."

"If you promise never to suggest such a thing again, I'll promise that my master will be there."

Mary laughed. "You don't care to show off your best student?"

"I'm thinking of the safety of everyone of influence in Boston."

She pulled a light shawl over her dress, a pale lilac fringed in fine silk tassels. "So August is writing a book on sorcery, then?"

"He hasn't shown it to me."

She made sure that her hair was neat. "It has to be. Or magic."

"Not necessarily. It may very well be a book about books."

"Books on magic."

"I'm sure Doctor Rush wouldn't take kindly to such an endeavor."

"Doctor Rush? Darling, I've seen more magic come out of my own hands. He's grown irritable. Tired. Shrinking stride. Worse, the poor man is positively harried by my father. Ever since John was murdered, everything is about killing those rebellious Rattlesnakes. Hunt them down. Round them up. Search every shadow. Father is losing his mind. The man barely sleeps, and still Doctor Rush offers little beyond making it all worse for him."

"Worse?"

"To be fair, he's made a few gestures. Efforts. Honestly, they seem to take everything out of the old gentleman. Still, what advice he offered my father wasn't particularly well received."

"Such as?"

"Such as that we ought to move out of the governor's manse."

"Move out?"

"The good doctor has never been happy with various governors living there," Mary said. "It's haunted, you know. Or so he claims. Has been since the original Doctor Rush's time."

"Fletcher."

"Pardon?"

"Archibald Fletcher. The first Doctor of Magickal Sciences."

She waved her hand at me. "I'm sure it was something like that. I've never noticed anything more than horrible draughts near every window and hearth. I suspect it all to be no more than rumors passed down among the servants. Guards. That said, Doctor Rush has poked around in the cellar once a fortnight since John's murder, which does nothing to soothe my father. Of course, it occurred to me that if it hadn't been haunted before, it would be now, what with John's ghost roaming the place. I doubt I'll ever work up the nerve to set foot in that cellar again. Father won't hear of moving, of course. It would look weak."

Mention of the scene of John Whitelocke's murder shoved thoughts of Clara once again to the forefront of my mind. The image of the wall giving way and her dragged off into the demonmere remained vivid. I put a hand to my chin. "Can I see it?"

Mary straightened out her sleeves. "See what?"

"The cellar."

She shivered with a grimace. "Whatever for?"

Because it was the one place I'd seen the demonmere that hadn't been checked since Swaine and I had escaped and all other entrances had vanished. "I can tell you if there's any real danger," I said.

"If my father won't listen to his unhappy Doctor of Magickal Sciences, I find it hard to believe he'll listen to you, darling."

"No—but he'd listen to you. You're always saying that we women need to stick together, that we need to prove ourselves the equal or better of the men of this colony. What better way to do it than by allowing your father some peace. Information he can trust, delivered by you. Surely that's worth something?"

She smiled. "You've been listening, after all. See? We can teach each other. I think it's brilliant, and I shall absolutely put it at the top of my list. I promise."

"Should I worry that your list is yet another dandelion, ready to puff apart?"

"Now, now. My obligations have a way of sorting themselves. In time. When next we meet, I'll have a delightful cover story in place and we can get you in there without worry of too much gossip, too many eyes. And in the meantime, do tell August that if he continues his silence, I will have no other choice but to see it as a snub which I shall take quite personally." She set a silken hat on her head, angling it so, clearly not putting much more thought into my request. My hopes faded. "Good Lord, you would think food, drink, and dance are toil to that man."

To my master, they were. I smiled. "I'll do my best, but you know how he gets when deep in a project."

"Even groundhogs and bears and whatever else that hibernate the winter away eventually crawl from their dens into the sunshine."

"Perhaps I'll use another metaphor."

"Or some magic."

"Let's hope it doesn't come to that."

I curtseyed. She smiled and slipped out the servants' door. Like so many other of Mary's declarations, I didn't put too much faith in her commitment to get me down into the cellar of the governor's manse. If she couldn't, I'd have to find some other way to get in there; I could think of no other lead in discovering how I might rescue Clara. And, as Mary told me so often, we women needed to stick together, even if one of those women had pointed a pistol at the head of the other. However unpleasant she'd been to me, no one deserved her fate. I was determined to help her.

I waited for another quarter of an hour before leaving. Once back outside, a warm gust drew at my skirts as I followed the trodden alley until I came out on Ann Street, between the workshop of a plate maker on one side, a wine merchant on the other. The wooden sign reading *John Abbot, Fine Wine Imports* creaked on the breeze. Union Street ran wide coming out of Dock Square, filled with midday traffic on foot and in dray, on horseback and within four-wheeled open carriages. Off across Boston, a single bell tolled, followed a heartbeat later by another, both announcing the half hour past noon. Men in hats and waistcoats passed by, the wool scarfs and greatcoats of winter stored away until next fall. Women wore bonnets and light dresses, their hair hidden. Workers in vest and shirt, boot and breech, laborers and servants in varying degrees of homespun or hand-me-down, all alive in the warmth.

I passed beneath a weathered witch-pole. It remained unlit. As for my confidence around witch-poles, I'd had a breakthrough in January while practicing a small version of a glamour known as a *springfire*, often used as a trap of sorts, sending a fast-crawling silver fire over anyone who might pass over it, one that sought flesh. A proper version could be fatal, but I was working on a cricket-sized instantiation that would deliver only a painful snap of heat. As I'd run my palm over the tiny springfire, feeling the sharp pinch of the glamour as my skin passed over the boundaries, my mind had drifted into a curious state where I'd no longer felt the pain. From that, I'd discovered that I could indeed hide my nature from detection. Did any of the Bostonians I passed on that fine spring day have any idea that an infernal witch walked among them? I very much doubted so, and I allowed myself a smile.

Still, no matter how lovely the day had become, I admitted that I had no further cause to linger in Boston. I soon had the wagon loaded with supplies: fresh bread enough to last for the week; two tins of tea; parsnips, rutabaga, and more winter root vegetables; fresh cod, for making a stew; two armfuls of lumber and a bucket of penny nails requested by Mr. Twelves; a case of beeswax candles; three books for Swaine; a wooden box shipped from Paris that contained the femurs, humeri, and finger bones from several murderers. As I guided the wagon along a busy stretch of road that passed alongside a row of dogwood trees perfuming the air with their white blooms, I decided there ought to be a better collective noun for murderers—a *gallow* of murderers? A *throttle* of murderers? A *hang* of murderers?

The day only grew more lovely as I rode back to Andover, keeping my worries at bay with such questions.

3

—————

THE SORCEROUS MIND

Chores were a break from my studies, studies a break from my chores, and sleep a break from all of it. Any moment that wasn't one of those three was a rare moment indeed. A daydream, staring out the window—perhaps twice each week. A song hummed softly to myself—maybe less. Laying this or that dress sent by Mary Whitelocke across my front, examining the image in the mirror—hardly ever. Yet I was doing the latter the next morning during one of those fleeting moments between responsibilities. I'd practiced my wards, taken notes on my reading, and spent an hour frustrating myself with a glamour designed to enchant silver filings into forming a perfect circle (I could get a portion of an arc to emerge from the spill of filings, and no more). Before I set about my late morning chores, I took the opportunity to see if any of my dresses might create the effect on me that Mary's had had on her the day before.

I remained unconvinced.

Bertram Nagle might stammer and flush if I were to wear any of the dresses in his presence—but he would likely do the same if I wore my plainest frock. Swaine would mock me, if he noticed at all. Twelves, handsome enough in his own way, seemed more interested in tools and ale than in the fairer sex. (Since joining us, he'd learned the rigors of being in the service of August Swaine. There were a few bumps along the road as he discovered our master's extravagant ideas of what a workday should entail. After a fortnight or two of oversleeping, talking too frequently of taking breaks or of going to town for an ale or two, he'd learned, rather the hard way, the frequent thunderous moods of Swaine. I was convinced he was going to flee during the dark of night, never to be heard from again. For my part, I offered him a different perspective on working for Swaine: yes, the peculiar moods needed navigating, the work was demanding, sleep was always insufficient, plans might change in an instant, excuses weren't much tolerated, all true. On the other hand: endless innovation fueled by the finest in resources, freedom and the authority to decide the course of work within Swaine's generous boundaries, the chance to work alongside a man whose genius was as infectious as it was indisputable. And besides, I'd not so subtly implied, if a young lass such as myself could keep up with it, he ought to have no issues.)

I turned in the mirror, admiring how the cut of the dress framed my throat. No, Twelves looked at me as one might a sibling.

Of course, I might flit through any number of stand-ins before my thoughts inevitably landed on Francis Knox, as though convincing myself that by putting him far down on the list he was actually far down on the list. He wasn't, though I grew angry every time I realized it. So as I stood there, wondering if the green silk of the dress could ever make me as incandescent as Mary, I found myself wondering, not for the first time, where Francis had gone. And wondering about his location was, in truth, little more than an excuse to wonder if he ever wondered about me as I often wondered about him.

I shook my head and hung the dress over the edge of the mirror. Ridiculous. Trouble, peril, betrayal—Francis was the undisputed source of the most shameful of my problems. As far as I could tell, he'd thought no more of me than it took to decide how to best use me. I straightened the front of my house dress and went to the door of my room, thinking that if I might somehow find the demonmere and Clara, immediately asking her if Francis had ever talked about me might also be in poor form.

Stepping into the hallway, I paused for a moment. The Andover house had become quite respectable, thanks largely to my efforts. Swept, ordered, neatened—and I managed to keep it so in the face of the whirling chaos that surrounded my master in every sphere except his work. Any disruption leaped out at me. Beneath the door opposite mine poked a clump of soil, no larger than a finger joint. I fetched the straw broom tucked by the landing at the top of the stairs and went to sweep it up. When I opened the door, it bumped into something on the other side, only swinging in a few inches. I pushed. I had to lean my shoulder into the door to get it open.

With a gasp, I saw Mrs. Turnbull sprawled across the floor of Swaine's bedchamber.

A robust woman of middling age in life, she was my master's best revenant, and one of only three we'd brought with us to the Andover house. The circumstances surrounding her death and later retrieval by Mr. Preston weren't passed along to us, yet she'd been in decent enough condition, all things considered. She'd displayed both a fine and gross motor function that made her far and away the most competent revenant of the ever-growing lot, able to stitch a tear in a shirt, able to retrieve a book by the title alone, and able to serve tea without spilling a drop, for example. Swaine had begun referring to her as Mrs. Turnbull, for apparently she bore a comforting resemblance to the governess Swaine had been raised by. I found it strange he'd name a revenant with what appeared to be a name of affection.

We kept two other revenants in Andover. The second was the

corpse of a slender gentleman who'd come in deep in the winter, his misfortune to have choked to death on a large chunk of stew beef, but to have been otherwise fit. The ground having been too frozen to dig a proper grave until the spring thaw, he'd been interred in an unstable crypt whose roof had collapsed under several feet of ice and snow, thus preserving his corpse. Swaine referred to him somewhat uncleverly as Mr. Winters. The third, the young woman whose presence consistently annoyed me, had proven adept at keeping the mice who inhabited the cellar at bay, and Swaine had overruled my objections to bringing her along.

Why those three should stand out was a mystery. Some revenations were more effective than others: the corpse was in a fitter state; the demon in question more pliable; the incantations more concentrated and better delivered; the materials purer; the magic used in preparations more potent. Perhaps it involved a better day of the year, a better hour of the day, a better planar alignment of the subtle energies. Or a fortuitous combination of all such influences. Even my master couldn't predict the precise outcome, admitting once that one could never perform the same revenation twice, with a nod to Heraclitus's observation about rivers, and stepping into them.

As I pushed into Swaine's dim bedchamber, I spotted glimmering hints of magic falling like embers over Mrs. Turnbull. I readied a ward, but nothing happened. She lay on her back. The soil I'd seen came from her shoe, as we kept the revenants in the cellar when not needed. The revenant's eyes stared at me.

"Toadstool," she said.

A moment later, she rose into the air, lifted on unseen magic. Her neck craned back, her arms and legs dangled. Before I could do more than step back, the corpse floated to the ceiling, rotated counterclockwise, and dropped to the floor with a cracking thud.

"Finch?" Swaine called up from his study below, his voice muffled by the walls and ceiling. "What was that?"

Mrs. Turnbull lay motionless, her eyes closed. I neither sensed nor saw magic.

"Sir—you'd best come see," I called out the open door. "In your room."

As I heard Swaine's steps head toward the stairs, I glanced around the room, finding it in its typical disarray. My gaze landed on the table Swaine kept beside his bed. The *Occultatum Ostium* sat like an overturned gravestone. Since our venture into the demonmere, my master kept it under lock and glamour in a cabinet in his study, for the most part. Not that he'd lessened the time he spent with it—if anything, his obsession had deepened. As for me, my wariness of the tome was implacable.

Next to the book rested notes, a few scratches and corrections apparently made by Swaine at the shores of exhaustion the night before. The quill he'd used had fallen from the inkwell during the night, leaving drops on the topmost piece of paper. I shook my head; I had to help him rest more. He was too tired—four hours of sleep one night, maybe five the next, his days too busy.

"You might restrict your acrobatics to the outside," he said as he came up the stairs.

"It wasn't me, sir. It's Mrs. Turnbull."

He took in the scene quickly. Kneeling by the revenant, he muttered a spell, his eyes narrowing. After a moment, he ran a hand across his mouth and glanced up at me. "The demon is gone. Shorn away. Did you see anything?"

"Magic, sir—or an energy of some kind."

"No figure? No presence?"

"No, sir. Nothing." I described what I'd seen and heard.

Swaine stood when I mentioned the word *toadstool*. He stared at the corpse.

"Does that mean something, sir?"

"I should like to hope not, Finch." His gaze flicked to the *Occultatum Ostium* and back. "But I don't like it."

"Sir?"

"*Toadstool.* My father called me that, and it wasn't a term of endearment."

He'd never told me a word about his childhood in the time I'd been in his service. "Your father?"

He investigated the room, hands extended, eyeing the corners. "The man was an absolute thunderstorm of anger—and I so often found myself caught in it. Yelling. Backhanded blows. Pulling my hair. Do you know he kicked me so hard once that my hip wrenched and I couldn't walk for several days? I bore a painful limp for the rest of that year. I was no older than five or six. A dreadful man."

"I'm—I'm sorry, sir."

"Yes, well—I've chosen to leave such memories behind me. I harbor no nostalgia for a moment of my childhood." He went to the window. "There's nothing here. No signs of the infernal."

"I'm sure you deserved none of it," I offered. "The abuse. From your father. Sir."

"Kind of you to say so, Finch," he said. He turned. "But I suppose that we all confront the chaotic unfairness of life at some point. A universe of which overwhelming swaths remain immune to even the strongest applications of will, or wish."

"But you were a child."

"Yes. Some confront it sooner than others." He rubbed his chin. "Did you notice anything odd before you found her?"

"Nothing more than usual, sir." I didn't mention I'd been looking at dresses in the mirror, of course. As for what had become usual since our escape from the demonmere at the start of the winter, we'd both experienced a fair share of curious incidents. Vivid and peculiar dreams. Spells going sideways on occasion. Small charges seeming to follow us around, rearranging small items on tabletops, separating pairs of shoes from one another, knocking over coatracks, chairs, opening drawers. "Might it be connected to the book, sir?"

"In what way?"

"The magic I saw. In Gilbert's account of the Baron of Beynac, he noted several references to the *ghostly glimmer* that appeared near the book itself—only seen by the light of a full moon. He theorized that this pointed to the possibility that the book emanated a harmonic response. Shadows of the fourth and fifth order, his postulate being that these were the connections that allowed the book access to such planar energies as to allow its unexpected movements. Fifth order shadows being linked to what Koeffler referred to as the *Great Hidden Passage*."

Swaine retrieved the book from his bed table. "I didn't know you'd read Gilbert."

"Only his *Chthonian Scourge*, sir."

"Half of which is rubbish."

"Well, he certainly seemed to enjoy folklore, sir. Maybe too much. But he'd mentioned the book, so I was curious."

"It might be best not to sleep with it so close, in any event."

"Does it, sir?"

"Does it what?"

"Demonstrate a harmonic response?"

"It's possible." He stepped over Mrs. Turnbull and headed to the stairs.

I followed him from the room. "You've never tested it, sir?"

"I have not."

"There are ways. Koeffler's *Tap*, for instance." The tap was a technique devised by the magician Gustav Koeffler to probe beyond the present dimensions as a means of assessing the intensity of planar currents in a specific region. We walked to the stairs.

"Might as well chase an ant around with an axe. Far too powerful for the job at hand," Swaine said. His boots were loud on the stairs. "And that's forgetting that I don't have more work than the days might accommodate even were they to sprout another dozen hours each. No, Finch. This book is a tool. A gift.

Not a relic to be probed, prodded, and stuck under glass somewhere."

"But if it's somehow disrupting the planar barriers—"

"A leap, Finch."

"Gilbert suggested that—"

"Gilbert thought hobgoblins stalked the unlucky thirteenth child. So, no. Once we have the sorcerium built, there will be time anon for investigating such fancies. Until then, the book shall slumber in its proper place."

"Could it—or anything else—pass unbidden through a weakened barrier?"

"Such as?"

I thought of General Whitelocke's ring, now hidden away beneath a loose floorboard in my room. "I don't know—an object? A relic?"

"Are you suggesting the book came through a channel between the planes? Thoughtfully wrapped in paper and twine?"

"No, sir. I was—just curious if such a thing could happen."

"The planes and the rocky shores where they meet are everchanging, dynamic, and complex beyond reckoning. I wouldn't discount anything."

"And Mrs. Turnbull, sir?"

"I supposed we'll have to drag her out of my room. Bury her after dark. It's a pity we couldn't pay Mr. Preston to sneak her *into* a graveyard for us."

"He might."

"Don't give me any ideas." At the bottom of the stairs, he turned to his study. "For now, however, I think we'd best give you a demon."

"A—what? A demon?"

"It may be nothing more than chance that my revenant was abandoned by its demon in or near your presence—the house isn't large, after all—but there may be something to it." He put the *Occultatum Ostium* into the glamoured cabinet in the corner of his study and locked the door after he closed it, slipping the key into his vest pocket. "I ought to have thought of it sooner, to be honest."

I followed Swaine out the door, across the yard, and into the workshop in the barn. "Am I to—summon one, sir?"

"One day. But I think a bit more than eight months of study is called for before one attempts the highest expression of unseen arts, don't you? The answer is yes. That said, with my guidance—and decade worth of experience—we might give you a minor demon to control. Something of a watchdog, if you will, capable of alerting you with more precision as to the proximity of stray demons."

"I already can, sir."

"As a witch, yes. But as a sorcerer? It's different—and that difference might be quite useful to us both." He searched through the supplies on his bench and on the shelves along the wall, gathering an armful of materials. "More than simply giving you the ability to instruct a revenant, this will allow for a relatively benign communication of wills. Aside from the practical considerations, it will afford you an opportunity to experience firsthand the feel of a demon. If I'd had such training early on, it would have shaved years off my learning. Rather clever of me to think of in the first place." He swept aside a number of brass crucibles, flints, candle stubs, and glass beakers from the table in the corner. The strong stench of sulfur hung in the air. "Nothing like the lingering malodor of an experiment gone wrong."

"Was it the one with the adamantine spar, sir?" A rare form of *corundum*, the mineral had taken months to procure, having originated in the far reaches of the King's Empire. It had cost a small fortune.

"My ideas for the titrimetry proved overly complicated, I'm afraid. All that effort for a trail that petered out to nothing." He put the new ingredients down in the cleared space and stoked a small iron stove to life. "But not every investigation succeeds, and not every intuition bears fruit. Guesswork, hard work, and rework, Finch. All the while plagued by doubt, frustration, and fatigue—this is the truth of sorcery." The flame growing, he straightened and wiped his hands together. "For every success or flash of brilliance, many long nights will be spent burning away expensive ingredients. Bah."

He selected several instruments. "Let's hope you develop a better feel for the alchemical branch of the art than I. It's never come as naturally as summoning, or spell casting. And there's never enough time to master it. If only a lifetime might extend to five hundred years, or a thousand, so that one might give the proper consideration due to all the things worth studying and learning. To mastering."

"I can't imagine having any better luck at it than you, sir." It was false modesty on my part—I'd shown a knack for it. In fact, I suspected that my witch nature allowed me to intuit the tempo and subtle proportions of such alchemical procedures rather well.

"Bear in mind that if you don't become a better sorcerer than me, then I shall have failed as a mentor."

"Better? I never thought of it that way, sir."

"Well, let's not get ahead of ourselves. You're not there yet." Swaine rolled up his sleeves.

"Will this work with me being a witch, sir?"

"We're about to find out." He fetched a book from a shelf by the corner. "Moreover, giving you influence over a demon may aid us in locating another entrance into the demonmere. Another set of eyes, if you will. The longer I consider it, the more convinced I am the demonmere holds the key to my work. Funny, that. For years, I dismissed mention of it as a curiosity, a fringe theory. But if in fact it's not simply leftover energies occupying a peculiar interstitial space, it may be the very thing that connects the planes, the waystation through which all demons must pass. As such, it teems with potent energies. Pressed on by innumerable planes. The heart of the universe. Being effected by magic as it is, it must be inextricable from the generation of magic, the source of it. So I would say it's worth finding, wouldn't you?"

The thought horrified me, considering we'd both nearly perished in the demonmere. "Well, yes."

"That's the spirit." He slid a folded sheet of paper out from where it nestled inside a small book and opened it. "I've selected a demon that has a rather well-documented history. Desiderius Holbein wrote of summoning the fiend in 1523, having followed a trail of older mentions dating back to the twelfth century. I suspect it to be the same demon once mentioned by Witiges, the sorcerer who served Anicius Manlius Severinus Boëthius in Rome. I've encountered no more recent indications of activity, and so suspect that Holbein was the last."

The idea filled me with a sense of unease. It was one thing to have grown used to working around various demons, named and unnamed, tamed and untamed, all the while protected by layers of glamour and watched over by the age's greatest sorcerer himself. It was another to forge a bond with a demon. To bend it to my will.

Swaine looked up at me. "Of course, we will proceed only if you're willing. You're my assistant, not my servant."

"No, I will, sir," I said. "I'm honored."

He put the paper on the bench. "Excellent. We'll be using Heinrich Knutzen's *Verstricken* protocol to bind the demon into a ring. You are familiar?"

"No, sir."

Swaine sorted the materials, readying them. "Knutzen is widely regarded as the father of German sorcery. Seventeenth century. He modernized the older strains of the art with an emphasis on precision, documentation, and clarity. Tragically, he was executed at the behest of a Prince-Bishop—Dornheim, I think it was—after being imprisoned and tortured in the notorious *Malefizhaus* of Bamberg during the violent waves of witch-hunting that plagued the region in the early 1630s. The *witch-house*. Such foolishness."

I helped Swaine ready the various elements. A tarnished silver ring from a small box of unmagicked rings. Three dark candles, the wax imbued with dried ox blood. A vial of silver dust. A vial of ground azure. A raven feather. A glamoured nub of chalk. Coins that had rested on the eyelids of dead men, one for beneath each candle. Three scraps of magicked parchment. A quill, and a bottle of warded ink with which to inscribe the demon's name for the burnings.

"His method of ensnarement—the *Verstricken* protocol—is designed to imprison a demon within an object, most often a ring or a jewel. The demon will remain thereafter within the item, only to be released at the beck of the sorcerer. In this case, the demon shall be under your thrall, even though I'm the one summoning and binding it. At the precise moment, I'll have you recite an incantation that will give you the control over the demon." He looked through the various papers he'd assembled and slid one over to me. It contained a long incantation. I read through it several times, keeping my gaze light on the words, as was prudent with a powerful incantation. It was of a form I was familiar with and committing it to memory wasn't difficult.

Swaine took up a quill and wrote out the name of the demon in his scrawling script on three small pieces of paper: *Inverres-sayte*. I took the papers, reading over the name silently.

"The proper state for your awareness," he said, "should be focused into what I refer to as the *sorcerous* mind: observant, nonjudgmental, supple, and fluid. The practice is designed to enhance this shift, nudging the mind into concentration. Each step, each ingredient has a role to play. The summation of them drives the mind to a heightened awareness, ready to tangle with a demon."

Swaine ignited a circle of protection with the silver, the candles, the azure. Inside it lay the ring, vibrating with the preparatory magic. He finished the proper chalk glyphs that ran along the outside of the circle.

The flames of the three candles wavered. On the workbench sat the three scraps of paper with the demon's name. I took them in hand, careful not to smudge the writing. My palms were slick.

"You're ready?" Swaine said.

I relaxed my shoulders. "I am, sir."

He stepped to the summoning circle. "I shall begin the summoning. When I signal to you, speak the demon's name, and burn the paper. Repeat it two more times, using the other scraps of paper. Then, recite the incantation."

What he didn't say was *And if anything goes wrong, I'm right here, so don't worry.* That wasn't how sorcery worked.

After a few minutes of Swaine bowing his head and not moving, he began the incantation. As the words took flight into the channels created within the glamoured circle, I felt a chill as the air in front of us straddled the boundary, half in one world, half in another. The sensation stole my breath. Not only did sorcery touch the unseen, sense it, reach out to it as though it were every bit as tangible as the walls that held the ceiling up, but it seemed to shift my ability to concentrate, as though I might hold more than one thought at a time, see from more than one perspective.

As the summoning grew in strength, I felt the energy before us shift, crackling and snapping, as a church steeple just before a strike of lightning. The vibrations coursed through my skin. After another ten minutes, Swaine reached the crux of the summoning, raising both palms at the edge of the circle and reciting: "*Reiþ goþr Grana gvllmiþlandi, þars fostri minn fletiom styrþi. Einn þotti hann þar ollom betria í verþvngo. Hvartki knatti hond yfir annat átta nottom occart leggia.*"

And the demon arrived.

The true appearance of a demon is never only one thing. When they enter this world, they stay within their plane of origin, and the physical shape they evoke is but a projection cast from one plane to another. My first impression was of movement in a poorly lit environ, a presence obscured by swaying shadows.

A demon summoned from the hidden planes was often disoriented for a short time, pulled into this world with no warning. That was when a demon was most dangerous, as many react with a thrashing fury, arching, lashing, chomping, and clawing. Many demons possessed potent natural defenses—massive expulsions of foul magic, bursts of electricity fatal to a human, poisons that might fill the air with a fine mist capable of blinding, choking, or paralyzing. Others lunged at the summoner, seeking a crack in the summoner's will or concentration, hoping to possess the sorcerer before a binding occurred.

Inverressayte knew better. A demon once bound before is wary. While they might be surprised, it wasn't the first time they'd been drawn into the world, and they recognized the danger. They knew the game that was afoot, and would do all they could to wriggle free, to prevent the invisible tethers from clamping them with more finality than steel shackles. At that moment, it became a contest: Swaine's will, and the demon's. My master held the advantage. The magic was his, the opening to the channels in his hands. The only leverage that the demon still possessed was that the binding itself was tricky, and required Swaine's full concentration—which he was unlikely to get, as demons had unending techniques for distraction, for feint, for deception, for intimidation.

As Swaine circled the glamoured region of the floor, Inverressayte followed his progress, turning, revealing its true form in shifting glimpses. Within the warping darkness, I made out the demon's features. A slender form emerged that looked like melting wax, covered with boils and welts. At its top loomed openings I took for eyes, pitiless obsidian hollows that filled me with dread. Three long appendages waved, many jointed and thin, while at the bottom, more spread out in serpentine roots, moving. Thin curtains of deep red crosshatching surrounded it, glowing and fading in a fine brocade burning to embers, which I took to be a planar membrane or cloak—an aspect of the demon that held no counterpart in this world.

As Swaine made his assessment, Inverressayte hurled itself at him, crashing against the potent magic of the glamour and glyphs. Pressure ran along my arms and torso as the glamour strained. The demon flailed and howled and battered itself within the confines of the circle, each time looking and attacking the barrier. Shoots of bright light ran along the column of magic as the planar energy collided with it. It wasn't unheard of for a demon—particularly one bound multiple times—to react to a new summoning with extraordinary violence.

Swaine held his ground. He turned to me and nodded.

I held out the first scrap of parchment, then lowered it to the first candle and spoke the demon's name: "*Inverressayte.*" The written name glowed like molten gold and then flames erupted around the edges and consumed it. I released it and watched the curling embers drop into the circle. I repeated the naming and the burning with the second scrap, and finally with the third. As I spoke the demon's name the third time, the air around my outstretched hand grew so cold as to burn. I watched as lines of frost crawled along my skin. Flames devoured the scrap.

I raised a hand and spoke the first of the binding incantations. "*Duguð eal aras wolde blondenfeax beddes neosan, gamela Inverressayte,*" I began. The demon slunk back as far from me as possible. As I spoke the words, a connection between my awareness and the demon's opened—a most curious, frightful, and exhilarating sensation. Experiencing a demon's thoughts is unsettling when first among them is the unrestrained desire to kill you, and that's what I got from Inverressayte. "*Ða com beorht scacan,*" I finished.

The demon went still, its strange eyes fixed on me.

You're the one they want. How curious. The words sounded in my head as an insistent whisper. Inverressayte's words. I found the effect disorienting.

"Silence," I commanded.

But no wonder—with such ravishing blood.

I balked for a moment before starting the second verse. During that pause, Inverressayte shifted, and I felt him straining at the first binding. I noticed Swaine's attention, off to the side of where I stood—his eyes had shifted. Raising my other hand, I began the second, more powerful, incantation.

"*Scima ofer sceadwa. Scaþan onetton—*"

I can stop them, of course. I'd be pleased to stop them. I'm sure they can be reasonable—and if not, I can be perfectly persuasive.

"*—wæron æþelingas eft to leodum—*"

There's no need to go any further with this nonsense. I've no quarrel with witches. Certainly not a witch with such beguiling power, something I haven't seen in ages and ages. This is all a terrible misunderstanding. All I wish is to be left alone.

"*—feorran hæle farenne. Wolde feor þanon—*"

Please, I beg you. Let me talk with them. Convince them to leave you be. You leave me be, I'll get them to leave you be.

"*—Cuma collenferhð ceoles Inverressayte.*"

No—they'll kill us both!

I ignored the shouts of the demon that clattered around in my skull. I needed to finish the binding. The words wanted to rush out in a wild, panicked tumble; I slowed them to maximize their potency. "*Gumena dryhten, Inverressayte. Oððe fyres feng, Inverressayte. Manigum dryhtguma, Inverressayte.*"

The howl of frustration that filled my head also filled the barn, and from the corner of my eye I saw Swaine straighten up, facing the glamoured circle. He couldn't hear the words of Inverressayte, only I could. My hand trembled, and I fought to bring my concentration back to the proper focus. The demon went berserk—spinning, whirling, slamming itself against the barriers that contained it, shuddering, and vibrating back and forth so fast as to confuse my eye. Inside my head, it tugged, twisted, and pulled at the tethers—and then it slithered forward, looking to overpower my will.

"Back, Inverressayte," I ordered, but he was so wild that the frantic thrashing grew worse. The candle flames shook, and the floor shuddered. Papers slipped from the table. I stepped forward, raising both my arms. "*Freonda findan, feorcyþðe beoð. Selran gesohte þæm þe him selfa deah. Hild heorugrimme, strang eaferan, Inverressayte.*"

The moment the last syllable of the demon's name passed my lips, the most peculiar stillness descended and hung poised, two forces in perfect balance. With the smallest of mental gestures, I leaned forward, and tipped the balance. The ring in the center of the glamour flared with a brilliant gleam as it rose a foot into the air. It fell back to the floor, bouncing and tinkling before coming to a rest and dimming.

The ring held Inverressayte, and he was mine.

Swaine, no surprise, was sparing in his praise. After a perfunctory *Well done*, he catalogued in perfect detail the flaws in my technique: my tempo had been uneven; my pronunciation barely worthy; my admonitions to the demon lacked vigor; the gestures could have been smoother; the ring rose too high, it could have rolled out of the circle; I'd been too tense, overall.

"Still," he continued, straightening the items on his table, "it could have gone worse."

"High praise, sir."

"Now, now. We all have to start somewhere."

I smoothed the front of my dress. My limbs still tingled from the magic and planar energy. "There's so much happening, all at once. That was the hard part, sir."

"Yes, it's sorcery, that's always the hard part. That will never change. If you're looking for something easy, best look some-where else."

He wanted to tamp down my enthusiasm, but I wasn't having any of it. "But it was also—amazing, sir. That moment, just at the end. It was like being in four places. Having two minds. Balancing half a dozen thoughts. I still feel—well, incredible."

Swaine nodded. "It's an accomplishment like nothing else, Finch. Little else can clarify the mind like touching the consciousness of a demon and living to tell the tale."

He checked me over for any signs of possession. The powder flared blue, showing no signs of a demon about my person. He brushed the remnants of powder from his hands.

"And now, sir?"

"And now you keep your demon with you. For now, only when you're in the house, and even then only for an hour a day to begin with," he said. "See what it senses. If my thinking is correct, it may give us insight into anything untoward being drawn by your presence."

I dismantled the glamour, snuffing the wicks on the candles and defusing the glyphs. Finally, I picked up the ring. The silver felt different, as though alive. Revulsion and edginess bordering on dismay passed from the metal to my skin as I held it. That was expected. As I focused on it, I touched the awareness of Inverressayte. As his master, I could reach out for him as I wished.

Inverressayte remained silent. Sulking.

4

CHARM IS A WEAPON

A forge filled the glassworks with heat. I'd ridden to Boston to order the glassware my master and Mr. Twelves needed for their new device. The warm air in the workshop held the scents of beeswax, of charred wood, of thick gloves that had been scorched and dampened. The shop's owner, Hugh Keefe, stood next to me with a heavy leather apron and a wooden pole. Red beard shot through with gray, a wide set of shoulders. I pulled two pages of crisp paper from my pocket and unfolded them for him, drawings of the enclosures. "These are bigger than we've had before, but not too different."

Keefe looked them over. His mind held a sharp edge—and none sharper for glass, so claimed both my master and Mr. Twelves, neither one an easy man to impress. I could see Keefe's mind working, his eyes tracing the figures next to the drawings.

"Let me guess—he needs them next week," he said.

"Last week would suit him better."

"I see."

"We know you're always busy, so we're willing to pay thrice your normal fee."

"Thrice?"

I nodded. "More, if you could go back in time."

"Seems there's profit in the past, leastwise." He nodded. "Fine. I can clear out a few other jobs. Still be a week."

We settled on the price, and I took out a leather pouch and handed Keefe a fair number of silver Spanish dollars. He jingled the coins for a moment before putting them into his pocket. "A lot of money to be carrying around on your own, Miss Finch."

As I slipped the pouch back into my pocket, I lifted the edge of my riding jacket and showed him the small pistol I wore on my waist, purchased from a gunsmith on Queen Street. Conducting as much business on my own for Swaine as I did, it was a comment I received with regularity—the pistol answered their concerns without another word, if not a note of admiration. My skills at shooting were only fair, so the weapon served mainly as a prop.

"You're a surprising one at that," Keefe said, chuckling. "Perhaps it's for the best I lack a son to court you—doubt there's many as could handle a young woman as yourself without coming away feeling six inches shorter, dumb as a knob, and likely heartbroken, on top."

"Oh, I'm just a dainty thing, Mr. Keefe."

"So the lads might think until someone warns them."

"Then it shall be our little secret, sir."

"Indeed it shall, Miss Finch. Indeed it shall." He lifted the papers. "I'll have them ready by Monday next."

As I opened the door to the outside, a figure stepped aside. Doctor Ephraim Rush leaned on his cane, a snug tricorn on his head, a scarf around his throat.

"Why, Miss Finch," he said.

I stepped out of the doorway. "Doctor Rush. You're—looking well, sir."

He waved away my half-hearted compliment. "Bah. I'm an old tree, hoping to remember how to sprout a few last leaves before the final winter snows topple me."

"Nonsense, sir. You've outsmarted winter this long. I think you know something that the rest of us don't."

"Winter knows everything we all don't, Miss Finch—though I suppose I'll learn it soon enough. As we all will, if I may be so dour."

Boston blurred under a soft spring rain. The green of new leaves trembled with drips and windows shone with streaked lantern light. A pair of regulars watched our conversation from the carriage half a dozen paces away.

His gaze didn't look addled as Mary Whitelocke had implied, but rather as sharp as Keefe's had when looking over our plans. "Is your master a fan of Mr. Keefe? Or are you the connoisseur of his craftsmanship?"

"He came recommended. For some lantern work, sir." *Lantern* work? Had I lost my mind? I couldn't have picked a worse phrase, but the words careened from my lips before I could stop them.

"A sound recommendation indeed. I've used Mr. Keefe in that capacity for years. At this point, I quite expect his handiwork to outlast me. Or my own handiwork, frankly. Would that I were as skilled."

"I'm sure you're—quite skilled, sir."

"How kind of you to say. Yet I seem to have a knack for shattering much of my glassware when it comes to my work these days, much to the profit of Mr. Keefe." He moved to the door, which I still held open for him. "Please tell your master I'd enjoy a conversation with him in the near future. I'd value his opinion on some matters."

"Yes, of course, sir. I shall mention it to him today."

He lifted his walking stick in farewell as he entered Keefe's shop. "He'll know where to find me. Adieu, Miss Finch."

I waited until he was fully inside and closed the door. As I let my breath out, I tried to look more composed than I felt as I passed by the regulars, my mind racing along one possibility after another for why Rush had decided to pay a visit to Mr. Keefe—most of them ending with the construction of new witch-poles, or lanterns devised to illuminate all of Swaine's and my secrets.

I dodged puddles as I made my way along King Street, the name of which never failed to bring back memories of my first night in the province. *On both sides runs the King.* A shiver—not from the rain—ran along my neck. A row of tulips edged the front of a home, red and yellow blooms seeming to glow from within against the gray afternoon. Three seasons had passed since that horrible evening, and the world had kept spinning right along. Wilkes, Flynn, my strangler—all dead, and life continued. If I'd met my end on that night—as to all rights, I should have—these same flowers would shine on this same spring day in the rain. My father, my brothers, all gone—and yet I continued. My other dead masters, nothing but memories. The world didn't care about the life of any one person. Or the life of every last person. The seasons would pass, springtime would come, new life would come reaching out of the dark soil. As I stepped around an ankle-deep puddle, I wasn't sure if the thought was a comfort, or worthy of the deepest dread.

As I turned the corner, I came up behind an officer in Whitelocke scarlet atop a massive white stallion. He patted the flank of his horse, squinting into the fine rain. For a moment, I thought him the ghost of General John Whitelocke, come to add his name to the list of the dead that my mind had conjured. Then I saw: Grayson Whitelocke.

"I see that no one took your warnings about making you an officer seriously," I said.

He looked around for a moment, then reined his horse in my direction. He doffed his hat and inclined his head. "They never do. But don't let this dashing uniform give you an impression to the contrary. The commission my father paid to make me a major will no doubt prove a poor investment indeed."

The horse skittered, but Grayson held it still with a confident hand on the reins. He'd filled out, and the resemblance to his deceased brother was hard to ignore, especially as my memory of that horrific death held exceptional clarity. "Does my sister still have her claws into you, or has she moved on to some other hapless plaything?"

"She's quite charming."

"Her charm is a weapon she wields better than I do a rifle or pistol. She's devious, which I'm fairly certain I'd warned you of. She will beguile you with what she thinks passes for wit, shower you with pointless advice until you're uncertain of which direction is up, dress you like she's a fairy godmother of silk, satin, and lace—all to lure you into her service. And—like magic—most young ladies fall for it and gather about her as though she's royalty."

"She's not like that at all."

"She's precisely like that, but to each her own."

I strolled again, and he set his horse to walk alongside me. "Are you enjoying your new rank, then?"

"Let me tell you what my father insists that I do, Miss Finch. He insists I dine with the regimental officers. A twice weekly affair wherein I shall develop a bond of trust and respect with them. And as I glance around at the sullen faces staring into their mince pies and custards, listening to the aching silence, the shift of napkins, the clink of fork on plate, I realize that I'm hardly the only one who doesn't believe me fit for my rank, regardless of the perfectly good coin paid for it."

"No doubt your father feels it important that his son earns respect."

"Yes, well, I'm sure he feels the wrong son was murdered."

I'd heard Mary say precisely that, but I held my tongue. "It must be fascinating, commanding troops."

"If one is a sadistic accountant." We paused at the corner of Merchants Road while a two-horse carriage passed. Grayson raised his voice above the clomp and racket. "Honor among officers consists in an unending amount of scorn and yelling delivered to anyone of a lesser rank. The lesser, the crueler. I'm spared the shouting from our two generals due to the shouting that my father may cast down upon their heads should they dare. Still, their curt answers and patronizing side looks hardly put a spring in my step. As for accountancy, I'm daily given lists of cannons to stare importantly at." We started forward again. I noticed that most people glanced at Grayson, discreetly in most cases. "I may report that our regimental artillery, across the companies, counting three-, four-, and six-pounders comes to thirty-six. We have a dozen similar guns in reserve, outside the city at several garrisons. At the fort, our park armaments include half a dozen five-and-one-half-inch howitzers, four eight-inchers, and the big guns: six twelve-pounders, and a pair of twenty-four-pounders." He looked at me. "Is your heart beating faster? Feeling swoonish?"

"It certainly sounds interesting," I offered.

"Then you possess a quality I lack, for a long list cataloguing various rock types, or thread colors, or daily catch at the wharves holds no more interest for my taste. Which is to say, none. I've men rattling off such numbers about muskets, about horses, about powder—and I find it nothing but dreary."

"Well, you look dashing in your uniform. That must count for something."

"Does feeling a fraud count for something? If so, then perhaps you're right."

"The young ladies of proper society must find you irresistible," I said.

"Their parents find the prospect of my family's wealth and influence irresistible, I'll say that much. As for the young ladies themselves, it's apparent that they've been coached to bat their lashes and dangle their pillowy bits enough for me to catch a calculated glimpse."

"Pillowy bits, Major?"

"Please, call me Grayson. No need to taunt." He rode on ahead of me and dismounted, tying his horse to the hitch in front of a chandler's shop. As I drew closer, he took off his riding gloves and tucked them into his belt. "Whilst I'm not entirely immune to flattery, no matter how forced, and even less so to pillowy bits—particularly the flawless sort, who couldn't find those enticing?—I find the unmistakable transactional nature of such encounters to be rather cloying for my tastes."

I came to a stop in front of him. I still had further errands to run, and Swaine was clear he needed me back before the afternoon grew long. "So if I wanted something from you, it wouldn't work to bat my eye—just the one, as I believe you kindly pointed out—and heave my chest?"

"Not you, too?"

"Why not me?"

"I thought you made it rather clear which Whitelocke you were fond of."

"Perhaps I haven't had enough time with you."

"Pray tell."

"I'd like to see your manse again."

"Why?"

"Because it's lovely. Because I spend my days repairing books. Because I didn't come from a wealthy family."

"Ask your good friend Mary—oh, wait. You have. But she's found one reason after another not to."

"I'm sure she's quite busy."

"She's lazy and easily distracted. I, for one, don't bat my eyelashes and play coy, Miss Finch. I was rather hoping for more from you." He straightened his hat. "But I must admit to being intrigued—what might I get in return for such a favor from a bookbinder's apprentice such as yourself?"

"Well, we've ruled out batting and dangling, I believe."

"Have we?"

Oh good Lord. "I suppose we didn't technically rule anything out."

"Why, Miss Finch, I believe you have something that the other giggling hens who my sister surrounds herself with quite lack. I'm not sure I've put my finger on it. Yet."

Shall I kill him for you, Mistress?

The voice buzzed inside my ear, inside my head—Inverressayte. I tried not to show the shock on my face. How was he communicating with me? The ring the fiend was bound within was safely—or so I thought—stowed away in my room in Andover. It made no sense.

I could do it before the drool spills over his pouty lip. I don't care for the way he's looking at you, no indeed. But I am ever at your command, Mistress.

"No, don't," I whispered quickly.

"Pardon?" Grayson said.

Really, it would be for the best. The stench of curse wafts off him. That won't do anyone any good, no. Gutting him here and now would spare him—and you—the bother, Mistress.

Had the binding gone wrong, after all? Or, more worrisome, was the binding somehow different because I was a witch? And what was the demon capable of this far from the ring?

"No, no. I—I'm sure you're fine. Right, I mean. You're right."

Grayson raised an eyebrow. "You're purposeful. Feisty. Sharp. Tall. Capable."

Oh dear, there's someone else coming who certainly won't care that you'd prefer this simpering flap-bag to keep flapping. I've noticed he seems worryingly interested in you, Mistress. I might even take my leave. I don't like him. Nor he, me. Adieu, Mistress.

The strange tickle in my mind ceased just as I became aware of another presence. Before I could figure out how to extricate myself from the conversation with Grayson, a second demon made his presence known. The last time I'd been with a Whitelocke hadn't gone well under such circumstances. With a whinny, the stallion rolled his eyes and tossed his head. A small cobbled walkway led from King Street to a small green.

"Come with me," I said. I grabbed Grayson's hand.

"That was easier than I expected."

"Now." I led him along the walkway. A bronze statue of a man stood astride a marble plinth. "This way."

A pair of enormous chestnut trees bordered the green, across from a row of trimmed hedges. A curved marble bench sat before the weathered statue of bronze, which as I drew closer showed itself to be of a man with a proud head and flowing uniform, a sword at his hip, a torch held aloft in one hand. *Hon. Governor Warren Peabody* was carved into the front of the base. Drips of rainwater fell in fat beads from the outstretched arms. Beneath his name were smaller words carved into the marble base: *In Eternal Watch Against the Devilry of Vile Witchcraft*. I wondered if he could help me protect Grayson from the demon. I had no pendant to give him. I readied a ward. A shadow trailed us.

At the statue, I turned to Grayson. "Do you recall the evening we danced at the ball—and what you told me about pretending? About the costumes we wear, or are forced to wear? That we hide behind?"

"No one listens to me."

The demon drew near, a dim shape coalescing behind Grayson. I extended my natural protections. "I did." With that, I threw my arms around him, pulling him tight, crushing him against my chest. I put everything I had into raising my witchcraft around the both of us.

"You are full of surprises," he muttered in my ear.

"Katie. Call me Katie," I whispered into his. I tightened my grip on him, not letting him pull his face back to kiss me.

The demon prowled, circling. The same shade I'd seen kill others in my life, on both sides of the Atlantic. I tried to think of what to do. So far, my protection seemed to have kept the demon from Grayson, but I didn't think I'd be able to keep him wrapped in a hug all day. I could cast a ward—and reveal myself to yet another Whitelocke, which had already proven unwise. Grayson's hand slipped down my back, landing on my rear end.

Inverressayte, I thought. I reached for the connection again. *Inverressayte, now.*

There it was, the tickle in my thoughts.

This really isn't safe, Mistress. This hideous maniac—a monstrosity, without question—would like nothing more than to take advantage of my gentle nature and rip me to shreds. I beg you, don't risk the life of your poor, tender servant.

Draw him away, I commanded. *Right this minute. Lead him from this spot, lead him five miles north.*

He'll catch me without question—and a slavering hulk like that will make me suffer, breaking me slowly, when all I offer are the finest of intentions of service toward—

Now, Inverressayte! I command you!

The feeling of a desperate sigh washed through my mind. *In which case, Mistress, may I say what an honor it's been remaining at your behest these many hours and days. You are a witch and a sorceress of uncommon grace and—*

Grayson's hand tightened on my backside.

Inverressayte, lead him away this moment! I put as much force behind the silent command as I could. Inverressayte—with no choice—obeyed. As he did, the other demon darted off after him, no doubt driven half mad with fury at the presence of the weaker fiend.

I reached back and lifted Grayson's hand, then released him from my embrace, attuned to the presence of any demons in our corner of the green. I sensed nothing.

Grayson smiled. "I stand by all my assertions of your character, and then some. I'm almost at a loss for words." He leaned forward, toward me.

I stepped back, smiling as prettily as I could. "Wouldn't you care to show me—your room."

"When?"

"Now."

"How bold. What will people think?"

"Don't worry—it can be our little secret, Grayson Whitelocke."

"Not too little, I hope."

"Big enough." I reached out and straightened the facings on his uniform. Still no demons.

"You are refreshingly direct, Miss Finch."

"It must be the uniform. And call me Katie."

I kept the smile on my face as I followed him from the green. I glanced over my shoulder. No demon. Only the rain-swept bronze face of the late governor, still busy keeping his never-ending watch against witchcraft.

5
———

GHOSTS OF WITCHES

Half an hour later, we stood just inside the delivery door in the cellar of the governor's manse, our clothing damp from the rain. It hadn't been difficult to convince Grayson that discretion was called for—a way into the manse that didn't involve guards or cooks or any other servants who might make a note of comings and goings. Just beyond a row of casks was the spot where General John Whitelocke had been shot by Francis. The sight of it set my heart to racing.

Grayson closed the door. "Now, where were we?"

I lifted a finger. "Behave."

"I thought we came here to do the opposite of behaving."

"We'll see."

"And if you can't resist the allure of my uniform?"

"I shall gird myself."

I glanced beyond to the stairs. Leaving Grayson by the door, I crossed past the casks of beer and racks of wine, now repaired since my magic had given the dirt floor an expensive drink. I ignored my unease and looked over at the spot on the floor where John Whitelocke had perished. Had his ring tumbled free and— what? Rolled across the floor into the demonmere when it appeared? Unseen and unnoticed by the guards who swarmed the cellar? Turning, I glanced at the wall where Clara had disappeared. *Down and down I was dragged, deeper and deeper, bruising me, cracking my ribs down stairs. And when I stopped, I was afraid.*

"One of my favorite rooms," Grayson said. "Or it used to be before my brother decided to die in it."

"This is where it happened?"

"Somewhere near the stairs, yes." He stood near the casks and retrieved a silver flask from behind the farthest one, pulled the cork and took a swig. He held it up for me, but I shook my head. "I daresay we both resented being each other's brother. Both quite sure there'd been some divine mistake involved. His torment of me rarely ceased. And in fact it hardly ceased with his death now that I've inherited all his appalling duties and expectations."

"I'm sure he loved you," I said. Glimmers of magic—faint at first, but growing more clear as I neared—sparkled in the nooks and corners of the wall. As far as I could tell, it had nothing to do with the demonmere. Rather, I suspected I was seeing Doctor Rush's handiwork, Mary's contentions about his dwindling abilities notwithstanding. What had he found?

"Loved me?" Grayson said. "When we were young, he cost me years' worth of decent sleep with tales of the witches—or the ghosts of witches, he wasn't clear—coming to my window in the night with the aim of devouring me. Or cursing me. Again, he wasn't clear, though to be fair, what he lacked in imagination, he more than made up for in the bully's instinct. And if that weren't enough—by the way, what exactly are you looking at? The wall?"

I straightened. "Come here."

He put the cork in the flask and slipped it into his pocket. When he stopped before me, I took him by the shoulders and spun him around, pushing him gently against the wall. He didn't tumble into the demonmere, so that was something.

"Feisty, am I?" I whispered.

"More than I'd guessed, apparently." He leaned forward to kiss me, but I leaned away.

"What's on the other side of this wall?"

"What does it matter?" His breath smelled of brandy.

"Somewhere a servant won't walk in on us?" I nodded to the stairs to my left.

"Ah, thinking like the officer I ought to be thinking like." He patted the wall and raised an eyebrow. "A storage room."

"Show me."

"Yes, ma'am."

He led me past the stairs and around a corner, to a door. He opened it, revealing a long, dusty room that ran beneath ceiling joists, crosscut by shelves packed with books, bundles of paper and parchment, and rolled-up documents. A single small window let in the dreary daylight, most of the room dark. "The residence of Doctor Rush's predecessors, as I've heard it. Kept close to protect the various governors from the infernal. Doctor Rush once slept here until he prevailed upon one of my father's predecessors to fund the purchase of a separate house one street over."

It struck me: Archibald Fletcher had slept and worked there. So had Henrik Kraus, his successor. Peculiar, then, that I should find myself in that very spot. I scanned the nearest shelf, finding birth records from Boston and nearby towns, death records, certificates of debenture, and decades of tax records, separate volumes covering each season. Trade records, land titles, armloads of maps. Grayson followed behind me, rather close.

"All these important scribblings," he said. "And all to mark the passage of money to and from people who have no use for a column of it as they stare up from the black of their graves."

"How cheery." I went deeper into the stacks, looking for the wall adjoining the spot where the demonmere had appeared.

"Season after season, decade after decade, it all means less and less." He followed me, poking through the dusty folios. "For instance, here we find the ever-popular *The Treasury*

Warrants of the Towne of Cambridge, 1708. If that's a bit dry for your tastes, we have *Sheriffs Returns on Tax Executions 1692–93*. And of course the titillating *Navigation Acts of the Massachusetts Bay Company*." He pulled it out and blew the dust from the top of its pages. A breeze sidled in around us, rustling papers along the way.

"Have the spirits heard us?" he said. "If you're worried about ghosts, I can wrap you in my arms."

"Ghosts don't exist, but thank you."

"I've swallowed half a cup of dust already." He took another swig of brandy.

I ducked beneath a slanted portion of the ceiling that indicated where the stairs were. As I neared it, I paused. The wall next to it appeared as sturdy on this side as it had on the other. Nestled in the corner was a small trunk that caught my eye, appearing to have more color than anything else in the long room. Magic of some sort, though I couldn't tell much more than that.

Grayson put his hand on my hip, sidling up next to me. "The servants shan't find us. As long as we're quiet."

"Has Doctor Rush been down here lately?"

"You think he might walk in on us? How exciting."

I eyed the trunk. "Has he?"

"I would imagine so, if only to keep up the appearance of helping locate Rattlesnakes." He kissed the side of my neck. I gently pulled away.

"Did he do any magic?"

"Magic? My father wouldn't have it, especially now that Lord Middlesex has ensconced himself in the midst of our affairs, no doubt penning furtive letters to His Majesty and sending them on ships bound for London on a monthly basis, furthering the case that my father is steering the colony straight into the blazing pit of Hell."

He raised his hand on my lower back, but I stepped sideways, looking over the trunk. A subtle and peculiar magic tickled my senses.

"Why would he do that?" I said.

"To curry favor? Because he's a true believer? Either, neither, both? He certainly *appears* to smell the whiff of brimstone everywhere he looks. The corrupting nature of our deviancy. The hand of Lucifer. And it goes without saying that what hurts us helps him—so my father has been quite clear to Doctor Rush: no magic, not even so much as sparking a candle to life without a tinderbox."

I reached over to Grayson, pulling him close to me by the collar again. "That's what we need—candles."

"Candles."

"Don't you want to see more of me?"

"Very much so."

"Then fetch some candles."

"Is that any way to speak to an officer?"

"Oh, Major Whitelocke, sir."

He smiled. "Perhaps it is. Stay here. I shall find the nearest candles."

"And a tinderbox."

"Yes. Father's orders." He leaned over and kissed me on the mouth.

Shocked, horrified, and somewhat ashamed, I let his lips linger on mine for a moment, then put my palm on his chest and eased him back. "Candles."

"Candles." He turned and hurried back to the door. I waited until I heard his steps on the stairs before turning and regarding the trunk. I didn't have much time. With care—for certain magic could be an alarm, or even a trap—I placed my hands on the lid. No visible countermagic activated, that I could see. I tried to open it, but it didn't give, locked. I looked closely at the hinges, which appeared to be steel—not easily broken with elemental magic, at least not by me. I only knew one spell of proper unlocking,

Chance Harlow's *Revelation of the Unseen*, but it required quartz dust, an iron nail, and several other ingredients I didn't have with me. With no better solution at hand, I closed my eye and held my palms over the chest. Relaxing my shoulders, I allowed my witch-craft to seep down my arms, out my hands—and into the wood.

After several breaths, sensory impressions of the wood filled my mind. Grain that marked the barrier that marked one year to the next. Unseen hollows that had carried the water between the fibers. Strength that ran in one direction as unyielding as steel; the fragile weave of vulnerability and lightness that ran in the other.

I twined my will and intention around that latent structure and started to nudge it to movement. Along one axis, then another, finding the rigid resistance, and finding the give. Once I found the give, I pushed more of my energy into it, feeling out the pattern and the structure, seeing how it might yield to my efforts. The trunk sounded with whispery creaks. A snap, as some long-stored tension released. A pop, as the glue in one of the joints that held it together lost its grip. The close air filled with hints of varnish and the sweet breath of raw wood as the boards warped. Feeling the wood reaching its point of failure, I released the smallest push of further energy. Joints and miters strained, and the trunk slumped. A yawning gap opened up between the lid and the front panel.

I withdrew my witchcraft. The sense of subtle magic was stronger now. I leaned forward, peering into the trunk. Overhead, the cellar door opened and footsteps—Grayson's—started down. Not waiting, I reached an arm into the trunk. The interior smelled of old resin. A bundle of letters and papers, tied with a brittle string, sat off to one side. The interior was otherwise empty. I snatched up the letters, barely giving them a glance as I shoved them deep into the recesses of my coat and stood. Leaving the trunk behind, I met Grayson by the door.

He came around the corner holding a candelabra shining

with four candles. "The kitchen staff think me daft. I hope they're not right."

"Of course they're not. You're clever, skilled, handsome."

"Oh, do go on."

I cringed. "Forgiving?"

"Forgiving?"

"Because I have to leave."

"Leave? Why we haven't even—"

"I know. I'm so sorry, but my master is already expecting me to—"

"I was gone for four minutes."

"I've lost track of the time, and—"

"This is an excuse. I thought we weren't hiding behind—well, if not clothes, then polite lies. Verbal costumes."

"Fine. It's not that—or, not *only* that, because I am going to be late and my master, in the wrong mood, will not be pleased. Or possibly furious."

"Then what is it?"

"I just—as I waited, I thought about where I was, and I thought about Mary. And what she would think."

"Let her think what she wants. She will anyway."

I reached out and laid a finger on his chest. "Easy for you to say. You're her brother. I'm her *friend*. And that becomes difficult."

"Not that difficult. It's never kept me from her friends before."

"It wouldn't be right for her to find out there was something between us after the fact. Secondhand."

"Then shall I run and tell her now? See what the kitchen staff think of me darting down the hall yet again?"

"No. I need to talk with her. Myself. Soon."

"Since when does my sister's approbation dictate my peccadillos? What sort of catastrophic punishment is this?"

"Now you're being melodramatic."

"You underestimate your allure."

I pushed the candelabra aside and kissed him on the cheek. "I didn't say never. Just not yet." With a pat on his chest, I slipped by him and hurried back past the stairs. He followed me.

"When?"

"After I speak with Mary."

"Don't believe half of what she tells you about me. *Most* of what she tells you. She has an agenda. I have terrible siblings, always happy to snuff out the tiniest spark of my own happiness."

I hurried past the spot where his older brother died. "I'll handle it delicately. And don't forget—I have my *own* opinions, as well. About you, for instance."

"As you flee from my presence. Rather telling."

"You won't have to hear from my master." I reached the delivery door. "I will."

"Then when shall I hear from you, Miss Finch?"

"Katie. And soon. I promise. No batting eye. No costume, verbal or otherwise."

"Yes, and no pillowy bits."

I pushed open the door into the misty yard and turned to him with a smile. "Behave." With that, I hurried out into the gray afternoon, leaving the governor's manse to dwindle behind veils of spring rain beneath a low sky. The letters remained snug against my ribs.

6

MAGICK OF THE DARKEST SORT

"Ah, there you are, Finch."

My hopes of returning to the Andover house unseen vanished the moment I turned around to hang up my muddied and soaked cloak on a peg by the kitchen door. Swaine bustled in from the hallway carrying a kettle, dressed in shirtsleeves. He barely glanced at me. "Mr. Keefe will push aside all other work for us, I hope?"

The rains had grown torrential as I'd ridden north, leaving me drenched to my skin, my hair heavy. I don't know that my master even noticed. The tone in his voice hinted at a mood not altogether light.

"He promised a week, sir."

"A week? He could have it done in two days."

"I urged him to do it quickly."

"A week doesn't sound like you urged very much." He filled the kettle and hung it in the hearth, tossing a quartered log on the huffing embers.

I didn't fall into the trap of further defending my—or Keefe's—actions; there was no easy path out of those woods, I'd learned. Swaine in a dark place would find fault with any answer I could give, whereas his annoyance with my silence might be the better course.

"How comfortable to take a week," he said. "I can't seem to fit more than eighteen hours in, day in and day out, and still find myself half a dozen hours short by the time the cock crows. Ah, but I'm only looking to elevate the course of human achievement. It's not blowing a few glass pieces, after all."

"Can I fix you some soup, sir? And there's bread from yesterday."

"Not hungry. I just need tea."

I'd get him soup anyway. He was hungry, I saw—petulant because of it, enough to refuse an offer of food. I couldn't exactly hold him down and shove a slice of bread into his protesting mouth, but if I took away as many barriers between hot food and his stomach as I could, it often did the trick.

He looked at me. "You're dripping all over the floor."

"Rain, sir."

"I assumed you hadn't gone for a dip in the pond fully dressed." He sniffed, crossing his arms. "Well, don't just stand there. You have a rather ostentatious wardrobe full of perfectly dry, if not necessarily practical, clothing. No need hunting around to catch a chill on my account."

"Yes, sir." I took a pair of steps to the hallway.

"But before you do, a moment." He brushed past me and led me to his study. In the time I'd been gone, he'd hung up a large map on the wall across from the fireplace. I noticed the *Occultatum Ostium* on his writing desk. He hadn't been away from it for very long. "I'm not altogether confident that even with Twelves's new technique we'll be able to locate further access into the demonmere. Frustrating, but there we are. But I've started wondering if the sources of planar energy—which have most certainly shifted over the past month—might demonstrate other effects to help narrow down the possibilities. What do you see when you look at the map?"

His concern for my shivering had been eclipsed by work in an instant. Looking over the map, I saw that he'd notated with red ink the progress we'd made ridding Salem of its planar infestation. He'd marked up the various rises and stretches of abandoned buildings, dividing them into five sectors. Roughly equal sized, they appeared to correspond to the greatest infernal activity.

"As you can see," Swaine said, "that first sector—the area between the lane to the manse and the bridge, tracing along the river's edge and stretching to one of the large coves that opens into the harbor proper—is where we've trapped the most demons with our planar clocks. Assuming we've been somewhat thorough, let's say it's taken two months. Appallingly slow. Still, do you see a pattern?"

As I stared at the map, tracing the southwest corner of town where both a smaller river and a brook that fed into a small pond made for easy boundaries, I nodded. "They're clustered, sir. In these three spots." I lightly tapped the map.

"It might be a coincidence."

"Or it might not, sir."

"Exactly. It might, in fact, reveal a grander, shifting pattern." He stood beside me, looking at the map. He tapped it with a dry quill. "If we were to see a repetition of these sorts of clusters, it might indicate the strongest possibilities for finding another entrance. Do you see?"

"Yes, sir."

"How many planar clocks do we have out there as of today?"

"Four, sir."

He turned. "Four? We had fourteen out last week—and now we have only four?"

"We ran out of the silver foil, sir."

"And no one thought to order more?"

"We did, sir. A month back. Mr. Winslow assured us it would

arrive within a fortnight. Then it was supposed to be last week. Then this. It's coming up from the Carolinas."

"Why not just order it from China and wait a year?" He tossed the quill to the table. "You're telling me there's nowhere closer than the bloody Carolinas for this?"

"Mr. Winslow assured me he's checked with all his other contacts."

"I find that doubtful."

"I'll ask him to check again, sir."

"Two weeks ago might have been a more opportune time to do so, Finch." Swaine flipped through several papers on a writing table he's stationed by the window. "How lovely it would be if I didn't have to do everyone else's job besides my own."

I had asked Mr. Winslow to check again two weeks earlier, but I saw no value in saying so at that moment. I could only hope that my silence, again, wouldn't provoke further argumentativeness from Swaine. I'd noticed that it wasn't unusual for my master to have his mood change—sometimes notably—after he'd been deep in one of his frequent studies of the *Occultum Ostium.*

Swaine spent a few minutes scanning the papers, then put them down. "The point, Finch, is that I have more than enough to grapple with already. I need you to be more diligent. I've tasked you with what I trust you can handle. Please don't force me to rebalance the ledgers—my column is already overfilled."

"If we reused some earlier clocks, sir? Or stripped the silver from them?" I offered.

"You do know this is *sorcery* we're talking about here? Not barrel-making?"

"There are techniques to return the silver to a neutral state. Summerfield mentioned one or two."

"Summerfield ignored the disharmonative half-life of Holzian glamours, which are precisely the glamours we've used through-out. Really, Finch. How is that—" He stopped himself, frowning. After a few moments of his staring off into the middle distance, he straightened, glanced at me, waved for me to leave. He followed me to the door. "I'm not to be disturbed. At all."

With that, he closed the door.

I can't say I wasn't relieved to be excused, and not just for the sodden clothing keeping me shivering. The letters I'd taken from the governor's manse seemed as conspicuous to me as though they might erupt in flames and reveal themselves to Swaine. So when I shut the door to my room, I took them out and tossed them into a drawer in my bureau first thing, hoping the dampness they held hadn't ruined them. After quickly changing into dry clothes, I stood by my door listening for a moment for signs of Swaine deciding that he needed me, after all. Silence.

Fetching the letters once more, I went to the window to look at them in the gray light of late afternoon. With care, I peeled off the old string that bound them together and unfolded them, laying the pile on the edge of my bed. Water stained their edges, but thankfully the writing was still legible.

The first pages contained what appeared to be a list of soldiers and companies who'd taken part in the efforts against Salem in the infamous summer of 1657.

I frowned.

Most citizens of the Crown were familiar with the details, from the insidious settlement of Salem by a pilgrimage of witches cast off the ship *The Westenshire Bell* to the eventual victory of the faithful Christians under the stern leadership of Governor Warren Peabody. So went the official tale, left to posterity in the ubiquitous Major Thomas Abbott's *Accounte of the Defeat of the Infernal at Salem*, a poorly written hagiography in praise of the stout-hearted governor and his officers, who had remained flinty-eyed in the face of terrors that drove others to despair. While it had no doubt made Major Abbott and his printers wealthy men —having become popular throughout the colonies, and a minor phenomenon in London, several decades back—my master insisted it was largely nonsense. I read the paper, which indicated that the company of soldiers who'd mobilized against Salem had been broken up two months afterward, shipped off to a dozen other colonies and locations.

Looking over the next page, I paused, my gaze landing on the name at the bottom: Archibald Fletcher, the first official Doctor of Magickal Sciences for the colony. Reading from the top, I found it to be a handwritten proposal recommending an expedition into Salem to map out the powers there:

...to explore the signature patterns of the curious passageways which I fear may honeycomb the abandoned ruins. With the guidance I possess, vigilance and care might spare us from calamity of the sort we've witnessed.

I reread the passage. More intimation of the demonmere, the Great Realm he'd alluded to in his book. How much had he known?

Folded up along with the proposal lay a handwritten reply from Warren Peabody, Royal Governor:

In no fashion will I countenance your presence in or around that ghastly location, Doctor Fletcher. Your charge is to keep the malign forces of Salem at bay, not to tamper with them. I cannot be more insistent that you abandon these troublesome notions.

The signature of the governor might well have been carved with a knife, so fierce was the scrawl.

I picked up the next letter, unfolded it, squinting at the faded writing. It appeared to be addressed to Fletcher.

Esteemed & Honorable Doctor Fletcher,
A woeful dread has taken hold of me, and I could think of no recourse but to reach out in hope to you. Despite the differences that

have kept us apart, I believe a time approaches when we must turn to each other for help. My heart tells me we stand on the cusp of darkness.

Even as the days grow longer, the nights keep me wary. I daren't tell you more save in person—and I fear nothing as much as not having grace enough to convince you of our plight.

Please, let us meet.

In earnest,

Bridgette

Bridgette? The name felt familiar.

Whatever the witches of Salem had been, autobiographers they were not. To my knowledge, there had been no account of Salem written by a witch. I'd found no mention of any such book existing in any of the books I read. The closest thing to it was *The Spirit Treatise of Issac Levy.* Levy, cast adrift alongside the witches from *The Westenshire Bell,* had been a grifter of some note, but had provided a firsthand account of the settling of Salem. According to his book, the settlement had been led by women, and among the inner circle of leadership was one Bridgette Close, daughter of Helen Close, regarded as the de facto leader of the town. Could it be the same Bridgette?

I unfolded the next letter. Written in the same hand, it began:

Archibald,

I've no reassurance that my prior missive reached you, but I must relay that my suspicions have deepened. There are stirrings. Shadows. Something has taken root and now watches us from the dark eaves of the forest.

I don't feel safe keeping the children here as this darkness waits for our vigilance to falter.

We are doing all that we can, but I fear that it won't be enough. You could make others understand. You could find a place for the innocent until we're safe again.

Can you find it in your heart as you once did?

Bridgette

I looked up, my gaze running over the pile of letters. Had Fletcher known one of the witches? One certainly didn't need to read far between the lines with talk of *finding things within the heart.*

The writing on the next letter was harried as if scratched out under a speeding and trembling quill.

Archibald,

I tried to see you, but was once again rebuffed by the governor's men. I fretted and wept bitter tears—but I kept my promise to you, and though I could have slid past your guards and your locks, I didn't.

I know now that the threat that is eating away at us is nothing that a musket or a blade can dispatch. I don't ask for your strength of arms, I ask for your strength of character.

Please help us. The shadows burrow through this place. Infect it. Demons, of the darkest sort. We've tried what we can, but our strength is overmatched, and our efforts draw more darkness. All I ask is for shelter. For the young ones, and the infirm.

Our town has grown rotten with hidden passageways spawning fiends. We dig, we plumb, we reinforce such entrances as we seal off. Unless we can find each and every incursion, I fear we will not survive. The map I've included marks the worst locations and where we've anchored our most powerful efforts—you should have it in case we fail.

I beseech you, my old love.

B.

My gaze lingered on the final phrase. It made no sense, given how the story was commonly understood—but there it was: lovers.

The next sheet wasn't a map. I turned the letter over, nothing. The next sheet in the pile looked to be an official report, written by a Major Giles Fuller, and had a date upon it: August 27, 1657.

We manned our post along the Salem Road, five miles from the town. Once night fell, we saw lights shooting into the sky and heard screams on the wind. Strange shapes prowled the borders of the forest, and men quailed. One family begged us to let them pass. We drove them back. I fear that some escaped our watch.

Throughout the night, horror held fast.

Unholy fires burned, and cries of lament rose and fell in the distance. When blessed sunrise arrived, a darkness remained over Salem. For seven days now, it has not moved.

In that time, no one else came from that direction. No person, no bird, no fowl, no legged creature at all.

My mouth went dry. Salem had attacked no one. It'd been attacked, by demons emerging from hidden passageways.

One final letter remained, an old stain of water or tea across the paper. Written across the back was the instruction "BURN THIS." I opened it and read:

September 18, 1657

Good Governor Peabody,

I write you with little hope. The terrors are gone, the fight won at great cost. We spared nothing in sealing out the threat, digging by hand, reinforcing with fieldstone, all we could do to reinforce our efforts at holding the shadows at bay. Only a handful of us remain. We need to reach areas to which only you can grant us access if we're to keep the dangers at bay.

Please, my lord. I beg you—allow us into Boston and the towns to the west of it to build stronger defenses.

This plague that has taken my people will take yours next if we can't work together to finish what we've begun.

Ginny Lane

I reread it. *Only a handful of us remain.*

At the bottom of the page was a note scrawled in a different hand, the same writing that had directed that the letter be burned.

A woman plain in appearance confronted His Lordship the royal governor. He remained polite as he dismissed her concerns. The woman grew heated and waved her hands, speaking in a strange and frightful tongue. Shadows, like those of ravens, filled the room, sweeping along the walls, the ceiling, the floor. The shadows of ravens gathered on the governor, who became much distraught.

She was taken, to be thrown in the gaols, but she vanished in plain view of the governor, the guards, and myself. We have not found her.

I stared at the letter. I looked through all of them again, searching for the map mentioned by Bridgette—nothing.

The map I've included marks the worst locations and where we've tried to seal it—you should have it in case we fail.

I reread the letters, one after another.

...hidden passageways spawning fiends.

The demonmere—it had to be. I put the letters down. I'd seen phrasing like that before.

In Fletcher.

Where Swaine bemoaned the imprecise logic and breathless adjectives, I found Fletcher's descriptions of the region captured an essence that many authors of the unseen arts missed. As Swaine had largely given up on Fletcher's *Unclean Remnants of Witchcrafte & Devilry in Salem*, the tome had found a permanent home on one shelf in my room. I stood and crossed to the row of books on the bottom shelf of my bookcase and slid Fletcher out. I flipped through the pages, scanning the faint ink until I found the passage the letters had called to mind:

There's not been a midnight that didn't embrace your humble narrator. Midnight last, I made my way round the periphery of Salem beneath the glint of ten thousand stars tracing the silent structures and wharves.

It burrows through this place. Infects it. It turns the benign into the harrowing. Magick—magick of the darkest sort, twisting and tangling about stone well and gate, passing through wall and across lane, pooling and gurgling and seeping like a river blown its banks. An incredible power courses, unchecked and dangerous, along the hidden passageways beyond time's watch.

Within, I hear the dim tolling of an infernal cacophony, the clang and ring of all the irons of Hell, sounding in their depths.

I strengthen my resolve and put aside my fears.

I LOOKED IT OVER AGAIN...THE *hidden passageways beyond time's watch.* That he should have used the identical phrasing mightn't have been a coincidence. And if a map existed, was sent to him— maybe that's why he wanted to explore Salem, only to be forbidden by the governor at the time.

They're going to notice those, Mistress. They're tainted, stinking with the horrid stench of witchcraft—if you'll pardon me saying.

I dropped Fletcher's book as Inverressayte's voice crawled along the inside of my skull. "I didn't call you." I glanced over at the box that held the ring where the demon was bound.

I humbly beg your pardon, Mistress. I only value your well-being, unerring judgment, stirring presence—

"What do you want?"

The letters. I shuddered as soon as you touched them. As soon as you brought them with you into this place. Most distasteful, but I assure you my unhappiness is of no concern, and no reason why I should trouble you with my revulsion. I'm not the only one who sees them, however. The others do. Especially that uncouth brute who feels it necessary to threaten to tear my very essence into wailing shreds every time he notices your timid servant. The farther away you put them, the better for us both. Perhaps there's a way to burn them, divide the ashes, scatter them in a dozen or more locations—

"Witches, or witchcraft?"

I beg your pardon, Mistress?

"Do they stink of witches—or of witchcraft?"

There's a difference?

"Look closely."

Oh, I'm mistaken. Forget I mentioned anything. I shall retire to the barren prison you keep me in. Quiet and humble.

"No, Inverressayte. I want you to look closely at them. There they are. Tell me." The sensation of a long sigh rippled through my mind.

As you wish. I shall contain my disgust—no easy task, given the putrid reek I'm sure I shan't find relief from for years. Ugh. Sounds reminiscent of gagging and choking rattled in my ears as the letters on the bed stirred. *Witchcraft, Mistress. And witches. But only faintly with the witches—your scent is much more pungent, if you don't mind me saying, only because you're near, of course. These whining scratchings exude witchcraft. Brightly enough to draw the attention of a number of horrid monstrosities, any of whom would find you—or your helpless servant—a delightful morsel.*

"Is there another?"

Another?

"Another letter—or a map—anywhere in the colony with the same witchcraft?"

I'm afraid I don't know what a colony is, Mistress.

"Anywhere near here?"

Your chamber, Mistress?

"Within fifty miles?"

Miles, Mistress? I'm afraid I'm unfamiliar with—oh, dear. My other tormentor. He's coming. I beg you, Mistress—put them away. Hide them, somehow. I'm only a tender-hearted servant, but if you can spare me further indignation, I'd rather not be mauled out of existence at just this moment.

"Finch!" Swaine called from his study. "Come. You're a genius."

I looked to the door. "Coming, sir," I yelled.

He's using you, Mistress. They're all using you.

"What do you mean?"

Swaine knocked on the ceiling below me with what sounded like a fire poker. "This one idea alone might be worth putting up with all your blasted questions and half-formed theories. Nose out of book, come!"

You're worth more than gold to them.

I shook my head. "I don't have time for this. Back to your ring, Inverressayte. I'll hide these."

The sensation of the demon wicked out of my mind. An uneasiness wafted over me—perhaps Inverressayte was right, something neared. I quickly scooped up the letters and folded them, placing them inside Fletcher's book and placing it inside the glamoured circle of protection next to my bed. I tossed a shawl over it. The presence grew for a moment more, then dissipated.

Swaine beckoned me into his study before I reached the bottom of the stairs. He pointed to the map. "I've been thinking too small about the matter. Picking away here, picking away there. Looking, testing, probing. What we need is a wider vantage —see the forest, not just the trees."

"I don't understand, sir."

"Your mention of Summerfield—and my much more informed understanding of the man's blind spots—sparked an idea. In short, the reason why the silver I glamoured can't be reused is because I made use of Holzian glamours. Such glamours direct a portion of their magic back into the initial incantation, thereby creating a low-level, self-perpetuating reinforcement of activation. The added longevity and integrity are worth the extra effort." He walked over to the map. "The problem with such glamours, however, is that this very longevity and integrity render them impossible to neutralize until the eventual decay of their activation falls below a certain threshold. Fair enough. But there's another curious effect to such glamours: they create a disharmonative effect on the upper orders of planar sympathy. Such disruption results in a minor expulsion of magic, sometimes capable of shifting nearby wards, glamours, even objects. Generally nothing more than a nuisance. For my purposes, I barely even thought about it." He pushed back the cuffs of his sleeves. "Now, what does any of this have to do with our continued search for the demonmere? Any guesses?"

I hadn't the faintest. "No—not at all, sir."

"Well, in making pinprick attempts to map the variations in planar energies, I've been hoping to leverage the principle of *concordant alignment*: locating and identifying regions of planar sympathy, those moments when two or more planes come into alignment. One of the more interesting aspects of planar cartography, and most certainly not child's play. Even Doctor Rush likened it to trying to deduce the location of the white pieces on a chessboard from only seeing the movements of the black pieces." He stared at the map, arms crossed. "And why? We can start with the fact that the unseen planes are exceedingly difficult to connect with, let alone isolate. They're constantly shifting in relation to both our world, and other planes. There are an unknown number of planes, perhaps infinite. What cycles as have been identified with several of the known planes appear to be, upon long-term observation, cycles within cycles within cycles. So even in identifying and connecting with one particular plane, we're starting off in a good deal of darkness. And when things appear as unstable as they have of late—I think even the new device of Twelves might not keep up with the shifts. The instability."

Our work in Salem had been plagued by a series of tremors passing through the planes over the preceding month, unexplained and unpredicted. The most recent had occurred a week earlier. Glamours had strained under unseen forces for the better part of two hours—setting my master to anxious pacing as he worked through several spells to reinforce his bindings—and then it had passed, offering no ready explanation nor cause.

Swaine turned to me. "But what if there's a better way? What if we could leverage the disharmonative impact of Holzian glamours to reveal the contours of the planar forces? A controlled release of energy that could, in an instant, outline all the planar intersections in and around Salem?" He walked over to his writing desk. He moved aside the *Occultatum Ostium* and pulled out a large drawing that I recognized from his work in the autumn.

"The resonance clock, sir? But isn't that what caused the problem in the first place?"

"In its prior form, yes." He ran his hand across the drawing. "But the same principles used in the creation of a resonance well could theoretically generate a Holzian glamour powerful enough to reveal the upper orders of planar sympathy—the intersections, the contours, the temporal displacement. And if my theories are correct, such indications will almost certainly lead us to the demonmere once again. The signs should be unmistakable."

"I see." I thought I understood, at least in principle, what he'd explained.

"Exactly, Finch. *You* see. The one characteristic of the disharmonation of planar sympathy I neglected to mention is that they've only ever been inferred—and as with most magic, never seen. Hidden. *Occult.* Now, we might carefully, painstakingly, one point at a time, as we are now, set about trying to log and map and triangulate such forces using sensitive detection techniques." He opened his palms wide to me, revealing the final ingredient to his plan. "Or we could use a witch who might simply observe the spectacle with her own eye, and guide us straight to the demonmere."

My master's mood had improved considerably.

7

TINKER'S PACK OF SECRETS

I felt like a tinker of old, carrying on my back a sack fair to bursting with tools, old pots, solder, and sundry, clanging with each step, announcing my arrival well before I rounded the bend. Except in my case, my sack rang with guilt, lies, and worries, with no room for any more. That anyone I spoke with didn't immediately see me for what I was—fraud, fool, take your pick—was a source of continual surprise on my part. Maybe they were all too preoccupied with their own troubles to notice. The curse and blessing of life. Perhaps I'd developed a skill at deceit. After all, as I frequently lectured Mary Whitelocke, there's no secret, only practice.

My worries weighed on me, whether others heard the clamor or not. So as I hitched the wagon at Knox's Inn & Tavern, I tried to ignore my pack of troubles, even though just seeing the inn gave my guts a twist. That the walls hadn't given way with poor Iris's grief astounded me. A young child and a new baby, every day a reminder that she was a widow. When she spoke of Ethan, which was almost the entirety of her conversations, I could only cringe on the inside, feeling the lie fester between us. I could never tell her how he'd really died, a decision that became a third party to our friendship, one I couldn't banish, one that might never let us be who we were before again.

The relief I'd once felt stepping through the door had been taken, like so much else in my life, by demons. Leaving Swaine and my work behind had been my one chance to relax, if only in short, sweet draughts. Now even that was ruined, replaced with a shame that trailed me like my own shadow. Maybe I would learn to ignore it, in time. As I walked to the door, mist lifted from the tulips, the lilac bushes, the fragrant grass, the roof of the inn, the rains of the days before warmed off by the midmorning sun. Cardinals, jays, and robins carried on, filling the inn's yard with their chatter.

"There's a lass I know isn't a witch."

I stopped in my tracks. *Witch?* Drawing a bucket up from the well by the corner, Bertram smiled at me, fat drips of well water falling from the rope. Since his brother-in-law had died, he'd taken up much of the work at the inn, and some.

I shaded my eyes. "What did you say?"

"Witch. You're not one." He hauled the bucket off the hook. "At least, I'm *hoping* you're not one. Otherwise I'm sure to find myself a toad or a salamander one morning on account of saying something foolish to you. Which I've a habit of, you might have noticed." He gave me a lopsided smile.

"What are you talking about? Why would you call me that?"

"Call you that? I was saying you *aren't* a witch. Oh, there I go again." He walked toward me, leaning against the weight of the full bucket. "I'm sorry. Another lighthearted jest misses the mark. Or hits the wrong mark, more like it. I've an aim problem, especially when I can't keep a story to myself."

I went ahead of him and opened the door for him. "You've kept it to yourself so far." The public room of the inn was empty.

He nodded thanks and went inside. "I might just stop before I dig myself any deeper, begging your pardon."

"Bertram. Just tell me."

"Better—I'll just show you." He plunked down the bucket and went to the small table at the corner. Reaching behind it, he pulled out a folded pamphlet from the pocket of his coat. "Saw this over in Reading, in the public house along the Boston Road. Heard a fellow saying he's seen them up in Cambridge and Boston proper. Bit of talk they've made."

He unfolded it and handed it to me. The title along the front nearly stopped my heart: *A Witch Roams the Province and Your Governor Quails.* Below, the print, neatly type-set, filled the inner fold of the pamphlet in a great block:

Whereas the rightful duties of our Royal Governor Hamilton Whitelocke, chosen Magistrate of our Beloved Sovereign King George II, ought first and foremost exhibit full fealty to the Welfare and Safety of the citizenry of this Bay Colony, it is with Shock and Despair that we attest to the unmolested presence of a Witch within the borders of our long-suffering Province.

Irrefutable evidence, arisen and announced with the widely noted Spectral Illumination of Doctor Ephraim Rush's Witch-Pole Lanterns early on in Winter, continues to accumulate in such a Woeful Tide as to press the question of whether or not we Citizens have been abandoned by the man flailing inside the Governor's Manse. Does he not hear our entreaties to save us? Has he so ensconced himself behind the silken coats of his benefactors that our Peril leaves no impression on his Soul?

Are we to return to a Damnable time when a Witch might open the door to Lucifer himself, set loose to prowl the dark coast, bedding innocent young lasses and turning them into witches? Be witness to midnight negotiations at crossroads where greedy and weak-willed men are seduced into becoming warlocks, conjuring gold and silver in exchange for their souls? Mourn babies hexed? Tremble beneath a night sky filled with swooping silhouettes? Wake to find our well water cursed, our animals sickened?

Where is our Governor when the eastern half of the colony is at Utter Risk of sinking into the Flames?

One might only surmise he cares not, gripped by a Corruption of the heart so poisoned by Greed as to render his Soul blind to Duty.

Thomas Truesight

I HANDED it back to Bertram, furious. "Where is he?"

"He? He who?"

"Francis."

"Francis? He's off in New York, far as—"

"Bertram. It's *Thomas Truesight*. That was Francis's pen-name. Has he contacted you?"

"That was never Francis." He took the pamphlet and stared at it. "Was it?"

"Of course it was. That and the other one—*Solomon Fairmind*. They were both him, everything the Rattlesnakes believed, printed up and hung all over Boston. You haven't heard from him?"

"No. Of course not. He wouldn't come back and not tell me. Or Iris. With his nephew and babe niece—would he?" He waved the pamphlet. "And with all this about witches—why would he have anything to do with that? I thought it was just another frightening tale. Course, it lodged in my head soon as I saw it, and you know how that is. Tales like that. Witch-wells. Haunts. Always drawn to them. I never thought—" He let his words drift off as he looked at the name at the bottom of the printed page.

I hadn't believed Francis would come back, either. And if I had—in a stray thought or two, I may confess—I certainly hadn't considered he'd take my secret and use it as a weapon against the governor. Or, the idea dawned on me, against *me*. All lies and air, his promises. He saw an opportunity and he took it. Everything else went by the wayside. If he thought he was going to pressure me—well, I wasn't going to be fooled twice by his honeyed words and hazel eyes. I promised him I'd rescue Clara, if I could. Nothing more. The more I thought about it, the more infuriated I became. As if I didn't have enough problems to face without half of Boston being reminded of witches and my unfortunate incident with the witch-pole on the night John Whitelocke was killed.

"When did you see that?" I said.

"Just last evening. Had to run to Cambridge to meet with a creditor—me, if you can imagine. Poor Iris is in no state, even now."

"How long had it been up?"

"I don't know. I just—took it. Because of the witch business. Not the other business. Never thought once it might have been Francis. You must think me a fool. There you are, seeing it in an instant, while here I am worrying about witches, working it left and right in my head all morning."

"You're not a fool, Bertram."

"Kind of you to say. But we both know better. Francis. Who would have thought?" He folded up the pamphlet. "He's bound to come by. I for one would be glad for a bit of his help around the place."

I looked him in the eye. After a moment, he nodded.

"Right," he said. "This is Francis. Any sweeping he'll do will be sweeping in, loading up with half the pantry, and sweeping out again. A few words. A wink. A pat on the shoulder for old Bertram. And the broom will remain stood up in the corner, waiting for me as ever."

"Don't tell Iris," I said, touching him lightly on the arm. "I don't think it'd do her any good. If he does show up, he can explain himself."

"Oh, he can explain himself, all right—though never quite what anyone's after, when it comes right down to it. More words than answers, if you follow."

"As I said—you're no fool."

"Debatable, but thank you again."

Iris came around the corner from the kitchen, holding the hand of her oldest, Jude, all of two and a half years old. Her dress and apron were clean and well-kept, as always—but her face and hair looked washed out to me, a cloth doll left out for a season in the yard. The spring sunlight didn't appear to have touched her skin at all, leaving no freckle, no blush of hale warmth. Jude took half steps, looking down at the floor with a frown. Iris glanced at me and flashed a momentary smile that looked as strained as her eyes.

"This one won't be quiet while his sister is napping," she said.

"But I will," Jude said, his voice loud.

"There you are again. Hush. Whisper talk when they sleep, remember?"

"I am whispering." His voice was louder.

"Whispering is quiet," Bertram whispered. "Like a mouse."

"But mice don't talk," Jude said.

"They most certainly do. All the time. Perhaps just not to little boys—unless they're quiet enough to listen. Maybe you can help me bring this bucket of water to the kitchen, where—if we're lucky like we've been the past few days—we'll see a little mouse in the corner. Maybe he'll tell us a story."

Jude looked doubtful, but helped his uncle with the bucket, off to the kitchen.

"He's good with the children," I offered once they were out of sight.

"I can't do it on my own." Iris stared out the window. "It's not right. Not for me. Not for the children. Jude especially—he misses his father so much. He asks after him every night. Every night."

I recalled Ethan's death, yet another horror in a day full of them. The memory clung to me like a stench, so eye-watering and pungent I didn't know how Iris missed it.

"It's hard," I said. "For all of you. And—"

And—what? *It will get easier, with a few years behind you.* Or, *Be glad, he's in Heaven.* Answers? There weren't any. He'd been decapitated by a demon and would spend the rest of eternity as dead as all the rest whose brief—or long—lives had winked out. *But don't worry—we're trying to get a handle on the demonic infestation, even though our work appears to be making worse at the moment.*

"—I'm sorry you're having to carry such a burden."

"I'm worn out."

"You have help. Bertram. Me. We'll bear part of the load. You're not alone."

Behind me, the door opened. A half-dozen soldiers entered, following their officer, filling up the public room with voices and taking seats at two of the tables near the hearth. Iris nodded at them, giving my arm a thankful squeeze as she passed me and went to take their orders. Bertram came around the corner.

Witch-wells. It came to me in a flash: *witch-wells.* I motioned him over. "I need you to show me something."

"You weren't too pleased with the last thing I showed you, begging your pardon."

I turned for the door. "Come. Please."

Flustered or not, Bertram followed me. As I knew he would. Outside, I led him away from the tavern door, stopping by a rail fence. No one watched us. Still, I kept my voice soft. "What are witch-wells?"

"I thought you said Francis was behind this witch business?"

"He is—but that's not what I asked. You've mentioned them to me, before this. What are they?"

"Witch-wells? Well—they're wells, of a kind. Old wells, sealed up. With stone, sometimes old boards. I don't rightly know much more about them than that, save that I've only ever heard them called *witch-wells.* As lads, we'd dare each other to peer down into them, listening for the whispers of witches. Or even to get near one after nightfall. They are a bit queer, now that I think of it—

not necessarily where you might dig a proper well." He scratched his jaw. "Why do you ask?"

I chewed the inside of my lip and thought about how much time I had before I needed to get back to Swaine. "Show me one."

"What—now?"

"Now."

"I only know of three. Nearest is out by the pond, in those rises on the eastern side, the woods. Where those girls drowned."

It might only have been coincidence—where the girls drowned, where their corpses disappeared, where I'd cast DeBurgh's *Grave Raven* on the bodies of three members of the Rattlesnake society—but I didn't like it.

Still, I needed to see. "Please, Bertram?"

He glanced back at the tavern. "Well—if we're quick."

Twenty minutes later, Bertram had me pull the wagon over at the foot of a wooded rise a few miles from the tavern. Through the trees, the waters of the pond gleamed like metal. Boulders nestled among a carpet of dried pinecones and rust-colored needles. The hillside rose through a stand of hemlocks. Bertram hopped down.

"It's just up the top of this ridge." He wiped his hands on the sides of his breeches.

I climbed down and followed him through hazel, buckthorn, and chokeberry. Our steps crunched on the thick carpet beneath the boughs. A few stretches grew so steep I had to grasp nearby trunks and branches, my fingers coming away tacky with dried pine-pitch. As we neared the crest, I felt a strange energy. Gnarled trunks of hemlock rose around the clearing at the top, broomstick branches coming out parallel to the ground. Beneath stood a weathered stone wall, a flat field stone in the center laid atop a circle of stones, strands of thorny rosebush in front. I stopped in my tracks, winded from the climb.

"There it is," Bertram said. He took off his hat and wiped the sweat from his forehead.

Witchcraft stretched from the stones of the wall to the edge of the clearing, beautiful and orderly, an intricate tapestry. Curls, spirals, long parallel lines, spun and carved and sculpted out of colors and hues that echoed dawn touching a weathered stone, the sun shining through a spring bloom, candlelight on a porcelain edge. I sensed motion, as if the witchcraft were a delicate gear work that turned on hidden principles of nature, and time. The wall itself hummed with wards and well-crafted seals.

The terrors are gone. The path here was won at great cost. We spared nothing in sealing out the threat.

A shiver ran through me; it was clearly one of the protections put in place against the evil that had enveloped Salem. A monument to the dead, left by the witches who'd struggled and died in the darkness, those who'd survived long enough to seal out the threat. I approached the wall and crouched before the lichen-dappled stones.

The shadows burrow through this place. Infect it. Demons, of the darkest sort. We've tried all that we can, but our strength is overmatched, and our efforts draw more darkness. All I ask is for shelter. For the young ones, and the infirm.

Stones here and there had come loose and tumbled. Strands of witchcraft glowed in and around them.

"Even in the daylight, still gives me a shiver," Bertram said. "There's a bit of a crack near the edge of that lid. You can see into it—not that you can see much."

Leaning over the large flat stone, I felt a chill breeze coming up through the weathered crack. As I held my hand out, a slender filament of witchcraft twisted and connected with my palm. A powerful charge ran through my arms and torso. Without even trying, my own witchcraft slipped into sympathy with the energy around the stones, and I sensed it extended beyond this plane through passages glamoured and bound, straining at unseen forces like the sails and lines of a great ship that bound the wind itself.

"Katie, are you—"

"Give me a moment."

The wild energies woven throughout the stones shifted, dappled with bright reflections. As I looked more closely, I saw darker strands. Faded. Moving my hands through them, the sensation changed to something tattered and uneven. Frayed across gaps, stretches where it had loosened or torn. I sat back on my heels.

"Now don't try to frighten me, pretending to hear a voice," Bertram said. "One calling for *Bertraaaaaam*. Old trick. My cousin sent me home crying with that one when I was about six."

"Does it look the same to you?"

"Unreasonably terrifying? Yes. Maybe a tad more decrepit. Couldn't really say."

Strands of faded witchcraft wriggled, and I reached out and put my hand through one. A charge ran through my hand. My own energy flared from my palm—and color filled the shadowed witchcraft, the blue of an October sky. I watched as the color traced its way back to the heart of the stones.

"Is there a breeze coming from it?" Bertram said. "What are you doing?"

I closed my fingers and the connection broke, as though I'd pulled my hand from a swift stream. "Maybe I'll just have a look —it's quite interesting. You go on without me. You take the wagon —I'll walk back to the tavern in a while."

"What—leave you here in the woods? Alone?"

"Bertram, I'm fine."

"So were those girls who drowned. Fine. And then they walked back into the murky depths, right down there. Fine."

"I'm not going near the water."

"Doesn't seem right. Not what a gentleman ought to do."

"A gentleman ought to respect a young woman's wishes." I

smiled. "And don't forget, I run errands on my own all the time. Here. Boston. Towns and woods in between."

"I still don't feel right about it."

"Because you're considerate. A lovely quality. But go—shoo." I flicked my fingers. "Iris will be needing your help, no doubt—and I don't need her scolding me for taking you away for too long."

He looked at me, at the witch-well, down the slope toward the water, then back at me. Nodded. "As you wish—but I don't know what else you'll find. Rocks. Well. That's about it."

"I'll let you know if it gets more interesting—I promise."

"Fine." He doffed his hat, frowning, then set off down the wooded hillside.

I watched until he was out of sight, then waited for another few minutes. Turning back to the witchcraft, I felt along the faded stretches of energy, running my hands as though working my way across a bolt of cloth, feeling for broken threads in the weave. When I found a loose end, I connected it with the thicker strands of energy that rose from the heart of the stones, letting instinct guide me. The interchange of witchcraft drew me in, and I found it exhilarating. For all my blind fumbling with my own witchcraft, I'd never encountered the work of another witch—yet there it was, all around me, connecting with my own.

The further I went, the more I grasped how it worked. Had I not studied wards and glamours with Swaine, I'm not sure I'd have been able to make heads nor tails of it—in fact, I most certainly *wouldn't* have known even how to start, or what I was even confronting. Yet, between that and my own intuition, I discovered a manner in which the frayed bindings might be reinforced by knitting them together with more potent streams. At some point, I got to my feet, manipulating the magic in broad sheets, gesturing with both arms, tucking, straightening, checking how true it was, running my awareness over the connections I'd made.

So intent was I on the work that I failed to register the footsteps snapping twigs and dragging through the fallen pine needles. For a brief moment, I thought it Bertram, driven back over my objections by his budding sense of a gentleman's responsibilities—until I heard singing.

"Oh! woman, woman, woman. What have you been and done?"

I spun, startled from the witchcraft. Two young girls crested the hilltop, holding hands, their sodden clothing dripping streams of brackish pond water. Their skin had grown puffy and swollen, while their eyes glinted, black and brooding. Above them, their hair floated as though swept upward in a gentle current. Horrid smiles cracked their faces, and when they sang, they sang together, voices high and tremulous:

"You have killed the finest butcher, that ever the sun shone on!"

Hints of shadow passed over them, even as the sunlight and branch shadows wavered.

"With my hey, ding, ding, with my ho, ding, ding. With my high, ding, ding, high dey!"

A sickening dread crashed over me, flooding my senses. I wanted to retch, to scratch my own skin off, to grip my bones and wring them clear of the leaden doom that seeped into them. My ears felt as though they crawled with bugs and my nose filled with the sweet bruised stench of decomposing flesh. The corpses stared at me with a fulsome hunger. They sang:

"May God keep all good people from such bad company!"

I recognized it then—a lullaby called "The Three Butchers." I backed off, raising my hands to ward them away, raising my cloak. That helped with the assault on my senses. They stepped closer, still gaping at me, but they paused at the boundary of the witchcraft flowing from the stones. I held my ground.

"I don't think you can come any closer, can you?" I said. "You can only sing."

"With my hey, ding, ding, with my ho, ding, ding. With my high, ding, ding, high dey!" The younger girl clawed at the edges of the flickering lines of witchcraft.

I let the energy on the ground surround me again, reaching out with my senses. Power rolled down my arms. "The lullaby is a nice touch, demon. Very disturbing."

"I watch everything you do, witch." It was the older child who spoke this time, a girl of about nine.

"Then you know you don't belong here."

"I hunger for you." The child licked her pale lips.

"What's your name?"

"Eternity."

"The song was more creative."

"Be careful."

"If you've watched me so closely, you know that I always am."

"Not as careful as you think." This time it was the younger girl who spoke. Her pretty hair floated about her head as though she were underwater, her skin pale like a dough, bloodless. "And your secrets and your shame fester. Ripening. You won't be able to resist."

"You're fooling yourself—just like all the others of your kind."

"There are no others of my kind." She opened her arms in welcome. "Join me, witch. Save yourself the struggle. I can give you a key. A beautiful key, just for you."

Of course, I made no move forward. I didn't let my awareness waver. Corpses, voices, song—it was all distraction. "You don't like what I'm doing."

"I don't care what you're doing."

"Yes, you do, demon."

The corpses shuddered, pressing forward against the boundary that they couldn't pass beyond, horrible expressions of pain on their faces. They groaned.

"But you can't get close. I've made sure."

"You did nothing, witch. Nothing is all you are. Nothing is all you feel. Nothing reaches to nothing. Nothing knows only nothing." An expression of malevolent glee broke across each of the corpses' faces. The effect was ghastly. "Oh, tell us what you know.

What you've guessed. What your lippy-lappy insides tremble with. Fumble, bumble. We want to see you grasp, blind as you are, every lovely, longing, lingering moment until you see what we really are. What we've become. What we will make you feel, you simpering, succulent, dumb, blind witch. You're already too late."

With that, the two girls hurled themselves at me, their faces twisted into rage. Of course, I had a ward ready, Hume's Seventh. As I spat out the words, a flood of energy filled the glade, bright enough to draw my shadow across the ground in firm strokes, bright enough to illuminate the smallest detail of every stone, every branch, every root, every cranny in the soil. An intense power flowed along my arms, the crown of my head, at the point just below my navel. The colors shifted toward indigo and slate gray.

The corpses of the girls crashed back through the branches, bashing along one tree trunk after another. My witchcraft fueled the ward, taking on a character I'd never imagined. High screams filled the woods as the demon fought in vain against the power banishing it from my presence. Down below, the bodies dropped to the ground by the water's edge, rolling, tumbling, cartwheeling back into the pond, leaving only pale trails of bubbles. A moment later, the air over the witch-well shifted, then stilled. The demon was gone.

Beside me, the strands of witchcraft above the stones narrowed, twining and winding into three narrow columns. They rose to the height of the surrounding hemlocks, then joined and burrowed back into the stone wall in one graceful arch. The shift in the atmosphere was profound—trees rattled, branches swayed, my own dress fluttered from the hems to the collar. I glanced at the columns of witchcraft. Shining, spiraled, compact. Powerful beyond anything I was capable of. I put my hand to my mouth, stunned by the connection I'd made.

"Good Heavens."

I spun. Bertram stood at the edge of the clearing, his right arm steadying himself on the trunk of a canting birch tree, his eyes wide.

"I—it's not—what it looks like," I stammered. "Bertram, it's not."

He looked at the freshly broken branches snapped by the corpses, then back at me. "You—they. But, how—or what—I'm sorry. I'm not being clear." He motioned over his shoulder. "I felt wrong leaving. *Bertram*, I told myself, *it's not right, leaving a young lady like that, all on her own.* And so I came back. Thought you'd appreciate the ride."

"What did you see?"

"I can see I should have kept riding. And that I needn't have worried." His words were light, but his face looked drawn and more pale than usual. He kept his hand on the white bark of the birch trunk.

"Please don't say anything. To anyone."

"I'm not—altogether sure what I'd say."

I glanced back toward the water. No sign of the corpses. I felt no presence of the demon. Turning back to Bertram, I went toward him. "You can't say anything. I'll end up in jail. Or worse."

"Because...?" He dragged the word out, his voice low, not looking away from my eye.

Down on the pond, geese argued with one another, their honks echoing up into the trees. Witchcraft rose all around me, more powerful, stronger than when I'd found it. "Because of what I can do," I whispered. "Because of what I *am*."

After a moment, Bertram nodded, slowly. He pointed to the pond. "They tried to kill you."

"They did."

"Corpses."

"Corpses."

"But you—drove them off."

"I did."

"With—" He motioned to the stones, then to my hands.

In for a pence, in for a pound. "Witchcraft."

"Witchcraft."

"Yes. Witchcraft."

"I see." He rubbed his chin. "Which would make you—a witch."

"Who's your friend. Who will stay your friend."

"So that pamphlet is true?"

"No. Nothing in it is true. Save for—well, for me. But he invented the rest. He's using what he knows. About me. For his own ends."

"So once again—I was wrong."

"Wrong?"

"When I said *Here comes someone who's not a witch.*"

"I suppose you were."

"Well, I can see why you wouldn't correct me."

"The colony hasn't been kind to witches."

"No, it hasn't." He took his hat off, ran a trembling hand across his hair, put the hat back on. "Though I hasten to add I had nothing to do with any of that. Nor would I—now that I've a friend who's a witch."

"Bertram."

He approached me. "I won't say anything. If you promise, of course, not to turn me into a newt. Or a toad."

"As long as you behave."

"Ah, I see how it is with you witches."

"How it is with *friends.*"

"Friends—who are witches."

"I'm still me."

"I hope so."

I stepped forward and threw my arms around him, pulling him into a hug. "Thank you, Bertram."

He stiffened in alarm, only gradually relaxing. "I'm still terri-fied, by the way. Corpses."

"Let me handle those." I pulled away, smiling to see the radish-red blush that blazed on his face.

"Well, if you need someone to weep and cower, I can handle that part of it quite well."

"You've done more than you know already."

He'd shown me the witch-well, true—but even more, he'd allowed me to lighten my tinker's pack of secrets, if only by a little.

8

THERE ARE NO SHORTCUTS

The weather turned to showers later that afternoon, heavy downpours that continued day and night through the rest of the week. Still, Swaine brooked no delay in his new plan to reveal the demonmere, and we spent the next few days soaked and miserable as we placed sixteen magicked steel spikes in an elaborate, precise pattern around Salem. In the center of the arrangement, my master's new device would be activated as soon as it was ready. If his theory was correct, the activation would reveal—to me, through my witch nature—any indications of the demonmere. On the fourth day of placing spikes, we stood before the river, the current fast, the water high from days of steady rain.

Swaine squinted at the river, then down at his hand, where he consulted a compass in his palm. "Whoever placed this river here deserves a good talking to. Glass."

I handed him a glass marble, glamoured with a variation of Benjamin Harker's *Pure Line*, a spell that imbued the marble with a chromatic sensitivity, changing the light that shone through it from dull red to bright blue as it neared the exact distance from its entrained twin. As Swaine held the marble up, his foot slipped

98

on a muddy lip and plunged into the water. He steadied himself and shook the drops from his shoe.

"Map."

I handed him the map. He looked it over and consulted the compass again. "This river obviously hasn't read this map."

"The spot isn't on the bank, sir?"

"Now you're taking the map's side. As would I, were I not convinced that reality shall have the victorious cut. Damn it all." He stared at the river as though his displeasure might move the waters by ten feet. "It's right there. Right bloody there."

"How close?"

"Not close enough." He lowered the glass. "We must move the rest. Adjust them all—I don't know, two rods clockwise."

"Wouldn't that put the one near the hillside into those rocks, sir?"

Swaine closed his eyes. "You're right."

"And if we go in the other direction, the one near the old pier would end up—"

"In the harbor. Yes, I see."

"Can't we just put it in the riverbed?" I said. "Aside from the difficulty, that is?"

He considered it for a few moments. "From a functional standpoint, yes. But unless you believe I'm capable of walking underwater, I don't see how it can be installed."

"What if you say the incantation and then dive in?"

"It would still require the gesture."

"You could do that in the water, sir."

He pulled a kerchief from his pocket and blew his nose, having developed the sniffles. "My father tried more than once to teach me to swim, you know. It always ended in swallowed water, choking, and tears. My father, infuriated. Me, half-drowned and trembling. He shouted at me. Struck me." He cleared his throat. "And even after all that, I still can't swim."

"Then let me, sir," I said. I took off the hat I'd worn to keep the rain from my face, placing it atop a bush. "I know the incantation, and the gesture. I've seen you do it fifteen times. I can swim well." I undid the ties at the back of my dress, a sturdy cotton affair in a deep plum. "I don't think you want to repeat the work of the past few days, sir."

Swaine straightened. "God knows you're right on that score, Finch. Well said. That's the spirit."

I slid the satchel I wore over my shoulder to the ground, and then slipped out of the dress, still in my linen shift. After I kicked off my shoes, I picked up a foot-long length of old branch. "To test the bottom first. See how deep, and how soft."

"And how far out." He held out the marble, which I took.

"I'll do that first," I said. I took off my eyepatch and rested it on my folded dress. With the marble and length of stick in my hands, I stepped into the lapping edge of the water. It grabbed at my ankle with a cold grip. "Chilly."

"Don't go drowning on me," Swaine said. "You're the only apprentice I have."

"And you would miss me terribly, sir." I stepped farther out into the water. "Because I'd be dead."

"Well, yes—that's what I meant."

"I'd make a poor revenant, too." The water pushed the air from me as it rose past my knees and thighs. A gasp escaped me as I took the next step, the current tugging at my shift, up to my belly in the flowing water. The bottom fell away.

"The talkative ones always do," Swaine called after me.

Holding the marble tight, I pushed off and floated out. The fresh rain turned the water painfully cold, and I wondered if the whole idea was foolish. Kicking my legs against the current, I swam out until I trod water, then lifted the glass to my eye.

"Aim for the crown of that tall elm," Swaine called out.

I nodded and did so. The color of the marble was a pale violet —nearly there. I paddled out a short distance farther and tried again. "It's blue." I gripped the marble, took in a deep breath, and ducked under the surface, kicking my legs. The water was murky, but I found the bottom quicker than I expected—it was only a foot or so beneath my feet when treading water. I peered at the marble again—it shone soft blue. Good. I jammed the stick into the river bottom. It was sturdy enough for the spike—packed silt, with the consistency of clay. Once it was embedded, I placed the marble next to it, where its glow would help me find it when I returned. I pushed off from the bottom and broke the surface.

My jaw shivered. "It'll work, sir."

I swam back to the shore, standing when I had firm footing. Water fell from me in strands. I noticed that my shift, sodden, had become rather revealing, and I put one hand across my chest—not that Swaine had ever shown the slightest impropriety toward me. (Although I might add that he'd startled *me* more than once by suddenly striding down the hallway from his bath, pink and naked, modesty and manners eclipsed by whatever idea had propelled him from the copper tub. Having had six brothers, however, I wasn't altogether shocked by what I saw.) Swaine met me at the edge, averting his eyes from my body and handing me the spike.

"Now listen carefully," he said. "You must say the incantation at the surface. But I also want you to repeat the phrases silently as you set the spike. I assume the words at the top will be sufficient, but let's not take any chances."

I nodded, wiping the river water from my face, taking the spike.

"You're sure you can do this?" he said.

"I can, sir."

"Be careful."

I nodded, and headed back into the water. The mud of the riverbed smooshed up between my toes. I swam back out and looked for the tall elm again. With a glance back to shore, I nodded, then closed my eye, focusing. It took several moments before I found the proper concentration—the chill faded from my thoughts, my legs and arms kept pace with the current without requiring my attention, and my awareness both focused and expanded into the proper mindset for magic. I gripped the spike and lifted it from the water.

"*Betsta mære cempa. Oððe gripe meces, oððe gares fliht, oððe atol yldo, oððe eagena bearhtm. Forsiteð ond forsworceð. Weold under wolcnum.*" As the words brought forth the glamours embedded in the steel, I gestured with my free hand, struggling not to gargle half the river as I did so. There were five gestures—combinations of bent and angled finger joints, thumb positions, and alignment of the palm—and it took all I had to work through them while staying in the same spot. The steel awoke in my grip. I blew out a long breath and inhaled as deeply as possible, then flipped over, plunging to the bottom, arms and legs straining to get me there.

I'd drifted from the spot I'd marked with the stick, so I had to fight against the current to reach it. The blue glint of the marble shone as a beacon, and I headed straight for it. Pausing at the bottom, my shift caught the current like a sail and wanted to draw me away. I kicked my legs and poked the bottom of the spike into the silty mud. It slid in more easily than the stick had. I pushed hard until the flattened top was flush with the bottom. My lungs hitched, hungry for air.

As I pushed off for the surface, the shadowy muck next to me rose in a ghastly shape—larger than me, and shaped somewhere between a spider and a person with multiple limbs. Like a grotesque fish that had lain in wait, motionless, blending in with the bottom, the demon had gone undetected. In the murky water, I saw flashes of white teeth, spikes that lined the churning limbs, and a cluster of orb eyes as the bubbles and debris filled the water in front of me. The fiend caught my legs in a powerful grip and wrapped other limbs around my torso.

Panic is a strange thing. Time slows to a tenth its normal speed. Thought constricts to a single point. An extra jolt of strength fills the limbs. Within an instant, I realized that I wasn't getting to the surface, no matter how much my lungs protested. Worse, none of the wards I knew would work, for not only was I underwater, I had no breath left in me and the words needed to be spoken.

I thrashed, trying to break free of the repulsive grip, but the entity only wrapped me harder, crushing and bruising me. Once again, I found myself at the threshold of life, about to slip to the other side. I wasn't frightened (though I should have been) nor was I particularly shocked (another proper response), but rather gripped by disappointment, as the thought *This is how I die* appeared with absurd calm and clarity in my mind. My vision filled with throbbing black spots, and I wondered if it mightn't be easier to take in a deep breath of water before the beast crushed me.

But no. In what might have been my last, flickering moments of awareness, I rebelled against death: I'd had cornbread and tea, ninety minutes earlier; I'd put on my scuffed work shoes; it was Tuesday.

Somehow, I turned that sense of implausibility, the connection to the most banal details of life, into a great swelling of natural witchcraft. Without thinking, I pushed out a pulse of energy. The power ran through the vile appendages, and it loosened its grip. That's when it jolted me with a massive shock of lightning. The water lit up with the strange zigzags of current. Without realizing how, I deflected the charge, directing it right back into the fiend. I screamed, my last lungful of air burbling up from my open mouth: a war cry. As the limbs retracted from me, jerking back and forth and filling the water with burst scales and skin, I swallowed river water, trying to push myself away. My back hit the bottom. With so much witchcraft roiling the water, I had lost track of down from up. I shoved off from the river bed.

Hands grabbed my collar. For a moment, they felt as though they were shoving me down deeper, holding me from rising. As water flooded my nose and mouth, the arms hoisted me up. A confused moment later, my head broke the surface of the river. Blessed air taunted me—with mouth, throat, and nose full of water, I couldn't inhale. I did something between a retch and a cough, water spilling out, water swallowed, water seeming to come out my nose, my ears, and my eye. I couldn't get a breath. Coughing, choking, spitting, I flailed.

Above the sounds of my desperate attempts to rid the river from my lungs, I heard Swaine crying out. The demon fled as the banks of the river rumbled. Water raced up the ground and retreated—leaving only the gurgle and sigh of the river, flowing again with no disturbance. My limbs tingled, and I managed only gasping, rattling breaths.

"Finch?" Swaine shouted. His hands clamped underneath my arms and he dragged me to shore. On the damp ground, my feet free of the river at last, he placed me on my stomach and pressed on my back. More water sieved out my mouth. "That's it—take a breath. Come on."

My lungs felt as though they'd crumpled to a quarter their size, and they wheezed and crackled as I fought air into them. With a lengthy fit of coughing and cramping, I rid myself of the last of the water in my throat and nose, light-headed. I dug my fingers into the earth to keep myself from swooning. Swaine got off my back, apparently satisfied that treating me like bellows would produce no further liquid.

"Are you all right?"

I nodded weakly, simply grateful for the sips of air I could finally take in.

He sat back on his heels and put his face in his hands. His shoulders shook. "Oh God, why did I do that? I never—I couldn't —" He leaned over me. "I'm so sorry. Are you hurt?"

As he stared at me, I saw that his left eye appeared a paler gray than his right, which I'd never before noticed. "Just—" I squeaked out before another round of hacking took me. With effort, I whispered, "I'll be fine." The world tilted sideways, but I remained upright as it soon corrected itself.

Swaine nodded, and shook his arms, drips and threads of water falling from his sleeves, his coat, his hair. He wiped his eyes and turned back to the river. "My demons took care of it—though not without a struggle."

With my lungs mostly working again, I calmed my breathing. "You swam in. After me."

"An overly generous description of what I did. Thrashing and panicking was more like it. I sensed the demon and luckily saw a flash of your shift beneath the surface. You're sure you're fine?"

I nodded. "I couldn't say a ward, so I used my witchcraft—I think it might have worked, if only a little."

"Well, desperate measures and all that." He sniffled and came closer. "Let me make sure."

I nodded. He stood over me and spoke the words to a spell of detection, looking to see that no demon had gained a foothold on my mind, that no remnant remained. He followed with a second incantation, then nodded.

"You're clear, thank God," he said. His voice shook. He wiped his wet hair from his forehead. His eyes showed a concern I'd never seen. In that moment, I saw that I wasn't just a servant. Nor was I just an apprentice, a mirror for his ego, a receptacle for his copious knowledge, a spare hand for his work, a pupil whose progress was yet another burden on his time. No, the fear—and thankfulness—in his eyes told me I was closer to him than perhaps anyone else in his own life had ever been. I was the family that his pursuit of sorcery had supplanted. "Thank God, Finch. It was foolish. Desperation. There are no shortcuts, and my mistake nearly cost us. No. We'll do it right. We'll replot the locations. If they don't fit, there's a variation with fewer nodes I think might be effective, in which case—"

"I got it in, sir."

"Sorry? You what?"

"The spike. I got it set properly. Right before that—thing rose from the murk."

"You got it in?"

I nodded. "Set it. Just like the rest."

"You're positive?"

"We can test it, I suppose."

He stared at me, and his expression softened. His voice broke as he spoke. "Bravo, Finch. Bravo. That's magnificent."

I tried to stand and found my legs had gone weak. Swaine stepped forward and took my hands, helping me to my feet. He turned and handed me my eyepatch, and dress. "You've impressed me again."

Impressed him? Again? I don't believe I'd heard praise any stronger than *That should do* or *Adequate* in all the time I'd devoted my efforts toward learning the fundamentals of magic from him. We may have come into each other's lives through reasons unknowable, too complex to be ever understood, but it was clear that we'd grown into—well, if not family, then something rather more than what either of us had imagined on that fateful evening when I'd arrived in Salem, tossed in a wagon full of corpses. I found nothing to say to Swaine's remark beyond a mumbled "Thank you, sir."

9

———

UNENDING TROUBLES

The next day brought a respite from the rain, though not the cold my master had caught from four days of working in the deluge. He sneezed, honked his nose into a rag, and muttered his displeasure at the frailty of the flesh for the entire ride into Boston to retrieve his glassware from Mr. Keefe's shop. I drove the wagon, tending to my own worries between *Bless you, sirs*. More than once, I noticed Swaine wiping at the corner of his left eye. When I could finally hold back no longer, I said, "Has something happened to your eye, sir?"

"Yes. It's attached to my failing body, unfortunately."

The wagon bounced over a stretch of washout as we drove along Orange Street.

"The color—well, it looks lighter than it once did," I said.

"I beg your pardon?"

"The iris, sir."

Swaine blinked half a dozen times, tears pooling in his lashes. "Now it's all I can think about, thank you very much. Lighter, you say?"

"You haven't looked in a mirror?"

"My apprentice has monopolized the lone looking glass in the

107

manse, believe it or not. Admiring herself in a succession of outrageous, impractical outfits. I haven't had a moment to gaze dramatically at myself ever since."

"Did you do something to it, sir?"

"I may have. Interesting that it should appear different in hue." He sneezed twice, groaning in between. "My first attempt at glamouring the glass marble must have done it. It didn't quite work, for reasons that elude me. One rather blinding flash while I was staring closely at it made the misfire abundantly clear. Some stray magic must have reacted with my eye. I suppose I can be thankful it wasn't worse."

"Thankful indeed, sir."

He waved away *my* tone this time. "Now, now—no implied critique or comment on your condition, Finch. You do more with your lone eye than most people do with a full set, so don't go trawling for pity from me. My vision hasn't changed. Minor irritation. The mortifying appearance of weeping. I shall make a note of it when I have a spare minute, which is to say probably within the decade. Give or take."

By the time I pulled the wagon to a stop down the corner from Keefe's shop, Swaine's complaints about his eye had taken on the tenor of blame directed at me for having called attention to it. He kept it shut as he climbed down to the ground.

"If I recall, there is an apothecary just down that way," he said, motioning with his rag. "Be so good as to inquire after a balm or ointment that might tamp down the irritation of an eye. And anything to help with this blasted ague. A noose if all else fails, there's a good apprentice."

In spite of the warming sunshine, Swaine wrapped his scarf more tightly about his neck, shivering. Without another word, he turned on his heel and headed into Keefe's shop. I followed the street, searching for the apothecary shop. Women walked in pairs, baskets tucked in elbows from the marketplace. Two men, wigged and well-tailored, argued with one another, the taller pointing the stem of his pipe, the shorter shaking his head with vehemence. A lad in front of a chandler's shop swept a mound of manure off to the side of the doorway, squinting at the cloudless sky as a clutch of gulls winged past, their cries echoing off brick and cobble.

You're being followed, Mistress. Inverressayte's presence crawled into my head. I stumbled, nearly tripping over my own feet.

After a pause, I kept walking. "Where have you been?" I whispered.

Where all lowly servants reside. Lonesome. Cold. Alone.

"I was almost devoured by a demon yesterday. I could have used a warning then."

I stay well away when he's around. The big one. He frightens me.

"Who's following me?" The lad with the broom glanced at me, overhearing my whisper. I smiled at him and kept walking.

I could kill him so we could find out, Mistress. Tear him from crevice to crown. Spell his name out in his intestines.

"Awfully aggressive for a demon who frightens so easily. I just want to know who he is."

A puny, gasping, sloshing ant—like all the rest, begging your pardon, most noble Mistress.

"How do you know he's following me?"

He has something of yours—something that carries your inimitable scent. The same scent that make so many of my kin want to devour you. I can hardly blame them. Not that I ever would, Mistress. Your obvious succulence pales before your towering will and glaring spirit, the sureness of purpose that—

I paused at the corner of a timber and plaster tavern whose sign read *Willow's Walk.* "Enough. Which one is he? And where?"

Just out of sight, but watching you. Watched you since the terrible man you keep company with discharged his nasal passages across the past three streets, Mistress.

"He's still following?"

Indeed.

"You can't get near him, can you?" I whispered. "You're lying about gutting him."

I would never lie about something as delightful as that.

"Except you're lying now."

You think so little of me, Mistress. I'm only here to serve. I could easily have said nothing, couldn't I? But even my most benevolent assistance is taken and twisted, smeared with imagined ill intent, I see. Any other servant would have been more than happy to see your pursuer do his worst, I hope you know.

"Then why tell me at all, Inverressayte?"

I felt the demon hiss at my use of his name.

I'm here to serve, Mistress. And my greatest—nay, only—hope is that the service I might render you will be of such spotless utility and good will that you will see it in your heart to release me, to let me live out the rest of my dwindling days in peace. Harmless and thankful, forever indebted to your kindness.

That sounded perfectly fine to me. I didn't enjoy communicating with a demon. The unpredictability. The comments. Never knowing when he was there, when he wasn't. Yet Swaine was insistent I learn the foundational skills of sorcery—so here he was. Perhaps the demon found the arrangement as odious as I did.

"We'll see about that," I whispered. "Now—where is he?"

Behind the barrels, just over there.

As casually as I could, I looked back. A cooper's workshop occupied a corner at a cross street. I didn't see anyone following or hiding, but I wanted to see if Inverressayte was telling the truth. Turning, I headed past the apothecary's and slipped down a narrow lane that ran perpendicular to the road. From there, I ducked behind the back wall of a stable and waited.

"Did he follow?"

He's coming closer, Mistress. I can hurl something at him—one of these fence posts. Slates from the roof. Cleave his head from his shoulders—should you desire.

"No. I do not."

Yes, Mistress. Guile suits you better, I must say.

"Silence."

The clank of a farrier on the other side of the stable rang out into the lane. I didn't have to wait long before a man sauntered past the spot I'd chosen. He wore a brown coat and black breeches, while an unruly beard reached down almost to his collar, longer hair tied back beneath his tricorn hat. Hands in his pockets, he glanced about—perhaps an ordinary Bostonian coming from a coffeehouse, looking for anything of interest, or maybe someone looking for me. As he passed down the lane, I extended a hint of witchcraft—and there it was: my pendant.

I stepped from the back of the stable. "I'm not at all happy about your damned pamphlets."

To his credit, Francis didn't quite jump—though he startled. He turned to me. And there they were, the same eyes I found so disarming; this time they rode above a beard that glinted with hints of copper in the sunlight.

"And that's the last time you ever mention anything about *witches* again," I spat.

He raised his palms to me as though unfairly accused. "There wasn't—"

"No. I'm not interested in your excuses. Word after word after word of them. If you set that particular string of letters into type once more, I shall see to it that you don't have any fingers left to ever lift another letter from a type case again."

He lowered his hands. "A fine welcome back, Miss Finch."

"I hope you're listening."

"I'm working on that skill, believe it or not. Here's an example. I'm happy to listen to you when I ask you this: Where's Clara?"

"Don't change the subject."

"You *did* promise. Or wasn't I listening?"

I stepped closer to him. "I've been looking for her ever since she disappeared—it's not as easy as you seem to think."

"So you haven't found her."

"I'm closer than I've managed to get so far."

"What does *closer* mean?"

"It means I may have a chance—*may*, mind you—unless I'm clapped in irons because of your idiotic pamphlets putting half the colony on notice. What were you even thinking?"

"It's not about you."

"No? It's not? '*A Witch Roams the Province and Your Governor Quails*'? I'm sorry—were you referring to some other witch?"

"It's about the governor. It's *all* about the governor."

"Because that's the word that's catching people's eye. You must think I'm stupid."

"Far from it. In fact, you're surely smart enough to see that it's just a rhetorical device. A conceit designed to pry at the existing cracks in the foundation of the governor's already crumbling support."

I held up my hand. "Sorry. First off, I'm not one of those to grow weak-kneed at your vocabulary. Second, I actually read your pamphlet, and your 'rhetorical device' takes up about four-fifths of the text and I fail to see how that won't have people looking over their shoulders for—oh, I don't know—women with a touch of the unseen about them, just to name a far-fetched example. Or should they be lowering their brows at the governor as a result of your clever leveraging of a conceit? Because if that's what you think, then I don't think you've thought it through well enough. To exactly no one's surprise."

If I'd expected him to wither at my pointed words—well, he didn't. In fact, the half smile on his lips, just visible through his unshaven bristles, remained infuriatingly steadfast. "It's not as though I printed your name and residence."

"I wouldn't have been so nice about this if you had."

A stable boy led a mare out of the gate behind me. Francis stepped aside and we waited until the lad had the horse to the corner.

"Listen," he said after the boy was out of earshot. "Everything is different now. This is real change getting ready to happen. It isn't just me and a handful of apprentices anymore. There's money. Funding. Resources. I'm getting support. Volunteers. I have places to stay. Ways to get around. Access to a press."

"Clearly."

"Word got around about the witch-pole. No one needed a pamphlet of mine to hear about that. But what you're missing is that it might very well prove to be the key to undermining the governor. And a key is just a little thing. A tool. It's the unlocking that matters. Trust me, no one will learn about you from me."

"Francis—you printed a pamphlet about me."

"Not *Miss Katie Finch*. We just needed to catch people's eye. Something to stand out above the gossip. And, after all, one of the tensions between His Majesty and the governor is precisely about the special status we have. Different from all the other colonies. If that status isn't even working—well, it's not going to help the governor keep the King happy."

"So now you're fighting for the King? That's what this is about?"

"No—it's about justice. Governor Whitelocke is fattening his own pockets, fattening his friends' purses, making the rich richer and the poor poorer. I've been told there are men of integrity ready to have their names put to the King, ready to step in and turn things around."

"Who told you this?"

"As I said—I have support now. They've seen what we started."

"Killing General Whitelocke."

"You know it was an accident."

"Do they?"

"We can make a difference here. Don't you see?"

"I promised you Clara, if I can rescue her. I didn't promise one inch further as far as anything else."

He stared at me until I wanted to look away. I didn't. "Or maybe you've grown a little too close to the Whitelockes?" he said.

"You've been *spying* on me?" I stepped closer to him. "Of course. You were spying on me just now."

"I just happened to see you ride past. That's all."

"But before?"

"This is a movement. We have eyes and ears."

"You listen to me—I'm not part of your plans. I have more than enough trouble at the moment. I have eyes and ears, as well. Better than yours. If you so much as breathe a word of my comings or goings—none of which are in any way your business —I will make sure you regret it."

"You haven't denied it."

"There's nothing to deny. I do what I have to. Think what you will, I don't care."

His half smile remained. My skin tingled, itching to cast a spell on him.

"I think you're going to change your mind," he said.

"Think again." I held my hand out. "Give me my pendant. Now."

A flash of uncertainty crossed his eyes, I was pleased to see. For a moment, I thought he might deny he had it on him, but he reached beneath his beard and collar and pulled it out. I yanked it from his hand. The smile finally left his mouth.

I shoved it into my pocket, noticing his warmth on the metal. "Don't think I'm at your disposal. I'll let you know when I find Clara, if I do. Until then, back off. Don't make the mistake of mentioning me to anyone again—and I'll consider doing the same. Are we clear?"

He didn't dare tell me I'd change my mind. He raised his hands. "Fine."

I turned and headed back to the corner where the apothecary's stood.

Mistress? Inverressayte cooed in my thoughts.

It wasn't the worst idea I'd ever had. "Don't hurt him. Just frighten him," I breathed.

Thank you, Mistress. I didn't care for the tone he used with you.

I glanced over my shoulder. Francis stood by the stable, no doubt struggling to bite down on one last condescending remark to leave me with. His hat leaped from his head. Both sleeves of his coat tore off, wrenching a cry from his throat. The front of his coat and the shirt beneath erupted in rips in the pattern of claw marks.

"That's enough, Inverressayte," I whispered.

I can do so much more, Mistress. I beseech you—let me show this guttersnipe to mind his tongue when he talks to you.

"No, you're finished. Back off. Now."

The demon said nothing further, but made his disappointment known with a long, dramatic sigh.

"You owe me yet another shirt," Francis called after me.

I ignored him, hurrying along to fetch Swaine his balm. Maybe the apothecary had a balm for unending troubles.

10

A SHADOW AMONG SHADOWS

As midnight neared, I sat back and yawned, bleary-eyed from my studies. Books spread out around me, their pages marked with scraps of paper, with ribbons. I'd only half focused on my work, my mind returning again and again to Francis, to witches and their wells, to the letters, to the demonmere. The house was quiet. I'd convinced Swaine to go to bed soon after dark, his chills turning to a fever, his mood scratchy and self-pitying. He'd surprised me by agreeing. Robert Twelves puttered around in the workshop until a few hours later, then knocked a goodnight on the door jamb to my room as he headed to his own room, our bond based in part on mutual exhaustion.

I reached for more tea, but had long since finished it. The hearth was down to cinders. Wax trailed out from the bases of the candlesticks. I was done for the night. Before I snuffed the candles, I took a cloak down from the hook by the door and stepped into the hallway, needing to use the outhouse before I slept. I stepped softly to the stairs. As I reached the bottom, I stopped. A figure sat on the floor outside the door to Swaine's study: the revenant of the young woman, the one who unnerved me with her constant lurking. I plunged my hand into the pocket of my dress and took hold of my skeleton key.

"Get back to your spot," I said. "In the cellar. Now."

She lifted her head, giving me a demure smile. Her hands were on a book in her lap. "You'll find the answer in here." Her voice was a silken whisper. A tremor ran through her—a demon might dawdle, but they must obey a command. As she turned to the kitchen and the stairs to the cellar, she clasped her hands around the book and held it out toward me.

"Don't touch any books from now on," I snapped. "And while you're at it, stay out of any place that isn't the cellar. I forbid you to leave that spot. Do you understand?"

"I'll always be there for you."

"You'll always be there—you're right. Now give me that." As I reached for the book, I pulled up short, yanking my hand back. "How did you get that?"

The book in the young woman's hand was the *Occultatum Ostium*. I'd seen Swaine lock it away earlier.

"Answer me!" I lifted the key from my pocket and held it out before her. The demons found direct line of sight to the key to be woeful.

She recoiled. "I plucked it from the air."

"Liar. Tell me the truth."

"The air. It floated down the hallway. It spun."

"You're forbidden from entering your master's study."

"I didn't."

I wasn't about to get drawn into a debate with an insidious, lying demon. "Put it down. On the floor. Now."

"Your answers are here." She grimaced at the nearness of the key, but placed the book on the floorboards.

"The cellar, now. Go."

She headed to the cellar door, still watching me. "It's all for you."

"Silence." There wasn't a demon whom I disliked more. I

watched her open the door and step down into the darkness. Once she was out of sight, I turned my attention to the book. I didn't want to touch it—but I wasn't about to wake Swaine from the sleep he so desperately needed. I slipped the key back into my pocket and knelt. With a surfeit of caution, I brought it back to Swaine's study, uneasy with the way the weight seemed to change in my grip. It had a strange heft to it—at one moment lighter, at another heavier. Crossing into Swaine's study, I gave a quick glance at Mr. Winters. The revenant stood next to the glamoured cabinet, unmoving. In the dim moonlight falling in through the window, his eyes tracked me.

The locked cabinet stood open. I looked at Winters again. "Who did this? Was it that one?" I said, nodding my head toward the hallway.

"It was no one," Winters said in his curious voice.

"No one? Then what did you see?"

"Nothing."

I pointed to the cabinet. "The door is open. It was closed. Surely you saw how that happened?"

"It opened."

"Yes, I can see that. How did it open?"

"It opened."

It was in keeping with the uneasy history of that tome: appearing and disappearing, directed by subtle magicks that rendered its presence as unpredictable as luck, as likely to stray as a memory, as restless as a ghost.

"*When* did it open?" I said.

"Earlier."

"How much earlier? What hour?"

"The hours are endless."

"Answer me: What hour did the door to this cabinet open?"

Winters's eyes shone with antipathy. "The twelfth hour."

On the mantel next to him ticked a clock. The hands said it was four minutes after midnight.

"What—do you mean just now? Four minutes ago?"

"Yes."

"And it opened on its own?"

"It opened. Creeeeeeeeek."

I regarded the cabinet. I knew the squeak that Winters referenced, a hinge that balked. As I neared the cabinet, the open door slammed shut, catching the corner of the book as it did and knocking it from my hesitant grip. I yelped. The book landed facedown and open.

"No, no." I bent to get it, lifting it by the spine, finding two pages toward the middle bent in half, folded flat. Balancing the book, I attempted to smooth them. The curious paper held up well, I was relieved to see—much of Swaine's collection was so fragile that even trying to turn a page was a fraught endeavor. I folded back the page, and there I stopped with a small gasp.

The page beneath my fingers showed an illustration in faded black ink, flecks of dull red and gold scribed around the edges of the drawing. The drawing depicted a figure peering into a standing mirror: a woman wearing a plain dress and cloak, only visible from behind. The hair, the dress—I recognized both, for it was Clara, as I'd last seen her the night of the governor's ball.

My fingers trembled. "Mirror," I whispered. She'd mentioned a mirror she'd found within the demonmere. *But I see you in this mirror*, she'd said. *And this mirror flared with a beautiful light when I saw you.*

I lifted the book and peered at the drawing. Within the mirror's glass was what looked to be a workshop that stretched the length of a house. Slanted ceilings marked a gabled roof. The long tables held an abundance of instruments, diagrams, mechanisms, books, quills and ink-wells, maps, glassworks, and sundry items I couldn't identify, other than that they were of a magical nature. In the center of the image was a map, tacked to a board and stood on end before one of the workbenches.

Scribed beneath the drawing were words: *The Doctor has the map. The Ring is the key. The Crypt has the answer.*

I looked more closely at the page, bringing the book over to the window so the moonlight might better reveal the details. The map? Small as it was, it appeared to have detail, showing marks and notations over what was clearly the northeastern portion of the colony—the harbor in Salem was clear, as was Boston's.

The map I've included marks the worst locations and where we've tried to seal it—you should have it in case we fail. So had Ginny Lane written to Archibald Fletcher. Was that what I was seeing?

I'm not sure how long I stood there, my eyes drawn back again and again to the image. A brush of eldritch light wavered across the page. The lines of the drawing flared like silver—and then faded. I touched the page as though to stop the disappearance, but by the time my palm landed on the book, Clara, the mirror, along with the image of the workshop and map vanished as though sinking below the surface of a pale lake. A shiver ran along my spine. It seemed impossible—or so I might have believed, had I not been holding the *Occultatum Ostium*, the strange enigma that had bedeviled the occult arts for centuries. Did it know my thoughts? Was it answering, in one image, the question I'd scoured a dozen other books in search of?

I wanted to flip through page after page after page, trying to draw forth yet more answers. No. Swaine's first caution rang in my mind: *know when you're nearing a mistake.* I may not have honed my instincts to the level that my master had, but in this case, I didn't need to. Exhausted, my head brimming with possibilities I'd never considered, and alone, it wasn't anywhere near the time to go traipsing through a book that had its own agenda.

I closed the book and again approached the cabinet. Before my fingers reached the knob, I spun sideways—a strange combination of slipping on the smoothest ice imaginable, and being pulled by the wrist.

"Wonderful," I muttered. I tried again, and the same thing

happened, as it did from every angle I attempted. Worse, my arm went numb. As I'd guessed, Swaine had left the cabinet heavily glamoured. I turned to the revenant. "Mr. Winters, please open this cabinet door."

"Doubtful."

"Do as I say."

He approached the cabinet and stopped. "It is wound and bound. Chained and restrained. Rather like me."

"I don't need your comments. Please open it."

"I can cross no farther to it."

"Try."

His head ticked to the left several times, but he raised a foot—and flipped head over heels. He folded to the floor, then righted himself.

No, neither one of us could get the cabinet open—only Swaine.

"Damn it," I whispered.

I settled for placing the book in the middle of Swaine's writing desk, under the watchful eyes of Mr. Winters. Would Swaine realize I'd touched it? Could I deny ever having seen it? What if it vanished altogether? Whatever would happen would have to happen, I decided. What else was I to do?

Winters had no comment.

Leaving it so, I hurried out to the privy, listening to the wind sough through the new leaves of the maples beneath the stars. The image I'd seen haunted me: Clara gazing into a strange mirror.

The Doctor has the map. The Ring is the key. The Crypt has the answer.

And I dragged myself back into the house, a shadow among shadows, and headed up to my room. Snuffing the candles, I burrowed beneath my blankets, wondering how many nights I might spend rummaging through riddles. Slumber came slowly.

11

BURIAL SILVER

Morning found me busy with chores. I'd heard Swaine moving about around dawn, but he'd continued resting after that. Quite unlike him. I made enough porridge for the three of us, listening to Twelves slurp his up as he confessed to me he'd taken a fancy to a lass whose father owned the sawmill over on the Shawsheen River.

"She's big. Tall," he said. "Seen her lift a wagon wheel over her head."

"Have you spoken with her?"

"Twice. And both times, I panicked."

"Panicked?"

"I don't know what happens. Words just come dumping out of my mouth. In clumps. Don't even know where they come from. Last time I told her I love deep snow. In the woods."

I laughed. "Why did you tell her that?"

"I've no idea. It just blurted out."

"I've only ever seen you curse about the snow."

"Not the kind in the woods. The deep snow."

"Since when have you tromped about in the woods? In the deep snow? *Is* that even something you enjoy?"

He pointed his spoon at me. "Exactly."

"She probably found it endearing. Especially if you were blushing like you are now."

"I'm ridiculous."

"Don't give up. Just be—genuine."

He finished up his porridge and tossed the spoon in the empty bowl. "That's my worry—I might be genuinely ridiculous."

"You're not. You're talented. Ambitious. Clever enough to be impressive. Awkward enough to earn sympathy."

"Promise to carve those last two lines on my tombstone if I embarrass myself to death." He stood and pulled on his coat. "I'm headed over there this morning to pick up more lumber."

I patted him on the shoulder as I picked up his empty bowl. "Smile. Look her in the eyes. Ask her how she is this morning. Listen to what she says."

"I'll probably end up praising parsnips. Lord help me." He went to the door. "Thanks for the porridge. And the advice. Tell him I'll be back before noon, when he gets up."

After he left, I brought in firewood for the hearths and gave the downstairs a sweep. In Swaine's study, the *Occultatum Ostium* remained where I'd left it, which left me half-relieved (for I'd had dreadful thoughts of it disappearing for good with me to blame) and half-anxious (for Swaine might blame me for not fetching him during the night). Nothing I could do, so I ignored it and the knot in my stomach. As I stood in the open front door, sweeping my pile of dust and debris out into the warming air, a four-horse carriage rounded the bend from the lane. I stopped sweeping.

A soldier and driver in scarlet uniforms sped the carriage along, slowing only as they neared the house. With Swaine still sick, I hesitated to wake him. Instead, I leaned the broom in the entryway and went out to meet the carriage. The enormous carriage rocked to a stop in a cloud of dust from the lane.

Mary Whitelocke leaned out of the window, waving her

porcelain fingers at me. "If you can't bring Mohamed to the mountain, as they say."

"Madam Whitelocke." I curtseyed. The soldier and driver had no need to learn of our familiarity.

The soldier climbed down and opened the door for Mary, lowering an iron step from within. Demure in a violet dress and petticoat, a cape of black silk draping her shoulders, Mary exited, shading her eyes with one slender hand. "No more shall your master dodge my written invitations. He can't avoid my recital through silence."

"Begging your pardon, madam—Master Swaine has taken ill and is still asleep."

"A transparent ruse."

"No ruse at all, madam. Fever, sweating, weakness. I'm sure he would be mortified to see you in such condition."

She looked closely at me. I nodded. She sighed. "How unfortunate. I say, as long as I'm here, a quick tour of the grounds. I've heard so much about it from August, I'd at least value putting a visual to all he's referenced."

"Of course, madam. As you wish."

She turned to the soldier. "Give me a quarter of an hour. We shall have plenty of time to reach Reading for my visit."

"Yes, ma'am."

She turned from him and walked alongside me. "Show me the vaunted orchards, if you would be so kind, miss."

"Yes, madam. This way."

When we were out of earshot of the driver and guard, she leaned in. "Is he really ill?"

"He really is. He never stops and it's catching up with him. He just needs rest."

"You'll give him my regards. And convince him to attend my recital. In a way, it's not the worst of circumstances—I did want to speak with you before our next session."

I led her alongside the vegetable garden I'd planted a few

weeks back. Slender sprouts already stretched from the earth. She looked back at the carriage, then put her hand on my arm as we passed beneath a trio of birch trees dappling the ground with shadows. "I've gotten hold of something I understand is quite rare. It's called *argentum inferi*. Have you heard of it?"

Conscious that the soldier or driver might be watching us, I managed not to come to a full stop. "Burial silver?"

"That's it exactly. Are you impressed?"

Impressed? I was dumbfounded. Argentum inferi—also known as *burial silver*—was one of the rarest of ingredients used in the unseen arts, as it could only be produced from century-old graves of magicians, individuals who deliberately planned to use their own deaths to add to the world's quite limited supply. The metal possessed a tremendous potency, and was known to have a particular usefulness in bindings, capable of rendering glamoured objects impregnable to countermagic. It was also prone to violent and unpredictable interactions with other magic.

"How did you even hear about burial silver, let alone get any of it?" I said.

"I happen to have made a connection back when I was in London. He recommended it—it's quite rare, you know."

"Mr. Chesterton of Southwark? Mr. Hill of Chiswick?" Having corresponded with both men on Swaine's behalf numerous times, I was certain that neither of the aforementioned dealers would sell such an item to an unknown practitioner.

"I don't know them."

"Then please tell me it's not Israel Benedict." Her silence said I'd hit the target square in the center. "Mary, the man is a fraud. No scruples. My master will have nothing to do with him."

"He assured me it was genuine."

"The gentleman would assure a blind person a pebble was a diamond. Not to mention what happens if various ears in London were to learn that a Whitelocke of Boston was practicing magic. If anyone could find a way to profit off that morsel of information, it's Benedict."

"I didn't use my own name."

"If you're purchasing burial silver, you hardly have to. Who else in Boston could afford it?"

"Oh, dear." She frowned. "But you'd be able to tell if it were real, wouldn't you?"

"What in the world were you planning on doing with it?"

She waved a hand as though dismissing all such niggling common sense. "I can enchant a mirror with it. Quite easily, apparently."

The mention of the word *mirror* gave me a shiver, thinking of the image I'd seen. "Mirror magic? I've only just started studying it—and I can't do it. It's difficult."

"Not with the burial silver."

"Yes with the burial silver. Moreso with the burial silver. But let's assume what you have isn't burial silver—I promise I'll take a look at it as soon as I can. Please don't touch it until I do."

She sniffed. "Fine."

I tried to choose my words with care. "Mirror magic isn't something to attempt without a strong, definitive grasp of the fundamentals."

"You saw me with the fire. The coins."

"Which is a wonderful start."

"Start? I spent months practicing them."

"You did. It showed. Mirror magic is delicate work. Subtle. Of more than one dimension."

She took her hand from my arm. "You can just come out and say I'm not good enough."

"Yet. You're not good enough *yet*. Nor am I."

"We're not all witches, darling."

I glanced over at the soldier and driver. Well out of earshot, but I didn't like her using the word. "Mary, I just said I wasn't good enough yet."

"But you will be. And you'll still make me stare at coins."

I decided to take another tack. "What did you want to do mirror magic for in the first place?"

"Not for what you seem to expect me to say."

"What do I expect you to say?"

"That I want to spy on Rebecca Chase to find out which pastor she's sleeping with. That I'd like to learn what Victoria Abbot has been telling her sisters about the teas I've invited her to. That I'm eager to find out which of the young merchants is smitten with me." She adjusted the hem of her riding coat. "I already know all that, in any event: Pastor Mears; that I'm jealous of her beauty; and all of them—if you're curious. No, it's not that."

"Then why mirror magic?"

She whispered, "To learn what my father won't tell me. He absolutely refuses to include me in his thinking. He barely tells Grayson anything. He only ever really trusted John, which is probably why he's grown so obsessed with his restless bones in the family crypt."

The Doctor has the map. The Ring is the key. The Crypt has the answer. I recalled Mary's description of the controversy surrounding locating John's ring prior to his burial. *The Ring, the Crypt.* My mind raced.

"The system doesn't work properly," Mary continued. "The dreary Rattlesnakes at least have that right, not that they have any idea what to do about it. Guns, force, intimidation, threats— where's that going to get us? Nowhere. Only more of the same until all that's left is distrust, lying when it suits, and violence. And for that, we may confidently blame the men. Why wouldn't we, when half of the smartest people I know aren't even given a seat at the table? Such as you. Or me. What if we could do more than just look pretty? Not that we'll give up an inch on that front, mind you—but you take my point."

"And the mirror magic would—what?"

"Lay my father's plans clear for me to see. *His* plans. Others' plans. Information is power, isn't it? I already know how to play the strings of trivial gossip—why not move up to knowledge that is more delicate? Subtle? Of more than one dimension?" She smiled.

"I see. What if they found out?"

"We'll make sure they don't."

"There's talk of a witch already."

She waved a hand at me. "That nonsense? I'm sure people see it for what it is."

"Which is what?"

"Politics. Lionel Sackville may as well sign his name at the bottom of those pamphlets. Lurking around as though no one sees how desperately he wants to drive my father from his position. Drive poor Doctor Rush from the colonies altogether. Your master—don't think he's not unaware of him, either. Of course, he'd burn you at the stake, if he knew about you."

"Good thing there aren't pamphlets suggesting anything about witches papering over half of Boston."

"They're his pamphlets, I told you."

"You're certain?"

"No one else fits the bill, darling."

I held my tongue about Francis. "Look—don't do anything yet about mirrors. I'll help you do it. When I can figure out how it even works. Done wrong, it can be dangerous."

We crossed back alongside the other end of the garden. "Now—my recital. Although August might well feign illness to keep at his work when prestigious visitors come by unannounced—"

"He's really sleeping. And ill."

"—I shall in no way countenance yet another snub. I must be losing my touch if I can't lure a gentleman with a personal invitation. He does appreciate the fairer sex, doesn't he?"

It was a good question. My master sacrificed all else for his work, I knew well. Did he begrudge it? Not that I could see. Had he ever hinted at being attracted to a woman? Not that I could recall. "I assume so," I said carefully.

"I knew more than one scholar in London who was rumored to be drawn only to other men."

"No—I don't think that's the case with my master."

"It would be a pity if it were. I hate wasting my time." As we approached the carriage, she tapped my arm again. "My singing voice will put it to the test, then—every time I perform, I have another half-dozen gentlemen following me around for months like ducklings following their mother, full of this professed love, or that. If August resists even after that, you and I may raise eyebrows and investigate further. It's this Sunday. Arrive at noon. I shall begin the aria at half-past. Wine, punch, victuals. Cream of Boston's society. My latest dress from the young genius—Bartholemew Goodman—colors to rival the spring around us, fit to tempt even the most committed scholar. You'll see."

At the carriage, she smiled and stepped to the door. The soldier opened it for her. "Please do give your master my best wishes. Hopes for a robust recovery. My invitation."

I lifted the sides of my skirts and curtseyed again. "Yes, Madam Whitelocke."

"Adieu, Miss Finch." She entered the carriage. I stood and watched the driver set off a moment later, waving.

By midafternoon, the sky had turned pewter and low, lending the leaves a radiance as they fluttered on a rising wind. I smelled rain blowing in from the west. Returning to the house after weeding the garden—and my thoughts—I brushed off my skirts. Swaine coughed from his study. With no small amount of trepidation, I went to the doorway. He sat in his reading chair wearing his dressing gown over his nightshirt, his hair taking flight at an angle that reminded me of the branches on the wind outside. The *Occultatum Ostium* sat in his lap, unopened. "Sir?" I said.

"Ah, Finch." His voice was a fragile husk. He looked pale.

"There you are. I woke up rather—" He hunched his shoulders and cough after cough racked him. When he finally wheezed in a steady breath, he shook his head. "Bugger this plague."

"Can I get you something, sir? Tea?"

He held up one hand, with effort. "I'm parched. Just water, if you would."

"You don't look well."

"I feel even worse. I'm going back to bed. Let the cure of sleep do its work." He wiped his running nose with a handkerchief. "We have spare sheets? I seem to have drenched mine."

"You rest, sir—I'll get you water. Change your sheets."

"Well done."

I left him to his misery, shocked and relieved he'd made no mention at all of the book. Perhaps the fever had blurred his memory. He guzzled half the water I brought him. I carried another pitcher up to his bedchamber and changed his sheets. He hadn't exaggerated; the sheets he'd slept in were sodden with sweat. As I put the clean sheets on his bed, fat raindrops spotted the window panes and soon the steady murmur of a downpour sounded on the roof.

[Image: image1.png]

Back in his study, I helped Swaine to his feet. "This goes away," he whispered, approaching his cabinet and saying the phrases to unlock the glamours. Once the spell was spoken, he put the *Occultatum Ostium* inside and reactivated the glamours. "Now, I rest."

"If you need anything, sir—just ask."

"Sleep is all. Quiet. Darkness." At the stairs, he paused. I heard his lungs whistle. "You and Mr. Twelves ought to take the evening off. Enjoy yourselves—quietly. Maybe take him to that tavern for some of that ale he's always on about. You've earned it."

"I—well, thank you, sir. Perhaps we'll step out for a while."

After getting him back to bed, I shut the door to his room behind me, going to find Twelves. I was sure he'd enjoy the opportunity to sample Iris's ale—maybe he could get her advice on his new romantic interest, the big, tall wagon-wheel lifter.

I had other plans.

12

———

BONES

I leaned into the wind and rain. Gusts grabbed at the hood of my cloak as I entered the burial yard near one of the grazing commons in Boston. The downpour hissed on the gravestones. Nature Herself appeared to be warning me off after a horrid, drenching, muddy ride from Andover. Thunder sidled in from the west, muttering. Distant clouds flashed, veined with lightning. The flame of my lantern barely cut the darkness at the center of the cemetery. Set back from the rest of the graves, a crypt nestled into the slope of a hill, behind a tall iron fence. I held the lantern up to reveal an embossed *W* over the crypt gate. In the wavering light, I inspected the hinges and lock. Magic coiled around the ironwork. I suspected it was Doctor Rush's handiwork, but wondered of what sort it was. There existed an entire branch of magic related to the binding of tomb and crypt. Alarm. Witch-pole-style detection. It could have been anything.

"On any normal occasion," a voice rose above the rain and wind from half a dozen paces away, "a night like this would only be fit for a warm fire and a bottle of brandy, wouldn't you say?"

I confess I screamed. Staggering back, I saw a dark figure huddled against a headstone a few paces from the gate. He held on to his hat as the wind tried to send it sailing: Grayson White-locke. He raised a hand, holding a flask.

"What in the world are you doing here?" I said, regaining some of my composure even as my heart wanted to kick its way out of my chest like a startled hare. I stepped closer to him. He squinted at the light of the lantern.

"Me? What am I doing here? What are *you* doing here, Miss Katie Finch?" From the way he stretched out the *F*, I knew he was drunk. "Have you followed me? Not had enough fun taunting me?"

He attempted to get up, but his foot slipped in the mud. I reached out and steadied him, helping him upright. The alcohol vapors on his breath cut through the rain.

"I bloody hate graveyards," he said. "We get a few score years in the sunlight, and then eternity in dreary silence. Rotting coffins given way to earth and damp. Dead flesh devoured by pale life wriggling out of sight. And all that remains are bones left to hug themselves."

"Might I suggest you've come to the wrong place, then."

"Don't get cheeky with me, Katie Finch. I didn't plan on coming here, you see. Having a simple spot of Madeira and punch at the King Street Public House. The idea floated into my thoughts. A few more glasses settled it for me: I would come here and tell my sodding dead brother that he could kiss my arse for all the trouble he dumped on my head by having the ill manners to die." He turned to the crypt. "Do you hear that, John? I hope you're enjoying the peace and quiet." His shout was drowned out by a rumble of thunder. He turned to me, motioning with his free hand. "Now you may tell him what you came to tell him. Go on, then. Your turn."

I reached over and snatched the flask from his other hand. He grabbed at it, but I kept it out of his reach. "I think you might want to ease off."

"Ease off? I'm just getting started. And please don't suggest I *behave*. I've heard it all before."

"Maybe you ought to head home," I said.

"With you? You've come to your senses?"

"Before you pass out."

"Pass out? Couldn't be farther from happening. Further. Farther? Which one?"

"Further, I believe."

"Well, I trust your judgment, Katie—even after you've plucked at my heartstrings with a ruthless abandon. All in service of your agenda."

"Agenda?"

"Oh, you very much have one—I just haven't figured out what it is yet. But you're not half as clever as I think you are. Or as you think I am—no, you are. As you think *you* are." He came up next to me, staggering into my shoulder, and peered at the crypt. "Unless the brandy conjured you."

"No. I'm here."

He poked my arm with his finger. "Yes. Yes, you are." He reached again for the flask. I kept it away from him.

"Maybe it's best if I walk you to the gate—get you out of here," I said.

"I like the way you're thinking."

"Only to the gate."

"What—you'd send me off alone?"

"You came here alone."

"But now I have the opportunity to leave in the company of a beguiling, secretive, alleged apprentice to a so-called bookbinder. An admirer of storm-drenched graveyards. A prudish thief of perfectly good brandy. Come along—I'm growing parched. And lonesome."

He put his hand on my hip. I moved it aside.

A tickle erupted in my awareness. Inverressayte whispered in my mind: *Mistress—men approach. Eight of them. With weapons.*

"Where?" I said.

"My breeches," Grayson said.

Three the way you came. Two from the north gate. One behind you, close. Two more in front.

I lifted the glass on the lantern and blew out the flame.

"Good thinking—it's more exciting in the dark," Grayson said. To my horror, he started fumbling with his belt.

I turned and spotted a figure passing between gravestones twenty yards behind me. He marked us, stopped, and raised a musket. I turned to Grayson and shoved him in the chest, sending him reeling backward. The ball split the air in the spot where he'd stood, an angry wasp, then ricocheted off the iron fence. I kept Grayson down, kneeling on his back.

"My spine," Grayson grunted.

I peered into the darkness. Two men with drawn pistols advanced, crouching. They'd had luck when they got the jump on us, but the surprise was over. I felt for a connection to the headstones in front of them and extended a wave of witchcraft. The stone shattered and flew straight into the faces of the men. While they staggered from the unexpected projectiles, I kept Grayson low. He wanted to straighten, but I put one firm hand on his head and pushed down.

A second shot just missed us. "Christ," he said, flinching. "Who are they?" His voice had gone sober.

Another shot fired, cracking the corner of a tombstone. I leaned out and got off a second expulsion of witchcraft, sending a pair of stones hurtling at them, torn from the ground. A rumble of thunder rolled over the night.

"Stay low," I said. I held my hands before the gate, closed my eyes, turned my focus away from the chill rain that pattered on the hood of my cloak. The wind pried at my wrists, my ankles, my neck. I waved my hands across the gate, and then up and down. "*Un tenna a austrum torven,*" I whispered over the metal palings. Tiny blue lines appeared along the surface as faint as a spiderweb in the moonlight. The lines flared, and white sparks leaped from the gate onto anything metal—the steel of the lantern, Grayson's coat buttons, something he had in his pocket.

He patted the smoldering fabric on his greatcoat. Lightning flashed, a jagged strike coming down several miles to the west. "Miss Finch?"

I grasped the bar and gave a shake. The gate was heavy, but swung inward, unlocked. "Come," I said, reaching back and grabbing the lantern. "Hurry."

Crouching, we entered the space before the crypt.

"How did you do that?" Grayson said.

"I'll explain later. Quickly." I scanned the tomb before us. A sensation of tingling, of mites or tiny ants crawled across my face and the backs of my hands: more powerful magic draped the crypt. My spell left the air scented with the bite of iron. Before the granite walls and door of the crypt, damp juniper and broom filled the yard, heady with meadowsweet. Grayson followed me to the door, crawling on hands and knees. Out in the darkness, someone called out that we'd moved.

"I knew coming to this drear, cursed, lichen-crusted, seagull-shat-upon crypt in this foul storm was a terrible idea," Grayson said.

"Be careful," I said. "Don't touch the door."

They're still coming, Mistress.

"Distract them."

I wouldn't go in there.

"Just distract them."

"Another terrible idea," Grayson said.

"Not you. Just stay down."

May I hurt them?

"Do what you need to keep them away," I whispered. The door of the crypt hummed with powerful strands of energy. I lowered my head and concentrated, rubbing my hands together to begin the accompanying gestures. Raising my hands, I spoke, my voice steady. "*Geben sie ihre geheimnisse, eisen und schatten auf. Stein wird flüstern, metall aufsprengen soll. Dunkelheit mit dem willen meinen augen schimmern soll.*" The air took on a charge that crawled along my skin and stirred my hairs. My palms went numb as the magic flared from them. "*Ärger mich nicht mehr, sie haben ihr master ausgefallen. Ich durchtrennen solche bindungen wie mir trotzen!*"

The howl of a shrieking wind swept through the burial yard, staggering both of us. I held steady, lifting my hands. The lock at the center of the door sprouted a burst of white sparks and clicked. Grayson flinched behind an upraised arm. As we watched, the crypt door creaked ajar. A freezing black river of air poured out through the doors, straight from the deepest winter. I peered into the dark opening.

"Go," I said.

"What—in there?"

"We'll hide."

"Or I'll be murdered in the family crypt. How efficient."

"Here." I reached into my pocket and handed him back his brandy. "You might want some more of this."

He took it without a word and slipped into the crypt. I ignored the unease in my stomach and followed him. The air smelled of clay and stone, along with the stale must of rodent droppings. As soon as we were both inside, I pulled the door shut behind us, whispering a spell of holding. The sound of the storm softened, leaving our ragged breathing to fill our ears.

"Did they see us?" he whispered. His words echoed in the darkness.

"I don't know." Taking a few cautious steps, I heard nothing beyond the scuffing of my shoes. "They probably think we're fleeing." I risked a little light, setting the lantern ablaze with a whispered "*Ignis.*" Fungus bloomed between the stones of a square, low-ceilinged chamber. An arch in the far wall led to the main crypt. A cold hand of disquiet brushed the back of my neck.

We both stood by the door, listening. Beyond the wind and storm, it was hard to make out much. After a minute, we heard another gunshot, no telling quite how close. I thought I heard a scream, but wasn't certain it wasn't just wind whirling around the stones outside.

I focused on Inverressayte. "Where are they?"

Some here, some there, Mistress. Thank you. I can't begin to express my gratitude for you letting me assist you—serving you is my highest calling, filling me with a unique satisfaction.

Grayson made as if to answer me, but I held my hand up to him, urging quiet. The demon could well be lying. I met Grayson's eye. "Best if we wait it out. Make sure."

He took a swig from his flask and wiped his mouth with the back of his sleeve. He looked around. "With all my dead ancestors. With—John. How ghastly."

I stepped back from the door and to the arch, inspecting the opening. I sensed more magic. Threshold glamours could range anywhere from harmless to fatal, I knew, so I explored the energies. Concentrating, I allowed my mind to extend my witchcraft. The archway filled with glimmers of brilliant gold. As the light faded, Grayson remained quiet behind me. The inebriation of earlier appeared to have dissipated. His eyes narrowed.

"Your master is no bookbinder," he said. "And you're no apprentice."

"I'm very much an apprentice—and I just saved you."

"You do know my father is the governor, don't you?"

"Yes. And everything is—complicated."

"You were there. The night John was murdered."

"I told you it's complicated."

"Don't. Don't tell me."

I held his gaze. "Don't tell you what?"

"The witch-poles."

I said nothing.

"All the talk," he continued.

"There's always talk."

"Not this kind of talk."

"You mean the pamphlets. They're nonsense."

"And yet."

"And yet *what*?"

"Here we are. A Whitelocke. And a—whatever you are." He nodded toward the crypt door. "Are you working with them?"

"What? Those men? The ones I just saved you from?"

"Unless the point isn't to kill me."

"They certainly look like they want to kill you. Guns. Shooting. All that."

"Until you appear—and unquestionably protect me. A witch, protecting a Whitelocke. Seen by any number of men."

"In a storm. At night."

"They found me in a storm, at night. As did you."

"I didn't *find* you. I had no idea you were even here. Why would I know that?"

"Because everyone knows more than you'd think lately."

"I didn't come here for you, believe me. If I could have avoided you in any way, I would have, begging your pardon, Major Whitelocke."

"Oh, here we go. Well, Miss Finch—it would seem the mystery only deepens." He sipped from his flask, watching me. "Then answer me this: in your telling, you had no idea I was anywhere near here. Here. My family's tomb—which you decided to pay your respects to in the midst of a thunderstorm? I'm sorry, but I'm having trouble even making up even an improbable reason for it. Do you see?"

"Better if you don't know." I turned the lantern to the archway. A set of three stairs descended through the stone.

"I'll wager you're correct on that count." Grayson followed, but as soon as his foot broke the plane of the archway, a shadow passed from the darkness and hurled him backward. The stones around us ground together and spills of dust fell from the ceiling.

Grayson crashed into the wall and writhed on the stones. His hands clawed at his chest and throat, and his face grew red, then darker—he wasn't able to breathe. A demon coiled around him.

I panicked, leaping to him, dropping the lantern. I swept my hands over Grayson as he thrashed, making the complex gestures, speaking the proper couplet of Hume's Seventh Ward. It didn't work. The demon reared—but held on. Grayson pounded on his chest with his palm, his eyes bulging, full of terror.

Deciding I wasn't going to let yet another Whitelocke die in front of me, I jammed my hand into my pocket and grabbed the chain that held my pendant and shoved it into his palm, crushing his fingers around it. As soon as it left my touch for his, he gasped, heaving in air. He rolled onto his side, his chest shuddering, his limbs shaking—a man just shy of drowning, dragged to shore. I recognized the feeling. I turned from him. The demon lurked nearby. I released witchcraft and even more wild energy flowed, wrapping me, shifting and magnifying my own power. While Grayson wheezed and moaned on the stone floor, I stood, palms out. The demon fled, its absence immediately palpable.

"Inverressayte," I said.

Thank goodness, Mistress. You drove that brute off. Foul-tempered and hideous. I was just girding myself to attack the fiend. He would have been met with my full ferocity. A terrifying defense of you, Mistress.

I rolled my eyes.

"Oh God." Grayson wheezed, his breathing settling.

"Don't let go of that pendant," I said.

He only managed a weak nod.

"Wait here."

Taking the lantern, I entered the larger chamber. A vaulted ceiling extended past the edge of the light. My shadow stretched across the floor. The coffins of the Whitelocke family lay on stone biers and in openings built into the walls, beneath skeins of cobwebs and thick dust, more than a dozen of them. Generations of Whitelockes that went back to the founding of the colony, I guessed. As I walked among the coffins, I sensed witchcraft, similar to what I'd felt at the witch-well. Hints of movement caught my eye. I placed the lantern on the nearest coffin and stepped away from it. Strands of magic stretched up and out, through wall and floor and ceiling. Through earthly plane. Flecks of color danced about—the blue of a midnight forest, pale white like twilight sea spray.

"Good Lord, I will never cheat you at cards, forget my manners, nor make disparaging comments about your eye again."

I jumped at the sound of Grayson's words. His voice quavered, and he stood well back from the doorway, a dim outline in the lantern light.

"It wasn't me," I said. My words echoed in the space, fading to dark whispers. "It was a demon."

"Wonderful. I can rest easy." He glanced about the darkened crypt. "So Doctor Rush was bloody right."

"About what?"

"This crypt. He didn't want John buried here."

"Why not?"

"Planar this. Infernal that." He wiped the rain from his face. "Voluminous explanations. *Shifting planes. Sympathetic concordance. Unstable energies.* On and on, like so. Demons? There must have been something about demons. I confess I hardly knew what to make of the old man's prattling. I become lost within half a minute, and Rush hardly marks the way as he dashes off into a wilderness of strange terminology, quivering jowls, and his frail finger stabbing the air before my father's face."

"But your brother is buried here, is he not?"

"Somewhere just past your elbow, I believe. The doctor may have logic—no matter how peculiar or inscrutable—on his side, but my father is the governor. You can imagine how well he received the recommendation that we bury him elsewhere. It wasn't a pretty scene. Frankly, I was surprised the doctor didn't turn into a smelly old owl and fly off into the night, done with this colony once and for all."

The Doctor has the map. The Ring is the key. The Crypt has the answer.

What had the doctor suspected? I examined the energy before me, the waves of force leaning into my subtle awareness. The shadows of the coffins and biers fanned out into strange angles and shapes. "He wasn't wrong. There's something strange here."

"I believe the bruises on my throat confirm his instincts, yes." He ran his fingers lightly above his collarbones. "Good thing I have a bookbinder's apprentice to protect me."

A dark energy rose from the corners. Smaller coils criss-crossed it, reminding me of the bindings of the witch-well, extended through the floor and up in rises of the vaulted ceiling. I walked the crypt, taking pains not to touch the moving strands and windings. I approached the newest coffin, the wood fresh-looking after but a season of stillness. A small brass plaque was riveted to the end of the stone bier beneath the coffin. *The Honorable John Whitelocke, Devout Servant to His Majesty George II, General to his Beloved father, Royal Governor Hamilton Whitelocke, Born 1701 Died 1736*, it read.

I slipped my hand into my pocket and closed my fingers around the Honorable John Whitelocke's ring.

"Is that it? John's?" Grayson said.

"Yes."

"He's why you came here—isn't he?"

I said nothing, resting my fingers on the lip of the coffin.

"Father dreams of him," Grayson said. "When he sleeps at all, I'll add. He thinks John's remains have gone restless."

"He told you that?"

"I overheard him speaking to himself. He denied having said any such thing when I asked him what he meant—but the dark circles under his eyes said I hadn't misheard." Thunder shook the stone floor, reverberating through the wood of the coffins. "Have they?"

"Grown restless? I'm not sure."

"But you came to find out."

I looked over at him.

He nodded. "Go on, then. Do what you came for. Maybe I can put my father's mind at ease—a break from my usual disappointing him."

Nothing about my trip to the crypt had gone as planned. Nothing about much, of late, had gone as planned. Yet there was hardly much point in denying what I was capable of, having just fought off assailants with witchcraft, opened doors with magic, fended off a demon as it tried to strangle him.

"You might not want to watch," I said.

He turned from the main chamber, sipping brandy. "Terrible brother, John was. Tormented me without respite. As though I were put on this earth for his dark amusements. And do you know the first thing I felt when he died? Relief. Maybe *I'm* the terrible brother. Relief. And then—of course—a dawning horror that somehow, improbably and cruelly, I would have to become the new John. I've wondered how quickly my father came to the same horrified conclusion. Depressingly quickly, I'd assume."

Iron nails lined the coffin lid at six-inch intervals, the flattened metal heads cold to the touch. Iron, I could deal with; steel would have been considerably more difficult. I decided on Blackwell's *Iron Rot*, a basic spell that would give the metal the consistency of stale bread.

As I spoke the incantation to *Iron Rot*, the pressure increased, and from the corner of my eye I saw the windings of force rotate. Tendrils reached out in my direction. As I spoke the final word of the incantation, the iron nails sizzled, glowing bright red, and then dulled again. I moved my hand over each one and saw a puff of powdered rust rise from them as I did, accompanied by a soft grinding sound. When I finished with the last one, I tested the lid of the coffin: it budged, the crumbling nails giving way with ease.

I moved the lantern and heaved up the top of the coffin, not keen to see what the remains within looked like. Once the lid was free of its groove, I slid it over to one side, the wood creaking, then banging loudly on the stone floor. Before I even shone the lantern on the insides, I knew something was wrong—instead of must and stillness and bones, my nose met a peculiar mineral scent, carried on a breeze. I grabbed the lantern and held it over the side. The coffin contained no body—and had no bottom. Instead, a thin stone stairway reached through bier and floor, down and down. Around it, darkness. The emptiness stretched yards, fathoms, farther, beyond the light of my lantern. As I stared, a powerful vertigo rocked me.

The demonmere.

"And how is dearest John?" Grayson's voice jerked me out of my whirling thoughts.

The Crypt has the answer.

"I'll spare you," I whispered.

"Not moving, I trust?"

"No. Not moving." I lowered the lantern into the opening. Something shone, a dozen or so steps down. As the light fell upon it more directly, I gasped: the *Occultatum Ostium*, laid across a stone step, its cover and dimensions unmistakable. But how? Had it followed me? Had it traveled from Swaine's locked and glamoured cabinet through the demonmere itself? I rested my free hand on the edge of the coffin. A dozen steps—that was all. The stairs didn't diverge, I wouldn't get lost. "But you should go stand by the door. Don't look. Don't listen."

"What? By myself? It's as dark as the Earl of Hell's waistcoat over there."

"I'm trying to protect you again."

"Whilst pilfering my brother's coffin."

"Grayson. Please."

"Not fair, using my name with such a sultry intimacy. You seem to hold all the cards, Miss Finch." At least he turned and stepped away from the arched entrance to the chamber. "I shall need more comforting than remains in my flask, I assure you. Let's agree the responsibility falls on your fair shoulders, as you're the one committed to watching out for me so diligently."

When he was out of sight, I lifted one leg over the side the coffin, holding tight to the wood.

Mistress, no. Inverressayte's voice skittered in my mind. *Not here. Not now.*

I paused. "What?" I whispered.

Far too dangerous—it's a trap.

"You haven't always shown such concern."

Your wellbeing is my utmost concern, Mistress. I'm nothing if not a reliable servant. As well as a generous servant—returning a favor for your generosity in letting me...play with the maggots who came after you. But I beseech you—to descend into that realm will mean your death. And probably my own, as soon as they're finished with you, Mistress.

"Who?"

They're listening—best not say.

"Then fetch the book for me."

I will be devoured.

"Why should I believe you?"

When have I lied to you?

"Everything all right in there?" Grayson's voice drifted from the crypt entrance.

"It's fine—I'll be done in a moment." I looked down into the demonmere again. The book—I couldn't leave it there. I lowered my voice to a whisper again. "A trap?"

Of the most subtle kind, Mistress. There are places witches shouldn't go—and that is perhaps the most dangerous of all. They'll try everything possible to lure you inside.

I hesitated. *Never trust the words of demons.* Swaine had

drummed the warning into my head a thousand times. Better still, I'd heard nothing *but* lies crawl from the mouths of demons since coming into his service—yet some intuition held me back from dismissing Inverressayte's warning out of hand. Something about the situation felt wrong: the clues from the book, the appearance of the book within the demonmere, the strange witchcraft throughout the crypt, the magic outside of it.

Another of Swaine's aphorisms: *Know when you're nearing a mistake.*

At first, I'd thought such a pithy piece of advice self-evident nonsense; the nature of a mistake is that you don't expect it, it simply happens, thus the very definition of the word. Yet on further reflection—and hours upon hours of learning to practice basic magic—I began to appreciate the truth of it. Mistakes happened unexpectedly, yes. But in hindsight, there are inevitable hints, signs ignored, intuition brushed aside, lines crossed, advice disregarded. Even the advice of a demon.

I pulled my leg back from John Whitelocke's coffin. "Fine," I whispered.

Your wisdom serves you well, Mistress. I'm honored that my humble suggestions proved worthy of my service to you.

"Who wants me in there?"

My whisper hung in the air—but Inverressayte didn't answer, his absence from my thoughts sudden and disorienting. I glanced about. From the coffin, a draught rustled my hair. The lantern at my side dimmed. A dread unlike any I'd ever known rolled from the demonmere, carried on an exhalation of despair. Around me, the witchcraft grew taut. Something approached from the darkness below.

I hauled the lid back onto the coffin.

"Good Lord, you almost stopped my heart with that bang," Grayson called from just outside the chamber. "Extra comfort required, thank you."

"We should go," I said. I straightened the lid atop the coffin.

Frigid air streamed from the gaps and a bleak terror gripped my heart—I wanted to cry out, to flee. No demon had inspired such fear in me, which said a lot. I steadied myself, holding back panic. Inky tendrils of shadow seeped from the coffin.

I held my hands out and spoke in a trembling voice: "*Vade, exiit dæmonium. Ab exterioribus ad te qui deleo Venitisne regna. Molestus nobis non magis diabolus.*"

In the palms of my hands, glimmering flames rose, the white-blue of lightning. I squinted, a crawling sensation gathering in my stomach, a sudden flex of vertigo. The crypt filled with light, streaming from my outstretched hands. The heavy strands of witchcraft flared, dozens of filaments breaking free and arcing over to the coffin. In the center of such force, I could barely get a breath in. Between the spell I'd cast and the witchcraft, the coffin groaned, pushed upward by whatever force surged from the demonmere.

"My God," Grayson said, his features lit up just outside the arch.

I closed my eye and focused, driving the wild energies out through my arms, twining and rotating them to knit together with the other witchcraft. Tapping into a power I hadn't guessed, I grunted as webbings of blue light snapped across the surface of John Whitelocke's coffin—a dozen, a hundred, a thousand. The coffin slammed to the stone floor. Light played across the ceiling of the crypt, fine filaments tracing every surface. As the light dimmed, the silence of the dead hung thick.

I remained perfectly still. The air by my feet spun up in little eddies. I lowered my hands—and one coffin after another shifted, banged, tilted, and rocked, from where I stood to the farthest corners of the crypt. Stones cracked behind me, followed quickly by the banging of the iron doors. On and on it went, and then with one last rattle, the clamor ceased.

"Let's go," I said, my heart pounding. I had no idea if what I'd done would hold. Scooping up the handle of the lantern, I ran to Grayson, tugging him along with my free hand.

"Bloody witchcraft," he muttered.

"Not now."

I stopped at the iron doors to the crypt and listened. The storm continued outside, but I heard nothing else. I hoped Inverressayte had taken care of Grayson's pursuers. Lifting my hand to the door, a wave of magic rose from the glamour I'd shut it with, sliding across the iron and breaking like the surf. Flecks of light glimmered, moving across the surface, seeking exit. One door and then the other shuddered. With a squeak and an iron sigh, the right-hand door opened. Fresh night air rolled in. I pushed the door open. The metal was frigid, an aftereffect of the enchantment. I pulled Grayson out into the dark of the burial yard, squinting in the rain.

"Still deluging. Lovely." He took another drink and raised the flask. "Congratulatory nightcap?"

I ignored him and scanned the area around the crypt. No movement, aside from the gusting rain. I turned back to the crypt doors and closed them, nipping them shut with a minor enchantment.

Grayson lifted his other hand, dangling my pendant, unsteady on his feet. "I don't suppose I might keep this delicate adornment? Formerly nestled in the heavenly embrace of your décolletage if I might hazard to say."

"I need it."

"And if I refuse to give it to you? I'm a major in the Governor's Own, I'll have you know."

"Then you'll have proven yourself ungrateful." I raised a hand. "And I shall still take it back from you."

"Relax, Miss Finch. Ungrateful I am not." He placed the pendant into my palm and I slipped the pendant back into my pocket.

With a final pull from his flask, Grayson stoppered it again, and slid it into his coat. "For the stormy journey. And a job well done. Bones—restful. Dead brother—still dead. Huzzah. Something of a spot of bother with assassins and witchcraft, but we'll keep that to ourselves. Our secrets. Just the two of us." He held a finger to his lips and smiled, swaying. "Perhaps there are other ways I might thank you, Katie. Put some truth to the scandalous pamphlets. Whitelockes and, you know, witches."

"Time to go," I said. The rum, or whatever it was, had done its work to his tongue, that was clear. I wasn't keen to see what else it would stir. "This way."

I steadied him by wrapping my elbow through his and led him back through the iron gate and out among the headstones.

"Ah, look at us," he said. "A handsome couple. Out for an evening stroll. Some good cheer. Fresh air and hearts pitter-pattering in the rain. What rumors we might—"

He pulled up short, nearly topping over after tripping on something. I kept him upright. A head lay on the sodden grass at his feet—shorn from the neck it came from. The face of the man —nose broken, old scars crisscrossing the bridge of it—stared up into the stormy heavens. As the lightning flared, body parts revealed themselves, scattered nearby. Hands. Arms. Viscera. A musket.

...returning a favor for your *generosity in letting me...play with the maggots who came after you*, Inverressayte had said.

"Christ on the cross," Grayson said.

"It wasn't me," I whispered. But I'd told the demon to do what he'd needed to keep them away. I felt my stomach rise.

"They wanted to kill me. Put me in the dark with dead John and the others. Sod them all—I wish it *were* you. Rattlesnakes."

I stared at the face of the dead man. What if it were Francis's face staring up into the storm? What if he were among the others no doubt gracing some expanse of the burial yard?

Know when you're nearing a mistake.

I glanced back at the crypt. The demonmere, sealed up inside.

My witchcraft holding the entrance closed. All around, dead Rattlesnakes. A Whitelocke on my arm, having seen it all.

"Come," I said, pulling Grayson through the darkness and rain.

Nearing a mistake? I feared I'd left that line well behind me. Thunder rolled across the sky, Nature herself seeming to agree.

13

A MEETING OF THE MAGICKAL MINDS

A day and a half later, the morning sun shone through the trees, casting a shifting light through the kitchen in the Andover house. I had a fire stoked, tea steeping, and buckwheat flapjacks cooking on our cast-iron griddle in the hearth. Fresh butter and molasses in bowls. Books open on the table.

A plan.

As expected, the aroma of the johnnycakes conjured my master. Wearing his dressing robe, he stepped into the kitchen. "Ah, Finch. There you are."

His color looked near to normal again, though his cheeks looked gaunt from missing meals as the ague had run its course. While he claimed to be impervious to exhaustion, needing only an ocean of strong tea to sustain his focus, his recent illness was as stark a sign of the limits of endurance. My gaze went to the book tucked in the crook of his elbow: the *Occultatum Ostium*. I hid my surprise. Inverressayte had been right, it seemed.

"It's good to see you up, sir."

He placed the book on the table. "By God, I've had enough of horizontal time in the bed. Unbearable."

"You needed the rest, sir."

"And I begrudged every moment. Days and hours gone. An inexcusable waste of time. Even now, I'm not sure I can be fully productive in my work."

"It's not time wasted if it gets you back to full health."

"It's tragic."

I poured him a steaming cup of tea—a new blend I knew he'd enjoy. "Tragic?"

"Don't act as though I'm being melodramatic."

"Never, sir. The important thing is that you'll be fine."

He pulled out a chair and sat at the table, resting the fingers of his left hand lightly on the cover of the book. "Until I'm not. One sad day illness shall inevitably win. Hence, tragic. And let's not forget pointless. Insipid. Ridiculous. And what would have happened to my work? My plans? All of it? All because of a random and fickle shift in my humors. A wayward draft. A four-day rainstorm and the want of an umbrella. I'm telling you, Finch —I've looked personal obliteration in the face, and am most displeased."

"A cheery way of looking at it, sir." At least he was sounding his old self again.

"There's nothing cheery about the darkness of one's own grave." Swaine closed his eyes and rolled his head one way, then the other. When he opened his eyes, he glanced at the books I'd set on the other side of the table. "Knausgaard? Well done."

"You'd suggested I study panlocational glamours. Why not dive in?"

"Straight into the unforgiving depths."

Kasper Knausgaard of Oslo struggled for years to assemble his daunting six-volume *Elementer og Deres Egenskaper av Magi* ("*Elements and Their Properties of Magic*"), that explored the specialized branch of magical sciences known as *polymorphic machination*, glamours operational in more than one plane at a time. His writing was widely regarded as a feast of language and insight that received the acclaim of noted practitioners throughout Europe, a high-water mark for Scandinavian magic.

Swaine sipped at his tea. "The twelve base metals suitable for a panlocational glamour, according to Knausgaard?"

"And one mineral, sir." I stacked his plate with four steaming flapjacks. "Lead, copper, zinc, nickel, iron, steel, tin, tungsten, bismuth, antimony, cobalt, and molybdenum. The lone mineral is beryl."

"Bravo."

I brought him the butter and molasses. "I wondered, sir—is the technique he describes as *lightning charming* similar to Hume's Twenty-Seventh Ward?"

He pushed his hair back and drizzled the molasses off a spoon onto his flapjacks. "Strikingly so—good eye. It's the same principle found at the heart of the medieval English spell *Iron Dēath*."

"I don't believe I've read of that, sir."

"An interesting web of principles." He forked a triangle of cakes into his mouth. "Ironically, to be subjected to the *Iron Dēath* is excruciating, though not, as one might surmise, fatal. The effect is of intense heat—described variously as wasp stings, glowing embers, or lightning—radiating out from the marrow of every bone in the body, so powerful as to render the victim immobilized, as though their skeleton has turned to a fixed iron sculpture for the duration of the spell. The victim merely wants to die."

"How terrible."

"Quite." He seemed quite pleased with my observation, horrifying side note on the spell notwithstanding.

Now for the next step. "It's the last Sunday in May, sir."

"Is it?"

"Today is Mary Whitelocke's recital in Boston."

"Good for her."

"We were both invited, sir."

"Yes, well. Listening to Madam Whitelocke sing an aria, hobnobbing with various affluent persons—I think not."

"Of course, sir." I poured another quartet of cakes, suspecting that Mr. Twelves would be down soon enough. "I thought it might be a nice break from your rest, though. Not too strenuous. Up and about. A change of scenery in advance of you returning to your work. I also thought it might be a fine opportunity to wear the indigo silk waistcoat and jacket you purchased in January."

While disavowing any preference for clothes (hence my master's wardrobe full of identical breeches, shirts, and coats ranging in color from coal to midnight) in an unguarded moment he'd surprised me by remarking on the appealing shade of blue of the aforementioned apparel at Winslow's during one visit.

"But if you don't feel up to it, sir," I said, going in for the *coup de grâce*, "I can get you some fresh sheets and more broth. We can give it another day or two of rest."

It hadn't been magic, but it had been close. Within the hour, I'd laid out his outfit, and readied the wagon while he washed and combed back his hair. Swaine looked in fine feather as we set off: somewhat paler than normal, but better than he had in days.

"Just the trick, Finch." The meadows buzzed with bee and bloom as I steered the wagon off toward the Boston Road. "Leave the dreadful tedium of bed rest behind. Take in fresh air. Well done."

"I'm sure it will do you well, sir." I eased the horse along the rutted stretch of road. "Mary Whitelocke will be pleased to see you."

"Somewhat too pleased, I believe. Half the time she looks at me, I can't decide if I'm being scrutinized for purchase, or about to be toyed with, the prey before the pounce."

"I'm not sure you have a price, sir."

"I very much do—just not one she'd be willing to pay, I'll venture," he said. "You of all people know the difficulties I present in the way of domestication."

"Then perhaps the pounce, sir."

"Well, good luck to her, I say."

I gave him a sidelong glance. His mood remained light. "You've never thought of marriage, sir?"

"No, I haven't. Nor have I ever considered sawing off my own legs below the knee."

"Oh, I don't imagine it's all that bad. My father adored my mother. Even years after she'd died, he still spoke of her with love."

"Ah, adoration. Is that the ideal we should strive for? To be adored?"

"You say it as though it's terrible."

"Not terrible. Maybe tawdry. Simple. Vain. And not much harder than luring a cat into one's home with the promise of fresh milk."

"There's more to it than that. What about love? Companionship? The other—*aspects* of marriage?"

"Aspects? How prim, Finch."

I felt my cheeks redden, but ignored his mocking. "One could do worse than Mary Whitelocke for a wife, sir."

"Yes, yes—she's a handsome woman. I'm not blind." He stretched his legs out. "And I'm sure she's wealthy—which is a good thing, knowing her tastes in finery. It's not that. I find the whole premise of marriage riddled with such obvious and substantial flaws I'm rather amazed how anyone papers them over."

"Flaws?"

"Flaws. Let's not forget that human beings are vile creatures to begin with. It's no wonder that once the fierce instincts of biological lust have faded, no one is particularly happy thereafter."

"A bold statement, sir."

A bend in the Shawsheen River glimmered in the sunlight, the water moving slowly, flecks of sediment carried along by the brown waters.

"As the truest statements are. People are, nearly without exception, selfish, confused, and delusional—on a good day. So eager to support their own self-image, their own pride, racing ahead to fill in the options that proper society has assured them they must, that they never even question the underlying assumptions. No, instead they accept the use of others as props to decorate the play, proclaiming to all, 'Look at my full life.'" He straightened the cuffs on his sleeves. "No, in every instance, you may boil it down to thinly disguised transactional commerce—I will give you this, if you grant me access to that. And if one thinks that's not the naked truth of things, then one's been sufficiently fooled, or is merely fooling themselves."

It all sounded rather cynical to me. "So you've never felt the sting of Cupid's arrow?"

"Well, of course I have. I'm not heartless, nor entirely bereft of the innate male temperament, believe it or not. Her name was Theresa Petain, all of twenty years. She had me in quite a swoon for the better part of a year when I was studying with my master. I wrote poems. I pined for the sight of her. I was ready to pledge myself to her love—and what a foolish mistake that would have been. It was only at the last moment I recognized the trap: love is a device the mind generates to further the organism through life. Not to say it isn't heady, nor all-encompassing, impossible to ignore. But it is a madness. A useful madness, if the goal is for humanity to continue, I suppose."

"How analytical, sir." I'll also admit to being curious, having never heard my master speak his thoughts on love and marriage. Oh, I knew his dedication to the work and his thoughts on maintaining a focus on it, but the image of him swooning for a woman was something else altogether. Theresa Petain? I found the idea difficult to imagine.

"You can stay lost on one side of it, Finch—or you can see it for what it is," he said. "It's a trick we play on ourselves. Or perhaps one that Nature plays on us. The physical draw. I hope

I'm not being too frank by pointing out that for every interlude of erotic anticipation and fumbling pleasure, measured in mere minutes, how many hours must one face dealing with the expulsive and extruding reality that is the human body?"

"Good Heavens."

Swaine smiled and continued. "We can start the list with cruel breath upon waking. Inevitable. Add in crevices from which one might detect the stink from a yard away. Flakes, seeds, and scrapings disgorging from every orifice. Gurgles, flatulence, the constant tyranny of the wet plumbing. Snoring, mumbling, coughing, clearing, picking, wiping."

A laugh burst from me. "We are wretched things, sir."

"Well, it gets worse. For all of that shudder-worthy list of insults to the senses, marriage will also force one to crash daily against the will of another who, as time goes on, will grow ever more contemptuous of the true gap between their desires, and your own. Ever more sensitive to unspoken critiques. Ever more demanding of having their neediness satisfied." He coughed a handful of times, our laughter having riled up his lungs. "No, I'll pass, thank you very much. If never-ending treaties and skirmishes and uneasy truces are the price to pay, then I've better ways to spend my time in this world."

I started the wagon off on the turn that headed to Boston, the warm wind rustling in the trees that shadowed the faint road. "But if Madam Whitelocke's singing voice is as lovely as a nightingale, sir?"

"Oh, you're a clever one."

"And now one mortified at the very idea of marriage from here out, sir."

"Now, now. My views are extreme, I'll grant you. One must make the assessment for oneself. While I'd be happy to see you become a sorcerer worthy of the name, should you decide that a more ordinary formula for happiness is for you, then you would have my approbation. Still, expect that if I'm presented with the possibility of losing my valuable assistant to some thick-shouldered blacksmith's apprentice, I shall be probing in my questioning, and unrestrained in offering my opinions on the situation."

I was touched by the remark. "I'd count on no less, sir. And we needn't worry of such a thing. I've more demons under my thrall than suitors."

"And how many young women in Boston may say that? You possess a rare intellect, Finch. You're fit. Hardworking. Accomplished. Hold your head high at the recital. There won't be a young woman—or man, for that matter—there who's your equal."

"And shall I hurl myself in front of you should Madam Whitelocke attempt to pounce, sir?"

"As though my life depended on it, Finch. As though my life depended on it."

Boston wore the late morning with uncommon grace, fragrant blooms lining the streets, expanses of yellow powder fallen from spring maple trees. Fine white petals carried on the warm breezes. The sky of deep blue, dotted with towering clouds of white that sailed across the city and harbor like great ships, trailing shadows. The governor's manse stood amidst sculpted hedges and gardens alive with fuchsia and crimson impatiens, white and yellow pansies, golden million bells, purple salvia. Carriage after carriage lined the lane leading up to it, shaded by chestnut trees. Liveried footmen escorted the guests past groups of scarlet-clad regulars who watched over the arrivals. I followed the directions of a servant and found a space to hitch the wagon. Giving Swaine a hand down, we joined the flow of well-dressed gentlemen and ladies toward the door.

"Better than bed rest, sir?" I said.

"Indeed. My body seems in shock after lying about for so long."

At the doorway, we were greeted by members of the household staff and shown through the grand foyer and a well-appointed hallway to a wide library. Walls of books—appearing all but untouched—lined two sides, while the far end opened through pairs of French doors to a pavilion set up outside. Soft-cushioned chairs stood in a semicircle before a double-manual grand harpsichord with sides decorated with a stunning floral pattern, the underside of the opened top painted with a lovely scene of children, soldiers, and a winged horse in a forest. The guests chatted in small groups, gentlemen with gentlemen, ladies with ladies. Perfume hung in the air, along with notes of brandy, coffee, and delicacies being carried on trays. I searched for Mary Whitelocke, and spotted her in the far corner of the room, surrounded by several young women, the group of them a riot of embroidery, satin, and lace in colors that rivalled the flowers in the garden. Mary noticed me and wiggled her fingers, continuing her conversation.

I was about to point her out to my master when Doctor Rush appeared at my elbow as though by magic. "Mr. Swaine. Miss Finch. I see you've been lured away from your quietude." The old gentleman wore a dark green velvet suit and white linen shirt with ruffled cuffs. His shoes shone, buckles polished, silk stockings rising to matching breeches. His pale eyes flicked from my master to me, and I managed not to yelp in surprise—in fact, I didn't miss a beat in smiling and giving him a dainty curtsey.

Swaine reached out and grasped Rush's hand, bowing his head. "Doctor Rush, a pleasure to see you again."

"Ephraim, please."

"One must lift the nose from the books at some point, lest the world pass by."

"More's the pity," Rush said. "I'd be pleased to have somewhat more of the world pass me by, if you would have the truth of it."

I watched him, trying to hide that my pulse hammered away at twice its normal pace. My stomach churned.

"I should think your benefactors would give you free rein to insert your nose into as many books as you wish, given the service you've given to this colony over the decades," Swaine said.

Rush smiled. "With benefactors like these, who needs tormentors? I jest, of course. No, I'm left to chart my course, mostly. The work is the relentless taskmaster, I'm afraid—and I fear that I have no one to blame but myself in that regard. The concept of leaving well enough alone eludes me, even in my autumn years."

"I trust your troubles with the infernal have subsided?"

Rush took a jam tart from a passing server. "Would that they had—but enough of my grumbling. I'm eager to hear more of your work, August. Surely you and the spritely Miss Finch are contributing worthily to the literature of the arts of practical magic? You had a particular interest in the sorcerous lineage if I'm not mistaken?"

"Many years ago, Doctor," Swaine said.

I got a tea for my master, and handed it to him as he spoke, careful not to spill any with my nerves. From the corner of my eye, a bustle approached, and Mary Whitelocke stepped up next to me. She rested a hand on my arm and smiled, then turned to the men.

"Why look at what my recital has conjured," she said. "A meeting of the magical minds. I wasn't sure that my spell would be strong enough."

I cringed inside. She might as well have levitated a coin with one hand while cocking her thumb at me with the other and winking.

My master bowed his head. "Nothing could keep me away from the promise of your singing on such a lovely day, Madam Whitelocke. I'm prepared to be delighted."

"I shall endeavor to delight, sir."

While the three of them exchanged pleasantries, I scanned the crowded room. The governor stood in the corner, chatting with several men whom I assumed to be among the city's more influential merchants or judges. Where was Grayson? After a panicked minute, I spotted him standing outside the open doors, talking with a pair of women. So busy were Swaine, Rush, and Madam Whitelocke with whatever they were all after with each other that I didn't even need to excuse myself to slip away unnoticed. I cut through guest and chair until I stepped out into the warmth of the outside, ducking my way between serving trays and women's hats until I reached Grayson. He held a glass in one hand while gazing with rapt attention at the woman before him. His cheeks wore spots of color and I guessed that the drink in his hand wasn't the first of the day. I motioned for him. He glanced at me—and ignored me. I waved again. He laughed at a joke, glanced at me again.

Ignored me again.

I approached the women, and as he saw me draw near, he used his free hand to wave me away. Not a chance. "Major White-locke," I said, putting a smile on my face. "Your sister asked me to fetch you. She says it's urgent."

The women turned and looked at me. One was older, wearing a pale rose colored dress, her hair lifted into an impressive arrangement, a silk choker around her throat. The other looked related, a much younger sibling or perhaps daughter, and wore a dusky blue gown, her hair somewhat more constrained.

"She must wait," Grayson said. He smiled, yet his eyes continued to wave me off. "I'm discussing rather important military tactics at the moment." Both women giggled.

"I'm not sure she can wait, Major." I smiled back. "Her tone was quite—grave."

He got the message. "Ladies, if you will excuse me for what I pray is just a few moments. Go nowhere, I beseech you."

"Major," the older woman said. She looked both amused, and hungry—and I wondered who on earth could be so bold with no outward signs of shame. I led Grayson back to the manse. Instead of going back through the doorway, I took him by the arm and pulled him off to the side, stepping behind the edge of the pavilion and into the narrow space between it and the manse.

"Do you know how much trouble you caused me?" Grayson said, pulling his arm free, but following me. I went far enough so that no one might overhear us and turned. He walked into me.

"Do you mean when I saved your life?"

"I mean when you managed to litter the burial yard with body parts. How do you think that looked? I needed six men to get it all picked up and disposed of before day broke. Their silence didn't come cheaply, either."

"Maybe next time I'll spare you the trouble."

"Let's just agree there won't be a next time, shall we?" He narrowed his eyes. "For as I was watching my most disreputable privates dump sacks of bloody remains into the harbor, it all came quite clear: you've played me better than my sister's drooling accompanist will pound away on the harpsicord in a few minutes while dear Mary croaks tunelessly along. Get you into the cellar. Get me into the crypt. Where do you need to get you into next, I wonder?"

I straightened my hair. "You just need to tell me where Doctor Rush lives—you said it's nearby."

He folded his arms in front of his chest, nodding. "Of course. It's always something—but never the thing you pretend. I shan't get my hopes up again. Besides, I'll have you know I'm closer now to conquering Juliet Davenport than I've ever dared hope. Do you know how long I've fancied her? Why, ever since her daughter Audrey and I went to school together. And don't go looking at me like that—she's only nineteen years my senior. But my God, just look at her."

"That's fine. Just tell me where he lives."

"Why not ask him yourself?" He dropped his voice to a whisper. "Or use some of your bloody witchcraft?"

"He can't know."

"And if he winds up dead—and I was the one who told you?"

I poked him in the chest with my finger. "I won't kill him, or anything like it. Just tell me. Do you know? You said it was just a street over."

"You seem very insistent."

"I'm glad you noticed. Shall I ask a fourth time?"

"Are you going to pretend to want me again? Lure me to the old man's front door with thin promises? What—you're not even going to attempt to make me forget about the delectable Madam Davenport for the time being? You're losing your touch."

"I could set your breeches afire." I began the spell for throwing flame, enough to manifest heat along his thighs.

He patted his legs and stepped back. "Unfair, unfair."

"Tell me."

"Number Two. Pudding Lane." He pointed behind me. "Brown house. Black door. That way."

A chime sounded. A servant announced that the recital was soon to begin.

Grayson shook his head. "Well done, Miss Finch. Madam Davenport was melting in my hands."

"You have all day to—melt her. Just tell no one what I asked you."

He turned and headed back toward the doors into the library. "Already scrubbing this unfortunate distraction from my thoughts. I would offer you some cotton for your ears, but you've more than earned the punishment of listening to my sister's squawking."

14

HOLD BACK THE SHADOWRISE

Inside the library, people took their seats. Swaine appeared deep in conversation with Doctor Rush, the two having taken seats off to the side. A bit of luck for me. I made my way across the crowded room only to be waylaid by Mary White-locke herself. "There you are, come."

She led me into a side room where a lady's maid held a delicate spray of garlands before a mirror. Mary bowed her head and looked at me in the mirror as the maid arranged the garlands in her hair.

"Do you see them talking? Your master and Doctor Rush. Like a fiddle and a bow. I knew it. Couldn't pick a better audience."

"For what?"

"Who better to assume the position than August?" She eyed me. "Although it may seem like it, Doctor Rush won't be around forever. And at some point soon, my father will consider who might replace him—though I'll wager the thought has crossed his mind once, twice, or a hundred times over the last few weeks."

"My master would never."

Mary shooed off the lady's maid. When she was gone, she held up a pair of long silk gloves. "Help me with these, darling." I took the gloves and held one for her as she slipped her hand in it, helping her to pull it up past her elbow. "August wants to make an impact. He wants respectability for his art. He wants to expand his influence."

I held the other glove. "Even if my master was interested—which he's not—wouldn't it require an appointment from His Majesty? I believe there were issues between my master and that Lord Middleton."

"Lord Middleton has done little but hyperventilate to the city's pastors about Doctor Rush. Scheming little fellow, all bark and no bite, as far as I can see—and I note he didn't deign to attend today." She finished straightening her gloves, admiring them in the mirror. "Issues can be worked through. All it takes is the right approach with the right people. Boston is important to the Crown, and my father delivers without fail. If only August would see that I have more to offer him than just beauty, the finest tastes, and my effervescent wit. Help me with my skirts, darling."

I straightened out her hems.

"And if August isn't interested—well, maybe the two of us together might do something. Take on the role. Can you imagine?"

"I have a hard time imagining *that* issue being worked through, Mary."

"Maybe you're not imagining hard enough. As I've said, we have to start believing in ourselves. We won't change anything by immediately accepting perceived limitations, will we? We simply need to get people used to certain ideas." She turned from the mirror and looked at me, lowering her voice to a whisper. "For instance. I've had a single rose placed on the clavichord. What do you think about adding a flourish to the end of the aria?"

"A flourish?"

"Yes. When I reach the final verse—it's about longing, memories of the nest, clearing grief from the chest—*Più non rammenta il nido, sgombra ogni duol dal petto, e il dolce antico affetto, solo spiegando va*—could you make the rose sparkle, or shine? Nothing outrageous—just an accent, a flash of light upon it, or a glimmer of dew shining like a diamond, just for a moment?"

My mouth hung open. "Absolutely not. My master, Doctor Rush—they'd both know in an instant."

"Limitation."

"The end of my apprenticeship. Or my arrest. No. Sorry. That's not how we change minds. And please tell me you haven't touched the burial silver? No plans to surprise me or anyone else during your performance?"

She flicked her fingers at me. "My word is my word. No, I haven't. Fine—I only thought it might be a nice touch." She lifted a glass bottle of what looked to be rose water and misted herself with it. She closed her eyes and sprayed her face. "Now I need a minute before I sing. Don't hold back at the ending if you change your mind."

"I assure you I will contain myself. Good luck." I turned and left before she asked me to levitate the clavichordist, clavichord, and herself at the end of the aria. I intended to be elsewhere during the performance, in any event.

Back in the library, I realized that it'd been a stroke of good fortune that Swaine and Rush had fallen into conversation—it made it easier for me to take a spot off along one side, where those guests of lesser rank stood, leaving the chairs for the more noteworthy audience members. Swaine looked up and caught sight of me. I waved, he nodded. I positioned myself in the rear, next to one of the open French doors. Grayson Whitelocke had seated himself as far away from his father as possible while still assuming a position of authority. He craned his neck, carrying on his inebriated wooing of the elder Madam Davenport. The scabbard of his dress sword jabbed the hems of the skirts of the woman next to him. He seemed not to notice.

Polite applause broke out across the room, soon picked up by everyone as Mary Whitelocke entered the library, resplendent in her silken gown of emerald, golden embroidery, ivory gloves, and matching shoes. I glanced at Swaine, who stared at a spot off on the floor, still engrossed in listening to Doctor Rush, even as he clapped along with the rest of the guests. Behind Mary came a well-dressed gentleman, her accompanist. Mary smiled, nodding her thanks left, right, center. The accompanist took a seat at the instrument and opened a musical score.

"Thank you all for coming," Mary said as the applause trailed off. "I'm more than honored, and hope to enliven your afternoon with a few of my favorite pieces. No hymns, of course—I'll trust that you all had your fill at services this morning."

A chuckle passed through the library. She commanded every eye. I admired her ease speaking in front of so many people—I could only imagine stammering and flushing a deep red at the prospect. The room grew quiet, the only sound that of the songbirds outside in the gardens. Mary closed her eyes. The music began. When she sang, the tune was clear, nowhere near as bad as her brother had intimated. My own singing voice was an unruly thing, not inclined to find notes, or move gracefully between them once found. Mary added tasteful gestures to her singing—a hand to her heart, an extended arm at some poignant crescendo. With all eyes watching her, I slipped from the library unnoticed.

Once on the terrace, I hurried along the side of the house, cutting between manicured shrubs and down steps. A flagstone path brought me to the corner of the house. Following Grayson's directions, I cut across a stretch of lawn until I came to the nearest street, not far from that edge of the house. Slipping between two of the carriages parked there, I found my way to the corner and spotted Pudding Lane. From there, it took only a few moments to locate the house painted a brown so dark as to be nearly black. Number Two, Pudding Lane: Doctor Rush's house. Even though it was the residence of the colony's Doctor of

Magickal Sciences, it looked little different from the adjacent houses—even to my eye.

Yet I suspected there was more to it, unseen.

I walked to the side of the house and around to the back where a smaller lane opened out. No one in sight. By the back door, I pulled a small hand mirror from a pocket of my dress, along with a glass vial. I knelt and laid the mirror on the ground, faceup. I paused and gathered my concentration. After several long breaths, I opened the vial. It contained a mixture of dried ox blood, sage ash, and ground flecks of glamoured glass. I poured the mixture onto the surface of the mirror, then shook the mirror back and forth until it assumed a uniform depth.

The wind carried a faint note of applause from the recital. Had Mary already finished her first song? I tried not to let the urge to hurry disturb the smooth surface of my focus. I spoke the proper incantation: "*Mægenes fultum, þær ðe bið manna þearf. Gif þu eart mægenes strang, ond on mode frod, wis wordcwida.*" The powder on the mirror vibrated. I reached out and traced a glyph into the center of it, ignoring the snap and grab of the magic as I did. Once I'd finished it, I lifted the mirror and blew. All the powder floated off, save for a fine outline of the glyph. The glass went black. Good.

I raised the mirror to my eye. The darkness cleared, revealing Rush's house as though the mirror were transparent. Yet over doorway and window shone traces of pale fire: the various glamours and wards he'd put in place. As I'd guessed, not only was his house well-guarded against the infernal and intruders, he'd made sure to hide as much of the magic as possible—in a colony once occupied by witches, it was no surprise. Looking through the mirror, I examined the back and side of the house. The doorway was, of course, most heavily glamoured. Several of the windows looked nearly the same. I did find, however, a narrow window by the corner that didn't look to have much more than a hint of enchantment about it. The problem was that it was six feet up from the ground. I looked around, but didn't see anything useful to boost myself up.

Fine—I would improvise.

Standing beneath the window, I whispered a spell of subtle sundering known as the *Gáttspial Gandr*. Each phrase brought forth a spiking headache that wanted to crack my skull. I almost dropped the mirror. Taking a gulping breath, I continued, not slowing the flow of the spell, wondering if it were the onset of something akin to *accersitus vomica*, the sorcerer's bane, or some reaction to the glamours Rush had put in place. I ignored the pain and finished the words around the sensation of grinding shards in my head. The discomfort subsided once I finished the last of the phrases. Inspecting the window through the mirror, it appeared as though the glamour had been neutralized.

"Inverressayte—come here, now."

Tell me you're not going into that horrifying fortress, Mistress. His presence swarmed into my thoughts like furious bees. *I feel ill even this close. I can't bear to look at it.*

"I'm going in, not you," I whispered. "But you need to lift me up so I can slip inside this window."

I humbly beg your pardon, but Mistress forgets that the cruel chains you've bound me with prohibit even the smallest touch of your divine flesh. Even if I wanted to—not that I would consider such an affront—all I would gain would be agony.

I put a hand to my chin. He was right. I looked around. A wheelbarrow lay tipped on its nose against the back of the next house over. "There," I said, pointing. "Fetch that. Lift it underneath the window and hold it. I'll step on it."

I find nothing but satisfaction of the noblest measure in menial service to you, Mistress.

"Just get it and do as I say."

The pleasure is all mine. A moment later, the wheelbarrow lifted into the air, floating across the worn patch of ground separating the houses. It came to a stop beneath the window.

"A foot higher," I said. It lifted. "And you will hold it completely still until I command you to place it back precisely where you found it. No movement whatsoever—do you understand?"

The job of a simpleton is well within my reach, Mistress. I shall endeavor to follow your single-step command down to the last syllable.

He could sound as aggrieved as he wanted, but he'd just as happily fling the wheelbarrow like the bucket of a catapult, shooting me a hundred feet into the air above Boston, if I wasn't specific. Still, I remained cautious as I stepped up onto the wheelbarrow. It gave, just a little.

I am so fulfilled at this moment, Mistress.

"Just do as I command." I reached up and grabbed at the bottom of the window. I pushed inward and found it hinged at the top. Looking around once more and spotting no one, I hauled myself up over the sill, wriggling my way inside. Blinking from leaving the strong sunlight, I found myself hanging into a parlor, above a musical instrument—a spinet, I guessed.

"Put the wheelbarrow back exactly where you found it," I commanded the demon.

Of course, Mistress—it was a delight to have risen to the challenge for you. I surpassed my own limitations, driven on by your inspiring command. From here on out, I shall regard this device as nothing short of a miraculous testimonial of personal achievement—and will return it with reverence.

I ignored him. Looking around, I resigned myself to the fact that there was nothing graceful to be done. I hung down, grasping at moulding on the wall, at the edge of a bookshelf. My skirt tore, and I performed half a handstand before I tumbled to the floorboards next to the bench before the spinet.

Getting to my feet, I saw the rip in my skirt hung a small flap of four inches—right in the front. I ignored it and quickly explored the downstairs of Rush's home, finding little out of the ordinary. A kitchen, a well-stocked pantry, a small study lined with bookshelves and writing instruments, a mud room. A pang of doubt stabbed at me. I paused at the staircase, spotting an embedded inlay of silver which I guessed to be some form of a glamour. Holding my hands above the first step, I gathered my witchcraft about me, wrapping it tightly as though it were an unseen cloak. With a grimace, I stepped through the glamour—and sensed no disruption.

I exhaled. I moved quickly from one floor to the next, from one room to the next. Bedrooms, sitting rooms, closets, an indoor privy, all with the imprimatur of Doctor Rush. A narrow staircase led from the second floor to a third, and there I found what I'd been looking for: his workshop, extending the length of the house beneath slanted gables. The far wall held a pair of glass doors, revealing a balcony of some kind beyond. Three tables occupied each long wall, chock-a-block with the equipment of the magical sciences: brass instruments, glassware, containers of powder and liquid, candles, bells, stacks of papers, writing tools, scales, hourglasses, and the like.

Exactly as I'd seen it in the *Occultatum Ostium*.

The Doctor has the map.

Lifting the mirror once again to my eye, I scanned the room for additional glamours and enchantments. Three large circles occupied spots between the tables, no doubt protections of a similar nature to the ones in Swaine's workshop. Other than that, it looked safe. Hurrying along the tables, I looked over each in turn, trying to recall exactly where the map had been. On a table next to a dormer window, I found it: a large map drawn on brittle paper. Several other maps sat next to it, all marked. As I scanned those, recognizing stretches of Boston and sections of the Merrimack Valley, I saw a word repeated in several places: *incursus*. I saw numbers written in a neat hand, indicating various locations.

Turning back to the large map, I recognized the northeastern shore of the colony, with particular detail extending out from Salem—the hills marked, including Ledge Hill where the manse stood, the north fields, the North River, the contours of the harbor correct, and the old lanes depicted. There were small circles drawn in a strange pattern, annotated with numerals drawn in fresher ink.

As I lifted the map to look at it more closely, faint ripples rolled across its surface, lines of silver. The edge of the map lit up like glowing embers, then faded. I cursed. Had Rush glamoured the map itself? Why hadn't I been more careful? About to put it down and sprint from the workshop, my heart slamming—I paused. The map changed, even as I looked at it. Thin lines of silver appeared, here, there, everywhere—a dozen, then a dozen more overlaid across the various lines, scratches, and contours. Connecting them were small circles with a keyhole symbol drawn inside.

What had happened?

As I gazed at the bottom of the page, more writing appeared in silver lines: *Behold, friend—the locks that hold back the shadowrise. Keep them strong.*

The writing glimmered. My touch—had it revealed the message? I placed the map down on the table. The words and symbols faded. When it picked it up again, they reappeared. *Behold, friend.* I shivered, recognizing that I held the map Ginny Lane had sent to Archibald Fletcher—more so, in realizing she'd designed it for another of her kind, another witch, to see the full picture.

And that witch was me.

Scanning the map, I confirmed my other intuition: one of the keyhole symbols appeared on the eastern side of Gray's Pond, where Bertram had shown me the witch-well. The exact spot, near as I could tell. That would mean the other locations would correspond to additional seals. Dozens of them, from—

The sound of shattering glass interrupted my thoughts, coming from downstairs. Folding the map and tucking it away into the top of my dress, I hurried to the stairs. The creak of a board and footsteps floated up from the first floor. I breathed somewhat easier, for my first thought had been that I'd tripped one of Rush's alarms of some sort. Still, I didn't relax by much. I crept down the stairs—only to stop at the bottom when I heard voices coming up to the second floor, arguing—seemingly—in whispers.

"You think he won't notice?" one voice said.

"I cleaned it up."

"Cleaning it up isn't putting it back."

"He won't notice. Relax. Barely looks up from his walking stick half the time—do you think he's going to go counting his window panes before he dodders inside, sloshing with sherry? We're fine."

I slipped back up the stairs to the workshop, looking for an escape—or at the least, somewhere to hide. As the voices drew nearer, I stepped softly along the length of the workshop until I reached the glass doors. The brass handles were locked—but from the inside. I pushed it open. Before crossing the threshold, I extended my witchcraft in layers around me.

A shoe sounded on the stairs to the workshop. "This way. We can wait until he settles down."

Passing outside, I just had mind enough to close the door without a click, hanging on to the handle until it shut all the way. I crouched off to the side, out of sight, my pulse galloping in my ears. The balcony appeared to be used by the good Doctor as an observatory of sorts. Two telescopes of wood and brass stood beneath an overhang from the roof. An iron railing surrounded three sides, while slate tiles formed the floor. Beyond the rail, I saw rooftops and chimneys. Turning to my right, I made out the grounds and side of the governor's mansion.

Turning, I peered in through the glass door by my shoulder. At that moment, a figure emerged from the stairwell, followed by another. Both appeared to be young men, and they carried pistols. Neither wore a uniform, and each wore a kerchief that covered the lower half of their face. One carried a dark sack.

"Jesus. What's all this?"

"Tools of the trade. What did you expect? Teakettles and bed warmers?" The one with the sack looked about. "No guns. No guards. All this is fine."

A third figure stepped from the shadows in the corner. "I'm glad you approve, young man," Doctor Rush said.

I swung back away from the glass door with a gasp. How had he gotten into the workshop? Quarter inch by quarter inch, I leaned back so I could see inside. Something crashed to the floor, both intruders slamming into tables in their fright.

The one with the sack raised his pistol and pointed it at Rush. "You just saved us a fair bit of time, sir—I'll say that much. I'm afraid you're coming with us."

Rush, his back to me, didn't do more than lean on his walking stick, seeming to be as comfortable with the situation as he'd been in the library before Mary's recital began. "How intriguing. And, pray—where are we off to?"

"Don't worry about that, Doctor." Both men pointed their weapons at him. "The less you know, the better."

"While I've often found that precept useful in life, I can't always help myself, I must warn you."

The one with the sack held it out with his free hand. "You're going to place that over your head."

"No. I'm not."

The men stepped nearer to him, the barrels of their pistols aimed at Rush's face. "We're not fooling around. Do it."

Rush lifted the end of his walking stick by no more than three inches. As he did, both men spilled to the floor, their legs swept out from beneath them. With another small wave of his walking stick, Rush sent their pistols clattering across the workshop and down the stairs.

"Now," he said. "As of this moment, the more *you* know, the better. You gentlemen may struggle—in which case the pressure you're both feeling between your shoulder blades will increase significantly, risking a crack or two to your ribs as you are driven more forcefully into the floor. I would urge you to relax your muscles entirely, at which point you'll find the resistance holding you down will exert little more pressure than a back rub. And who doesn't enjoy a good back rub from time to time?"

Both of the men ignored his advice. Their subsequent groans indicated Rush hadn't lied.

"As you will," Rush said. "I'll say that for the soldiers I've summoned, I've no guarantee on how gentle they may or may not be, so I'm afraid I have little in the way of helpful advice once they take you into custody. Best to be cooperative, I'd imagine."

From down at the corner of the house came the voices of several men—soldiers, I assumed. Doctor Rush leaned over the intruders. With a wave of his fingers, their kerchiefs tore from their faces. The man closest to the stairs frowned, his face red from struggle. He looked to be in his late teens, a wispy beard shadowing his freckled chin. The other man pressed his face against the floor, staring up at Rush.

My eye widened: Francis.

Rush smiled at them. "A proper invitation is usually preferable to a kidnapping, but I must say I admire your enthusiasm."

"You work for thugs," Francis groaned.

"I work for the well-being of the colony. Furthermore, I do so without hiding my face, or pointing pistols at anyone's face."

I ducked away from the glass. Fascinating as it was, I needed to leave, and fast. Scooting away from the doors, I stood up at the edge of the balcony. The drop was too far for me to jump without injury. An elegant willow tree shaded the corner of the house, but offered me no route of escape. Along the side of the house ran a vine-covered trestle.

"Inverressayte," I whispered.

Oh, that hideous man. I don't care for him, not at all. Glaring magic of a most irritating sort. His mode of travel is offensive and—

"Quiet, listen. You will reinforce the wood of this trellis, throughout. You can't let a single length of it crack or shatter or come loose. Even when my weight is on it. Do you understand?"

Slightly more challenging than lifting a wooden wheelbarrow. I see I've impressed you with my ability to follow the simplest of directions. I only aim to serve—

"Do you understand, Inverressayte?"

His pain at my speaking his name registered as a shudder in my skull. *Yes, Mistress.*

I hoped I'd thought through my instructions carefully enough. Swinging my legs over the railing, I kept my heels on the lip of the balcony—then flung myself to the trellis. I slipped and grappled with ivy and wooden slats, but caught myself two feet below where I hit. It held. Fast as I could, shielded from the lane by the willow tree, I climbed down. At the bottom, I paused. Looking around the corner, I saw three soldiers standing by Rush's door. I turned and hurried the other way, cutting across the lawn, then the lane, circling around back to the end of the governor's lawn.

Straightening my hair and dress, I walked with casual purpose, as though I belonged there—which, I suppose, technically, I did. As I neared the back doors and pavilion, I heard laughter and the clink of glasses, along with the murmur of conversation. I slipped my mirror back into my pocket and checked that the map was safely tucked away.

Looking up, I barely stopped myself from walking straight into Governor Whitelocke, standing next to a hedge in midconversation with a pair of gentlemen. The governor looked at me in surprise.

"Your Excellency," I said, giving him a curtsey.

"The guests are over there." His tone strained the edge of

polite. "And who are you?" The men behind him looked at me. None of them appeared pleased.

"Forgive me, sir. Finch, sir. Katherine Finch. Assistant to August Swaine, sir. I was—admiring the gardens, sir. After the performance. I'm very sorry if I shouldn't have—Madam Whitelocke's performance stirred me so."

He didn't look as though he believed a word I said—but he also didn't appear to care much who I was, what I said, or for hearing any more of my bleating. "I hope you found them satisfactory, Miss Finch. Now, if you would."

I scurried off with another curtsey and a mumbled "Forgive me, Your Excellency." As I saw the crowds of guests around the corner, I exhaled, beads of sweat tracing their way down my sides. No one paid me any heed as I reached the refreshments. Many of the guests lingered by the doors to the library. In the pavilions, chickens, sausages, and ribs roasted, filling the air with the aroma of sizzling fat. Pennants and the King's Colors snapping on the warm harbor breeze. Mary Whitelocke was underneath the pavilion, surrounded by well-wishers. My master stood next to her, so I cut through the crowd in their direction.

"Ah, Finch," he said, noticing me. "I was just telling Madam Whitelocke about the invigorating discussion I've had with Doctor Rush."

Mary smiled. "Drawn together like two powerful magnets, as I always knew they would."

"Is he still here?" I said.

"Called off on some emergency or another." She looked at me. "And did you enjoy the recital, Miss Finch?"

"Very much, Madam Whitelocke. Your voice is lovely."

"Yes, well. The ending might have been stronger."

I smiled. "I found it quite soaring, madam."

Her gaze flicked down to my skirts. "Whatever happened to your dress, dear?"

"This? I stumbled while admiring the roses, I'm afraid. Torn on the thorns."

"Not that you should feel at all obliged to bestow yet another beautiful dress on my assistant," Swaine said. "A sturdy apron or two might be more in order."

Mary swatted his arm. "Sturdy holds but a candle to beauty, August."

I quickly excused myself with an offer to fetch my master a drink and some food. Over by the tables, I put together a plate for Swaine.

"How very interesting, Miss Finch."

I looked over my shoulder. Grayson Whitelocke smiled, standing just behind me.

"Madam Davenport eluded you yet again?" I said. I didn't like the way he smiled at me.

"For the time being. Yet I'm nothing if not persistent." He took a biscuit off the plate I had and bit into it. "You'll see. And how did you care for my sister's warbling?"

"Much nicer than you'd implied."

"You could hear it from the lane?"

"I beg your pardon?"

"Nature called. Shrubbery being most convenient. And imagine my surprise to look up from my business only to see a lovely young woman in a teal dress hurrying across the road and onto the lawn. Mere minutes after Doctor Rush suddenly excused himself." He took a second bite of the biscuit. "I have the eagle eye of a trained officer, remember."

"Whatever you may or may not have seen—"

"I saw it."

"I'm sure you wouldn't speak of it to anyone."

"Sure, are you?"

I stepped close enough to him that I could see the flecks of green in his irises. "I've helped you. You can help me. All you have to do is say nothing."

"And what will that get me?"

"My gratitude."

He wiped the crumbs from his chin. "You are a curious one, Katie Finch. Curious indeed. One of these days, I'm going to figure you out."

I turned, bringing the food to my master. Torn dress. Stolen map. Grayson Whitelocke figure me out? I couldn't imagine he'd have much better luck than I'd ever had at it.

15

MIRRORS, MAPS, AND MAGIC

Three days later, I rode into Andover to pick up supplies as the morning slipped toward noon. Swaine, reenergized after his conversations with Doctor Rush and his time spent in Boston's society, embarked on the construction and calibration of his new device to the exclusion of all else, including me and my studies. He and Robert Twelves saw both dawn and dusk from the confines of the room in the Andover house where they worked. It fell to me to keep them in tea, cider, and meals, the larder stocked, the hearth stoked. It also afforded me time to confirm my suspicions.

Inside the tavern, I found Iris sweeping the front room. Her children played on a blanket off by the fireplace. Iris hummed a tune in her pretty voice as she worked. She smiled when she saw me—and it struck me that I hadn't seen such a genuine smile from her in months.

"You look lovely," she said.

"Thank you." I ran my hands along the sides of my dress, a pale green affair that Mary Whitelocke had sent me off with after her recital, sturdy enough for daily wear, yet with superb stitching in a fleur de lis pattern across the waist. "You look lovely yourself."

She leaned on the broom. Her color looked healthy after the wan months of winter grief. "Ethan came to me in a dream last night. It was—I can't describe it, not really. It was him."

"Oh," I said.

"It was lovely, not sad. He sat on the edge of the bed, and he held my hands in his. He sang. So softly. And it felt somehow more real than being awake. His presence. His warmth." She smiled at the memory. "He told me it was all going to be all right. That we'll never be apart—not in our hearts." She waved a hand at me and shook her head. "It sounds silly."

"No, it doesn't. It sounds beautiful."

Iris swept again. "It was. The most beautiful dream I've ever had. When I woke up—I don't know. It's as though I've woken up into my life again. Not all the way, not yet. But a little. Ethan is still gone, but maybe not all the way. Not like I'd felt before. A touch of hope, that's what it is. Something beneath me where there had been no footing before."

"You'll make me cry." I put a hand on my chest.

"Me, too—but this time it doesn't feel terrible."

She opened her arms, and I stepped into her embrace, we gave each other a tight hug. After a few moments, we separated. She wiped the corner of her eye with a knuckle. I flicked a tear from my own with my index finger.

She swept again. "None of which I expected to happen at all, mind you—not after last night. I went to bed in a fury."

"Fury?"

"Do you know Henry McAlister? He and his brother make saddles up in Haverhill?"

"I don't think so."

"Well, he's in here now and then. Has a sharp tongue, but funny." Her strokes with the broom grew brisk. "He was down in Boston and heard Francis is back. And he's in jail."

"I thought he was in New York?" I lied, hating myself for it.

"He was. But he couldn't stay away, could he? Not that he could come here. Help his niece and nephew. Make an actual difference in someone's life. Of course not."

"Why's he in jail?"

"Why do you think? He couldn't leave bad enough alone. More Rattlesnake nonsense. This time, he tried to kidnap Doctor Rush—that's what Henry said. Doctor Rush. That won't end well."

"Are you going to see him?"

She stopped sweeping, but when she spoke, her words weren't hard. Instead, she spoke as if she'd answered a question she'd struggled with, and answered it with kindness to herself. "No. No, I'm not. I can't—not after all that happened. I suppose I thought I should, for Ethan's sake. But maybe that dream was him telling me it was fine if I listened to my heart."

"And your heart says no."

"It does. I feel for Francis—but I warned him. Ethan warned him. Over and over. He never listened. Look what it's cost us. His choices are his own now. Imagine it—stuck in prison and not a soul missing you." She looked at her children. "No, my heart is right here."

Her son played with a cloth doll, while her daughter lay on her back holding her feet, cooing. As far as my heart went, it wasn't resting any easier at the thought of Francis in jail, being questioned by the governor's men.

After chatting with Iris for a short time, I found Bertram mucking the stalls of the tavern's stable.

"There you are," I said.

"And a glamorous life it is, isn't it?"

"You'd be surprised what people can envy."

He leaned the handle of the shovel in my direction. "You are free to partake. I'll have no one accuse me of hogging the glory."

I pulled a map from my pocket. It wasn't the witches' map I'd taken from Doctor Rush's. I kept that glamoured away in my room after hiding it off in the woods for several days, worried that he'd tethered it to his awareness in some fashion, and would track it down with little delay. He hadn't, leaving me somewhere between unnerved and relieved. What I handed Bertram was a section I'd copied by hand showing the location of the three nearest seals. "Do you recognize any of these places?"

"Do I want to know why?"

"You already know why."

"That's what worried me." He took the paper and looked it over. "Did you make this yourself?"

"Why? Does it make sense?"

"It's well done, is all. Makes more sense than anything I might cobble together." He squinted at the lines and put a finger on the map. "This here's that old stone dam, I think. Was a mill by the river there. Burned years before I was born, but I've seen the stones it was built on. Was the original one—now it's the one nearer the quarry. But, yes—must be near there. It's a witch-well?"

"I think."

Bertram put a knuckle to his lip. "Down there? Never heard of one around that area. How'd you figure this out?"

"Don't ask. Can you show me?"

"What, now?"

"Yes."

"Mucking these stalls is looking better by the moment, I'll just say."

"Don't worry."

"I'm fairly sure you said something of the kind last time."

"I took care of that problem, didn't I?"

"Except my poor granddad's had to put up with my jumping at shadows and scooting from the door to my bed like a frightened five-year-old every night, thanks to what I saw of you taking care of that problem."

"I wouldn't let anything happen to you."

"A fine sentiment. Course, for every hour I see you, there's probably a hundred when I don't, begging your pardon. Not that I'm saying you should watch over me. Or always be with me. We're not married—no, that sounds terrible, my mouth is running. Of course we're not." He leaned the shovel against the side of the stall. "I'll show you where it is before I go any closer toward being a jackass, instead of just cleaning up after one. Begging your pardon."

We took half an hour of riding and then another quarter hour of pushing our way through brambles and underbrush to find the ruins of the old mill, a stone foundation extending along a stretch of the Shawsheen River. The water ran the color of tarnished brass. A heron lifted off its spindly legs with a rustle of wing and took to the air, drops falling from its feet as it sought a quieter shallow to hunt in. A stream of sweat trickled down my back as I searched the stones. The scents of sun-washed rock and soil, of goldenrod and Queen Anne's lace, of old boards eaten away by termites and pushed into the earth by rain and snow over decades filled my nose. Drowsy bumblebees gathered nectar, adding their note to the hum of insects all around.

"Funny to think of the work that went on right here," Bertram said, searching around the side away from the river. "No doubt seemed solid and vivid enough at the time. Another day's work. Filled with the busyness folk carry in their heads without even noticing. Now it's disappearing back into forest. Like it never happened. Bugs and snakes keep it company, and that's about it. Fox passes through now and again, probably."

"Maybe it's not as vanished as we think."

"Or as we'd like." He leaned back, lifted his hat to wipe the sweat from his forehead, and paused. "Look."

"Did you find something?"

"Couple of hemlocks, right there." He pointed.

I followed the line of his finger. Three hemlocks rose, a little apart from the line of canting alder that leaned out over the river. I led the way away from the old mill until I reached the trees, the ground beneath them barren of all but roots and twigs, as was the way of hemlocks. As I neared, the backs of my forearms tingled with witchcraft. Off to the side, I pushed through a dead tangle of rose vines to uncover a low line of stones, stacked two and three high, a higher cairn in the middle.

"It's here," I called over my shoulder.

"Witch-well?"

Behold, friend—the locks that hold back the shadowrise. Keep them strong.

"Witch-well," I said. I wasn't surprised, having confirmed what I'd already suspected: the symbols—the locks—on the witches' map corresponded to the two locations I'd discovered, the witch-well near Grays Pond, and what appeared to be the exact location of the Whitelocke crypt in the burial yard in Boston.

My other suspicions, however, had only deepened, with no ready answers in sight. I inspected the stones. Kneeling, feeling around their bases. Looking for any signs of the demonmere. While the map made clear the location of the seals, it remained mute on the subject of that fell realm. True, the Whitelocke crypt had been both a site of the witches' handiwork *and* the demonmere—but the same hadn't been true of the first witch-well I'd found. Nor did the map possess symbols or markings anywhere near the three other locations we'd encountered the demonmere: extending from my study in the Andover house; in the center of the house of the warlock Thaddeus Rivers in Salem; the cellar of the governor's manse, where Clara had disappeared. Adding to the mystery was that all signs of the demonmere had vanished from all of *those* sites after appearing.

All of which left me puzzling. Was the *shadowrise* the demonmere, or something different? With no better information to go on, I had to infer that some connection existed—and Clara's life depended on me teasing the answer out.

"Should I keep a lookout?" Bertram said. "For—you know. Corpses?"

"Probably."

"Probably? That's not comforting. What happened to *I won't let anything happen to you, Bertram*?"

"I'll try my best."

"I see you've made an allowance that didn't seem to be there before."

"You can wait for me back by the road, if you like."

"No need to say it like that. A simple, reasonable question on my part. I shall remain alert." He sighed, crossing his arms across his slouching chest. "For corpses."

I ignored him, focusing on the energies in and around the stones. Unlike what I'd found around the witch-well near Grays Pond, the currents of witchcraft here appeared to have retained more integrity. The pattern was balanced. As I extended my own energies, the faint ripples of light moved across the stones, climbing up a larger trunk of witchcraft rising from the center of the cairn. I found only two small threads unwound from the rest and could connect them back with the others as I'd done at the first witch-well. Moving my hands back and forth, I directed my witchcraft to stitch the ends together. When I finished, a greater power surged through the bindings, one of strength and suppleness.

Awe washed over me. Not at what I'd done—but at what *they'd* done: Ginny Lane and the others. Frightened, hunted, desperate, they'd put everything at risk to stem the infernal tide that had already swallowed up all they'd cherished. What they'd left held for scores of years, an expression of a talent far beyond anything I was capable of. Fixing a few stray strands was nothing. Humility was all I could muster in the face of their achievement.

Part of me wanted to sit there longer, in tune with the witch-craft, in touch with the lineage I'd become a part of. Another part knew I didn't have all day. I rocked back on my heels and stood. Bertram looked toward the river.

"No corpses," I said. "Well done."

He jumped at the sound of my voice, putting a hand to his chest. "Did you do that on purpose?"

"No—I'm sorry."

"Well, you almost made *me* a corpse, thank you very much. You did all of your—" He waved his hands around. "Work?"

"I did, yes. And I apologize for startling you. You've been very generous. And accepting. I owe you thanks. Not a fright to the death."

"You're welcome."

I started back through the trees, the way we'd come. "I'm glad we didn't see anything. Corpses, I mean."

"I heartily concur. Every shifting current in the river gave me a turn—and here I thought I'd been frightened of water before."

The wind whispered among the reeds. We passed over the foundation of the old mill.

"Not that I'm terrified of everything, mind you," Bertram continued. "Just most things. Wound a few turns too tight, my mother always says. Always been this way. Jumpy. Or, as I like to think of it, *alert*. A few alert fellows are useful to have around."

A movement to my left drew my gaze. The remnant of a burnt timber sat angled across the foundation, the far end thrust into a cluster of bayberry bushes. Three dark shapes stirred within the shrubs. I slowed.

"Course, there's such a thing as being *too* alert, I'll say." Bertram kept walking. "When it's half-past three in the morning and I'm alert to every sound in the cabin and every thought in my head, I'd give a respectable fortune—not that I have one, but if I did—to join the ranks of the less observant."

"Bertram," I said.

He stopped, looking at me.

I pointed. Just as I did, a trio of birds took to wing from the bayberry: sooty shadows, the edges of their wings trailing fine traceries of black. Crooked beaks, obsidian eyes ringed in glimmering gold.

Ravens. Shadow ravens.

Without a sound, they climbed into the air, above the old mill, above the alder and hemlock, off across the river, flying south.

"I've never—were those ravens?" Bertram said.

The ravens skimmed the roof of the woods beyond the river, diminishing to three points against the blue until they vanished.

"Of a kind," I said.

Imagine it—stuck in prison and not a soul missing you.

I wondered how I'd ever thought I might play a game of mirrors, maps, and magic against the formidable Ephraim Rush without being quickly overmatched.

16

BLIND SPOTS

Such paranoia as stalked me had little time to pounce, for when I returned to the house, Mr. Twelves announced the device was ready. My master was in the midst of gathering everything needed, unwilling to wait until even the next morning to test his theory.

"You're quite confident the trip to Salem shall not disturb any of the mechanisms or the magic?" Swaine said.

"Not if it's packed up right." Twelves wiped his hands on the sides of the canvas apron he wore, various-sized pockets lining the front of it, most of them home to the rulers, scribes, marking charcoals, and tools that Twelves used most often. His elaborate workbench stood chock-a-block with more: compasses, small drawers filled with brass and steel fittings, springs, screws, gears, weights, steel plates, vices of metal and wood, clamps, varying gauges and jigs, and more. Neat and ordered, a sign that Swaine had told me he took as reflecting the crisp intellect of his clockmaker.

As Swaine double-checked the various spells and glyphs on the resonance clock, I looked over the detailed map of Salem I was to use. The contours of the harbor and inlet, the hills and old lanes were familiar to me from having set the witches' map to memory—I could practically see the keyhole markings showing the seals they'd put in place. If Swaine's plan worked—the massive Holzian glamours released within boundaries of the spikes we'd set, revealing the breadth of planar intersections riven throughout Salem—my task would be to transcribe all I saw onto the map. How much of it would match what the witches had left? I suspected quite a bit.

And as for the demonmere itself—well, the knowledge that I'd already located one entrance into it burned inside me, an ember of pure guilt.

Swaine blew his nose into a kerchief produced from his coat pocket and motioned us to the wagon. "Then let's get it packed up properly, post haste. The hour is already much later than I'd hoped."

Twelves gathered up a few tools and shrugged on a coat. I followed my master out into the warmth of the late afternoon. I glanced up into the sky, terrified I'd see more shadow ravens watching me. Robins and sparrows carried on around the maples and lilac bushes, but no sign of ravens, magic or otherwise. By the time we had the wagon properly loaded, the device packed into blankets and tied down to prevent damage if the wagon jarred on a rock or a bit of rain-washed road, shadows started reaching eastward. Swaine climbed onto the wagon's bench. Twelves remained in the back, where he might keep a hand on the device.

"Come, Finch—aren't you excited?" Swaine said.

I headed around to the front, climbed in, and took the reins. "Of course, sir."

"Does she sound excited to you, Mr. Twelves?"

"She must've taken your advice, sir. Not letting her emotions color the clarity of observation. Keeping them at bay."

"Now, now," Swaine said. "The two of you may have your fun —but there is a time for enthusiasm. If not now—when we're about to embark on the unknown, about to bend the will of

Nature to our own ends—then when? If this works, and I'm confident it will, this is a day we shall long remember. Worthy of a wide-open heart. Pride in what we've achieved, together. Genuine good cheer."

He clapped his hands, then reached over and patted me on the leg. I loosed the brake, flicked the reins, and started the horse forward to the lane winding through the woods—wondering how long it would be before Doctor Rush's shadow ravens darkened the horizon.

By the time we reached Salem, the moon climbed from the Atlantic, a copper-colored eye peering through the twilight. The western hills behind us glowed with sunset. The sound of the waves rolling onto the shore carried, growing louder as we approached the old town. Across the rebuilt bridge that spanned the river, my master kept silent, no doubt working through the various steps and contingencies that lay ahead, again and again going back over the order of his calculations, the binding glamours he instated, the materials, the subtle foundational spells he'd imbued into the wood, the gearing, the springs of the device. His enthusiasm of earlier had sharpened into a profound focus.

Rising to our right, between the road and the harbor, a decrepit barn lay on its side like the corpse of a long-dead behemoth, collapsed joist, timber, and beam poking through the rotted planking. Beyond it, several buildings and small houses stood empty, sagging and canted in their sea-battered disrepair, home to nothing more than faded twists of paint chips, mildew, and draughts. It marked the epicenter of the glamoured spikes that circumscribed the eastern half of the town.

"The hour of truth," Swaine said.

I pulled the wagon to a halt near the location we'd marked. Swaine and Twelves carefully unpacked the device. Winds from the harbor whistled through empty windows, setting a stray wooden shingle to clapping, unseen. Waves shifted the stones of the rocky beaches and lapped against the rotted pilings. Despair seeped from the ground, the stones, the weathered wood like a poison. As I looked about, I sensed not only the handiwork of the witches, but the presence of demons. A map was one thing, I realized, but what it represented was altogether more frightful. I climbed down and went around to the back of the wagon.

"It's fine?" I said.

"Looks it," Twelves said. His chatter from the ride had ceased. He'd never ventured this deep into old Salem and from the way he kept glancing over his shoulder, I could tell he felt the mournful weight of the place.

"Let's get it into position," Swaine said. He and Twelves carried the long case to the proper spot and placed it gently down.

Twelves crouched by the device. I had brought with me a pair of lanterns, which I lit and placed nearby. The flames snapped on the breeze, reflecting on the glass in the spectacles Twelves wore. Swaine stared at the device, his arms folded across his chest, a slight frown on his face. He said nothing as Twelves worked the inside of the clock.

"Pins are set. Gearing looks fine. None of those bounces on the road did it any harm," Twelves said.

Swaine kept staring. Twelves looked up at him.

"I've gone over the calculations for two days," Swaine said. He coughed into his fist, shaking his head at the annoyance. When he continued, his voice had a hoarse note to it. "I'm confident— though I must confess to a moment or two of concern where I couldn't entirely eliminate the possibility that the activation of this might so disrupt the planes that it could open a rift capable of spiraling out of control, exposing this world to catastrophic planar energies."

"Did you say *world*, sir?" I said.

"The possibility is small."

Twelves and I exchanged a look.

"Salem itself is a chaotic collision of planes and energies," Swaine said. "We are harnessing such instability for our purpose. I assume you're both fine moving forward?"

Neither of us said anything for several long moments.

"As long as it's just the world," Twelves eventually said.

"Well done," Swaine said. He turned to me. "Finch?"

"The possibility that my emotions might not remain at bay is small, sir."

"Then let's proceed."

Twelves stood up and dusted off his knees. "Ready for the winding. The energy. And the flames." He held out a pair of steel keys, each with broad tooth. "I believe you and Miss Finch have the honors."

Swaine took the keys and handed one to me. The device featured a complex arrangement of brass hammers, silver-lined chambers, glass enclosures, warded candles, and delicate gearing. One notable deviation from the earlier version was the presence of a plum bob that hung from a fine chain of copper; an addition not, as one might guess, for assuring that the device sat level at its appointed location, but rather critical for releasing the massive Holzian half-life energies that imbued the sixteen spikes we'd placed. My help was required, for we needed to activate the device with a pair of incantations spoken at the exact moment. We'd rehearsed the timing multiple times.

Swaine checked his watch. "Then we shall begin. Once we've completed the activation, we'll have twenty minutes to clear the boundaries. No delays. We'll observe from the hilltop back there." He turned to me. "You're ready?"

"I am."

"And the sorcerous mind?"

I'd heard the precept scores of times. "Has but one point of focus, sir."

"Very good."

I clasped the key in my hands, and Swaine did the same. We

grew silent in our concentration, leaving nothing but the hiss of the lanterns and the susurration of the waves to fill the night. Swaine nodded, and we began the primary incantation. "*Óminnishegri heitir, sá er yfir öldrum þrumir...*" As our words filled the air, I felt the power grow around us. At first, it reminded me of the way the air felt before a bolt of lightning might strike—a pull, a heightened sense of the air itself, the hairs on my head stirring, tiny streaks of pale light rising from nearby surfaces. Then it grew more powerful. A trickle of power became a stream, became a fast-running, rain-swollen brook, became a river, became a crashing wave at the leading edge of a devastating flood. I heard Twelves shift, the ground beneath his shoes crunching—he registered it, too.

Both Swaine and I raised our hands. My muscles flexed as I pushed my palms forward, stretching my fingers apart. The potency of the incantation increased, making it seem as if the ground beneath us were tilting downward, as if a strange breeze pulled us along with it, dry leaves skittering along an empty lane. I steadied myself. The air crackled, sucking my sleeves to my skin, my skirts to my legs. Mirroring Swaine, I placed my key into the silver-lined chamber on the left side of the device, while he did likewise on the right side. Moving my hand over the spring-loaded door, I spoke the first words of the invocation used in a summoning. Swaine spoke in unison.

"*Biholen uuerden, uurisilic giuuerc. Barnun sie farstandan iuuuan modsebon. Iuuua uuerc endi iuuuan uuilleon.*"

I looked at Swaine, who nodded. We each reached forward and closed the small doors. Strange shadows gathered past the edge of the far glamours we'd placed; we'd attracted unwanted attention from the denizens of Salem.

I placed one hand on my key, Swaine did likewise on the other. I held my free hand over the four chambers near the middle and spoke "*Ignis*" and watched the wicks spring to life with flame.

"Good," Swaine said. "Now the keys."

We both spoke, our words in sync: "*Hverju ertu nú bölvi borinn, er þú þá móður kallar, er til moldar er komin.*" Both keys turned at the same moment. As we did, the plum bob in the middle spun, increasing in speed until it became a blur. I had to glance away, my stomach flipping from vertigo. The magic was potent. For a moment, the air disappeared. My ears stopped up and I couldn't hear anything but the fast beating of my heart, the sound of my blood thrumming through my veins. The surrounding air rippled as a firestorm of brilliant greens and blues swept past us and across the ground in a blazing few seconds.

Swaine leaped to his feet. "Let's go."

The air itself shifted like warped glass, and the magic sent out a vibration strong enough to shake the ground. We sprinted to the wagon. As I climbed up on the bench, I looked back and saw the device appearing to swell while whorls of bright white energy etched lines in the air above it. Without pausing, I slapped the reins and yelled, sending the wagon heaving forward as the startled horse leaned into its harness.

"By God, I feel it," Twelves called out. "Like something from the Old Testament."

"That ought to be your first clue, Mr. Twelves," Swaine said.

I drove the wagon out across the bridge and along the dark lane, guided in part by the flashes of light which rent the sky overhead. Waves of magic crashed over us, while debris lifted into the air, carried on the strong winds that the planar boundaries generated. Twig, branch, leaves from seasons past zipped through the air.

"I thought the effect wasn't supposed to trigger for some time," Twelves said.

Swaine gripped the edge of the wagon, standing up behind me. "It wasn't. The energies involved are stronger than I'd expected."

I knew my master well enough to realize that *stronger than I'd expected* meant something closer to *we might well die in a few moments*, so I whipped the poor horse to its breaking point, the tack and hitch and wheels of the wagon jangling and banging as I tried to get us as far away as I could. As we crossed the glamoured barriers that marked the edge of the most well-secured areas abutting the old town, Swaine leaned over next to me, pointing to the rise. "As soon as we stop, you need to start notating what you observe."

At the crest of the hill, I brought the frothing horse to a halt. When I looked back over the old village, I gasped. A massive coil of light rose from the device, lit from within by near-constant flashes of magic. Vermillion, chartreuse, azure, and more streaked the darkness over the town—the contours of temporal displacement. The air itself vibrated with a low rumble while the wagon rocked on the powerful winds. Points of light appeared among the shadows of the abandoned buildings, reflecting the same fell colors. As the Holzian glamours displayed their disharmonitive effects against the regions of planar sympathy, a great flare of light erupted, so bright that I had to raise a hand to shield my eye—it was as though a miniature sun had burst to life over the town, bathing it in an eerie wash of pale colors. I thought of Swaine's worries of a planar rift catching hold and tearing the world apart. The trees sighed and creaked as a massive wind arose. Again, my ears popped. Twelves's hat flew from his head. He tried to grab it, but it sailed away.

Swaine remained still next to me. "Finch, what do you see?"

"The planes, sir—colliding. The sky looks dented. Pried apart. Beyond, stars and flares." I squinted. "Sheets of light are arching above the harbor—like the ceiling of a cathedral. Columns stretch to the ground." Looking at it brought about such a sense of my minuscule nature that I struggled to find words for it: a spark above an ocean, a pebble at the foot of a mountain range, a whisper lost to time.

"Any signs of the demonmere? It would be on the ground somewhere," Swaine said.

I lowered my gaze. Throughout Salem, twists of energy lit up in peculiar colors. Among them, weavings of bright gold—witches' seals. One, two, three I identified instantly from the map, precisely where they'd been marked. More, several of a complexity I could scarcely comprehend.

"I'm not sure, sir—not yet."

"Mark down as many intersections as you can. Any form. Any color. Quickly."

Dipping a quill, I started sketching what I saw, as best as I could. There was no way my harried scratches could capture the magnitude of the planar collisions. I jotted down everything I could—save for the witches' seals. I wasn't ready to have that conversation with my master yet. Scanning the village, I spotted demons among the lines of magic, shadows moving among the glare, repellant shapes gliding between buildings. The more I looked, the more I saw—until the count extended into dozens, then scores.

"Sir, demons," I said.

"Drawn to our activity, moths to the flame," Swaine said.

"They're heading to the device."

"Ignore them—they can't harm it. Look for the demonmere."

The surrounding winds only increased in their ferocity, snapping our clothing, screaming in our ears, carrying off the terrified whinnies of the horse as he stamped and tried to buck in his harness. Behind us, a tree cracked with a sharp bang, half of it toppling with a ground-shaking thud near our wagon. I saw strands of strange magic lifting from the ground, as though a fire burned just beneath the topsoil. The wagon shimmied sideways. Twelves struggled to keep his footing.

Demons gathered around the device. I followed Swaine's instructions. As I searched the frantic scene below us, I paused. Some of the witches' seals were damaged, tattered strands fluttering off into nothing, stretching, reduced to threads. One in particular caught my eye, quite near the location we'd first attempted to use the original resonance clock. That seal looked as though it barely held its shape. In other spots, I found the same thing—and staring at the map, looking back up into the night realized they were in spots where we'd placed planar clocks. Had our work somehow damaged the witches' seals?

"Do you see it?" Swaine said.

My gaze returned to the center of the chaos. A dim red glow surrounded the device, seen through the ghastly shapes of the demons drawn to it. A slender strand of pale light rose above it, whirling into existence like a living thread of lightning.

"Something's happening to the device, sir," I said.

Swaine steadied himself and peered at his watch. "It should go for another six and a half minutes."

"A light is rising from it. It's growing brighter. Bigger."

From the corner of my eye, I saw a similar glow entwine itself around the house of Thaddeus Rivers—where we'd found the second instance of the demonmere, the exit from which I'd rescued Swaine at the start of the winter. As I watched, the light flared—and then the house collapsed, roof, walls, and all crashing in on itself, sending a plume of dust and debris skyward. Light streamed from the ruins.

"The Rivers house, sir," I said, pointing.

"Remarkable," Swaine said.

Back by the device, the crowd of demons looked to have thinned. Worried, I looked to see if they were rushing in our direction—but as I looked, I saw two of them disappear into the light surrounding the device. More demons lifted, ones and twos at first, then in clumps of what looked to be a dozen or more. Once airborne, they darted—pulled—into the area from which the glare emerged.

"Sir—the demons—they're disappearing!"

"What do you mean?"

"At the device. They're being pulled in." Demon after demon disappeared into the opening until none remained.

Swaine checked his watch. "I don't understand."

I ignored the map and the quill in my hand. The light around the device flared. I spotted the device itself rotating in the air, twenty feet above the ground, casting a spinning shadow beneath it. Without warning, the device slammed down to the ground. The winds stopped at once, the blazing light winked out. Swaine and I both staggered forward, having held ourselves with such force against the winds that vanished. For a moment, the only sound was of trees settling upright again, stray branches falling to the ground. Coming up from the town, the creaking and collapsing of various old structures.

Twelves lifted his head. "Is it—"

The boom which shook the air was the loudest sound I'd ever heard. Everything within a mile shook, and we all carried a distinct ringing sound in our ears for days afterward. I looked all around and saw no signs of the planes, the glamours, the effects of the device. I didn't even see the device, the entire scene having plunged back into darkness.

"Well," Twelves said, his voice somewhat less than steady, "world's still here."

We spent the next hour investigating, first at the perimeter, then within the boundaries of the circle of spikes. Neither Swaine nor I detected any demons. Nor did there appear to be any residual distortion in the planes, visible or otherwise. I saw faint outlines of the witches' seals, but said nothing of them.

"Whole place seems different, that much is sure," Twelves said.

"If only I could explain why," Swaine muttered. A series of deep coughs racked him. As we neared the location of the device, the light from our lanterns revealed fissures in the ground, no wider than an inch or two in places. The air was noticeably more chilly. Twelves crouched, holding a lantern out.

"Hole," he said.

"The device?" Swaine said.

"Good question, sir."

Swaine and I approached. In front of Twelves opened a wide hole in the ground, about the size of a large table. Mist seeped from it and a cold breeze exhaled from the darkness within. Just beneath the edges of the opening, stones, like granite. As I drew nearer, I made out the first of the steps.

The demonmere.

"Sir?" I said.

"I see." The look on his face was beatific, and tears welled in the corners of his eyes. When he spoke, his voice was unsteady with emotion. "We just pried up the corner of the universe. And peered beyond."

"But how?"

"I've no good idea."

"And the demons are gone."

Swaine ran a hand along his chin. "How strange." In the flitting light of the lanterns, it appeared as though the shadows around us were living things, surrounding us like predators. It almost looked like Swaine emanated a dark glow, himself. A chill ran down my back. "Could it be that we've wiped clean the slate on this fabled town? Did we do it, Finch?"

August Swaine—a man of remarkable genius, sorcerer *par excellence*—had saved me, a one-eyed orphan girl without a shilling, a friend, or a living relative to call my own. He'd revealed to me the deepest truths of who I was, and what I could achieve.

Yet even a great man may have his blind spots.

In my endless drive to keep my eye on Swaine's blind spots, the great calling of my life, I needed to be a better apprentice than I was. I needed to be a better person than I was. I can't help but think, even now, that what I'd really wanted to say in that moment—*No, sir, we didn't—stay away—don't ever set foot in there*—might have been the one thing that could have saved my beloved master.

"Yes, sir," was what I said, torn and uncertain. "It seems so."

One can always wonder: *What might have been?* Four of the most haunting words in the English tongue.

17

A BEGUILING PUZZLE

A week later, I woke to the sound of my master knocking on the ceiling below my bedroom with a broomstick.

"Coming," I called out. I tossed the blankets aside and swung my feet to the chilly floor. The first light of dawn turned my room to a colorless sketch. Books, writings, maps, a few satchels and sacks still unpacked from our move back to the manse in Salem. I shifted and my hand touched the quill I'd drifted off holding. Three spots of ink now dotted my blanket where the nib had fallen, soaked to the sheet beneath, and dried. They weren't the first such stains. Of more concern was the small map which lay faceup next to me, my own notations marking the witch-wells I'd investigated in Salem since we'd moved back.

I folded the map and went to the corner of my room, moving aside a small trunk to pull up the loose board beneath, a six-inch length I'd cut with one of Mr. Twelves's saws and fitted over a small space between joists. The letters and maps lay inside the space, folded and tied with a length of hemp string. I put the map on top of the others and replaced the board, then with a wave of my hand glamoured it to make the cut section appear to be contiguous with the rest, just another bit of scuffed and faded floor. I slid the trunk back over it and vowed not to be so careless again.

Such secrets as I kept gnawed at me, true—but I listened to my heart. For what was the human heart if not a map? A map grown ever more detailed, charting the battlegrounds of life, the boundaries between right and wrong. A guide when the way became uncertain. The crucial atlas to tracking the ever-changing landscape of choices that one faced.

Splashing my face with water in a basin, I dressed, selecting an eyepatch covered in green silk. Swaine knocked on the ceiling again.

"Here I come," I said, raising my voice as I hurried out of my room and down to my master's study.

Swaine sat at his writing desk, hunched over a spread of papers, a candle casting the side of his face in light. The broom leaned against his desk. Embers glowed in the fireplace.

"Morning steals upon the night, melting the darkness," he said. His voice was rough, a touch of croak to it from the ague that no amount of tea and honey seemed capable of driving off.

"Don't tell me you haven't slept, sir."

"I slept. Until I couldn't." He stretched his arms and rolled his head on his neck. "Driven from my slumbers by an idea half-conjured in my dreams. Look here—I believe I've solved the mystery of those bothersome chambers."

I stepped into the room and approached. Swaine pointed with a quill at a curious arrangement before him. He'd cut three sheets of paper into circles of decreasing size, and stuck them with a pin in the center, the smallest atop one bigger, and that larger than the one at the bottom of the stack. As I stood looking over his shoulder, I wrinkled my nose. He needed a bath. A delicate matter grown worse as long days and nights moving back to Salem to grapple with the mysteries of the demonmere had pushed such matters of personal care—for him, at least—farther and farther down the list of priorities. (I'd learned the hard way that suggesting he stank was unwise. For all he ignored the matter, he was touchy on the subject, and deflected the observation into a stinging critique of my dedication, the implication—I'd guessed—being that if I wasn't sufficiently unwashed, then I couldn't be working hard enough.)

I ignored his sour aroma and peered at what he'd put together. Each of the circles was scribed with evenly spaced hash marks, larger ones corresponding to cardinal directions (only there for reference, for such notions as *cardinal* had no place in the demonmere). Swaine turned the top two pieces of paper, just so. "Look here. We have but one chamber, extending off the corridor beyond the pair of doors down stairs *A.III.*, as we found during our initial exploration. Now, we shift by six degrees—allowing for one degree for every twelve hours—and there are two. One atop the other though appearing side by side. Do you follow?"

I studied the papers. We'd made three careful expeditions into the demonmere, my master increasingly regarding the strange realm to be the key to understanding Salem itself. The walls of Swaine's study were now tacked over with maps and notes detailing the ever-shifting nature of what we'd found so far.

I nodded, understanding. "They're shifting—and somehow occupying the same space."

"Exactly. In something of a *multi-planar transposition*. Or *pan-planar shift*. I haven't decided on the proper term for it."

"So mapping any of it accurately is impossible."

He stood. "Let's not mistake difficult for impossible, Finch. We can leave that to the masses. It simply calls for a touch of ingenuity." He reached over and moved the circles, demonstrating. "This is our starting place."

Swaine swept out of the room, his night-robe flaring behind him. With one last glance at the collection of paper circles, I followed him.

"I'll make tea and porridge, sir," I said.

"We're just unlocking this—who can eat?"

I could.

Instead, I stood by Swaine as he slipped his bare legs into his boots and slung a cloak over his shoulders in the entryway. He looked at me, a glint in his eye. "Like a boy counting the days to Christmas. You don't find it exciting?"

"Of course I do."

"Then what's all this talk of breakfast? We'll eat later. Come. Let's see the dawn break on the opening." With that, he neutralized the glamour by the front door and shoved it open. I followed him into the crisp air, grabbing a cloak from a peg as I left the entryway. The sky over the ocean brightened, setting thin clouds ablaze before the sun crested the horizon. Tall hemlock on either side of the manse held the shadowed remains of night. Swaine raised his arms as he walked. "This is life, Finch. Here. This place. Each day our own. Isn't it magnificent?"

Frost held our footsteps, even on the lane. "It is, sir." I eyed him. He seemed buoyant enough for me to risk asking the question that had come as I'd looked at his paper maps. "Do you think the pan-planar shift could be related to any of the work we've been doing?"

"Ah, back to the notion that clings to the mind—some minds, at least—as a fleck of nasal waste sticks to the flicking finger. You have some new insight to bring to bear on the matter? Or shall I repeat, again, why it's nonsense?"

"You said it was unlikely. Not nonsense, sir."

"We're parsing words now, are we? Pray, go on." He kept up his pace, perhaps even increasing it. I matched his strides and continued. In for a penny, in for a pound.

"Well, if there were an actual concordance of planes, as Doctor Rush wrote of, aligning one atop the others—"

"I understand the theory."

"And if the displacement were being caused—sped up—by our work, then the shifting could be explained."

"How would that explain it?"

"Because—well, we're seeing just such a shift."

"You know that how?"

"What you just showed me, sir."

"I just showed you a theory."

I tried to keep my thoughts clear, so as not to make an obvious mistake—but he had a way of attacking my logic that reduced me to a stammering child, and it was difficult. "Yes, a theory, sir. But a theory that would appear to fit. Not just the demonmere discrepancies, sir—also the disappearance of the demons."

"And here I'd thought you'd trotted out your favorite hobbyhorse for the last time, Finch."

"You don't think it's at least possible?"

He withdrew a handkerchief and blew his nose wetly into it. "It grows no more possible via constant repetition."

As we neared the river, we passed by stacked piles of slab, board, and stanchion set up by Twelves—the first tangible progress on my master's long-dreamed of sorcerium, to be built adjacent to the opening into the demonmere.

Swaine paused, and he eyed me. "It's about trust, Finch. Without that, there's nothing."

I nodded. His words still carried an edge. Best let him have it out.

"We're on the cusp," he continued. "Men will speak of Salem in the same fashion they once spoke of the New Kingdom of Egypt, of Alexandria, of Florence. History will be made here. History that will bend the arc of mankind. You're part of this, don't you see?"

"I do, sir."

"Have I not fulfilled my promises to you—of instruction, guidance, access to my thoughts, my work?"

"You have, sir."

"And what do I ask in return? Very little, when you think of it."

I kept my face neutral. *Very little?* I dedicated virtually every waking moment of every day to assisting him. Some of that time was magnificent, no question—but the toil was endless. And what did I have beyond my apprenticeship? I knew the barest joys of friendship, nothing of romance. While I loved the work—from the studies to the practicing to the challenges to the unlikely route to understanding myself that it had given me—I wasn't unmindful of the cost. The ease of a normal life would forever elude me, I often thought. Relaxing, laughing with friends, or family. The pleasures of the mundane. Sleeping soundly. Having time for song, or prayer, or whatever else a typical Bostonian might do in the evenings. Such luxury. But, no—the sacrifice I made to be August Swaine's apprentice was as opposite of *very little* as could be.

"You're right, sir," I said instead.

Swaine watched me, then walked again. "And don't think I'm not sympathetic. I know what it is to be a young sorcerer. Full of brash thoughts. Wanting to make connections, to take the next big step forward. To think yourself more than you are. I know it well—which is why I'm trying to spare you some of the more painful lessons that I learned. I thought myself great before I should have. My hope for you is that I can make you a great sorcerer without all the delusions. Do you see?"

"You know I'm forever indebted to you, sir." I wasn't lying.

"And there are more days than not when I don't know how I'd cope without you, Finch, though you shan't hear me admit it often."

Reaching the entrance to the demonmere, I relaxed somewhat. On the ground stood a collection of gin poles, blocks, and ropes. Further signs of Twelves's efforts (often assisted by pairs of revenants) lined the roads: wide pilings, laid abreast, being readied to become supports for the sorcerium; supporting logs, peeling irons, and piles of timber dogs to hold them in place; broad-axe and foot adzes for the hewing, squaring, and shaving of joints. I followed him past stacks of cedar shingles, the ground well-trodden, the air still strong with the scent of sawn lumber and pitch. Three concentric circles of glamours spread out around the hole in the earth. I noted their integrity as I passed through them.

"Now," Swaine said. "If my rough calculations are correct, we should find two chambers plus a glimpse of the third extending off in the corner. Shall we take a look?"

"I think Mr. Twelves is still sleeping, sir." It'd been our practice to have Twelves remain outside the entrance each time we'd ventured into the demonmere, watching the time and maintaining an eye on the ropes we secured to ourselves as a safety measure.

"Just a peek," Swaine said. He lifted a fist to his mouth and coughed, a rattling hack that shook his shoulders and reddened his face. I worried that he wasn't getting anywhere near enough rest to lose the ague that plagued him for weeks.

"I can fetch him, sir."

Swaine waved away my suggestion. "Let the poor man sleep—he was working until well after midnight. Trust, Finch. Trust. We'll be fine." He slipped one loop at the end of a rope over his shoulders and around his waist. "They'll wonder, Finch—those in the future. They'll read it in their books, and they'll try to imagine what it was like for those of us who stood at that crossroads of civilization that separated the dark centuries from the enlightened epoch that came after it. Well, *this* is what was like." He stomped his boot on the ground, raising a puff of dust. "This." He raised his hands, pointing to the day breaking over Salem. "This." He turned and lit a pair of lanterns, took one, then stepped down the first stairs into the demonmere. "Come."

He has no idea what he's talking about. Inverressayte's words, like claws scratching the inside of my skull, made me jump.

"Not now," I whispered.

Mistress, pull the rope, pull him out of there. One of you needs to be thinking clearly.

I ignored him, pulling the second rope over my torso and cinching it around my hips. "Yes, sir," I said.

I've grown rather fond of you, Mistress—you're not nearly as cruel as the others who enslaved me—and would hate to see you hold the torch to light yourself on fire. Every time you go in there, the flames spread. You're dancing the dance they want you to. An infernal tune that will bring down the most important walls.

"Is there a problem?" Swaine called.

"No, sir—here I come." I grabbed the other lantern and stepped to the opening. Cold air poured forth. Looking to the side, I whispered, "I can't not go."

More's the pity, Inverressayte purred.

Seventeen steps led straight down, opening into a narrow corridor. As the ground disappeared, the sounds of my steps and the flame hissing in the lantern grew loud. Swaine waited for me at the bottom.

"How interesting," Swaine said. He held his lantern out, the circle of light revealing yet another lantern, dead center in the corridor.

"That's not one of ours, is it?" I said.

"No, it's not." He inspected the lantern. "It's a rather convincing facsimile, I believe. The dimensions are accurate—but the materials are strange. Not quite right. Let's not touch it."

As I neared it, I saw Swaine was right. The glass was milky and warped. The base was stubbier than our lanterns, the handle lacked the grips in the wood. "Where did it come from? Is there some test you could do, sir?"

"I don't think it's untoward behavior for the demonmere," Swaine said. "But here it shall remain. My research has impressed upon me the imperative that nothing native to this realm be removed and introduced into our world under any circumstance. What little documentation I found is harrowing. The complete destruction of the original town of Fladungen in the Rhön Mountains of Bavaria in 1656, for instance."

"Complete?"

"Complete. An otherwise unheralded magician by the name of Erwin Müeller claimed to have retrieved a chalice of *schädliche eisen*—noxious iron—from what he described as a passage he'd discovered behind an enchanted mirror of silver. Within a week, the town met with catastrophe. Every bit of nonorganic materials within a two-mile radius had become stippled with an unidentified metal. Worse, it had transformed all organic materials into something that resembled cold ash—a condition which had also taken every living resident, many of whom were found intact, only to crumble like cinders at the lightest touch."

"That's terrifying."

"Indeed. Let's leave it then, shall we?"

"Yes. Please." We continued along the corridor. "Is it made of the same types of materials as the rest of this?"

"One would imagine. Theories are sparse. Such construction is clearly not the handiwork of demons, as has been suggested," Swaine said. "Though such suggestions clearly didn't come from any actual sorcerer. I've warmed to the theory of Alf Bostrom of Gotland. Fifteenth Century magician, quite insightful. His claim is that these realms are the byproduct of subtle expressions of planar manipulation as instigated by the unseen arts themselves. If true, it suggests that every act of magic or sorcery might in fact draw upon the forces of the unseen planes, and as a consequence links the awareness of the practitioner to the demonmere in such a way as to fashion more and more features of human experience in an ever-expanding, pan-dimensional mansion of sorts. Think of that, Finch. An unspoken collective architecture beyond the heavens that grows more intricate with each glamour, every summoning, and all spells ever cast."

"Do you think witchcraft would affect it?"

"I don't see why it wouldn't."

The corridor, from our initial measurements, ran seventy feet at a four degree incline, with walls of smooth stone, the floor of a rougher stone. At the end stood a pair of stone doors. They were open, as we'd left them. Two flights of stairs followed, the first of stone, the second of a dark wood that curved to the right by fourteen degrees. A second corridor ran for just twenty-six feet. The farther we went, the more often we checked our ropes, keeping them trailing after us, not binding or catching. Echoes of our passage floated off in both directions, creating the illusion of a greater company that I found unnerving. Halfway along this second corridor, we'd found a rectangular opening in the left-hand wall, beyond which there appeared to be a vast space. Our attempts to see anything within range of our lanterns had proven fruitless, and the only sound was a faint, mournful sigh of wind. My flesh broke out in bumps as we passed it by, a touch of vertigo forcing me to steady my hand against the opposite wall. At the end of the corridor, a strange room opened to the right: ten feet long, but only half a foot tall, with what looked like miniature chairs, tables, and utensils arranged in the far corner. Across from it was a larger room of rounded stone walls that opened onto one, two, or three chambers, depending on when we looked at it.

Swaine held his lantern aloft and went into this second room. "Ha!" he said before even taking more than four steps. "Two chambers. Narrow sliver of the third. Narrower than I'd thought —but there's something to the theory. And there you thought it impossible, dear Finch."

"Very impressive, sir." I stood beside him. Each chamber opened from an arched doorway that ran the height of the wall, nearly eighteen feet.

"Civilization leaps forward care of the impossible, doesn't it? Sail across the sea—impossible. Climb onto that horse's back and ride it around—impossible. It's only impossible until someone actually does it."

"What of the person who thinks *I'll climb onto that tiger's back and ride it around*, sir?"

"You're a clever one." He stepped into the first chamber. "It's merely a way of thinking through a problem until the true problem reveals itself. Not giving up at the first brush of resistance."

I followed him, tugging my rope to give it more slack. The chamber was square. Two windows occupied one wall, but the glass was opaque and neither window opened. As I stepped inside, I stopped.

"My calculations are likely off," Swaine continued. "A more precise series of measurements are called for, obviously."

Along the top of all four walls ran what looked to be a sculpted and painted border: soot-colored ravens in flight, one after another after another; behind them, a faded and peeling field of blue.

"Sir," I said.

"Although I suspect we'll have trouble with accurate timing," Swaine said, looking at his pocket watch with a frown. "Nothing seems consistent. According to this, we've been in here for eighty-one minutes, and it's barely been ten."

"Those—ravens, sir. They weren't there before." It felt as though my heart rose into my throat. The very thing I'd been furtively scanning the sky for since the week before. Ravens. Of course, ravens had another connection to the demonmere, as well; my clumsy, desperate attempt at raven magic had led me to finding Swaine when he'd gotten lost inside the corridor that appeared in the manse.

Swaine glanced up from his watch. "They weren't?"

"No, sir. They definitely weren't."

With a snap, he closed his watch, and walked the perimeter of the room, inspecting the border with the upheld lantern. "No, you're right. The stone went completely to the top. I remember. How curious. Has anything else changed?"

I searched the room, consciously trying not to hunch my shoulders against the accusatory gaze of the ravens, quite sure my face beamed with nothing but the purest guilt. The same strange wood as the stairs behind us formed the floorboards. I inspected the corners. In the first two, I found nothing unusual. The third corner brought me to a halt. What appeared to be a porcelain tile was inlaid into the floor, showing a green tree against a white background.

A hemlock tree.

Every time you go in there, the flames spread. Inverressayte's words. The words of a demon, true—but what if he were right?

"This wasn't here, either," I said.

Swaine came over and knelt by the strange tile, running a finger across its surface. "Ravens? A tree? How strange."

"Could it have been—someone's magic, sir?"

"Not mine. Not yours."

"Someone else?"

"Such as?"

"Doctor Rush."

"I've never met a magician more averse to doing magic—though my impressions are hardly more than superficial. What do you suspect?"

"Suspect? I—well—nothing, sir. Or, nothing specific. It's just that he's the only other practitioner in the area."

"It's unclear what degree of influence proximity exerts on the demonmere. For all we know, this change could be related to something done four thousand miles away. Or two hundred years ago." He stood, gazing at the borders again. "Though it is curious. Your use of raven magic when you rescued me certainly comes to mind. You haven't done any tree magic you haven't mentioned, have you?"

Oh, how close I came to spilling out everything. *Well, I did witchcraft with the witch-wells and seals I've kept secret from you, and those were typically near hemlock trees. Where demons attacked me—*

but don't worry, I fought them off. And shadow-ravens took flight. Probably Doctor Rush, because I stole his map when he caught the Rattlesnakes I'd been involved with. The map the Occultatum Ostium told me about when I looked inside it. But I'm just desperate to find Clara, another Rattlesnake, who slipped into another entrance to the demonmere, which I also didn't tell you about—because John Whitelocke was killed after I used magic to sneak the Rattlesnakes inside the governor's manse. Yet another demon in the infernal vox expander told me about Clara, which I also haven't spoken a whisper of. On and on, there was so much. Any one bit of it sure to infuriate my master. Disappoint him beyond measure. Shatter his trust in me.

It's about trust, Finch. Without that, there's nothing. He'd just said it to me.

"Tree? No. I don't even know any tree magic, sir."

"If we weren't standing in the demonmere," he said, "I might make a jest about the various branches of tree magic—but this isn't the time, is it? We'll make note of it, see if it changes further, see if anything else pertinent arises that might explain the change."

Lantern in hand, he led the way out of the room. I glanced back at the tile and the images of the ravens before following him. *Pertinent?* The word took on a shameful weight.

The second chamber was narrower than the first, but twice as long.

"Does this look even narrower than before?" Swaine said, standing just inside the doorway. "You didn't think to bring a measuring line, did you?"

"No, sir. I thought we were just taking a quick look."

"Twelves has it right: clothing with enough pockets to keep our tools with us." He walked farther into the room. Before I even got a good look, I knew the room had changed—and not just in its width. My stomach tightened. Along the top edge of the wall, another decorative motif banded the room: coffins; black coffins, end to end, against a gray background that appeared to be streaked with fine lines of slanting rain.

I was suddenly glad I hadn't eaten breakfast, after all.

Swaine held his lantern high. "Look at this—coffins. Now I know these weren't here before."

"Coffins?" I said, scanning ahead, dreading that I might see likenesses of Grayson Whitelocke and myself traipsing through the burial yard.

"The change is evident in both chambers," Swaine said. "Perhaps not altogether surprising, if my theory is anywhere near the mark. A disruption of some kind, the influence of some magic somewhere, could very well leave its mark across all three chambers, transposed as I suspect they are across the same multiplanar coordinates. But why coffins? Ravens? The tree? A strange riddle."

I volunteered nothing, struggling as I was to keep the tightness of my chest from showing.

"Of course, it might be random," Swaine continued, walking the length of the chamber and inspecting the coffin border. "Or it might somehow be reflecting something we're bringing in here. Or it might be a message, directed at us. Intriguing possibilities, those last two. What do you think?"

I think I'm going to throw up. I cleared my throat. "I don't— those all could be possibilities. But why this time, not the others?" To me, it sounded like desperate babble. Swaine didn't appear to notice.

"Yet another good question. We're acquiring questions faster than we're finding answers. I find it rather thrilling." He lowered the lantern and swept the light across the floor. "No unusual tiles, this time. Interesting. All else appears as it was earlier. So. Dimensions certainly different. The appearance of the coffin motif. I want to see the third chamber, don't you?"

"Yes."

I didn't. I didn't at all. Still, I stayed close to Swaine as we left the second chamber and strode over to the last one. The air felt even colder than earlier, driving me to shiver—though some degree of that was worry about what I'd see next. Not fully realized, the third chamber's doorway was only two feet wide, and the inside not much wider, by only half a foot on each side. Unlike the other two rooms, this one had smooth walls of a dusky hue, cornice work around the edges in pale ivory, and a narrow chandelier set into the middle of the ceiling.

The walls were without a mark. No fresco, no border, no images of any kind. I didn't see anything break up the evenness of the floor, either. Pale floorboards extended neatly from one side to the other, unbroken by a tile of any kind.

Swaine continued forward. "I don't see—wait."

That one word hit me like a blow to the stomach. Due to the narrowness of the room, I couldn't see past my master. "What is it, sir?"

"Come see. Remarkable."

He'd stopped at the far end. Peering over his shoulder, I managed not to gasp.

"Do you recognize this?" he said. "I do."

Before him stood an elegant table on carved legs, with a single drawer.

"From that corridor, sir. Beneath the Rivers house."

"Exactly. My God—what a beguiling puzzle all this is becoming."

The sight of the table ran chill fingers down my spine. I didn't want to see what was in the drawer—so much so that when my master reached out to open it, I almost cried out for him to stop. The drawer slid quietly open. As I looked past Swaine's shoulder, I bit the corner of my mouth, cringing.

A gray velvet pillow sat in the drawer. Atop the pillow sat a single key, three inches in length. It shone, polished silver, or perhaps pewter.

"A key, sir?" I said.

"Do you see a keyhole anywhere?" He made no move to pick up the key.

"No."

"Ravens. Coffins. A key. No more confounding than anything else we're likely to encounter in here, I suppose—yet intriguing that they should all appear simultaneously, or near to it." He slid the drawer closed.

As it shut, I straightened, remembering the high voices of the drowned girls, their song, their words: *I can give you a key. A beautiful key, just for you.*

None of what we'd discovered in the chambers related to my master. No, every change was explicitly tied to me. No other explanation offered itself. But how? None of it made sense.

"You have thoughts, Finch?" Swaine said.

"No. I mean, I'm not sure, sir. I can't guess the logic."

"If there is logic. We've no specific basis for assuming so—though I suspect it won't stop us from dwelling on it. More research is certainly in order."

Above the fluttering of the lantern flames, I heard a faint sound when my master stopped speaking. I cocked my head. Music, faint and delicate. A distant melody, plinked out, metallic. The skin on my arms broke into gooseflesh.

"Sir—do you hear that?"

Swaine looked off to the side, listening. "No. What do you hear?"

"It's—music. A tune." As I listened, the melody revealed itself as familiar—though I couldn't, at first, place it. My mind followed along. I almost had it.

"I don't hear anything," Swaine said. "Several inadvisable explosions in my younger years did my hearing no favors, save for leaving me a ringing in my left ear that plagues me to this day."

...hey, ding, ding, with my ho, ding, ding...

The words snapped into place. *May God keep all good people from such bad company.*

"The Three Butchers." But it wasn't a voice, wasn't sung—just the tune, tinkling faintly from somewhere out of sight. Then I remembered Clara's words:

They said Hell was a fiery pit. It's not. It's room, after room, after room, after room. Bridges. Courtyards. Hallways that go on forever. Tiny doors. Windows that open out into dead worlds. Twists and turns and trapdoors. Teakettles. Music boxes. Footsteps. Forever. And it never changes.

Music boxes.

"A song, sir," I said. "As though from a music box. You don't hear it?"

"I don't." Concern darkened his brow. "Best if we leave, I think. It may be my damaged hearing preventing me from discerning it. It may be something else. Your nature as a witch. In either case, more caution is prudent. Let's go."

As we headed back through the corridors and staircases, the music grew faint, to the point where I couldn't tell if I was still hearing it, or merely imagining I was hearing it. By the time we reached the final flight of stone steps, I heard nothing of it, lost beneath the scuffling of our feet, the soft sound of the ropes we dragged with us. Swaine started up ahead of me. I glanced back over my shoulder, into the black corridor beyond the light of my lantern.

Clara was still in there, somewhere. *Please—please—please— get me out. Get me out and I'll never do anything wrong, ever again. I promise on my soul.*

I hadn't forgotten my promise. Yet it seemed the demonmere was now more than aware of me, as well. Fear, pity, and worry weighed on me as I turned and followed Swaine, leaving behind the darkness of the demonmere.

18

———

UNIMAGINABLE

There is a fragile line we all walk, each day of our lives: life on one side, death on the other. From that boundary, which we must all cross at some unspecified hour, stretches eternity. We console ourselves that such a line is absurdly distant in time and therefore unimaginable. Unworthy of more than a stray thought or two, unwelcome thoughts at that. Draped in tales of redemption and reunion to leave the true contours only guessed at.

But, no. Death is no further from us than our own shadows, likewise carried around with us wherever we go. What a state we find ourselves in. Outright terror wouldn't be uncalled for. If someone invited you into a great home with but one simple caution: *Any of these boards might give way beneath your feet at any point, hurtling you to your demise*—who in their right mind would step across that threshold? Yet that's the great home we all inhabit for our entire lives, short or long, blessed or full of cruelty and deprivation, just or unjust, until the moment that our next step becomes our last, and that most irreversible line is crossed, its promise kept.

I bore no less guilt than anyone in my delusion that what

currently was, would ever be. More foolhardy in my case, given how I'd seen my life stripped of loved ones and significant figures as they'd been snatched into the black. Yet I wasn't at all prepared for August Swaine to drift over that fragile line the night we returned from the demonmere.

My first tickle of real concern came when he stood in his study, reviewing the plans for the sorcerium with Robert Twelves. Swaine leaned over the drawings that Twelves presented him. Still bedeviled by the cough, he held a cloth in his hand, using it to dab at his mouth after yet another racking fusillade. His cheeks and forehead flushed, he nodded along without comment as Twelves guided him through the drawings.

"As you suggested, sir," Twelves said, "the first floor has eight walls of equal length, creating the octagonal enclosure. Seventy-five foot span at the farthest corners. Pairs of windows here, here, and here."

Swaine followed Twelves's fingers as he tapped the drawing.

Twelves continued. "Second story has the four gables, aligned east, west, north, south. Larger windows. Glass will get expensive. Might delay things."

I waited for my master to let fly a tetchy complaint about the mere suggestion of delay, but he said nothing. Twelves looked at him, perhaps sensing himself the uncharacteristic silence. With raised eyebrows, he shifted to the third drawing. "And the final floor has the circular observatory here. Dome above. Tall iron spire."

Swaine reached with a shaky hand for the back of the chair and helped himself into the seat, wheezing in a shallow breath as he did. "Go on," he said, his voice thin and wavering.

"Would you like me to get you some tea, sir?" I offered.

He waved away my suggestion. "Thank you, no, Finch," he whispered.

Twelves and I exchanged a glance. Twelves turned around a ledger book so that my master might see it. "Estimates of glass.

Shingling. All the finishing details. It'll be one of a kind. The cost, as well."

Swaine stared at the figures as though not seeing them. His breath hitched and he hunched over, covering his mouth with the cloth, coughing and wheezing so loudly that the sound of it reminded me of a dull saw tearing through a board: push, pull, push, pull. When he finally drew in a thin, crackling breath without it exploding back out, he reached forward and put his hand on the drawing. "This," he began, his voice a fragile ghost, "is how history happens. Vision"—another bout of coughing blotted out his words, followed by a whistling inhalation —"meets hard work." He sat back, looking up at the ceiling, blinking his eyes, which had gone glassy from the effort of getting the words out and a subsequent breath in.

"Sir, you don't look well," I said. I stepped over to him and put the back of my hand on his forehead. His skin radiated waves of heat, as though embers lay just beneath his skin. My tickle of concern grew to a sharp edge. Swaine closed his eyes. "We're getting you in bed, sir. You need to rest."

I looked over at Twelves, widening my eye to show the degree of my worry. Twelves came around the table.

"Can you stand, sir?" I said.

"History," he whispered, the word a thin scribble amidst the wet crackling of his lungs.

"Mr. Twelves, if you would kindly get his other arm." I waved for him to hurry. Between the two of us, we got Swaine out of his chair, only to find his weight balanced on uncooperative legs. Worse, I felt sweat soaking through his shirt beneath the coat he still wore.

"Bed," Swaine muttered, his eyes still closed.

"Oh, boy," Twelves said.

It took a good ten minutes for the two of us to get Swaine up the stairs, an awkward affair. Halfway up, he whispered, "I didn't mean to spill it," followed at the top steps by, "It wasn't fresh."

Along the way, we both heard the ghastly sound his lungs made, and my mind went back to my brush with death beneath the surface of the river. The fear took hold he was drowning from within. His pallor went from flushed to pale, a hint of blue around his lips. Sweat rolled off his scalp, pouring out of his skin, making it even more difficult to keep a good grip on him. As we staggered into his room, I whispered, *"Ignis,"* and the pair of candles on his writing desk flared to life. By the time we got him to his bed, his head lolled forward.

"Sir? Sir?" I said. I tapped his cheek, still hot. He said nothing.

"Not good," Twelves said.

"Fetch well water and some rags. Hurry."

Twelves rushed from the room, his steps breaking into a sprint as he raced down the stairs. I pulled the coat off Swaine, fighting back the dreadful shadow of fear that closed in around me. *Another death. They've all died, everyone in your cursed life, every last one of them. Now it's his turn.* The memories of my losses constricting like iron chains around my chest. Anger rose alongside the fear, as though some part of my mind wanted to blot out the desperate worry. *His unceasing drive did this—he let his persistent exhaustion strain his humors beyond their limits. He wore it like a badge, the single-minded commitment, the endless hours.*

"Master, don't," I whispered. "Don't."

The candles burned lower, the hours chimed through seven, eight, nine o'clock, and beyond, and all I could do was try to keep him cool with a steady exchange of soaked compresses held to his forehead. Twelves refreshed the well water to keep it cool. He stared out the window. He paced. He took a few turns holding the compresses against Swaine. At one point, Swaine called out for me, even as I sat with my hand on his arm, my other shifting the cloth on his forehead. His eyes fluttered for half a moment, then he slipped back into a stillness, his chest straining and gurgling.

"These compresses aren't enough," I said.

"I suppose none of those powders at his workbench are medicine?" Twelves said.

"I don't know. Maybe. Nothing I can put together, though."

Swaine's teeth clacked, his shoulders rising and falling, his arms trembling. The water glass on his nightstand shattered, water spilling out everywhere, glass shards flying.

Twelves flinched. "Did he do that?"

"No—a demon did," I said. Despite the myriad glamours Swaine maintained in his room, I sensed a demon. Weak groans escaped my master.

"They can't get away from him when he's like this—can they?" Twelves said.

"They shouldn't be able to."

"You don't sound certain."

"I'm not." Shivers coursed through Swaine's limbs. "Fetch another blanket."

When Twelves opened the door, Mr. Winters stood just outside it. He pushed past Twelves, his hands on his thin hips.

Swaine held the edge of his blanket up to his eyes, covering the bottom of his face. "I'm sorry, I'm sorry, I'm sorry." His eyes were wide and his voice a husk. "I only wanted to honey them."

Winters frowned. "You've made quite a mess, young master. Sticky everywhere. Sticky. Sticky. Sticky." He spoke in an unfamiliar accent.

"I'll clean it," Swaine whispered.

"You can't clean sticky like that. I've even tried my vinegar water. It's holding fast."

"Noooooo!" The wail that broke from Swaine's muffled lips ached with equal parts despair and terror.

"He'll know for sure," Winters snapped. "He's coming up the lane. Coming even now."

A gurgling cough shook my master, so hard and throttled that his face grew deep red and his eyes bulged. He bent over on his side, wheezing for air.

"Jesus—what's he talking about?" Twelves said.

"I don't know." I reached into my pocket and pulled out my key for the revenants, thrusting it into Winters's face. "Out, now! Speak no further! Go!" The revenant snarled at me, raising a hand to block the key, staggering backward.

"He'll not be pleased, young master," he said, his voice in that same accusing tone.

I didn't understand—I'd commanded the demon to be silent. Before I could puzzle it any further, a strange movement swept through the chamber, lifting the curtains, shifting any loose pages on desk and nightstand. From beyond the doorway, heavy footsteps clomped up the stairs.

"I just wanted them honeyed," Swaine croaked.

"That's it—out now!" I chased Winters back with the key, and when he tried to speak to my master again, I cast Hume's Eleventh Ward, my gesture viper-quick. The revenant flew backward, crashing into the door, held up off the floor by the force of the ward. Shadows bled from his open mouth, nose, eyes, ears. "Out!"

The latch slipped, and Winters tumbled out, slamming into the wall opposite Swaine's door. I followed. Half a dozen revenants gathered in the hallway.

"WHAT HAS THAT BEGGARLY STEM OF A BOY DONE TO MY BLOODY KITCHEN?" They screamed in unison, strange voices booming around me. Swaine shrieked. I raised the key and drove the revenants back, ignoring their growls and hissing.

Mr. Winters, the slender man, the young lad we used for chimney work, the man with the crooked leg who bailed water from the stone cellar, all stayed away from the key. "Down the stairs, all of you! Go!"

"AUGUSTUS SWAINE!" they cried out. "I'LL WHIP THE SKIN FROM YOUR HANDS—TEACH YOU TO MIND WHERE YOU EVER PUT THEM AGAIN, WRETCHED WHELP!"

More demons swarmed around the chamber. "Drive them back, Mr. Twelves—all the way down the stairs."

Twelves, his eyes wide, pulled his own key from his pocket and strode toward them, holding it up. "They're not moving!" he called over his shoulder.

A chill wind gusted, setting the air in the chamber to whirling. The plaster along the ceiling cracked apart, falling in jagged pieces. A distortion in the air slid across the floorboards and moved beneath my skirts, leaving my legs shocked with a ghastly grip. Whispers bounced off the walls. Behind me, Swaine sobbed and fell to the floor next to his bed, smacking his head, his feet tangled in blankets. The sight of it struck my heart with a heady blend of pity, panic, and anger. I turned back to the revenants, shouldering my way past Twelves.

"BACK!" I yelled, and then I released an explosion of the most potent witchcraft I'd ever generated. I coiled both of my hands and watched as the force spun outward in a massive wave. The revenants fell over like corn stalks before a line of artillery. Blinding curls of light sped across the walls, floor, ceiling, bodies, pale gold and wavering. My hands shone with it, and my arms tingled. My insides vibrated as though I'd sprinted full-out. I sensed every demon—their exact location clear. They weren't pleased. No, not at all—but at least I had their full attention.

I swept my arms, turning and curving them, releasing a tremendous wash of energy. The hallway lit up as though the ceiling had been torn away, the sun filling the space. The free demons fled while the revenants scurried and scampered away from me. I drove them to the stairs and chased them like vermin before the broom. They somersaulted and cartwheeled down the stairs, landing in a heap at the bottom.

"The next one of you who crosses this top step will be obliterated," I said. None of them made a move to return, so I hurried back to my master's chamber.

Mistress, I don't think you understand. Inverressayte's voice scratched the inside of my mind.

"Not now, Inverressayte."

But Mistress—

I didn't have time for the demon's snide commentary. "No, enough. Do not speak to me unbidden. I shall call you when I need you, and that is the only time you shall speak to me."

I ran a hand along both sides of the door frame, leaving fey blue tracings where my fingers touched the wood. Potent, like a glamour. Once I'd done the doorway, I held that same focus in my concentration and hurried around the room, leaving a trail of witchcraft that would keep my master undisturbed, for a time, at least. Twelves had his hands beneath Swaine's arms and heaved him to a sitting position, dragging him until his back rested against the side of his bed. "There we go."

Swaine's cheeks and forehead blazed, flushed deep red. He trembled. I knelt before him and slapped at his cheeks. His eyes fluttered, but didn't open. He shook his head back and forth, and muttered something that sounded like "May I keep him?" in a strangled voice. I put my hand to his chest and felt his heart knocking about within. He shook, his limbs jerking. At that moment, I no longer worried about demons—I panicked that he was slipping across death's doorway.

"What can we do?" Twelves said.

"Let me think." I closed my eye. What did he need? *Relief, cool relief. Calm, flowing movement. Gentle currents. Ease.* An image filled my mind: a clear stream, passing through a forest, winding among dark stones, soft banks, trees shading curves and drops, morning sunlight weaving golden lines across the bottom, opening to a wider pool that flowed more slowly.

"Keep him sitting upright." I put an index finger to my lip, as though to shush Swaine, and I blew gently. From within, power passed up through my lungs, coming from deep within my lower abdomen. It flowed out my mouth, my nose, the palm I raised.

This stream of magic rolled over Swaine, starting at his chest and flowing both up and down, expanding. Green and gold washes passing over him. I pushed out another long expulsion of this energy, not letting go of the image that filled my thoughts: the forest stream, wrapping Swaine, swaddling him in a blanket of sunlight passing through leaf and branch.

His limbs stilled. I continued to expel this strange magic, drawing from deep within me, as though from my bones, my organs. I suspected it was moving *through* me, rather than coming *from* me—but I didn't question it, only knowing I needed to keep it flowing. Breath by long breath, I maintained the image of the forest stream, connecting it with a sense of coolness, of nutrient, of life. With my other hand, I reached out and grasped Swaine's forearm.

I'm uncertain how long I knelt by his side, bathing him in magic. At one point, the door banged, shaking in its frame. The windows rattled. From the first floor came the sound of crashing and toppling. I ignored all. The manse soon stilled, the ruckus replaced with a brooding watchfulness I found even more distracting. Still, I was a stream—gentle, fragrant with mineral, moss, and soil, decorated with mist, dappled with sunlight. I kept my focus.

Eventually—it may have been an hour later, or double that—I let my breaths grow soft, the smallest of breezes, and then relaxed. I hunched over, holding myself up with a palm on the floor, drained. My arms trembled as if from an afternoon spent chopping wood. My right hand was numb. I looked up at my master. His eyes were closed, his breathing slow and deep. I laid my palm on his forehead. The fires had consumed their fill, the appalling heat that had poured from his skin had retreated. I hung my head in thanks.

"I've never seen anything like that," Twelves said. "You saved him."

"Don't ask me how." I reached over and patted his arm. "You stayed with him, holding him."

"All I could do."

"We'd best get him in bed." We lifted Swaine, getting him back into his sheets and blankets. He wasn't senseless, but whatever sounds he made weren't quite words. Worried about him getting a further chill, I stripped him of his damp clothes and settled him beneath a set of fresh sheets and blankets. He appeared to sleep through the entire effort, for which I was thankful. Twelves stoked a small fire to life in his hearth to keep the room warm in the hours before the dawn and refilled the water he kept on his nightstand. The protections I'd scribed across the floor and the doorway still glowed, which was reassuring.

When we'd finished, the manse quiet, the fire snapping, Swaine looked peaceful beneath his blankets. The panic that had swept me away had receded by then, but like a high tide, had left its mark, reminding me of how close I'd come to seeing the center of my life ripped away from me again.

"Come," I whispered to Twelves. "Let's let him sleep."

Twelves nodded and went to the hallway. Exhausted, I followed him, stepping across the glowing line of magic I'd painted on the threshold. Such a small step, across that line.

19

———

DEMON ON THE PROWL

Morning came with its peculiar silence. Though we'd rid Salem of its demons—seemingly—it hadn't been enough to lure back sparrow, gull, or crow. The sigh of the nearby water and the shifting winds were all the song that filled the air, unchanging from night to day to night again. I checked on Swaine first thing, half prepared to find him dead. His breathing was smooth and deep. His color looked good. The evening before stayed in my mind like a nightmare, the handful of hours I'd slept not enough to dull the frightful memories.

I ignored the revenants, back in their corners as expected, and made a breakfast of biscuits with molasses and cornmeal mush, steaming dark tea, fresh butter. Mr. Twelves—unerringly attuned to the moment a meal was ready—appeared in the doorway to the kitchen, a fresh change of clothes on, his face wet from his rinsing bowl.

"Hope I don't look as tired as you do," he said.

"Never say that or anything of the kind to your lady friend whose father owns the sawmill." I put a plate together for him and poured him some tea.

229

"Anne. I doubt she'd ever look this tired. Even if she was."

"One doesn't comment on the appearance of a woman unless one is using the words *ravishing*, *beautiful*, or *lovely*. No matter how tired she is. Or you are."

He took the plate. "You think I don't listen to your advice. But I do. All makes sense when you say it."

"Now there's something you may say to a woman as often as you wish." I sat at the table with my plate and slid the corner of a biscuit through the butter. Twelves sat across from me.

"How is he?" he said.

"Sleeping. He needs to sleep all day. For a few days, even."

"What's the chance of that happening?"

"He may not have much of a choice. He used up all he had."

"Wouldn't be the worst thing to have a day or two to get ahead," Twelves said, spooning up the mush. "The cross-ties I'm waiting for were delayed at the mill. Two broken blades. He wasn't happy to hear that. Not that it was my fault. Or anyone's." He put the spoon down. "That reminds me." He stood and went to the hallway, rifling through the pockets of his coat where it hung on a peg. Returning, he held out a folded letter. "This is for you. That fellow at the tavern. In all the madness last night, I forgot about it."

"Bertram?" I said.

Twelves sat back down and drizzled more molasses onto a biscuit. "Nervous. Looked at me like I might punch him in the face. For no reason. Sweet on you, though."

"Of course he is."

"You sweet on him?"

"I'm not sweet on anyone."

"There's got to be someone."

I glanced at him. Well, there was Francis, with his eyes that made me half as smart as I normally was—and the extortion, lies, and brazen self-regard which left me twice as angry as I cared to be. Also: in jail. Grayson Whitelocke? Brandy-fueled lechery, everything a jest, happy to use anyone who crossed his path, as much as he criticized his sister for exactly that fault. No. Lord, no. And dear Bertram, whose second-guessing had second-guessing, and whose fidgety nerves could probably power a mill? I adored him—much as I'd adored my brothers.

"No there doesn't," I said.

"So you're planning on turning into him?" Twelves pointed with his spoon toward Swaine's room.

"No." I dragged the word out for emphasis.

"Good. Because when you start flopping around like a perch thrown on the shore because all you do is work every minute of the day—I don't think I'll be able to save you like you saved him."

"Thank you for your concern. Now finish your tea. And you're welcome."

I unfolded the letter and read it:

Dear Miss Finch—

Good morning. I hope this finds you well. Should I have called you Katie? I suppose I should have. In that event—

Dear Katie—

Since your departure has necessitated less frequent visits, I wager this letter might reach you more quickly than awaiting your next visit to the tavern. Which I certainly await with pleasure. And no small amount of Excitement, given our last two jaunts.

It is on the subject of our last two excursions that I write you. The goal of our expeditions being "what it was," I expect you'll take great interest to hear that I've learned of yet another promising desti-nation, one bound to please. I've, in fact, heard it mentioned recently, very recently, by more than one traveler barely able to contain their excitement. What thrills they relayed to me, wide-eyed and bated-breathed.

I think you ought to go and see for yourself, before the word gets out and everyone interested in such Specimens beats a path there.

You clearly know how to find me.

Hoping you are well and finding your recent resettlement to your liking.

Your humble servant, etc.

B.

P.S. I believe it may have been one of your friends who first discovered this place.

P.P.S. I shouldn't wait too long.

I read the letter twice more. When I looked up, Twelves watched me, smiling.

"Love letter," he said.

"No."

"Not that I'd write one—tools and wood and gears suit me better than paper and words, I'm more of a hands-on sort—but if I did, I'll say this much: I hope it wouldn't make Anne's face do what yours just did. Poor fellow."

I shoved the rest of the biscuit into my mouth and got up, folding the letter. "Commenting on a woman's face, are we? I thought you said you listened to my advice."

"Well—yes. But you know I'm teasing. Come on."

"I need you to look after Swaine until I'm back. I shouldn't be too long."

"Me?"

"Yes. You."

"But I can't do—that thing you did to him."

"You shouldn't have to. He'll probably keep sleeping. But you can get him some water if he wakes. Tea. A biscuit, which I made already. Whatever else he needs. Except books or work."

"How am I supposed to stop him?"

"You're a hands-on sort. You'll figure it out." I hurried from the kitchen.

I made better time riding to Andover by taking the horse alone, saddled up without the wagon. For all of Mr. Twelves's teasing, he was as talented in the physical world as Swaine was with the unseen world, and had shown me how to ride a horse properly astride. Though Mary Whitelocke wouldn't have been pleased to see my habit and petticoats bunched as they were, it was much easier for me. What's more, having been stared at my whole life because of my missing eye, I'd grown largely immune to the looks I received in doing so. The frowns of disapproval I got from people I met on the road were left on the road where I got them.

By midmorning, I passed between the meadows of Andover, noticing in contrast the ruckus of life that Salem lacked. Chickadee, cardinal, catbird, blue jay, and, yes, even finch filled the meadows and woods with trill and chirp, while crow and hawk cried from their imperial heights. Cicada and cricket made for a soft bed of buzzing. Shifting branch and stalk revealed the patter and scurry of hare, of squirrel, of leaping deer with their ghostly white tails dashing off into deeper trees. Riding toward the center of the town, I smelled wood smoke and frying bacon, heard the chop of an axe, the squeak of a well handle turning. And singing.

My foot in the stirrup, I swung down from the saddle and hitched the horse. Iris stood behind the tavern, hanging white sheets and darker clothing to dry on her lines. Sunlight and shade crisscrossed her face as she pinned the wash to the ropes. Her voice rose prettily into the morning. Her little one lay on a blanket in the grass while the older boy darted in and out of the gaps between the sheets as the wind shifted them. When she glanced over at me, she broke into a smile and waved. I wiggled my fingers at her and went to find Bertram. The public room was empty save for a pair of older men at a table by the hearth, smoking pipes and gesturing with them as they chatted. I peeked into the kitchen and found Bertram chopping turnips and yams. His hair was tied back with a black ribbon and patchy red whiskers dusted his chin.

"Specimens?" I said.

He jerked at the sound of my voice, but, to his credit, didn't yell or slice off a finger. He put the knife down, however. "I should've known you'd sneak up on me like that. Practically appearing out of thin air."

I crossed into the kitchen. "I'll have you know I rode here on a horse, walked through the door, looked carefully around the corner before saying a word. Are you making soup?"

"Saving my sister some time, is all. She doesn't trust me enough to make the soup on my own. Not yet." He wiped his hands on his apron. "But one day, if I'm stout of heart enough, humble enough, wizened through her patient instruction, and well enough versed in the complex art of cuisine—I might be able to sweep all these chopped vegetables into a pot of stock and set them to cooking. Never say I'm not without a goal."

"I got your note."

"Bit of relief there, I don't mind saying. I thought that fellow might drop it down a well. Just to spite me."

"Robert Twelves is a man of his word. He would never." I sniffed at the pot of stock. Delicious. "You don't need to be afraid of him."

"Afraid? He said that?"

"No. You did, just now."

"I didn't say afraid. Spiteful is what I implied."

"Well, he's not that, either. He gave me the letter. He thinks well of you."

"Then what is—he said that?"

"He did. You don't give yourself enough credit for the impression you make on people. They like you."

He fidgeted with his hands, nodding his head. "Wait until they taste my soup one day."

"So what have you heard?" I said.

"Ah, yes. Specimens. Excursions, all that." He lowered his voice, looking to make sure no one else was about. "Nothing good. I heard it first from a cousin of Maryanne Rogers, who lives out by the forest leading to Reading. She's not that old, the widow Rogers. Three children. And her husband died of lockjaw last summer. Horrible way to die. Her cousin Henry came through here last week, telling tales of something in those forested hills on the far side of the Rogers farm. Said talk is on about a *nameless horror*."

"Meaning what?"

"Not quite clear. Some claimed it a headless mastiff. Others were calling it the shade of a crippled man who clambered about on his twisted legs and powerful arms. Now, a fellow Henry knows who's helped the widow with her planting swears he saw the devil slipped loose from Hell. A hungry scratch of moonlight passing through bough and hillock, haunting the moonlit lanes and ponds nearby." As he spoke, he picked up a cube of turnip and spun it, then tossed it into the stock. "Thought at first it might all just be talk. No one's forgotten the Hazleton sisters from last year."

The ones who'd drowned—then attacked me. I nodded.

"Stories like that get woven into the town, don't they?" he continued. "Brought back out on those nights when the wind picks up, clacking branches like bones, rattling door and shutter. So I thought maybe it was just people and their tales. But I heard the story, in one form or another, from three people over four nights. Two of those people I trust, mostly. And then, just yesterday, I heard that the widow Rogers decided to leave her farmhouse. Taking herself and the children to her brother's. He's a pastor up in Newburyport."

"Did you hear why?"

"Because she's terrified. Started hearing singing, from just outside her windows at night." He shook his head. "I'd never sleep again, something like that."

"What kind of singing?"

"She wouldn't say—only that it was evil. She heard it. Her children heard it. When she asked them about it—did they recognize the song? What were the words?—they refused to say. Youngest ones burst into fits of weeping. Couple of neighbors came to watch over, searched the outside with lantern and musket, didn't find a thing. The singing came again later that night. So she's decided to leave."

I didn't like the sound of what he'd said, especially after thinking of what the demon in the infernal vox expander had promised: *I could sing you soft lullabies below your window.*

Lullabies, coming from the night beyond the windows.

"Now," Bertram continued, "one of the neighbors is Bushrod Taylor, who knows my granddad. He came over, just to bring the tale. Mentioned coming across a strange little stone wall buried in the underbrush nearby."

"A witch-well," I said.

"Sounds an awful lot like it."

"Which is why you said it was one of my 'friends' who might have discovered the place, in your note."

"Bit more clever than I look, if I do say so myself. So there you are. Seems like—well, you know what it seems like."

"I do." I nodded toward the vegetables. "Finish up with that. We should take a look."

"We—no—I— Well, I thought it was really—for you. I only get in the way."

"I could use the other pair of eyes. Come on."

"But I can't. I need to help Iris."

I grabbed him by his sleeve and tugged lightly. "You knew what would happen if you wrote that letter."

"It was a favor."

"You knew."

He looked at the chopped vegetables and sighed.

Within the hour, we followed the split rails of a fence where it marked the boundary of a wide tract of land that extended from the skirts of two wooded rises. Young corn and clover rose in well-tended plots out beyond the lane. Where the fence rails ended, the boundary was taken up by a fieldstone wall. I paused, listening. No low of cows, no chop of the axe, no creak of rope pulling up a bucket from the well. No smoke rose from the chimney of the roughhewn farmhouse across the way.

What had driven the widow Rogers to flee with her family?

I could sing you soft lullabies below your window.

It occurred to me that it might be a message, designed for me. Or a taunt.

Or a trap.

Bertram peered past my shoulder. "What if we run into one of those—things?"

"I have what I need." Wards, spells, witchcraft. In my satchel, the materials needed for up to four glamours, all at the ready. A spare planar clock, ready to arm, and a few other sundries that might come in handy. So as I gazed out at the silent farmhouse where it stood in the shadows of the hills behind it, I inventoried my preparations. Looking back the way we'd come, I saw the break in the trees where we'd left the horses, hitched in a copse of birch trees.

"Let's go this way." I set a path to the farmhouse along the western side of the fields, the hills to my left. Pine and hemlock rose along the crest of the land, outcrops and boulders of granite showing between the trunks, half-buried in the rust-colored forest carpet. Coming closer to the house, we passed by a long line of dried cordwood.

The grounds around the house were well-maintained, neat rows of herbs poked from the soil, dandelions pulled from around the flagstones that led to the front door, the door to the privy closed and true. A clothesline sagged with a pair of small homespun dresses, an apron, and a blanket. The bucket for the well hung on its hook, the rope coiled next to it. It looked normal, and yet something stirred the skin on the back of my neck. Three gables topped the house, and a fair number of windows looked out. While so many windows might have made it a cheery place, the dim interior looked forlorn, mocking the bright afternoon that lit the fields and trees.

"Bushrod said the well was out past the corner of the house, in the thickets there," Bertram said.

"Let's look in the house first."

"*In* the house?" He looked about. "We can't just walk inside. Someone might see us."

"There's no one around. We won't steal anything. There's something I don't like about this." I swung down the satchel from my shoulder and knelt as I opened it, pulling out a small tin of glamoured iron filings. With a tablespoon's worth in the palm of my hand, I stood.

"What are you doing?" Bertram whispered.

"Quiet," I said. With my other hand opened flat above the filings, I spoke a spell in German called *Grässlich Präsenz*—the 'Ghastly Presence.' As I finished the Teutonic mouthful, I tossed the filings into the air. Instead of arching downward, the pieces hung in the air for several moments, glowing like a handful of stars. The shining flecks of metal shifted and formed a mask-like impression with a vile countenance: sunken eyes, twisting outgrowths of horns to either side, and a mouth that stretched for a good foot, a forked tongue lolling out between fangs. Bertram raised his hands and stumbled backward, tripping over his feet and landing on his backside with a yelp. The spell faded, the filings dimming and dropping to the flagstones with a soft hiss, leaving the air with the scent of gunpowder.

I turned and helped Bertram to his feet. "You can open your eyes," I said.

"What if I don't want to?"

"It was a spell."

"It was bloody Lucifer."

"Not quite." When he was stable, I wiped the flecks of iron from my palm. "But it confirmed there's a demon about."

"*That* was the demon?"

"No. The spell doesn't reveal the demon's appearance specifically. It's only an iconic representation, drawn from church art. A specialty of the magician who composed the spell, Arik Weber."

"Good to know. It was horrifying."

"Actual demons are worse."

"Noted." His gaze darted about nervously. "Chopping turnips does have its charms, I'm starting to realize."

"Well, at least we know the widow Rogers wasn't delusional." I straightened out my satchel. "Let's look inside."

As we drew nearer, a bang came from somewhere inside the house, a door or a cabinet being slammed shut. "I thought you said they left?" I said.

"They did."

"Then the demon knows we're here."

"Shouldn't we just leave, then?"

"I'll make sure nothing happens to us." Or, I'd try, at least. "You can wait by the horses, if you wish."

"What about needing another set of eyes?"

"I knew you'd stay." I readied a ward and followed the flagstones to the whitewashed door. Another bang sounded from inside. As I neared the door, the house erupted with the sound of wood on wood, knocking, bashing, tapping—as though a crew of coopers were knocking the rings around their staves, mallets hammering against push blocks. Before trying the door, I stepped up to a window to the right of the door. I saw little on the inside beyond a stretch of floor, pieces of dark-stained furniture, doorways leading to other rooms. The panes of glass rattled with the noise from inside. Wary but not overly frightened—demons loved to raise a racket—I tried the door and found it locked. With my hand over the keyhole, I spoke: "*Aperire cincinno.*" The tumblers within clicked, and the lock sprang open. With a gentle push, the door opened.

Leaning in, I saw what the fury was about—all the furniture

in the house shook, trembling as though the floors themselves were the back of a wagon speeding along a corduroy road. Various other items—lanterns, books, utensils, a clock—had fallen from their perches and vibrated where they'd landed. A pair of chairs covered in frayed fabric danced up and down.

Bertram went pale.

"Wait here," I said. I stepped inside. Ashes fanned out from the hearth along one wall, vibrating on the floor. Overhead, beams groaned. The plaster on the ceiling had fallen off in several places, and was cracked throughout the rest, lending a fine coating of white dust to various corners.

I raised my witchcraft, concentrating on projecting as much strength as possible as I walked carefully through the front room. In the kitchen, pots, pans, and tin plates danced on the floor. Shards of broken crockery vibrated in the corners and the cloying smell of spoiled milk filled the air. Beneath the noise and shaking, I detected another force, pressing in. I opened my satchel and rummaged through the interior until I found a planar compass I'd brought. I set it in my palm and watched as the demon-imbued needle spun wildly, first clockwise, then counterclockwise, then back and forth.

Bertram darted in after me. "It's somehow worse being out there alone," he said. He stood so close to me that our shoulders touched.

"Stay alert."

"You don't say."

I led the way throughout the rest of the first floor of the house, stepping over tumbled objects, avoiding anything that might shake loose from the ceiling. As we stepped through to a larger room where a door opened to the outside, the compass tried to bounce free from my grip. The line along my jaw buzzed and a moment later, a crushing headache tightened around my forehead. My stomach flipped. Just at that moment, glass shattered, first from the second floor, and then in the rooms we'd passed through, the panes in the windows imploding. I shielded us with my witchcraft, stopping the flying glass in midflight a yard from us. It dropped like frozen rain.

Bertram crouched, hands over his head, peering out from between his arms. "Maybe we should leave?"

"Not just yet," I said.

The malign presence of the demon grew into a disquieting sense of being watched. I turned. A glimpse of something moved past the stairs, visible through a wide doorway. A putrid stench rolled over us. Long noted among sorcerers, many entities from the hidden planes brought with them—along with better known fluctuations of temperature, some dangerously extreme—foul aromas, both from their origins and as this world reacted to their presence. To call them foul was an injustice. Swaine claimed to be haunted by a few of the more noteworthy fetors he'd encountered over the years, stenches so powerful that they conjured not just disgust, but despair.

Not taking my eyes from the opening that led to the stairs, I knelt, slinging off my satchel and reaching into it. I'd brought a number of items: a small wooden box that held glass flasks of ingredients, including saltpeter, ground bone, and powdered indigo; a pair of red candles; a bag of glamoured stones; a planar clock. The last was what I needed. I pulled it out.

"Here," I called out. "I have something. Just for you." I barely needed to look at the device to arm it, having done so scores of times. Once it was ready, I stood up and stepped back. "There. Isn't it lovely?"

The malignant attention shifted as the small demon bound within the planar clock was revealed—for while dangerous, demons were often startlingly dumb, their predatory instincts capable of being manipulated against them rather easily. As a cat couldn't resist the moving twine, so a demon couldn't help but lunge for a lesser entity. Still, I kept my wits—for there were demons, and there were *demons*.

Before I gave much more thought to which sort I was confronting, a shadowy blur leaped from the doorway, tainting the surrounding air, filling the room with a chill and a stench. The mechanisms in the clock sprang, and it slid half a foot across the floor as the demon was captured.

"Not the cautious type," I said.

Bertram looked around. "Everything's still shaking."

The rumbling of the house and its contents hadn't abated. I sensed more powerful energies, felt a thrumming in my chest. We passed through the kitchen.

"There's something else at work," I said. Continuing the search, the energies grew more powerful, the force thrumming in my chest. I pushed open the back door and stepped outside. To the right a barn loomed. A low stone wall wound along past it, marking the edge of a wooded hillside thick with hemlock and birch. The air whipped around in freezing currents. I searched for signs of witchcraft, but didn't see any. "Where's the witch-well?"

Bertram stayed less than half a foot behind me. "Corner. Past the stone wall. In the shrubs just up the hillside."

Past the far corner of the barn, we stepped over the stone wall and into the trees. Soon, we came to a line of rosebushes coiled along a furrow where hunks of granite peeked from the ground. I searched the thorny vines. The strange energy I'd felt inside the house was even stronger—yet curiously I saw no witchcraft.

"There," Bertram said, pointing to an outcropping where a number of stones stood next to a larger rock.

Pushing aside the surrounding thicket, I found the remains of a covered well, low to the ground, rotted boards still slung across the opening. The air whirled, frigid currents coming up from between the boards. Reaching forward, I placed my hands on the wood. The moment I touched it, strange lines appeared in the air before me, a crosshatched pattern that reminded me of markings scored into a pane of glass. Within these markings pulsed odd streaks of light, dim and red, the final colors of sunset. The mass of it rotated, spilling out across the ground, rising high into the air. Black strands of energy, tattered filaments, littered the boards.

I leaned back, hands on my hips, trying to figure out what I was seeing.

"Katie," Bertram said, his tone holding a question. "Your hands."

Looking down at my hands, I saw my skin had flushed a deep red, deeper than a blush, like a terrible burn from the sun. More alarming, pale markings covered my palms, my fingers, the backs of my hands, white against the red, as though the skin was untouched in those spots.

Coffins, ravens, and keys decorated my hands and halfway up to my elbows. I widened my eye in surprise. A faint tingle ran along my skin. Before I could do anything further, the boards over the well opening collapsed, dumping down into the depths with an echoing series of knocks and bangs. All across the inside of the well, drawings decorated the stones—the same images as my hands, save larger, white against the gray stone. As I leaned over it, I heard a sound.

"What's going on?" Bertram said.

"Quiet."

The tinkling notes of a music box drifted up from the opening, a tune I'd heard more than once. "The Three Butchers."

From the depths of what was unmistakably the demonmere.

I rested my hands on the edge of the well. The red drained away from them, the coffins, keys, and ravens fading back to my normal skin tone. I held them up.

"You see it fading, don't you?" I said.

"I do."

I didn't understand the strange magic that had affected my skin. A faint itching remained. That Bertram had witnessed it was both reassuring—and even more disturbing, for it wasn't typical witchcraft or magic, which only I might have seen.

"Do you hear anything?" I said.

"Not over my own heart pounding in my ears."

"Near the well."

"I don't want to touch it."

"Just listen."

He stepped to the well and inclined his head, frowning. He shook his head. "Nothing."

"Did the widow Rogers ever say if she knew the lullaby? What song it was?"

"Oh God, don't tell me you hear it coming from down there? Singing? A voice? That's terrifying."

"It's not a voice. Did she?"

"No. Not that I know of. What is it?"

I didn't want him any more frightened than he was. "It's not important." Crouching again before the well, I searched the ground. The odd filaments lay about like scraps. As I put a hand over them, the faintest of glows shone along their lengths, thin red, like a wick just extinguished. Lit up, they shifted, trying to clump together with other lengths.

And then I knew: they were all that remained of the witchcraft that had sealed the well. I held both my hands out and let my witchcraft flow down through my palms. Thinking of the earlier seals I'd repaired, I extended my energy into the frayed scraps. Hints of color, faint and flickering, ran through them— but instead of the strong eruption of witchcraft I'd experienced before, they merely stirred, dim. Were they beyond repair? Nothing I tried made any more difference. Somehow, the witchcraft had been breached, torn, unraveled. Worse, what had done it was linked to the demonmere. Like the gearing inside one of Robert Twelves's mechanisms, the connections in my mind meshed, driving yet further connections.

The witches' seals broken.

A demon on the prowl.

The demonmere opening.

Images of what Swaine and I had already found appearing on my hands, on the walls of the well.

It wasn't random. It was connected to the work we'd done, what we'd found, what had happened.

A cold hand clenched at my guts, and I knew: we were making it worse.

The gears turned faster, more smoothly, bringing in even more elements. The timing—it all fit. From the very first, our work had disrupted the witches' seals, introducing instability into the delicate balance that held back the unseen planes. The initial planar clock had preceded the intrusion of the planar umbra, nearly killing Swaine. All the planar clocks that followed—and suddenly there were tales of demons passing people's lips, talk of the infernal haunting field and fen again. My own casting of the *Grave Raven* spell by the pond, only days before the demons reanimated the corpses of the drowned girls. Swaine's failed attempt at clearing Salem of demons led to a temporal displacement— and ushered in the first appearance of the demonmere. Each step of the way, every breakthrough in our quest to tame Salem had tampered with the protections the witches had put in place.

And now more demons were breaking through into the colony again. I thought of all those fiends Swaine's latest work had eliminated. We'd assumed they'd been driven from Salem, out into—where? Swaine hadn't theorized anything, had he? Back into the unseen planes? But what if they hadn't been *driven* out? What if they'd seen their chance to *break* out? What if they were even at that moment clawing their way out of witch-wells and openings of the demonmere all across the colony? It was, after all, called the demonmere for a reason.

"Oh, no." I sat back on my heels, putting my hand over my face.

"Katie?"

Our town has grown rotten with hidden passageways spawning fiends. We dig, we plumb, we reinforce such entrances as we seal off. I thought of the desperation of Ginny Lane and the other witches. The work they'd risked everything for. The terror that had swept through Salem itself, cutting down a lonesome, isolated settlement of witches, shunned and abandoned.

The shadows burrow through this place. Infect it. Demons, of the darkest sort.

John Whitelocke's ring, following me. Clara, lost. My master's work—and my reckless uses of magic and witchcraft, no doubt—had started to unravel all they'd done to keep it out. Unwittingly on our part, it was true. Innocently, perhaps.

Fatally?

Devastatingly?

All the gears turned, one with another with another, and the mechanism of understanding ran smoothly in my head.

We had to stop it. Or *try* to stop it.

"What's this?" Bertram said.

I lowered my hand and opened my eye. "What's what?"

"It's turning." He stood a dozen paces away from the witch-well, hands on his knees, looking at something.

"Don't touch it."

"But what is it?"

I stood, unnerved. "Whatever it is, don't touch it." With a look back at the well, I went over to Bertram. On a level piece of ground just past the edge of the thorns stood a wood and brass tripod two feet in height, from which hung a chain with a plum bob made of metal, a silver alloy of some kind. The plum bob spun evenly, counterclockwise. Nothing marred the grass near it. I didn't see anything else—no signs of a glamour, no signs of magic, which was strange, for I'd normally be able to see such magic, and there was clearly magic at play.

My suspicion sharpened in an instant: Doctor Rush.

I'd read his book, *On Principles of Planar Magick*. The tripod was some form of his *invariable planar gauge*, a device designed to measure the unique frequencies within planar energies to help identify from where they originated, and of what strength they were. I watched transfixed as the chain and plum bob spun, round and round, a low whirring sound accompanying its motion.

Rush was aware of the planar breach. The cold grip on my insides tightened and turned. What else was he aware of?

As my mind whirred through the possibilities, a dread grew in me that Rush might be able to detect I'd been there—track the residue of witchcraft I'd attempted, follow it back to Salem. Luckily, I'd brought enough ingredients that I could cast a spell to mask our departure. Useful for demons, it ought to work against any other magic, as well. I reached for my satchel, only to realize I'd left it back in the Rogers house.

Before us, the orbit of the plum bob increased, filling the air with a low humming sound that rose in pitch as the speed of the rotations increased.

I turned to Bertram. "Run back to the house and fetch my satchel."

"What—on my own?"

"It's safe. I'll be right here. Just hurry, please."

He opened and closed his mouth, growing, if possible, even more pale.

"Quickly," I said, adding a touch of Swaine's impatient tone. That worked. Bertram hurried back across the property to the back door of the house. I chewed the inside of my cheek, trying to think through the spell I had in mind.

The sound of the plum bob grew louder. A blur replaced the chain and plum bob. I knew that an invariable planar gauge would react with any foreign planar currents by reaching a specific velocity, the speed of which could narrow in on a particular planar frequency. But as I watched, the tripod vibrated along the lengths of each leg. Before I could react, the plum bob spun out of control, crashing into the legs of the tripod and destroying it, sending out jagged shards of brass and iron. The bob and chain flew off like a cannon shot.

I flinched, only to have a torn curl of brass from the device scratch my cheek, just below my good eye. It burned like a wasp sting, and when I put my hand up to it, warm blood dribbled out from the rough cut. Dabbing the wound with the sleeve of my dress, I made sure I hadn't been hit anywhere else.

Just then, Bertram cried out, a wordless shout of fright.

I cursed and hurried back to the house—what had I been thinking, sending him back there on his own? How careless and stupid could I be? Berating myself so, I didn't even notice the flashes of scarlet moving through the windows of the Rogers house until a moment before the back door opened and a regular stepped out, a musket in his hands.

I darted behind the corner of the barn, stunned. Where had he come from? From somewhere beyond the house came the nicker of horses. The soldier strode into the yard. More soldiers moved throughout the inside of the house. Three more regulars came out of the house, two of them holding Bertram by his arms, an officer leading them. Bertram looked terrified. Behind them came a shorter, stout figure.

Doctor Rush.

Rush looked toward the witch-well. He held a device in one hand. I couldn't tell what it was, but suspected it to be akin to my own planar compass. I flinched as if I'd had a bucket of ice water poured over my head.

My planar compass. My satchel. The planar clock.

All of it sat on the floor inside the house where they'd already passed through. There was no way they hadn't seen it.

The officer turned to Bertram. "Where are the others?"

Bertram shook his head rapidly back and forth. "There are no others. I came on my own. Just out of curiosity. Tales—tales. I heard tales—had to see for myself."

"We found your things in there. Stop lying."

"I'm not lying! They're not my things—they were there when I slipped in. I shouldn't have, I absolutely shouldn't have. I know that now. Please, I didn't mean to cause a fuss. Or cause anything. Just—the tales. I was so curious."

I slipped back from the corner. He was buying me time.

Rush spoke. "I want every inch of this property and house searched, Captain. Every bit of material, anything unusual, find it."

"And the items inside, sir?"

"Pack them up. Don't, however, touch my equipment out back —I need to investigate that myself."

"Yes, sir."

Not waiting to hear any more, I slid off, shoving my way through the underbrush at the foot of the hillside. Keeping the barn between my escape and the soldiers, I ignored the scrapes and scratches from wayward branches and fled as fast as I could. By the time any of them reached the stone wall, I crested the hillside, a flash of movement hidden by trunk and bough, sped along by my own dread.

20

———

GRAVE ROT

Sunset drew out the shadows in Boston as I hurried along street and lane. The briny scent of the harbor mixed with cooking smoke, manure, and the day's catch. I kept my face hidden beneath the hood of my cloak, alert to groups of regulars, giving them a wide berth as I moved among the carriages and horse travelers. By the time I reached the governor's manse, only the highest peaks of the roof remained in sunlight. Across the sky, a quarter moon rose between two bright evening stars.

Regulars guarded the entrances. More since Francis's failed kidnapping of Doctor Rush, no doubt. With Bertram in their hands, I had to assume that simply walking up and asking to be let inside wasn't wise—for if he'd panicked and told them everything, the description of a one-eyed lass wouldn't have been a difficult one to spread throughout the city's garrison. I prayed he'd held his tongue.

Still, there were other ways to reach Mary Whitelocke unseen.

I waited for the twilight to deepen, lurking by a pair of wide chestnut trees down the street. By the time I slipped across the

250

street and made my way closer to the governor's manse, the sunset dwindled to an orange smudge silhouetting rooftops and chimneys, high clouds overhead draining of color. Windows of the manse shone, one after another, as candles and lanterns were lit within. Regulars stood in pairs around the edge of the property, at the corners of fences and hedges. I approached from the side where an arched entrance of iron fencing opened into a path to the servant entrance. The two regulars stood four paces away from the opening, muskets slung over their shoulders.

I concentrated my mind for a moment, then waved a hand in front of my face, drawing in the shadowed night, using the darkness to cloak myself. The spells of disguise I was familiar with gave me a sense—a framework—for how it would feel, and within a few seconds, I felt a chill wrapping me, as though I were being swaddled in sheets dipped in ice water. I slid along the angle of the hedge, silent.

Trying not to breathe, not to make a sound with my steps, I turned sideways and slid behind the guards and through the entrance. *The sorcerous mind has but one point of focus* as Swaine had told me so many times. One step after another: quick, silent, focused. A witch—like my foremothers before me—passing through the Boston night.

Through the iron gate, I lengthened my strides, not looking back, not breaking my concentration. Passing along the footpath, I let out a long exhale. I hurried along until I reached the entrance into the cellar. In the starlight, it seemed forgotten.

The door was unlocked, probably an oversight. I let myself into the cellar and closed the door behind me. Crossing through the dark room, I maintained the witchcraft shadows around me, passing over the spot where John Whitelocke had died. Tiptoeing up the stairs, I paused at the top, listening for voices in the corridor outside. A faint murmur reached me, likely from the kitchen to judge by the sounds. I inched the door open and peered out. The corridor was empty. I crept out and sidled along the wall until I could see into the foyer by the main doors. Another pair of uniformed guards stood watch near the bottom of the stairs, talking in quiet voices about a sergeant from another company who'd been forced to ride the wooden horse for some infraction or other. I paused.

Distraction.

Checking that no household staff approached, I summoned another surge of my witchcraft, envisioning the ballroom. When not used for such events, tables and chairs occupied the parquet floor—so I suspected that a quick gust of energy would make a noise worthy of investigation. I closed my eye for a moment, allowing the essence to stream down my arms like small rivers, flowing out my palms and fingertips to connect with the greater energies of the world around me. The connection was unmistakable, and after a moment, I heard a satisfying scrape of wood on wood, followed by a pair of crashing thuds.

I stepped into the shadows of the library. Both guards, as I'd suspected, stopped their conversation and came down the hall until they stood across from me, at the ballroom doors. One went into the ballroom, and the other followed. As soon as they were both inside, I padded out of the library and hurried to the stairs, praying that no one else had chosen that moment to wander down that way. The first landing was clear as was the second. The doorway I wanted was at the far end of the hallway to the left. Gritting my teeth, I hurried down the hallway to the far door. Pausing for just a moment, I listened, and heard nothing from within, yet the keyhole shone with light. With a glance back toward the stairs again—no one—I pressed down the latch and stepped inside the sitting room to Mary Whitelocke's bedchamber.

A fire crackled in the hearth beyond the settee. Everything matched, as ever—the silk of the furniture, the embroidery on the curtains, the pattern on the wallpaper, down to the fresh flowers in their vases by the window and on the mantel. Deep green, a calming cream, and highlights of gold. That was this season. Before, it had been pale pinks with touches of ruby. Before that, royal blue and bone white, and so on, a steady river of money flowing to decorators and artisans.

As quietly as I could, I crossed the sitting room to the doorway to Mary's bedchamber. She sat at a dressing table, a mirror in front of her, a glass of wine by her side, staring down at a box of jewelry. I stood in the doorway and released the shadows gathered around me, feeling the warmth of the room wash in on me. "Mary."

With a cry, she jerked her arms, craning her neck, eyes wide.

I lifted my hands and approached her. "I'm sorry—I'm so sorry. I didn't know how to not startle you."

"My God you almost killed me." She looked me up and down. "What are you doing here? How did you get in?" She reached over and grabbed a fan, spreading it open and waving it at her face. The delicate aroma of rosewater reached me. "No, don't tell me. My heart will stop galloping in a moment." She glared at me, then forced a smile onto her face. "Of course you couldn't make your presence known. I suppose I shouldn't have been surprised at all." The frown reappeared, and she swatted me with the fan. "But if you *ever* sneak up on me like that again, my witchy little friend, I shall never think of giving you as much as a silken glove ever again. I *hate* being startled."

"I'm so sorry."

"So you claim--but is that not a hint of amusement around your eye?"

"There's not much amusing about the last twenty-four hours of my life, believe me. If I could have—" I paused. "Wait. Why aren't you surprised I couldn't make my presence known? Is it because of Doctor Rush?"

"Doctor Rush? What would he have to do with it?"

"They aren't looking for me?"

"Doctor Rush?"

"Who's looking for me?"

She closed the fan and put it back onto her dressing table. "Not you, per se—though I believe there was mention of August's one-eyed assistant. The price of traveling through the right social circles. Visibility."

"Someone's looking for my master?"

"Sir Lionel Sackville, Earl of Middlesex. King's minister. Fomenter of trouble. Bane of my father's slumber." She looked at herself in the mirror and adjusted her hair. "Ever since he arrived, he's been slithering betwixt all the various men of influence who don't care for my father. Pastors. Councilors to my father. Members of the General Court. Spreading rumors that His Majesty is displeased and is on the verge of appointing a new royal governor. Any guess who that might be?"

"Sackville."

"Of course."

"But that has nothing to do with my master."

"Until it does. Sackville regards August as his own personal *bête noir*. Fine. The man has plenty of enemies. Here, however, he's trying to use August as the fulcrum with which to pry my father from his position."

"I still don't see the connection."

"Because there *is* no connection. Or, at least, there wasn't until Sackville began whispering. Now the mere fact of August's residing in the colony is being spun as proof of the corrupting influence of magic. First, Doctor Rush—grown ever so feeble, more so in Sackville's telling—and now August. With rumors popping up in every alehouse and wayside tavern of haunts and unquiet graves, it's given more fodder to Sackville than he might ever have hoped for. He made an 'impromptu' speech at the Town House just last night condemning the dalliance between August, my father, and Satan himself that left a poor taste in the mouth of anyone who prefers rationality to fiery demagoguery. It doesn't bode well and has left my father several degrees past perturbed."

I paced as she spoke. "So if the wrong person sees me here, they'll assume it's all true."

"This is why we should have a hand in events," Mary said. "We understand with no preening speeches, grunting mobs, and the fuses that come with them. So I supposed I should be grateful you floated in here unseen."

"Doctor Rush has said nothing?"

"The good doctor has been riding about the colony in his carriage, in the company of half a dozen bodyguards, sampling meat pies at every inn, in spite of my father's wish that he remain as unseen as possible for the time being." She sipped her wine. "You'd have thought an attempted kidnapping might have given the old gentleman pause, but it seems to have only wound him up further. Father isn't pleased. By any of it."

"Where is he now?"

"Down in his study. Up in his rooms. I don't know."

"Not your father—Doctor Rush."

"I haven't the faintest."

"If he'd—apprehended someone? Where would he take them?"

"Who would he apprehend?"

"A friend of mine."

She turned. "What friend? Should I be jealous? Don't tell me it's another witch."

"No." I glanced at the door, lowering my voice. "No witch. A friend. Who was with me."

"A romantic friend? If you've been keeping such a delicious secret from me, I shall be very cross."

"No, he's not—no. Just a friend."

"Do I wish to know why he was apprehended?"

"He was helping me with something important."

"Important how? Important to August?"

"Important to me. To all of us. And—maybe to Doctor Rush."

"I trust it wasn't any Rattlesnake business."

"No, of course not. Just—nothing anyone should know about. Least of all Doctor Rush."

She puckered her lips. "You're dancing around the truth."

"I'm not dancing by much, Mary. His name is Bertram Nagle. He lives in Andover. Where would they have brought him?"

"Well, if he were just another criminal or traitor, they'd bring him to the city jail. Orange Street." She stood.

"If Doctor Rush didn't want to make it well known?"

"I don't know. To his house? Anywhere else in the city?"

As I worked through this knot of possibilities, something caught my eye in the corner of her room. A small chest of drawers seeped threads of fine shadow. The grain of the wood shimmered. "What do you have in there?" I said, pointing.

"There?" Mary looked to where I pointed. "Various knickknacks."

"The burial silver?"

"Oh, yes. I'd forgotten all about it."

"You kept it in your room?"

She looked at me when she heard my cutting tone. "Where was I supposed to keep it? And besides—you swore it couldn't be genuine."

"I assumed it wasn't." I approached the chest. I sensed a potent energy from three feet away. True *argentum inferi* required special containment. Among the risks were subtle planar disruptions and physical contamination known as *grave rot*. It also attracted demons. More concerning was that it'd been sitting—unprotected —not thirty yards away from one of the few confirmed encroachments of the demonmere. "Have you touched it?"

"I looked at it." She might have gone a shade paler—from porcelain to chalk.

"But did you touch it?"

"I—may have laid a fingertip on it. I remember it was cold."

Burial silver was also sensitive to contact from the living. "When?" I said.

"I don't know. Weeks ago? Longer?" She crossed her arms. "Why didn't you warn me?"

"I did."

"Well, you didn't warn me well enough."

"I've been a little busy." On top of everything else, Mary's ridiculous acquisition of one of the most powerful ingredients in the unseen arts had, appallingly, slipped my mind. Before I opened the drawer, I raised my witchcraft around me. When I pulled the knob on the drawer, half the front of it cracked off in my hand, taking a chunk of the drawer's face with it. The back-side of the wood had gone pale gray, brittle and hollowed out with pinhole channels. *Grave rot.* I leaned over and peered into the drawer. The interior was largely gone, the rot having spread throughout the drawer itself, everything in it, and the adjacent drawers. My skin tingled with planar energy—and I half expected to see a staircase leading into the demonmere. "Bring me a candle."

"Tell me my finger won't fall off," Mary whispered.

"Let's assume it won't."

"You assumed it was faux burial silver."

"Candle, please."

"I never should have let you talk me into all this magic nonsense." She brought me a candle.

"You extorted me."

"Is this the time to quibble?"

As I peered into the dresser with more light, I saw the box holding the burial silver. While there appeared to be a glamour on it, it didn't look like much: uneven and weak; not the work of a competent practitioner. Everything near it had turned gray, more than half of it crumbled already. Still, the damage looked to be relatively contained—and no signs of the demonmere, which was something to be thankful for.

Before I could decide the best way to get the box out of Mary's dresser, a quick double knock the door from the hallway sounded, followed by the opening of the door and footsteps crossing her sitting room.

"Don't give me any grief for barging in," Grayson Whitelocke said, hurrying into the bedchamber. "We have a problem." He looked even more frightened than Mary. When he saw me, he froze. "What in the hell is she doing here?"

"Excuse me," Mary said, her tone sharp. "One doesn't come stomping into my—"

"I bloody said we have a problem." He looked back and forth between the two of us. "And I don't need a flood of words about manners, privacy, or frankly anything else right now. Why are you here, Miss Finch?"

"Since when do you get to interrogate my guests?" Mary said.

Grayson didn't take his gaze from me. "Did you do this? Are you the one?"

"What are you talking about?" Mary said.

"Father," Grayson said. He looked at the candle in my hand, then the peculiar deformations of the dresser.

"What about him?" Mary said.

Grayson looked over to her. For a moment, his mouth moved with no sound. Then he said, "He's dead. Torn to pieces."

21

SHADOWS AND EMBER

Outside the rooms the governor occupied, a pair of regulars stood at attention.

"No one's come through?" Grayson said as we approached.

"No, sir," one guard said.

"What about him?" He nodded toward the door.

"Talking, sir. We haven't let him out."

"Good. Keep everyone away until I say so. Everyone. Do you understand?"

"Yes, sir."

Mary looked like she was on the verge of fainting. I steadied her, grasping her elbow. The guards stepped aside, and we entered the front room. A fire and a pair of lanterns gave the room a warm glow. Bloody footprints decorated the floor leading to the inner room.

"Oh, God—where is he?"

"I thought you said he was dead?" Mary said. Her eyes fixed on the blood.

"He is. I'm talking about Hull. Harrison Hull. Father's barber —he was there when it happened." Grayson crossed to the inner door. "All of twenty minutes ago." He tried to push the door open, but something blocked it. Grayson leaned into the opening. "Hull? What on earth are you doing back in there?" He pushed at the door again, and when it contacted the man whom I presumed to be the barber, he pushed harder. The man moved away from the door.

Mary gasped.

Blood soaked the barber. Behind him the walls and ceiling of the inner room hung with gore. The mirror, the inlaid bureau, the embroidered blankets on the bed glistened with scarlet. Hull turned around to face us, a long pair of iron pliers in his hand. A giggle floated out of his mouth. "It got him, it did. Got him. All of him. And then he exploded. Ha, ha." Shivers racked the man.

"He was working on father's molars," Grayson said. "Always plaguing him. Complained all afternoon as we inspected the garrison by the harbor. Sent for Hull when we got back. I ate dinner. A guard fetched me—which is when I saw all this."

I stepped forward, looking at the carnage in front of me, above, underfoot. All about hung the bloody remains of the governor of the colony of Massachusetts. If there was a single piece bigger than a chestnut, I couldn't see it. I put a hand to my nose.

Behind me, Mary staggered. "Jesus. Jesus Christ."

That prompted a bark of laughter from the trembling Hull. His pliers clanged on the floor, slipped from his shaking fingers.

I opened my senses and detected the signs of a demon. I tried to pinpoint it, but the wake was growing faint.

Grayson crossed the room. He threw open the curtains and the window, letting the sea-tinged air in. When he spoke, his voice shook. "Right. First things first. The governor has passed away after a sudden bout of yellow fever. His heart didn't survive the strain. Tragic, but natural. These things happen every day in Boston." He gripped the sill and leaned out, drawing a long lungful of night air. I saw his fingers go white on the wood. Mary held the cuff of her sleeve over her nose and closed her eyes.

"What did you see, Mr. Hull?" I said.

"What, what?" The man smiled and looked as though he'd been asked his favorite childhood story.

"What happened, sir?"

"Work on the last molar," Hull said. A trembling smile hung to his lips. "No good keeping it, cracked and brown and seeping heat. So time to pull. A little left, a little right. And it splintered— the governor never had strong teeth, no, no—so I braced my knee on his chest and gave it a twist. Squeeze and twist, ha, ha."

He stared at the chair near the foot of the bed, which had gotten the worst of the blood and pulp.

"And what happened?" I prompted.

Hull's gaze snapped to the hearth. "The fire crackled. Louder and louder. We both looked at it. And a face was in the fire. A face. Not a nice face."

"Face?"

"Shadows and ember. Eyes." Hull giggled, an unsettling light in his eyes. "No one I've ever seen. Eyes it had. Five, eight. On stalks. And a mouth hung with tentacles. So many, many teeth." He ran a hand over his brow, smearing the blood there. "I screamed."

"And the governor?" I said.

"Was already screaming. Not enough rum, I'm sorry to say. Tricks of the trade not always working, you see."

"Go on."

"It came out. Slid out. Slithered. Sliding. Dragging ash and fire and smoke. And it kept coming, and coming, and coming. Legs working like a thousand little waves. Faster and faster, onto the walls. Through the candles, around our chair. It leaped." Hull shuddered. "It touched my shoulder. Left it filthy. Worse than filthy. Worse than the worms."

He'd lost his mind. I exchanged a glance with Grayson. Mary rested a shaking hand on my shoulder, holding herself up.

"What did it do to the governor?" I said.

Hull looked up and smiled. Tears welled in his eyes as he giggled again. His hands danced, tiny marionettes. "First it hugged him. So hard that his eyes burst from his face. When he screamed, it burrowed into his mouth. All the way. He choked. Hands to throat. Invisible noose, but on the inside, really." He coughed with a thick upchucking sound and spit a glob of bile, not bothering to wiping his chin. "And then it exploded him. Ha, ha."

Keeping my cloak up, I stepped around the room, alert for entities. At the hearth, I registered a brush of planar disruption.

"Is it still here?" Grayson whispered.

"I would have to—" I paused long enough to catch his eye. "Look more closely."

He understood and nodded. "Mr. Hull, let's get you cleaned up. Some rest is what you need."

Hull looked back and forth between us. "I—I—I don't think I can, well—look at a tooth again. No, no, no. Or eyes. Or—well, I might need a blanket. Oh, dear." Tears ran down his cheeks, erasing lines through the blood.

"Fear not," Grayson said. "We'll see you're well taken care of. Don't you worry. Somewhere quiet. Removed."

"What do you do with so many teeth?" His eyes pleaded with Grayson. "Can you tell me?"

"Best if you don't worry about it, Hull."

"I'm glad my dear mother never lived to see me so. Scared of a tooth. Teeth. An armful of teeth. More." He held his arms out as though they were mandibles. "I wish I could see her again. My mummy." At that, he dissolved into blubbers. I felt a stab of pity. Most people weren't prepared for exposure to a demon.

Grayson motioned to the door. "Come."

Hull nodded after a moment and reached for his pliers.

Catching himself at the last second, he lifted his hand away as though the tool burned him.

"I don't imagine you'll be needing those," Grayson said.

"Ha, ha. No. Mummy."

Grayson showed him through the door. I heard the outside door open, and Grayson giving orders to the guards.

"I didn't do this, did I?" Mary whispered, her eyes still closed. "With the burial silver? Keeping it down the hall?"

It was possible—but with the demonmere having already appeared once before that, who could say? "I don't think so."

"You're not certain?"

"Let me concentrate." I searched the room, glad for the harbor-scented air blowing in through the open window. With none of the materials with me for a proper glamour of demonic detection, I performed the next best thing: *Dæmonium Habes Indicare*, the traditional spell of shadow reveal. I paced the length of the room, my hands forming the proper gestures, whispering the incantation. Flecks of illumination leaped from my fingertips and ran along the nearby surfaces: walls, curtains, books, moulding, writing desk, fire pokers. No demonic signs appeared, though I noted a strange hint of magic around the hearth itself, where I'd sensed the planar disturbance.

I knelt, avoiding the blood, and found strange markings in the stones, thick scratches. Leaning in, I spotted a rolled-up piece of paper wedged between two stones of the hearth. I plucked it out. It held a scorched residue of magic, which showed itself as a shadowy haze that darkened the paper, shifting as the dying embers of a fire might. Unrolling it, it recalled the *Occultatum Ostium*—it had the same color, same texture. A repeating pattern in blackest ink decorated the border: raven, coffin, key. In the center was a detailed drawing. A woman's severed head stood upon a floor. Behind the head were limbs, separated at the major joints—hands, forearms, upper arms, thighs, calves, feet, sliced through, their interiors etched in detail—bone, meat, blood. The torso appeared to be standing. Before the head was the heart, gouged from the chest.

The face bore an expression of shock and alarm that no doubt echoed the look on my face as I stared down at the illustration and realized that it was of Clara. Accurate and close to life, there was no mistaking her. I scanned the drawing. A floor, body parts, and nothing else.

Before I could do anything, the paper incinerated in my hands, flames tracing the ink of the illustration first, then whooshing out across the entire sheet. I let it go, watching as the paper crinkled into ashes on the stones of the hearth.

The demon knew I'd find it—the message was mine alone: the demon had killed the governor and wanted me to know it. Clara was next unless it was already too late. My stomach clenched.

"Well?" Grayson closed the door behind him.

"The demon is gone."

He waved a hand. "From the room? The manse?"

"The room for certain. I'd have to check the rest to be sure."

He looked around for a moment, then lurched to the open window and vomited, hanging on to the window frame as he lost his stomach. After a minute of repeated heaving, he straightened up, flinging a thick strand of bile from his chin, spitting. His voice was unsteady when he spoke. "Lovely."

"This is ghastly," Mary said. "All of it."

"Well said," he said. "Glad you're paying attention."

"No one needs your attitude. This is terrible."

"As I realized the first moment I set foot in this nightmare."

While the Whitelocke siblings argued with each other over who had the better grasp of how dire the situation had become, I continued to investigate the area around the hearth. Using the iron fire poker, I nudged the spill of ashes. They flickered with vile magic. I didn't touch any of them.

"We should get out of here," I offered.

Grayson stared at me. "You know more than you're letting on, Miss Finch."

"There's nothing more to know," Mary said.

"She just happened to be here when it happened. In *your* room. With *you*."

Mary lifted her chin. "What are you implying? That I had Father murdered by a demon with Miss Finch's assistance?"

"You do know what she is, don't you?"

"I only came here to find where they took my friend," I said. "You suspect I did this?"

"You're the only witch I know of."

I stepped right in front of him. "And my grand strategy was what? Wait for months, knowing both you and your sister, then make my strike? And not only that, but come into the city on my own, stroll into all this, defenseless, soldiers all about? You're not thinking clearly. I'm trying to help you. As I did before if you recall."

"There were no shortage of people trying to help my father. Look what that got him."

"Listen. I've hidden nothing from you. I've helped you. When you've asked, and when you haven't. I did everything in my power to prevent this"—I swept my arm across the room—"from happening. I've no interest in politics, or—well, or murder."

He crossed his arms, his gaze drifting out over the brutal scene.

I reached over and grabbed his arm. "We ought to leave here, though. And I would leave the manse. Now. Tonight."

I led them from the room, and closed the door, glad to leave the horrific gore on the other side.

Grayson paced the room with one hand to his brow. "Good God. I'll be dead by morning. No later than sundown if I'm spared."

"What are you talking about?" Mary snapped. "You have your ring on. I have mine."

"And Father had his—it's probably nestled in his skin and bone, should you wish to lecture me about the protective quality of magical rings."

Mary turned. "Will they work?"

"I'm not sure," I said. "But leaving would be for the best. I wouldn't stay here tonight."

"Or bloody ever again," Grayson said. He stopped by a mantelpiece and steadied himself. "Let's not forget that horrors from fireplaces aren't the only monsters who want me dead. So if I leave the manse, how long before some other thugs who fancy themselves Rattlesnakes introduce the center of my head or my breast to a lead ball?"

"We have guards all about," Mary said. "We'll take them with us."

He hung his head. "The Governor's Own. Emphasis on *Governor*. And we're no longer the governor's children."

"Meaning?" Mary said.

"Do try to keep up, Mary," he said. "Father is gone—"

"Don't talk to me like I'm a child."

"Sackville has poisoned the council. As soon as word gets out, he'll step in himself. He's been waiting to pull out a royal appointment since he got here—he lacked the proper cause. Now he has it. He'll sweep in here tomorrow morning. And if he learns how Father died, we'll end up clapped in irons. Whitelockes consorting with the devil—all that nonsense."

"You say that as if we have no influence. You're wrong," Mary said.

"Am I? The cream of Boston hate us in the way that only the competent can hate a privileged dilettante—ruthless and dismissive in equal measure. And let's allow that whilst Father understood how to align the gears of power in Boston, without his hand, the entire intricate machinery of influence he curated might well all blow apart. Are the Adamses, the Cabots, the Endicotts, the Boylstons, the Quincys and all the rest going to bloody pledge their loyalty to us? Risk Sackville's displeasure to spare the two of us from whatever ignominious fate he has in mind? No, the scramble starts as soon as news gets out, and no one will hesitate to crush us." He swept his arm along the mantel, giving flight to a pair of candlesticks in silver holders. He turned and smiled. "Mauled by a demon, struck up on a noose, shot in the back—the possibilities are endless."

Mary shook her head. "They don't have to be. We'll find a way."

"You'll not buy or charm your way out of this one, I'm afraid."

"No—but we can *think* our way out of it. Nothing will happen instantly. We have the advantage of time. And knowledge."

"Mary's right," I said. "And we need to use every advantage we have—because the situation is worse than you know."

"My father was just shredded in his own bedchamber," Grayson said. "We'll end up in jail for dallying with Satan—for what better way to eliminate any remaining influence our family possesses. I fail to see how much worse the situation can be."

It was my turn to pace. "Oh, it's worse." I thought of the message I'd just seen burn up in my hands. I thought of what I'd found at the widow Rogers's house. The witches' seals sundering. The demonmere pressing in. Demons breaking free, all over the colony.

"How could it be worse?" Mary said.

So I told them. From the beginning.

When I finished, Grayson stared at me. "Wonderful. And, happily, now Lord Sackville's problem."

"He'll just make it worse."

"His problem. Not ours."

"It's everyone's problem."

"What about your master—what does he think?"

"She hasn't told him," Mary said, watching me. "Have you?"

"No. I haven't." Having said all I'd done out loud for the first time, I realized how I'd erred in not telling Swaine earlier. "But I will. There's no other choice."

"We must be careful," Mary said. "If Grayson's right and Sackville assumes the governorship, he will push us from the circles of influence. He's almost certain to arrest August. He loathes him."

"And you, Miss Finch," Grayson said. "Apprentice to renowned sorcerer, etcetera."

"Then he can't know what happened here." I resumed my pacing. "Not a hint. That will at least buy us some time. We can strengthen the seals and track down the demons as out of sight as is possible. How many people could you convince to give us cover? Quietly help?"

Grayson said nothing for several long moments. "People's utter lack of faith that I'm capable of anything more than swinging my privates around at the socialites and tarts of Boston while downing every dram and mug in sight may allow me a window of opportunity with which to confound all expectations. Deal with the body. Find help—though we won't be able to count on much, I'm afraid."

"More than you might think," Mary said. "I haven't offended everyone in sight."

"No one can know the real reasons," I said.

"Of course not. We'll be the only ones who know all that— but we can keep Sackville otherwise occupied. Get passage where we need. Learn if any talk is spreading. Help you find and repair these seals."

"That's all assuming none of us is torn asunder by a hideous demon," Grayson said. He put his hands to his face. "Maybe I should just string myself up now and save myself trouble."

"We'll have the most loyal guards clean up Father's— remains," Mary said. "Eunice Pemberton's uncle is an undertaker. We need a coffin—he'll get us one. I have favors I can call in. Left and right."

"None of this will work." Grayson kept his hands over his face.

"It will all work," Mary said. "Dear cousin James Emerson will vacate our old house on Princess Street—bit of a parasite, that one—so we can get out of here. As a sign of respect to the office, as a sign of mourning to Father, not to mention fear of the yellow fever that took him."

Grayson lowered his hands. "And if that—that *thing* follows us?" He looked at the door to the room where his father was slaughtered. The terror in his eyes was clear enough.

"I can protect you. There are glamours I can put in place." I rubbed my forehead with my fingertips. Paced more. And then I knew. I stopped pacing. "No one was looking for me."

"Sorry?" Mary said.

"Earlier. The Governor's Own. They weren't looking for me." I turned to Grayson. "Were they?"

"Ah—no. No one was looking for you—though I can see why you might think so, given what you said. But no, there was no talk at all of searching out you. Or your master."

"He knows."

"Who knows?"

I saw it all in a flash. "Doctor Rush. He knows—he's known all along."

"What are you getting at?" Mary said.

"The letters in the trunk—he put them there for me to find. The map—he left it out for me to find. He knew I'd try. The markings in the crypt. The device at the seal. He's been quietly guiding me. Leaving clues for me. Hints. Directions."

"He apprehended your friend," Grayson said.

"Or he tried to save him," I said. "He's known the threat. He's tracked it, seen it worsen." I spun to the Whitelocke siblings. "Where is he now?"

"I've no idea," Grayson said. "But if he knows what's good for him, he'll disappear as soon as he learns my father is dead. Sackville won't tolerate him. He'll have him shipped off to

London to stand trial for whatever infernal charges he can think of."

"We have to find him."

Grayson nodded. "I'll send guards to locate him. Now. Before the news gets out."

"What about you?" Mary said, watching me.

"I'll be fine—but I should leave. I have to tell my master. And I'm taking that burial silver with me."

"Please. Get it out of here."

"What makes you think I won't piss my breeches the moment you're out of sight?" Grayson said.

"Because we're going make it through this," I said. "We're *all* going to make it through this."

"Yes, and that's more than half the problem." Grayson nodded. "Fine. There's a back way. I'm sure you can hide yourself from being seen."

"I can."

At the door, Mary reached out and squeezed my hand. "Thank you."

I turned and embraced her. "I'm so sorry." I felt her chest hitch.

"As much as I'd like one of those, too," Grayson said, "best if you hurry."

I pulled back from Mary. Tears streaked her face.

"We'll get through this," I whispered.

Grayson led me out past the guards, taking me first to Mary's room where I took the silver, and then to a servants' door. He paused. "Finch."

I raised my eyebrow.

"Thank you," he said.

I nodded and then disappeared down the dark and narrow staircase.

22

A GOLDEN VINE

The moon rode high overhead by the time I reached Salem. After stabling the horse, I hurried along the footpath to the manse, stars glimmering through the lace of branch and bough. I found Mr. Twelves in the kitchen, making notes on one of his architectural drawings while polishing off a plate of biscuits I'd made two days earlier.

"How is he?" I said, taking off my cloak. I put the box with the burial silver on the table.

"Hasn't come out of his room once."

"Did you check on him?"

He put down his quill. "Every two hours. Sleeping. Not dead—he's flipped around a few times. Drank half the water you left for him. Heard him moving around about an hour ago. But it's been quiet since."

"Nothing else strange?"

"Nothing but my imagination." He leaned back and stretched. "Revenants didn't move, kept silent. Got a little uneasy around three o'clock—something didn't feel right, but I couldn't find anything. Glad I had my pendant. You?"

I filled the teakettle with water from the well bucket and set it to heat in the hearth over the fire Twelves had tended. "Oh, you know. Errands." I wouldn't implicate him any further than necessary.

"That's right. Katie Finch's *errands*."

"What's that supposed to mean?"

"It means you disappear for half a day at a time. And when you come back, you're wide-eyed and flushed." He pointed at me with a half-eaten biscuit. "I think you're hiding something. Something romantic."

If only. I grabbed the last biscuit before he could devour it as well and shook my head. "I already told you all about my lack of *errands* in that arena."

"You're terrible at keeping secrets. That's what I think. He's noticed it, too."

"Swaine?"

"Yes. Swaine. *One must allow for the infelicitous effects of being a young woman, I suppose—sails full of heartfelt nonsense.* Or something like that." His imitation of Swaine's speech pattern and facial expression would, under other circumstances, have delighted me. Instead, I frowned.

"He said that?"

"More than once."

"When?"

"I don't know—but more than once."

"Why hasn't he said anything to me? Why would he hold back?"

"He's frightened of women. All that feminine energy confuses him. It gets—intense."

I swatted him on the shoulder as I passed behind him. "It's never stopped him from calling me a fool a dozen times. More."

"He trusts you. You're more dedicated than his revenants. You've earned a little freedom."

I doubted that was it—*a little freedom*, to my master, would no doubt be followed by *to apply yourself even harder to your work, well done.* That he'd even remarked on it made it all worse, for my secrets hadn't even been as secret as I'd hoped. When the water finished boiling, I added the tea and poured some after it steeped.

No putting it off. "I'll go check on him," I said. I wiped the crumbs from my chest and headed up the stairs. Maybe it would be for the best he was still recovering from his terrible fever: his full fury might not boil over. When I reached his room, however, my knees shook. No, he would be livid—and I'd just have to weather the brunt of his anger and disappointment. Faced with the reality, I girded myself. Best get it over with, get on the other side of the unpleasantness as quickly as possible.

Listening at the door, I heard no sounds of movement from within. Straining to hear anything over the thumping of my heart, I thought I caught the soft breathing of his slumber. Quietly as I could, I lifted the latch on his door and peeked inside, opening the door a hand-width. In the darkness, Swaine's shape curled up under his blankets, pale spots of his face and one hand just visible. The blankets rose and fell with his breathing. Fast asleep.

I inched the door shut and lowered the latch so it didn't make a sound. He needed the sleep, and I didn't dare face him with my story if he was groggy and irritable for having been woken. No, I'd have to wait until he woke. My relief—short-lived, I was aware —nonetheless felt liberating.

Fine. While Swaine slept, I would store the burial silver—he would be flabbergasted that Mary had even acquired it. Fetching my tea, I told Twelves I'd be in the workshop for a while. Carrying the burial silver—along with the unpleasant collection of worries that swarmed me like a flock of cruel ravens—I cut through the dark yard and into the workshop. I lit three lanterns and searched for the proper ingredients to form a protective glamour. A bottle of ground violet quartz. Copper filings. Three dried roses, of which I required only the stalks. As I denuded them of their blooms, snapping off the flowers as though twisting off their heads, the image I'd found in the governor's room came back: Clara, dismembered and decapitated. I shivered. The clock over Swaine's workbench—the work of Twelves, of course—ticked softly, each second closing shut behind the sweep of the thin hand. Each second, gone forever.

What if Swaine slept for another twenty hours? What if the demon had already made good on its threat to Clara? I looked over at the pile of planar clocks stacked up in the far corner of the workshop. Then glanced back at the clock. *Tick. Tick. Tick.*

Putting down the rose stalks and dried petals, I grabbed the lantern on the bench and crossed to the planar clocks. Holding up the light, I searched the stacks until I found the one whose end I'd scored with a chisel.

Did you enjoy her pleading, witch?

I slid the planar clock out and carried it over to the infernal vox expander. Working quickly, I attached the clock to the pair of pins leading from the expander and set it down within the glamoured circle a yard away. I took a few moments to find the proper candle, but when I did, I set it by the expander. The corpse within the device—armless, legless—hung slack, its head bolted into a crown of iron, no different from the last moment it'd been activated weeks earlier, save for a thin layer of dust. As for the assistant, the heavyset revenant who worked the pedal that pumped the bellows, he'd been relocated to the cellar of the manse. With the focus of Swaine's work having shifted, there'd been no call, as yet, to bring him back to the workshop.

No matter, I would work the bellows myself.

I stood by the candle with a tinder stick lit from the lantern and recited the incantation to activate the process. Lighting the candle, I hurried over to the seat behind the foot pedal and pushed it down, feeling the momentum of the flywheel carry each stroke around for another. The metal squeaked—Twelves would scold me for not putting a touch of oil to each point of contact, but I was past being so thorough at that moment. As the familiar hiss and whine of air filled the tubes connected to the corpse, escaping through tiny pinprick holes in the various joints, flowing through the corpse's nose and mouth, I sensed a demon.

Was it *the* demon I'd encountered before? I wasn't certain.

In. Out. It's a thoughtless way to think. Planes are nothing. I'm everywhere.

The eyes of the corpse opened, lids fluttering, eyes rolling back in its pale head. A heavy sigh escaped its mouth. The mouth, however, remained still. It said nothing.

"Where is she?" I said.

Like earthworms brought from the soil after a rain, the corpse's lips wriggled before turning up into a sickly grin.

"Do you like what I've done, witch?" the voice croaked, dry and gasping.

I kept pumping the pedal. "Where is she?"

"I've shown you."

My heart tightened. I kept pedaling. "Why?"

"She deserved it. They all deserved it—knowing you as they did. Even the slightest contact with you is a death sentence. You believe me now, don't you?"

I didn't. Demons lied. Demons *were* lies, through and through. As I pedaled, I recited Hume's Seventh Ward. The corpse trembled in the jig, its face scrunched in pain.

"Clara," I called out when I'd finished the ward. "Can you hear me?"

The corpse groaned. I recited Hume's Ninth Ward. The corpse's mouth opened and closed, the dry lips making a flabby smacking sound. Along with the ward, I let slip a stream of witchcraft, channeling it into the connection the expander made.

"Clara—I'm here," I said. "Can you hear me?"

The corpse stilled, eyes closed. After a moment, the eyes fluttered open and gazed around.

"Miss Finch? Miss Finch?" the voice spoke. Still raspy, the words themselves took on a different lilt. "Please—please help me—everything is scary. And I keep hiding—but he keeps following. And there are knives. Everywhere. Knives. Flying and falling and trying to trip me."

"Where are you? Describe it."

"You can get me out?"

"Just tell me where you are."

"Stairs. I've been hiding in a room next to the big stairs."

As the corpse spoke, I saw tiny flecks of light spark from the wick of the candle—it was about to snuff. Keeping the air moving through the corpse, I raised a hand to it and said, "*Ignis*." The flame flared and continued to burn.

"Has anything appeared different to you?" I said.

"It's all different. That's why I'm so lost." The corpse shuddered with Clara's sobs. "Please. I'm so tired of being frightened all the time. Nothing I do—"

The corpse shuddered, the eyes rolling back in the head again. The terrible grin returned. "You're a clever one, witch."

"And you're a liar," I said.

"I won't be for much longer. Time to stop taunting this little friend of yours, entertaining as it's been. Time to slice—and each slice I make, I'll have her see your face."

Not losing my focus, I recited Hume's Thirteenth Ward, feeling an ache in my bones from the strain of casting three successive wards. The demon liked that ward even less than the others, rocking the frame that held the corpse, crying out in agony. After it fled again, the corpse went still.

"Clara—listen," I said. "Keep moving."

The corpse looked around again. "But I'm frightened."

"I know you're frightened, but you can't stay where you are. I need you to hurry."

"But to where?"

"Anywhere but where you are right now. Look for any signs."

"What signs?"

A thought had floated in my mind for some time—and I put it

to the test. I closed my eye and concentrated on my witchcraft. With the connection to Clara open, I extended energy from my core, envisioning it traveling through the pipes of the infernal vox expander, into the corpse—and through the planes, into the demonmere. As my witchcraft contacted the channel connecting the planes, my skin prickled as though a hundred mice scampered over every inch of my body. I pictured Clara—the way she'd looked while pointing a pistol at my head, my most vivid memory of her. *Seek her.*

"I see it—I see it!" the corpse spoke. "A golden vine. Oh, it's so pretty. Like it's made of light. I know it's you."

"Follow it," I said, maintaining the energies.

"It goes up the stairs."

"Follow it."

"What if he comes after me?"

"Hurry."

"I'm scared."

"But I'm with you—just run as fast as you can. Follow the vine. Are you following it?"

The corpse panted as though running. "I am. The stairs are wide and steep—but it goes to a door. Your vine goes through the door. In the middle."

"Push it open."

"What if it's locked? What if—oh, it opened."

"What do you see?"

"A long hallway. Stone. Tall windows on both sides. The vine looks like it goes up and through one window at the end."

"Keep following it."

I slowed my breathing, keeping the energy as stable as possible. The connection I felt caused my limbs to tremble. The pedal squeaked as I kept the air flowing.

"This window is different," Clara said. "It's littler. And I see into somewhere."

"Where?"

"It's a tavern—I recognize it! It's the tavern Francis's brother owns. Where I saw you."

"Knox's Inn & Tavern?"

"I see her, I see the wife. She's carrying a child. Locking the door. It looks late at night."

"Can you get to it somehow?"

"I don't know if I can—" The corpse grunted, as though straining. "It's only moving a little. The vine is curling on the glass. On this side. But I don't know if I can—"

"Try."

The workshop filled with the hiss of air, with the squealing of the pedal, the huff of the bellows, the tick of the clock.

"He's coming."

I opened my eye. "Hurry."

"No. He's coming—I hear him, stomping—he's so scary. I have to hide."

"Clara—push your way through the window!"

The shoulders of the corpse shook with panicked weeping. "No, no, no—I don't want him to get me—you don't understand —he's full of teeth, and—" A scream burst from the corpse's mouth, harrowing and desperate. My stomach dropped.

"Clara?" The corpse's eyes shut. I raised my voice. "Clara?"

The demon returned to the corpse, the face stretching into a vile leer. "I will kill them all. You've grown tiresome, witch."

Before I could cast yet another ward, the frame of the infernal vox expander shattered apart, iron and wood slinging apart into dozens of deadly projectiles. I raised my hands to protect my face, a sudden expansion of my witchcraft deflecting most of the shards that might have torn my flesh. Bottles on the workbenches shattered, posts and walls sounded with hard thumps, as though slammed with a dozen hammers. The corpse slumped forward, keeling over and landing hard on the floor, torn loose from the jigs that held it in place. Air gushed from the torn pipes. The planar clock connected to the expander had cracked along the woodgrain into half a dozen pieces, its internal mechanisms sprung. Everything went still.

I stood. No presence of a demon fouled the workshop.

I will kill them all.

Before I did anything else, I hurried to the workbench, rifling through several drawers in a panic. The third one I tried proved correct—I grabbed out a velvet bag that clinked softly from within as I jammed it into my pocket. I spun and ran for the door. I had to get to the tavern.

23

SPECTRAL BLAZE

Mr. Twelves's horse, a brawny stallion he lent me because my horse was spent, ate up the fifteen miles between Salem and Andover with vigor, muscles and lungs moving in concert as we flew through the dark night. The moon paced us, its light flooding the passing fields, winding rivers, and forested hillsides with silver. What few travelers we met on the blue-black roads raised a hand in greeting and then were gone. Fear and worry only tightened their grip on me as I passed through one small town after another, lone outposts between the stretches of dark woodland. The center of Andover was quiet. A few houses still shone with firelight. Most were dark. I pulled the horse up to the hitching posts outside of the tavern and swung down, tying the reins around the crossbeam. A pair of lanterns burned by the front door to the tavern and the merry light raised my hopes, beaten down as they'd been during the harrowing ride from Salem.

I pushed on the door, but found it locked. Moving over to the nearest window, I peered inside, holding my hand over my brow to block out the moonlight reflecting on the panes. The public room within stood empty, shadows of chair and table stretching out from the guttering fire in the hearth, the corners of the room grown dim. The room looked to have been swept and set to rights after another evening of service. As I hurried around to the back door, I wondered if I'd let myself be fooled by the demon. More lies. Worse, lies designed to take me from Salem. Worries went from a faint mutter to a louder whisper to something more conversational: *You fell for it, and now Swaine is vulnerable. Twelves is vulnerable. You rode off without thinking, leaving behind your best protections. You forgot what you were dealing with—the treachery of demons.*

Iris was likely in bed, the children asleep. The lanterns still burned outside the tavern because she forgot to extinguish them. Busy as she was, who could blame her? I paused at the back door. No, I'd been a fool—I had to get back to Salem. I was about to turn around and get Twelves's horse when I noticed the door was ajar by a mere quarter of an inch. I reached out and gave it a gentle push. It opened with a soft squeal of hinges. Nothing else disturbed the silence within.

Front door locked—back door not? I could well imagine Iris, at the end of another long day, children asleep in her arms, forgetting the lanterns—but forgetting to latch the door to the kitchen? My suspicions flared. I poked my head into the kitchen. Tin plates, stacked on the oak table. Broom leaning against the table. A pile of sweepings a stride away. All normal enough until I noticed a cloth on the floor—one Iris always kept tucked in her apron, or tossed on her shoulder, ready to wipe down or dry a table, a clean plate, a glass.

"Iris?" I called out, keeping my voice soft.

Approaching the table, I felt a chill current of air moving through the kitchen. Worse, I sensed planar energy. By the time I spotted a skein of frost along the floorboards and wall near the back stairs, I knew I'd been wrong about the demon—the lies were no lies at all.

Between the kitchen and the short hallway to the public room floated three bodies: Iris and her children.

They twirled, tipping head over feet as though caught underwater in a gentle current. I got closer. A small gasp escaped me as I saw that their eyes were open, and wide in terror. What brief hope I held that they were still alive was extinguished. Their mouths gaped, loose, and their eyes stared unseeing. They were dead. Tears blurred my vision.

"Oh, Iris," I whispered. I extended my witchcraft, wary of the demon. My fingers shook. I sensed the strong misalignment of planar energy, but no demon. Stepping past the planar shift, I looked into the public room. From the inside, the night outside appeared solid. I glanced from one window to the next. Which one had Clara seen through?

"Clara?" I called. "Are you here?"

Nothing. I stepped to the nearest window.

"*O woman, o woman, o woman, do you see what you have done? You killed the bravest butcher that ever the sun shone on.*"

I spun.

Iris stared at me, her feet and the hems of her skirt floating a yard above the ground, her pale eyes wide. She and her children still rose and fell within the powerful current, but it had drifted closer, only a dozen feet behind me. Hints of light appeared around them, gusting sheets of deep red, a spectral blaze that rose to the ceiling.

"*O woman, o woman, oh pray come tell to me. O woman, o woman, have you got any company?*" she sang. In the wavering light, her lovely skin took on a flush, her lips shining red. She'd never looked more beautiful as she clasped her hands and serenaded me.

And then I remembered what she'd told me about her dreams—dreams of Ethan coming to her, singing to her. *I'll sing you soft lullabies below your window... I know a beautiful song*, the demon had warned me from the infernal vox expander.

The demon. Even then. Getting ready, taunting me.

"*May God keep all good people from such bad company,*" Iris sang.

I couldn't stand the sight, nor bear the thought of what she'd gone through, what her children had gone through. I put my hand to my face and turned away, sobbing, unable to help myself. She'd been taken from me—just like all the others. My family. Masters, decent and not. So many, taken.

And I should have known.

The singing stopped.

"You like my handiwork, witch?"

Flinging the tears from my face, I spun. Iris watched me, her face a mask of gaiety. The voice that came from her throat deepened.

"Because I'm just getting started," she said. "Each one of them will be worse. The agony more appalling. Oh, what you'll find— do you see what you've done, o woman, o woman?"

I opened my arms. "I'm here right now. Why not just take me? Kill me—if you can? Leave the others out of it—if you're so frightful, so powerful, so cruel. I'm a witch—I'm the one you want. Take me!"

Laughter shook Iris's shoulders and her smile deepened. "Oh, I will. Soon. But that's not good enough. Your suffering is my sustenance—it always has been. I want you to see every last person in your life torn apart. Strangled. Flayed. Drowned. Crushed. Immolated. Smothered. Broken. Shredded. The frightened one, quivering even now behind bars. He's next. Then the proud one, near him. The vain one, learning magic. The drunken one. The clockmaker. All of them, for you. And you can't save a single one of them because I've out-thought you. And when I'm done with them, you're going to be mine. Whatever's left of you after you've come face-to-face with the corpses of all your dearest ones, witch. If you think you can—"

I screamed, hurling all the witchcraft I could muster at the demon within the planar disturbance. The red light flared, torn backward to ripple in blinding streaks, tearing loose to whirl through the room. Pale gold light shot from my palms to trace the strange contours of the planar energy. As it did, the bodies of Iris and her children crashed to the floor. The horrible sound of their lifeless limbs and heads hitting the boards further enraged me. I strode forward, witchcraft gushing from my hands.

The knot of planar energy burst apart, strange windings of it filling the tavern, knocking loose board and beam, sending plates, cups, candles flying. Chairs and tables slid across the floor to crash into the walls. Windowpanes cracked or blew out entirely.

I didn't need a planar clock. I didn't need a glamour or a sequence of summoning and binding sorcery. Wards. Spells. None of it.

The demon would learn not to trifle with me.

As the timbers of the inn groaned, I searched for the fiend—but couldn't find him. Up, down, around, in back of me, nothing. He'd fled.

After a moment, I lowered my arms, my chest rising and falling from the exertion. The last traces of witchcraft raced along the walls and then faded. I stared down at Iris and her children, still now.

"You'll pay when I catch you, demon," I said. "And I *will* catch you."

I would not lose another loved one to the fiend.

Ever.

24

A FEARSOME FIGURE

By the time I reached Boston, the darkness gave way, all but the brightest stars fading as the dawn sketched in the rooflines, the chimneys, the rope-lines and masts of the shipyard. I followed the edge of the harbor along the curve of Lynn Street. Water lapped at the tarry pilings of the shipyard where the spine and ribs of a trade ship under construction loomed. Talk and laughter drifted from windows of the houses I passed. I rode by, shivering, exhausted. How I longed for a normal life at that moment: the simplicity of a day's work, a meal, a laugh, a peaceful bed. Yet, there I was—alone and desperate, driven by harrowing fears. I shouldered my crushing worries into the city, along every turn, the horse path through the fens, every lane, every alleyway. I kept close to the houses that lined the rise before the water, hurrying until I reached Princess Street. I paused and watched the Whitelocke house from across the way.

Instead of the quiet house I'd expected, the residence of the Whitelockes was alive. Two wagons stood in front while servants and uniformed soldiers carried items from the backs of the wagons to the doorway. Chests. Trunks. Furnishings. Bundles of clothing. Leaving the horse hitched across the way, I straightened my cloak, then crossed the lane. A pair of soldiers stepped to the doorway carrying a bureau.

"Second floor," the first one said.

"Jesus, it's heavy."

"And not getting lighter with you complaining about it." They paused when they saw me. "What do you want?"

"Is Major Whitelocke here?"

"Out of the way." They passed me and headed to the door. "And you are?"

"Finch. Kate Finch. He'll know me."

"Wait here."

After a minute, Grayson Whitelocke emerged from the door wearing his scarlet uniform. The servants flowed around him. Seeing me, he smiled and led me by the elbow off to the front corner of the house.

"Lovely to see you, Miss Finch," he said, his gaze flicking over to the nearest guards. "What brings you around this fine and early morning?" Lowering his voice to a whisper, he said, "Walk with me. Say nothing."

I did. We strolled over to the corner of the residence.

"This should do," he said, keeping his voice quiet. "But word will spread."

"Word?"

"Sackville has moved faster than I thought possible." He kept a smile on his face, keeping my back to the activity at the front door. "I'm certain he's got half the household staff and most of my detail of Governor's Own on his payroll. All comings and goings noted. Young woman wearing a patch—that news will reach him before the morning is over, no doubt."

"He doesn't know who I am."

"Don't be so sure about that." He waved with his hand as though I'd just made a splendid joke. "He's asked about your master. Furthermore, he's made it known that Doctor Rush has reached the end of his Royal Appointment. Meanwhile, Sackville himself is going to be sworn in as governor tomorrow morning. No surprises there. And if he catches wind of what *really* happened to my father, things will take an even more vertiginous turn for the worse, trust me."

"Where's the doctor?"

"No one can bloody find him. I had men out looking for him. Nothing, anywhere. I'm not sure how long I have before Sackville makes it known the Whitelocke name is not one to advance one's military career behind, so I have no idea how much longer I'll be able to order men to keep looking for him."

"He wouldn't have left."

Grayson nodded. "One would think not. There's no other colony that would have him, to start with—and no city or township in the nearby colonies that wouldn't recognize his illustrious face. Even the King himself has made clear he is no admirer of the doctor. As a result, there are powerful men who would see him behind bars if they were feeling generous, hanged by the neck or even burned if they weren't. He's no fool."

"My friend—in the jail. I need to see him."

"No one's thinking about him right now. He'll be fine."

"No. He won't. What happened to your father—that's going to happen to him if I can't get to him."

"I can't do anything until later today, what with—"

"Now," I said. "Grayson, please. Take me to him. I'm begging you."

Within three-quarters of an hour, I followed Grayson into Boston's jail, a grim building of brown stone tucked away on a street by the ferryway and the water that stood between Boston and Charlestown. A flag snapped on the breeze, the King's Colors bright against the blue sky. Regulars stationed at the gate saluted him and unlocked the entrance.

"Tongues will wag," he said, after we passed into a chill

corridor lit by grimy lanterns. "Though with all my other rakish exploits, perhaps no one will give it a second thought."

"They think—wait. What will they think?"

"Let's just say you aren't the first attractive companion I've brought here."

"I take it I shouldn't feel honored."

"No. You really shouldn't."

We turned a corner into a small antechamber with a pair of iron doors on one wall and a desk and chairs against the other. An officer at the desk stood up on our entrance.

"Didn't expect you today, sir."

"Well then aren't you the lucky one," Grayson said. "I need to see one of your prisoners."

"Yes, sir." The sergeant looked me over. "Which one, sir?"

Grayson looked at me.

"Bertram Nagle," I said.

The sergeant nodded. He lifted a set of keys off a peg. "Down this way, sir."

Unlocking the iron doors, he led us deeper into the jail. Rows of rusted metal doors lined the long passage. Narrow windows at either end let in dank harbor air. We passed among the cells, most of which appeared to be empty, the heavy doors standing open. At one cell on the left, a face peered out of a small barred opening. I recognized him: Harrison Hull, the barber who'd been with Governor Whitelocke when he'd been killed. He looked worse for the wear, dark circles beneath his eyes, fingers trembling as they flittered through the iron grate. He stared right at me.

"My sister, thank God. Rebecca. Rebecca? Over here. I didn't kill him, you see. No, no. Ha, ha. It was the fiend in the fire. Not my steady hand. Ha, ha." His eyes looked fevered as they spilled over with tears. "What a sight you are, dear. Shining like an angel. Come to save me. Wake me from this frightful nightmare. Your warm hand. Gentle. Yes, ha, ha."

"Ignore him," the sergeant said. "Never stops jabbering."

I felt Hull's delusional gaze on my face as we passed his cell.

"No, no, no, no," Hull called after us. "Don't leave me. Or ever. Forever? I can't think, dearest Rebecca. Best ask Mother, yes. She'll know what to do!"

The sergeant pointed. "Nagle's in the last one on the right, sir."

As he slid the key into the lock, I extended my senses—and detected no demon. Still, I girded myself for what I'd see when the door opened. *The frightened one, quivering even now behind bars. Each one of them will be worse. The agony more appalling.* Was I already too late? The guard swung the door open. "Here he is."

I stepped past him and Grayson—and there was Bertram, sitting on a wooden cot against the far wall, wearing the same clothing as when he'd been captured. No blankets, no pillows. A bucket in the corner. A short window near the top of the wall let in a hint of daylight. Bertram blinked up at me, the fright on his face easing as recognition washed over him. He got to his feet.

"Oh, thank God." I rushed across the small cell and threw my arms around him.

Grayson turned to the guard. "I need to question this man in private, Sergeant. I'll call you when I need you."

"Yes, sir. I'll be back at the desk."

I pulled back and looked at Bertram. "Are you all right? Have you eaten? I'm getting you out of here."

"Well, I haven't slept much," he said. "Not much in the way of comfort. Or quiet. Food was barely fit for tossing out." His gaze went back to Grayson. "Begging your pardon, sir."

"I'll see if we can't get some roast quail and partridge sent along. Would you like some brandy with that?" Grayson said.

"I—brandy? No. I don't drink much besides beer, sir."

"Relax. It was a jest."

"Ignore him," I told Bertram. "I'm so sorry you've had to go through this." I turned to Grayson again. "Can you get him out of here? Now?"

"Well, I'm not really sure what he's been charged with," Grayson said. "And there's a process. I'm unlikely to have quite as much leeway as I used to, you see."

"What did they tell you?" I asked Bertram.

"Close-lipped bunch of lads they were," he said. "Er. Guards. Soldiers, sir. And that Doctor Rush. Questioned me for a good couple of hours. About—well, about some of the—expeditions. And specimens. Worried the whole time I was about to be tortured, but I wasn't. In fact, he didn't frighten me as much as I'd expected."

A shadow stepped from the corner of the jail cell. "Then I shall have to work on my demeanor, Bertram Nagle—a Royal Doctor of Magickal Sciences ought to be a fearsome figure, wouldn't you agree?"

I startled enough to bang my elbow into the wall while Bertram dropped to the floor. Ephraim Rush stood in the corner. The old gentleman's hair—what remained of it—had lifted off in several directions, and the spectacles roosting on his nose were askew, but he appeared otherwise hale. A hint of magic danced across the grimy stones in the corner of the cell.

"God, I *hate* when he does that." Grayson put a hand to his chest.

Rush straightened his spectacles and looked at me, registering nothing of the surprise that his appearance had engendered in me. "Miss Finch—how fortuitous, indeed."

I steadied myself. "Fortuitous, sir?"

"Quite so. If I ever needed the help of a witch, it would appear to be now."

25

MORE DIRE BY THE DAY

itch. To have heard it spoken so directly, so openly by the Royal Doctor of Magickal Sciences of the colony a week or a month earlier would have reduced me to terrified silence. Yet when faced with the very scenario I'd so long dreaded, what I felt instead was relief. Such was the mirror-world left in the wake of Fate's latest turns. I helped Bertram back to his feet. "You knew I'd come to rescue Bertram, didn't you, Doctor?"

"Forgive my crassness," Rush said.

"And you know what I am. You've been helping me."

"I have indeed, Miss Finch."

"When did you figure it out?"

"Well, I've known for months that a witch was present in the colony once again—although I've only come to suspect it was you in particular over the last few weeks."

I'd been correct—yet I still found his words stunning. "How?"

He smiled. "The man who invented the witch-pole would hardly miss that a witch had activated one."

"The ball."

"The ball, yes. Among my other concerns of that tragic

evening, I was stunned to discover that one of my devices had lit the snowy evening just outside the scene of the crime."

"I didn't kill General Whitelocke."

"I never said you did—though that seemed a most compelling explanation of events, at first. A man assassinated is alarming enough. A man assassinated in a room bearing strong traces of planar energies, a hint of demonic presence, his corpse drenched with a peculiar magic is another thing. Yet it was a bullet that killed him, fired from a pistol, neither of which bore the slightest trace of magic." He pulled a briarwood pipe from his coat pocket, tamped down a plug of tobacco into it, and brought it to life, watching me through the smoke. "Quite the riddle. The violence could be explained, given the troubles with the Rattlesnakes. As for the magic—well, there was your master, not present, as far as I could tell. How to connect the evidence? And then for the first time in decades, one of my witch-poles flares to life. What on earth was I to think?" He watched me. "Forty-three years. Eight months. Three days."

"Pardon?"

"That is how long the witch-poles throughout the colony had remained unlit. Forty-three years since the last remaining witch in Massachusetts died. An individual whom I'd feared to have been the last living witch anywhere in the known and civilized world. Uneasy years for me."

"Ginny Lane?" I said, remembering the author of the letters I'd read. *This plague that has taken my people will take yours next if we can't work together to finish what we've begun.*

"Possibly."

"You weren't certain?"

"If you were to ask me if I held any inklings, why yes. There remain several small towns and villages spread in the thick forests and valleys north of here that I suspected were once home to that small and secretive handful of surviving witches. Rumors and tales of that part of the colony never died down—and I maintained an obsessive interested in all of it. I kept track. I made myself mad with curiosity, in point of fact—but my commitment to leave them be never wavered."

"Leave them be?" Grayson said. "I'm sorry, Doctor Rush—but what about your commitment to the King, and the governors? Wasn't it the point of your position to keep the colony free from witchcraft?"

Rush straightened. "The point of my position is and always has been to keep the populace safe from threats of the infernal nature. Precisely what I've done, as had the two gentlemen who held my position before me. We all did what we could to make sure that those witches who remained, tending to the seals they'd paid such a terrible price to put in place, were never found, never suspected, and never interfered with."

"Says the man who invented the witch-poles," Grayson said.

"How many witches were apprehended as a result?" Rush said. "Not a one. Believe me, I've been battered by that question any number of times, by three separate governors. No, they were for my own edification. That they also served as a visible and noteworthy reminder of my usefulness—well, that too was of benefit. What better way to give the witches room to do what they needed to do than to draw the attention away from their real presence?"

"So you knew, from the beginning. From when Archibald Fletcher corresponded with Ginny Lane," I said.

"Of course. Fletcher knew, as you say. He subsequently told his successor, Henrik Kraus, a product of the Vienna school of magical sciences, whom I had the privilege of apprenticing with for five years. A man who brought the illumination of modern reason to bear on the oft-obscured workings of planar magic. Brilliant. He was a man of the highest integrity." He leaned forward, clenching his pipe, to emphasize the point. "It was, in fact, he who decided on the policy that we Royal Magicians leave the few remaining witches in this colony alone. We realized the danger they held back. What was at stake—for we've all seen it's not just the witches who pay the price of the weakening barriers between this world and the encroachment of other planes. Demons are drawn to witches with a notable fervor, yes—but they don't stop there. And yet somehow this desperate handful of witches kept it all sealed off."

"Until the last one died," I said.

"Until the last one died. And the seals have weakened in the interim, despite my best efforts."

"You've tried?"

"To little effect, unfortunately. While I'm somewhat adept at cataloguing and even exploring these intersections of worlds, the formula for preventing breaches has eluded me. No, witchcraft holds the key—as I think you've realized, Miss Finch."

With so many thoughts cascading through my head, I paced the room as the doctor watched me. "You left me clues."

"A few trinkets to help guide your own intuitions in the face of a growing tide of demonic activity."

"Goodness," I said. "Is there anything about me you haven't guessed, Doctor?"

"I suspect there's quite a story in you, Miss Finch," Rush said. "Yet the hours grow urgent."

"How much of this did my father know?" Grayson said.

Rush turned to him. "I tried to warn him. Of course I did. But your father had little patience for my—"

Grayson waved his hands. "Yes, yes. I was there. He didn't want to hear a word of it, staring at you as though you were reciting the alphabet before returning his attention to the politics that consumed him. Although, really—what consumed him in the end was a demon."

"Oh, dear." Bertram's first words drew everyone's attention. He put a hand to his temple. "Sorry. It's—well, it's all a bit much to take in. All at once, as it were."

"Bertram is correct," Rush said. "And perhaps the late

governor can be forgiven for struggling to grapple with the nature of the threat we face, one which grows more dire by the day. I've now identified the presence of demons in six towns, including here in Boston, just within this past week. The trend is unmistakable."

"There's been more," I said. "In Andover." I told them what I'd found at the tavern. I could barely look at Bertram, whose face crumbled at the news of Iris and her children. Reaching out, I steadied him with my hand. "I'm so sorry."

"Very concerning," Rush said.

"It's why I'm here—the same demon threatened Bertram."

Bertram's eyes widened. "Me?" He sat down on the edge of the bed frame.

"I'm here. I'll protect you."

"As will I," Rush said.

"Yes, it's not as though you're the duly appointed governor of the colony, Bertram," Grayson said. "Alone and vulnerable."

"You're not helping," I scolded Grayson.

Harrison Hull's plaintive nonsense rose again from the corridor. "Bit of a bother, bit of a bother. I mustn't let the governor look so shabby. That's what he always said. Can't be shabby, Hull. Clean me to vigor. Funny, I first thought he said *vinegar*. Never knew what he meant by that."

"The demon threatened Bertram specifically?" Rush said.

"Among others, yes." I looked out the cell door. "Francis Knox, too. He's one of the men who tried to kidnap you. I believe he's here, somewhere."

"It would seem Miss Finch's acquaintance is rather perilous," Grayson said.

"You made the list, as well," I told him.

"Of course I did. How else could things get worse?"

"No candles. No wicks, or pots, or tinderboxes. Ha, ha," Hull said, louder now, his voice echoing up the corridor. "No, no, no. No fireplaces. No flames. No, no, no, no, no."

"Forewarned is forearmed," Rush said. "We may have come together at just the right time."

"There you are, there you are, there you are, there you are," Hull called out, a curious singsong melody to his voice growing higher in pitch. "There you are, there you are, there you are, there you are."

While his words continued, something caught my eye closer on the door. The iron hinges sprouted fine scribing of black. Faint shadows crawled over the surface of the wood. I extended my senses—and felt a presence manifesting. "Doctor—something is here."

Rush looked at me, then glanced at the door. He gestured with his right hand. "*Revelare vires, videre lineae vis.*" A snapping sound erupted from the air, the crackling of dry leaves aflame. White sparks flared, riding the surface of wood and metal alike, bright enough to leave dabs of color hanging in my vision. I raised a hand to shade my eyes.

I glanced at Grayson, who squinted and tried to brush away the glimmering spark that spun around the topmost button of his uniform. It flared and popped like a squib. The brilliant light leaped from one surface to another.

"*Tergum in tenebris et silentio,*" Rush said in a commanding voice. The lights flared, then disappeared with a tearing sound. The wool of my dress lifted in a charged manner. Likewise my hair. I smoothed it down, residual static tracing my fingers and palm as I did. Rush's hair—those brave survivors who'd remained —extended around his head in a gray halo. He glanced around the cell. "You're right. There's a shift in the planes. We're not safe."

A ripple of pinpricks moved across my face and arms: a demon. I turned. At the far end of the cell, a shadow seeped from the corner. It reached fingers out, spiraling and stretching, dragging a darkness along with it. I saw Rush's breath condense in the air. The temperature plummeted, and a vile stench filled the space. Instinctively, I raised my witchcraft. A banging erupted in the corridor. Prisoners called out.

Rush turned from the door and placed his hands together, palms facing his chest, fingers overlapped. "*Sigillum seram et clausit,*" he said quickly. The door to the cell trembled, crashing against the stone wall, vibrating and shaking.

"We are in acute danger," Rush said, a tremor in his voice. "We need to—"

That was as far as he got before every door in the jail rattled, filling the air with a loud clanging. All four of us flinched. I ignored the clamor and stepped forward, executing the proper gesture of Hume's Seventh Ward with my hand, shouting out the words, "*Dagum cuomon ærest scipu, þa se gerefa þærto rad, hie wolde drifan to þæs cyninges tune þy he nyste hwæt hie wæron!*"

The air shook, and for a moment the door stilled.

"What's happening?" Bertram gasped.

"The demon," I said.

A series of bangs raced through the corridor—each cell door torn open and slammed shut, one after another, several of the bars flying off and clanging against the opposite walls from the force. Harrison Hull cried out in terror.

I turned to face the corridor, my skin breaking into gooseflesh as the demon raced toward me. The air fouled. This time, I used the Twenty-Third Ward. "*Her on þysum geare for se micla here. We gefyrn ymbe spræcon, eft of þæm eastric westweard þær wurdon gescipode, swa þæt hie asettan him on anne siþ ofer mid horsum mid ealle!*"

The floor shuddered. Wood splintered as the door to Bertram's cell tore free. Rush attempted an incantation, but as he spoke the words, the bed lurched sideways, the legs scraping the floor, one of them breaking as it slid with a wooden roar. Rush held out his hand and spoke, "*Primae autem quartaeque intervallum, quod habet duplam portionem, diastema facere.*" A multi-hued shimmer rolled out from his palm, stopping the bed before it could break our legs. Bertram cowered.

I extended my witchcraft as far as I could, the demon bearing down on us. The air filled with snarls and groans. Scratches appeared in the stones of the wall, gouges in the wood of the ceiling. Grayson urged Rush along, straining to clear the remnants of the door before hurrying into the corridor. I followed, dragging Bertram. A vile stain pursued us.

As soon as we left the cell, one and then another of the heavy cell doors ripped from its iron hinges and flew through the air. I just dodged getting my ribs broken, leaping forward. Grayson hurried the doctor along. Across the way, Francis stepped into the corridor, followed by a young man of his same age—the other would-be kidnapper of Doctor Rush.

Francis caught my eye. "That took a while. I'd expected you sooner, Miss Finch."

He thought I was rescuing him. Of course.

"Not now," I said, "we're—"

Before I could get any further, his companion lifted into the air, a look of uncomprehending terror on his face. He flew the length of the corridor, colliding with a sickening crunch against the far-off wall.

"Everyone must leave!" Rush shouted. "Now!"

As we hurried toward the front of the jail, I glimpsed Harrison Hull, still in his cell, rocking back and forth on his heels, eyes clamped shut. Shadows swept up the hallway after us. At the corner, half a dozen regulars emerged, muskets aimed forward. The officer in charge took in the scene, his gaze fixing first on Grayson, and then on Rush.

"There they are—seize them!" he called out.

"I knew I was being bloody watched," Grayson said. He straightened. "Captain, have your men step aside—this isn't the moment for any of Lord Sackville's nonsense, as you might notice."

"You can explain that all to the new governor, Whitelocke," the officer said. Turning his head to his men, he said, "Back them up. Keep those two apart from the others."

Before he could give another order, a smudge darkened the surrounding air. For a moment, he looked about, confused—and then his head cleaved from his shoulders, sending a jetting stream of blood across the floor as his body crumpled. The soldiers cried out, but, unsure of what had happened, pressed forward with their bayonets.

Raising my hands, I let fly as much energy as I could summon —and with a fuel of fear and frustration, it was potent. I cried out, and the soldiers lifted into the air, shouting. I hurled them back, and they crashed into the entrance to the front room to the jail, a good ten strides from where they'd stood. Grunts and cursing accompanied their broken wrists or collarbones. "Go, go!" I waved the others on, keeping close to Bertram. As we darted past the groaning soldiers, one of them caught my cloak on the tip of his bayonet. I tore myself loose. A scream erupted from the cells behind us.

We ran through the front room and out into the street. To the left, a group of mounted regulars spotted us. I grabbed Francis by the shoulder and pushed Bertram into him. "Keep him safe—but get out of here!" I reached over and took Grayson by the collar. "Grayson, too. Both of them, Francis—keep both of them safe!"

I reached into my pocket and pulled out the velvet bag, prying open the top. I fished out three glamoured rings, protection against demons. "Take one, each of you—put them on, don't take them off. Promise me!"

After what they'd seen, they didn't argue, each one sliding a ring onto whichever finger fit. Francis opened his mouth. I held my hand up. "No arguments. Rings on. Everyone kept safe, remember."

With a gleam in his eye, he spun. "Come, lads—you heard Miss Finch. Time for us to disappear."

"This is ridiculous," Grayson protested.

I shoved him in the back. "Go."

As the clatter of hooves bore down on us, the three of them dashed off down the street. Francis led them into a narrow alleyway. Other prisoners emerged from the jail, blinking in the morning sunlight. I heard Harrison Hull shrieking from deep within the cells, "*There you are! There you are!*" A few of the less battered soldiers limped out from the jail behind Doctor Rush and myself.

"Doctor Rush," I said.

Rush turned, reached out, and grasped my hand. "Our cue to leave, wouldn't you say?"

"The demon."

"Will follow us—but only so far." With a quick, sharp tug, he pulled me off balance to my left—and by the time the charging horsemen reached the spot we'd stood, a whirl of icy air rotated above the cobblestones, quickly dissipating.

We vanished.

26

A GLIMPSE OF THE SACRED

We tumbled into a large stone antechamber, hung with lanterns that drove back the gloom. A narrow window looked out over the harbor. The near side of the room had been turned into a workshop, its two tables strewn with brass fittings, pulleys and weights; glass flasks, beakers, and globes in a range of sizes; wooden vises and assorted clamps. Steel scribes, small glasses, lead plumbs, and inkwells held down sheets of notes. An empty cup and a teapot. A cane, leaning up against the chair. A coat, hung on a hook on the wall.

Doctor Rush released my hand and dusted off his coat. "Here we are. It's comfortable enough for my needs, though it gets rather chilly at night."

"Where—where are we, sir?" I steadied myself, disoriented from our disappearance and near-instantaneous entrance.

"Moon Island," Rush said. "In the harbor. This small fort was used for training regulars, though it's sat unused for most of the last decade, the various military officers coming to believe the chill breezes here made them susceptible to a peculiar ague. My guess is they tired of the boat ride, happy to commandeer various easier-to-reach meadows and fields to practice their drills." He grabbed an iron poker, stabbed at the embers in the hearth, and tossed in another quartered piece of alder. Books littered the table nearest an armchair, a few open, others with pages marked with black ribbon. Next to them, several pieces of paper scratched across with thin, fine writing—Rush's own hand, I presumed. A quick scan of the titles of the books—several of which I recognized—made the subject clear.

"You knew they'd come for you," I said. "The new governor and his men."

"Indeed. And where better to hide?"

"How did we—was that one of the *occulta proluo*?"

He put the poker back and smiled. "Under fairer circumstances, knowing my work had been read would have elevated my mood for a day, Miss Finch. Yes, you're correct. The *planar eaves*, also known as the *hidden outthrusts*. Small overlaps left by the collision of larger planes. I'm gratified to see that a witch may safely pass through them."

"You weren't sure, sir?"

"Well, I was sure that a bayonet would certainly pass through a witch—so I took the risk. Forgive me."

"Of course, sir."

"Now. How far have you and your master delved into the *Speculatum Somnium*?"

The demonmere. The name Rush used—meaning "Mirrored Dreams"—was used by both Koeffler and William Bostrom, but it referred to the same interstitial planar realm created by the residue of magic and sorcery.

"Not far." I pulled over a straight-backed wooden chair, leaving the more comfortable one for the doctor. "We've identified a dozen rooms and corridors. A few hundred feet, at most. No farther."

Rush watched the fire catch, the flames ripping upward. I was glad for the heat, as the chill that held me wasn't just from my dank clothes, but from our close escape.

"I see." The light shone on Rush's spectacles. "Since first discovering an entrance into the realm in the wine cellar of the governor's manse, I myself have identified three major crossroads, which I believe connect the planes that Gustav Koeffler identified as Seven, Twenty-Three, Twenty-Seven—though it seems a pity to ignore the Great Man's wonderful nomenclature. The soul of a poet, I believe. *Mitternacht Treppen und Türen*, 'Midnight Stairs and Doors.' *Die Beschatteten Tal*, 'the Shadowed Vale,' *Wo die Sterne Flüstern*, 'Where the Stars Whisper.'"

He took his seat with a grunt. I made a move to help him, but he waved me off. He gave me a wistful smile. "I wasn't always an old man. In fact, in my heart, I'm still twenty-seven, regardless of all that nonsense my hips and eyes keep on about. And while I love a certain amount of comfort, a certain amount of order, tall piles of books and papers to fill in the nooks and crannies of my other social engagements—well, there was a time when I loved nothing more than the forest, tracing rivers northward, following the coast."

He held his hands before him as though studying with surprise the knotted knuckles and liver spots. Not the hands of a young man. After a moment, he folded them into his lap and held my gaze.

"My mind has always been restless," he continued. "A fact which age has yet to temper. I may be better able to focus the darting and curious to-and-fro of my thoughts, but I still can't keep them still. And as a young man growing up amidst the bustle of Boston, nothing fascinated me more than stories of what happened in the river valleys to the north. The founding of the colony. All the tales of the settlers of Salem, the tales of the haunted forests."

"Witches."

He watched me for a moment, then nodded. "Yes, witches. When I was a boy—even until I was a young man—soldiers stood guard on every road and lane heading north, ten miles outside

Boston. The practice fell off, of course—but only after decades. Complacency. Money. Effort. Each took its toll. *North duty* became shorthand for any boring duty among the regulars. But what could have been more enticing to a young man with a mind that didn't still for a moment?"

A pocket of pitch burst in the fireplace, twirling embers up the flue.

"My interest in Salem grew to obsession. I read all I could about it. Letters, accounts from Boston, pamphlets. In time, I sneaked up into the surrounding forests and marshes on my own, defying the advice of my father, the advice of my teachers. The law." He shifted and straightened out his waistcoat. "I once set foot in Salem itself, for several hours on a chill winter's day. Quite foolhardy."

I wanted to wriggle under his gaze, but I held still.

He leaned back. "No one had dwelt there for decades. The sense of abandonment was profound. I found bones of houses, skulls of tumbled stone chimneys, all wearing the signs of untended years. Now, mind you, I was also carrying more than half my weight in imagination, and another half again of tales told to frighten. Even with those exceptions, however, I found something amiss about the spot. I had hardly begun my study of magic—but I considered myself a force to be reckoned with. Even as I near my seventy-third year, I blush at it. Quite unpleasant."

I watched him carefully. "You did magic there."

"I *attempted* magic there. Oh, I would tame the forces from beyond the veil. I would bring an enlightened sensibility to the matter. I would establish myself as the leading practitioner of the magical sciences in the Americas. Notes, instruments, different plans of attack—I was fully prepared. I was also seventeen years old with no comprehension of how foolish such an excursion was. Every day since has been a gift. An unearned, unlikely gift."

As he spoke, I had no sense of the musty ramblings of an older gentleman, lost in the past. Rather, I noted a keen mind moving from one relevant point to the next, drawing out a picture with precision. I'd spent enough time around my master to recognize the mettle of genius.

The doctor continued. "I plunged into a rather dangerous area of magic for even an experienced practitioner: harmonic shadow control. A vein of study that goes back centuries. Perhaps you're familiar with it?"

I nodded. "Somewhat."

"Excellent. Then I may spare you a pointed lecture on the currents of mirrored symmetry. It's a field that has fascinated me from the beginning." He turned in his chair and pointed to a rose sticking out of a quill holder. It had caught my eye as I'd come in, but I'd been too preoccupied to give it much attention. It had a fine source of illumination within it, a pale blush of pink fire on the petals, a faint sunlight-through-new-leaf glow on the stem. The light danced around in diaphanous strands while the rest of it was nearly transparent in spots.

"It never wilts," Rush said. "It bloomed in the spring of 1684. By extracting the second-order harmonic and discharging it from the source flower, I preserved its essence. It has faded somewhat over the decades, to what I attribute to a minor flaw in my process. That branch of magic can also create rather more distasteful effects, of course. *Il Gusto della Morte*, for instance."

"Something from *Magia Nera*?" I said.

"The very definition. Giambattista Ordine, an acolyte of Girabaldi. The tapping of a powerful negative current to embed a fourth-order harmonic into the threshold of a doorway, wherein anyone passing through it will taste their own demise. Ordine, like many of his contemporaries, had a rather cruel streak. Appropriate to the intrigues of the time, we must suppose." He sighed. "My experiment was brash, though with no such malice of intent. Through what I intended to be a cleverly devised sequence of spells, I would use these principles of harmonic shadow control to bring to life a marionette. Yes, a toy—but a toy

I had laboriously painted black with the proper glamours and then inscribed with several harmonic formulations of my own devising. The limbs were plugged with various metals designed to resonate with the correct forces."

"It sounds—rather dangerous."

He smiled. "Indeed, it was. Yet it gave contour and voice to what the eye and ear could not see. By tapping into the various harmonics of the energies woven throughout the silent town, this device would act as a guide, allowing me to map the topology of planar forces. As I said, quite foolish. Had I but known what I was getting into, I'd have never attempted such a dangerous technique in that locale. Rather akin to testing out floating shoes in shark-infested waters, or devising an eyedropper powered by a waterfall." He folded his fingers and raised his eyebrows.

"It didn't work?"

"Oh, it worked. Just not as I had intended, not by a horrifying Salem mile. The marionette came to life as I'd hoped. Quite a thrill that moment was. Nearly as thrilling as the rest of that afternoon as I tried everything I could to revoke the magical forces that animated that vile little puppet as it tried to kill me."

I put a hand to my mouth.

"Terrifying," Rush continued. "To this day, I still hear the clacking of those feet in my nightmares. Scampering over warped floorboards, climbing sills, leaping out at me from darkened doorways. Were I but a little less vain, I could show you the scars on my chest and stomach I still bear."

"That's horrifying."

"It was. I barely escaped with my life, let alone my confidence as a magician." He sniffed, folded his hands. "Still, I didn't let it go. And in time, I couldn't ignore the conclusion that all I'd heard until then had been only a damnable lie."

I recalled what I'd read in the letters. "About the witches."

"The witches, yes. As I suspect you are already aware, Miss Finch, the so-called *curse of the witches* is as black a lie as any ever uttered. The annihilation of the witches, is more like it. Salem is not the location of a crime, diabolic or otherwise—and it's never been. Rather, it's the location of a disaster. One quite relevant to our present situation."

"And the authorities of the colony lied about it."

"Correct. There was no trial, nor edict. There was no bargaining, nor demands, nor any parlay of any sort. There was no drive into Salem of armed men, no executions, no banishments. No cleansing of the colony. In fact, I would suggest that the entire story of the events as passed on from one generation to the next has been naught but a shameless twisting of the truth."

"Then what was it? What really happened?"

He stood up and retrieved a pipe. In silence, he tapped down a thick pinch of tobacco, then lit it using a long stick set aflame in the hearth, drawing in the fire until the tobacco shone with fine embers. "It was akin to a plague. Witches, as you well know, are distinct humans. To the eye, you are no different. But a witch's sensitivity to planar activity is pronounced. It's fair to say you have a sense that the rest of us lack—or to any useful degree, at least. Vision where the rest of us are blind, hearing where the rest of us are deaf."

He was right. "Yet one needn't be a witch to perform magic or sorcery," I offered.

"True. One can learn to navigate the world without eyesight. Memorize the layout of a dark house. Through memorization, through rote, through experimentation, through knowledge passed down—yes, I can do magic. That is the essence of the science of magic. But to a witch, such efforts must appear both laborious and unnatural."

He smoked in silence for a minute. I said nothing.

"It's this prime difference that led to their vulnerability," he finally said. "Their numbers were already small—for no love of witches came out of the dark centuries that Europe endured. Hated, feared, driven into their own communities, later driven out of those insular communities, driven into hiding, their numbers—they were already rare by nature—dwindled. More pertinent to us, I will contend that during the last decades of the sixteenth century and the first of the next, the remaining witches of Europe fell victim to a catastrophe that left normal humans untouched, one linked to a once-in-a-century sympathetic concordance of the planes. Measurements taken in Saxony at the time registered over six months of readings beyond the range of the most sensitive devices for tracking planar strength. And it was under such circumstance that one of the last groups of these set sail from England, under the guise of a community of Separatists, having arranged terms of passage and procuring a ship from Southampton, Hampshire."

"*The Westenshire Bell*," I said.

"Precisely." Rush returned to his chair and puffed at his pipe for several long moments. "Those unfortunate castaways were more vulnerable along the rocky shores of Salem than they'd been in England, sadly. They attempted to deal with the forces attacking them on their own as best they could. To all appearances, they weren't successful in their fight—although the colony was left with a strange assortment of relics. Cairns. Stones with carvings. Tombs. Dark wells, sealed shut. Each one a sealing of planar energies, the totality of which formed—and still forms—an intricate web of protections against the possibility of demonic incursion."

"Yet it's started failing," I said.

"Yes."

"What do you suspect?"

"Let's start with what I—and you—know, Miss Finch." He drew thoughtfully on his pipe. "And let's further categorize such evidence as we have into three distinct classes: the state and pattern of seals created, maintained, and then neglected by the last witches of Salem; our current understanding of the increase in planar activities, incursions, and energies throughout the eastern half of the colony; and, finally, such instances of the *Speculatum Somnium* that we have observed."

"You believe there's a connection," I said.

"Let's look at what the evidence tells us, and set conclusions aside for time being." He leaned forward. "The original work done to mitigate the deadly convergence of planes that peaked in the summer of 1654, as best I've been able to determine, involved somewhere between thirty-six and forty-two locations that appear to exhibit the signs of a planar seal. Often, these locations bear a construction that seems normal at first glance, but which upon further reflection is puzzling in some fashion or another. An old well, or cistern, boarded over, not near a home or lane. A length of stone wall, unconnected to any other. What appears to be part of a cellar, but which shows no sign of having ever had a dwelling atop it. The like, I'm sure you're familiar."

I nodded.

"And each of these spots possesses a corresponding feature related to the land itself—moving water, in many cases. Brooks, streams, rivers. Small groves of hemlock seem rather common. A dell, or a hillock. A spot between granite outcroppings. The edge of a marsh. Several near the shore. I've often wondered if these choices were made for reasons of landmarks, or if there was another rationale at work."

"The energy runs more powerfully in such spots, Doctor."

"Ah, I see. You've experienced this?"

I thought of the complex patterns of color and force I encountered around the seals I'd repaired and realized that I'd also noted such confluences of natural energy in other spots. "I have."

Rush shook his head ruefully. "I can only confess to the keenest jealousy, Miss Finch, having wondered my entire life what it must be like to see, to feel, to hear with senses I lack."

"Given what we've spoken of, Doctor—I'm not sure how desirable it all is."

"Nature is cruel. Yet beauty is beauty, and glory is glory, no matter how fleeting its existence, or how difficult a path it finds itself on." He pointed at me. "The gift you have is precious, Miss Finch. Secreted down through your forebears, given to you by, presumably, your mother—I believe the blood you possess to be a glimpse of the sacred. And trust me when I tell you I believe that were the world overrun by witches, it would be a better place for it. So enough of that dismissal. The witches I've observed from a distance were nothing if not noble."

The old gentleman only had but one kind of opinion: strong.

"So here we have it," Rush said. "A complex web of seals put in place to contain a planar convergence. And in time, the seals weakened. Connections opened again. Rumors once again took hold in tavern and distant village. And into this setting came—or perhaps was drawn—one August Swaine."

He stared at the fire for a moment.

"In Salem—in the very heart of this web of seals—your master begins introducing powerful magic and sorcery. Such work draws forth planar energy, and where the energies have built up pressures, leading to a cascading effect. Much like a dam giving way, where more water comes through, and the erosion quickens. The arrival of the *Speculatum Somnium* is no coincidence, I'm afraid, a consequence of such work, bringing with it a further degradation of the seals."

"My master is cautious."

"If he'd been in any way cautious, he'd have stayed well away from Salem in the first—but given the circumstances, we need not waste any time putting his character on trial. I well understand your loyalty toward him. He did what he did, and now we see the results. The measurements I've made are alarming. Spikes of energy that surpass even the highest classifications of Koeffler's Grand Scale of Planar Amplitude."

"I've repaired a few of the seals, though," I said.

"And perhaps that's been enough to hold catastrophe at bay

until now. You may have bought us enough time to prevent the worst of it from happening."

"Which is what?"

"Which is that an unstoppable tide of darkness bursts its bindings, leading to an event that makes the events of 1654 look gentle by comparison, this time with no witches to absorb the greatest blows. I fear that such a cataclysm would overwhelm my abilities to stop. The remaining practitioners of magic across the Atlantic would find themselves likewise bested. Those in the far corners of the globe, with no warnings or time, couldn't withstand such a flood. It's possible that such a collision of planes could render the entire world as uninhabitable as Salem itself once was. A demon-swept wasteland, from pole to pole."

The fire in the hearth snapped. For a moment, Doctor Rush, his features wound up in concentration, appeared to bear the weight of every one of his seventy-two years. Head stooped forward, gnarled fingers, gray hair.

"Then we have to stop it," I said. "It's not too late. I can repair the seals—I know what it takes. We'll just have to work around the other difficulties."

He met my eye. "Circumstances have conspired against us, indeed. Yet I think you have the right of it, Miss Finch. There's only one way forward—demons, Sackville's men, or not."

"Where do we start?"

"Your enthusiasm heartens me. Yet we need to be judicious in our efforts. I fear making the wrong decision would leave us with precious little time to backtrack. Above all else, I'm certain that we must put a halt to any further outlays of magic or sorcery, particularly in Salem."

"Which means my master." Surely Swaine would agree—wouldn't he? I chewed the corner of my lip.

"I shall speak with him directly," Rush said.

It was all too easy for me to picture Swaine growing defensive at the suggestion that he should cease his work, however valid the reasons—especially if it were coming from the doctor. "It might be best, sir," I said, "if I were to speak with him first. Not that he won't listen to you—it's just that his ability to, well... receive information can be a delicate matter at times."

"I see."

"And if he were to know that you and I had discussed this before he was aware—he might well see it as a betrayal on my part. If that makes sense, sir."

Rush leaned forward. "It makes perfect sense, and I shall rely on your insight into your master's temperament to guide us. But we don't have much time, I'm afraid. The growing incidents with demons tell me that the seals are failing at a more rapid pace than I'd feared."

I thought of Iris and her family. Of the governor's bedchamber. Of the threats the demon made against my friends. "I'll go to him straightaway, sir."

Rummaging through the papers on his workbench, Rush pulled out a piece of paper and dipped a quill. "Very good, Miss Finch. I shall concentrate my thoughts into a letter that you can present to him. The most pertinent—and convincing, I trust—facts alone ought to stir in August the same conclusion I've reached. It shall serve as an opening in a discussion that holds the key to averting a catastrophe. If we can't combine our efforts—magic, sorcery, and witchcraft—in the face of this threat, I'm not sure what else might succeed."

With that, he scratched out a missive in his neat handwriting. I watched the nib of his quill loop and whirl a trail of ink, wondering what Swaine would do.

A short while later, we stood at a pier stained black by the tides. A small skiff bobbed on the harbor swells. Next to the skiff, winds dragged sea spray, lifting my cloak into the air. Behind, the fort itself occupied a stretch of the leeward side of the island, dotted with a few gaunt trees.

"No shortcut through the planar eaves this time, sir?" I said. Rush's letter was tucked inside my coat pocket.

"A move made of desperation, I'm afraid." Rush puffed at his pipe, squinting as the wind blew the smoke back into his eyes. "The less we traverse the planes at this moment, the better, I should think. There's no telling who—or what—might observe such a passage. Can you handle a boat, Miss Finch?"

"Somewhat, sir."

I climbed down the weathered ladder, Rush offering me a hand as I made the transition to the boat. "Make for that point over there," he said, indicating the nearest stretch of shoreline. "You're not too far from where you said you left your horse. Don't worry about the boat. And good luck—August will surely see the gravity of the situation. We shall rendezvous tomorrow afternoon at the Bridges Inn in Reading."

I got myself settled. "Yes, sir."

"Our most difficult trials lie ahead, Miss Finch." He slipped the rope from the rusted hook.

Taking up the oars, I said, "They do—but we'll meet them, sir. With all we have." With that, I pushed off and got the oars digging into the waves. It wasn't easy, for I barely knew how to handle a boat. By the time the skiff rounded the tip of the island, Doctor Rush's figure growing smaller as he watched from the pier, my arms burned from the effort of forcing my way through the chop of the harbor. Rush raised a hand in farewell.

I stopped rowing for a moment, returning the gesture. The boat glided. Water dripped from the tips of the upended oars and the skiff sounded with the sigh of the prow passing through the waves. Beyond that, the distant surf rolled onto the island. The boat slowed, rising and falling on the swells. As Rush turned and headed back to his hideaway, I swung the oars back into the water and made my way toward Boston's shoreline, driven on by visions of a demon-swept wasteland.

27

THE VEILS OF INNOCENCE

orries. Fears. Secrets. They loom so large in the mind.

They darken the heart with their outsized shadows, grown over time and in silence into menacing, grotesque phantoms. So much so that one may be forgiven for believing the world itself is riven with darkness. Yet herein lies the power of speaking the truth: when such skeletons are dragged out into the daylight, one word at a time, one bone at a time, they often show themselves to be more shade than substance. A problem is still likely a problem. But a problem spoken is a problem brought down to size, sometimes going from vexing to solved in the speaking, other times from impossible to merely improbable. Even in such a case as the latter, there is blessed relief.

As I neared the manse in Salem, the better part of the afternoon behind me, I clung to the promise of just such relief—all the while bedeviled by the dozens of scenarios I could easily conjure in which Swaine would take it all so very, very poorly. Would his trust in me vanish forever? Would he throw me from the manse, tossing a few of my belongings out after me? Would he roar, moan, or howl disappointment? Or, worse, would he grow icy, his rage barely contained, his face gone pale, whispering for me to leave. I forced such vivid images out of my mind—he would react as he would react, and I would simply tell the truth. There was no other course.

Once I had the horse settled in the barn, I found Robert Twelves in the workshop, running a flat scraper along the sides of a board he was preparing for his next device.

"Is he awake?" I said.

"Aye. He's awake." He kept scraping, thin curls of maple rolling up from the edge to drop on the floor between his shoes. "And no admirer of my nursing skills. Banished me out here, if you must know. Not that I mind."

"How's his mood?"

"I don't think I lightened it. Didn't make the tea hot enough. Then I made it too hot. Apparently I can't butter a biscuit properly. I can't get the fire in his grate satisfactory. My footsteps are 'elephantine.' I forgot to wring out the cloth for his forehead. And a few more errors I'm happy to forget." He paused in his scraping. "Thank the Lord you're back, is all I have to say. You've got the touch with that one."

"I've heard worse from him. And more of it."

"And yet all I heard in his voice was disappointment when I told him, more than once, that you were still out running errands."

"Does he look any better?"

Twelves shrugged. "Color's back in his face and he's well enough to complain—so that's something. Did you get done what you needed to?"

"Some." I turned to the door. "I'd best get in there and see him."

"Best of luck. We can keep each other company when he banishes you out here." He resumed his work.

I crossed to the manse and paused at the door. I inhaled, straightened my back and threw back my shoulders, pushing my way inside. The door to Swaine's study stood open, but the room was empty. I hung my cloak and coat on the pegs by the entrance and made my way upstairs. From his bedchamber came the sound of pages turning. Leaning my head in, I found Swaine propped up on pillows on his bed, a lapful of books spread out before him. He wore his nightshirt and a dressing gown. Twelves had been right about his color—while not quite hale, he no longer had the pallor of one on the threshold of the next world. He glanced up at me.

"Ah, Finch—thank God." He left his finger marking the place in the book before him. "That man almost killed me, seemingly determined to make me as uncomfortable as possible in the process. Whatever sublime gifts he possesses in the world of material mechanics absolutely elude him when it comes to basic care of the unwilling infirm."

That sounded more like my master. "I'm sure he tried his best, sir."

"Let's not be too sure. A man who sweeps poorly may simply be a man who doesn't care to sweep, as they say."

"He was quite a help to me when you were ill, sir."

Swaine waved his hand. I noticed the *Occultatum Ostium* by his elbow. "Fine, irrelevant. You're here now. Listen to this." He turned back to the book in his lap. "Bostram again. *'Under the peculiar conditions engendered by the confluence of such realms as permeate the* Speculatum Somnium, *the question might arise: Could Time itself be subjected to influence of the collisional energies, bent and folded in on itself in such a manner as to be made a fundamental ingredient capable of integration into Magick of the highest order?'* The man had a razor-sharp mind, Finch. Think of it." He closed the book, tapping his fingers on the cover. "Harnessing even time itself, in endless supply. By tapping into the forces at play in the demonmere, themselves indicative of the planar collisions which generate such levels of energy, we might be able to remove so much tedium from incantations, spells, summonings. Rather than preamble after preamble, preparatory groundwork and spellcraft—we might get to the heart of the matter right away, essentially turning on a tap to inject the requisite energies. Including time. Think of it."

"Does Bostram indicate how to do this, sir?"

"No. He was much more a theoretician when it came to planar matters. Still, one must start with a theory. A vision. And there's something to this. I feel it."

I could tell he wasn't going to want to talk about anything else, his mind hot on the trail of a new insight, a bloodhound baying after the fresh scent.

"In fact," Swaine continued, "we've already seen evidence of temporal distortions, so we know we can influence the flow of time under certain conditions. The issue is of control. If there were a way to calibrate the flow of energies between the planes, drawing off such currents with some degree of precision—that's what we're looking for here."

I slipped a hand into my pocket, grasping the letter from Doctor Rush. "Sir, I—well." I pulled out the letter. "I have to tell you something."

He scanned the books on the bedcover, reaching for a slim volume near his knee. "What is it?"

"There's a problem, sir." How to even start? "A rather large problem—and I'm afraid some of it is my fault."

"Whatever are you talking about?"

I glanced up at the ceiling, then down at the letter in my hands. *Tell him everything.* Oh, how I wanted to. I'd told the tale more than once—just not to Swaine. *Throw yourself on his mercy. Let go of the burden.* Yet something held me back—something I couldn't explain in the moment, other than as a childish desire to hide my shame, to deflect some of the anger sure to come. Yet in hindsight, I believe a more subtle intuition took hold. Even though I mightn't have been able to put my finger on the source of my hesitation—I listened to it.

"Doctor Rush knows I'm a witch, sir," I said, making the decision to keep much of what I'd done secret from my master.

"You know this how?"

"Because he told me, sir. Directly."

"I suppose we should give the old gentleman credit. Charged with keeping the colony free from witches, it would be odd that he should overlook the first witch to walk these lands in decades. Yet I cannot help but note you're not clapped in irons. Tell me what happened."

Without pausing, I spun a tale of being confronted by the doctor while I was running errands, of learning of the governor's death, of the dispute between Rush and the incoming governor necessitating his going into hiding. I wove in a few reasonable-sounding denials of knowing precisely when Rush first discovered my presence. "He told me to give you this letter, sir," I finished.

As I'd spoken, Swaine had listened intently. He reached out and took the proffered letter. "He obviously knows more than he's let on to you, Finch. Which in all likelihood means he knows more about our work here."

"I'm sorry, sir."

"Nonsense. Nothing to apologize for. You're a witch. I'm surprised it took this long for him to realize it, frankly." He unfolded the letter and began reading it to himself. A frown appeared on his face. He glanced up at me, then continued reading. When he finished, he looked the letter over once more, then folded it, placing it atop his volume of Bostram. "Well, he was obviously using you to get to me."

"Sir?"

"He wants to meet. To discuss matters of extreme importance related to planar activity. Concerns about demons breaching into various locations around the colony—which is somewhat curious, now that he mentions it. Troubles with the new governor—and I shouldn't be at all surprised, given that Lionel Sackville is an ideologue of the worst sort. Craven, shameless, ignorant, as well. No fan of the doctor's, and certainly no fan of mine."

"Will you meet with him, sir?"

"As a fellow practitioner of the unseen arts, I fear I'm obliged to." Swaine ran a knuckle beneath his chin. "If there is a more cheerless word in the English language than *obligation*, I should strain to call it to mind, Finch. Effort explicitly stripped of reward —that is obligation. Expectation shorn of thanks, duty that eclipses protest, a requirement to be borne, irrespective of wish, preference, or enthusiasm. Deaf to argument, immune to recourse, obligation cuts through excuses like a scythe beheading daisies."

"He seemed quite earnest, sir."

"They always do." He rubbed his brow.

"And he is an expert on the planes."

"But is he truly? Has he delved as far as I have? Has he made the same leaps in insight? Is he willing to look at the situation with a dash of inventiveness? Of daring? Or—as I fear—is he going to barricade his mind behind stacks of books written by other timid magicians over the centuries?" His voice wasn't heated, but rather tired. Perhaps it was for the best that he was still recovering from his fever, in a place where his fiery pride had less dry tinder to ignite.

"I supposed it's worth hearing him out, sir."

"Yes, yes. How joyful."

He reread the letter. I'd certainly expected a more caustic reaction. Once more, I considered confessing everything to him —given his mood, it might be as good a time to do so as I might encounter.

Don't, the voice whispered in the front of my thoughts. *Just don't.*

Swaine put the letter aside. "Fine. Did he say when or where we might meet?"

"He mentioned a tavern in Reading, sir. Tomorrow."

"Wonderful. I can barely hold my head up enough to read."

"Shall I meet him there and postpone until you're feeling better?"

"No. With Sackville assuming the governorship, we haven't much time to delay before such travel becomes more risky. Soldiers out searching and whatnot." He looked heavenward. "Nothing is ever easy, is it? Oh what I'd give to be blessed to work in anonymous peace, once again. What we're doing requires intense concentration. Nothing less will do. All this distraction"—he motioned to the letter—"only serves to dilute such focus as I have."

"I'll do what I can to help, sir."

"Of course, thank you. Perhaps it's all for the best." He sat up, adjusting the pillows behind him. "Now, another few minutes of research, and then I should rest. Offer Doctor Rush my most clear-headed self. Blast this illness."

"Do you need anything, sir?"

"Peace of mind. A world happy to leave me to my work. Endless shelves of books and time to devour them all. The opening of mankind's mind around the globe. Barring any of that, a decent night's sleep will have to suffice. I'll see you at breakfast, Finch. Good night." He waved me off with a flick of his fingers.

"Good night, sir." I left the room, closing the door softly behind me.

There are moments in life when the veils of youth, unnoted and unsuspected, fall away, taking with them their shallow certainty and confidence. When the tales we tell ourselves prove little more than shadow plays of our own devising: the fleeting, mistaken for permanent; those individuals whose judgment we trust, revealed as just as flawed and bedeviled by doubt as we are.

Yes, Swaine was caustic in his frustration. Beyond exacting in the standards to which he held others. Temperamental, insensitive, dismissive, condescending, often fussy. Demanding to be coddled at all hours of the day. And yet he could just as frequently be witty, unreservedly generous, insightful, honest. He possessed the rare ability to instill confidence in the face of doubt. His lessons expanded horizons. His brilliance was unquestionable, his genius obvious.

But delusional? Wrong? His knowledge as overmatched by the unceasing swells of ignorance as the rest of us?

Unfathomable.

As I left him to his slumber, ready for him to help contain that maelstrom of the infernal we faced, I believed Swaine to be as in command of his future as anyone I'd ever be likely to meet.

How little I knew.

28

ALL MY SECRETS

I retired to my room soon after, exhausted. All I could do was think of poor Iris. When my heart ached at the memory, I consoled myself with the idea that everyone else I cared about was safe. Bertram. Grayson. Even Francis. Together, the three of them escaped the wrath of the demon. Whether they might escape the wrath of the colony's new governor was another matter, and one which I had no glamoured ring to provide them with—yet I suspected that Francis could see to it, if Grayson and Bertram could keep up with him.

After staring out into the darkness for some time, I turned from the window and got ready to sleep. A scratching sound came from the corner of the room. Annoyed that our efforts at keeping demons from the manse had been more successful than keeping mice from laying claim to the realm beneath the floorboards, I searched for the culprit. The sound came from behind a stack of books I'd been studying. Moving them aside, ready to reach for the broom leaning against my writing desk, I froze.

The spirit-tablet, stored away unused for months, bore a message in black ink, the nib and planchette tilted off to the side: *I've got Clara here now, and I'm going to kill her.*

As I watched, the paper tore from the tablet, careening around the room like a bat. On the sheet beneath, another message appeared, scratched out by the moving planchette: *It's fun playing with you, I'm disappointed you aren't a better player. You cheated with the others.*

With that, the planchette launched from the tablet at my face. I flinched, deflecting it with the back of my hand, where it left a stinging welt.

"No you're not," I whispered. I yanked open the small drawer on my writing desk and pulled out a small velvet bag containing the ring into which I'd bound Inverressayte. I took the stairs two and three at a time, racing to the front door. The revenants remained still, their eyes tracking my progress as I passed out into the night like a shadow.

Salem no longer crawled with its earlier infernal infestation, but it remained disquieting, particularly in the small hours. Naught but the faint sounds of wind and water filled the night. The heavens glittered and lent a gossamer tracing to the barn, the lane, the trees that lined the hillside. I sprinted. My shoes sent loose stones tumbling now and then, the loudest sound I heard. Two revenants stood watch at the end of the lane, both having been large men in life, now hulking, motionless statues in the faint starlight.

As I neared the dark bridge over the river, the sound of flowing water filled the night. Over the bridge, I passed an old well. A rotted pier. The tall meadow grass leeward of a slanting barn, blackened stones and the vestiges of burnt timbers half buried in the soil, hidden beneath decades of weeds and growth. As with much of the town, it bore faint traces of magic along with the residue of demonic presences. Running down the lane, I followed an uneven row of weathered gravestones, past the exposed doorway of a moldering house—until I reached the entrance to the demonmere. Leaning over, hands on my knees, I gulped in air.

"Inverressayte," I said, pulling the ring from the bag and clasping it in my hand. I reached for the bind of the demon. "I call you."

Mistress has missed me, I see. Oh, the trouble I might have saved you—but you chose instead to banish your humble servant, whose only desire is to spare you from the trials of—

"Quiet." I straightened up, sharpening my focus. "I need you to lead me to Clara. She's nearby."

Clara who?

"You know who I'm speaking of, Inverressayte." I felt the demon hiss in discomfort at the use of his name again. "I've spoken with her. She's in the demonmere—nearby."

Oh. Her. Hardly worth the effort, if you ask me, Mistress.

"I didn't ask you. I command you: lead me to her."

In there? You realize how dangerous that is for me, don't you? It's teeming with revolting brutes, any of whom would be pleased to crush your dearest servant. To turn and snap on me with jaws of venomous teeth. Moving through the darkest currents, hungry, hungry, hungry for a morsel like myself. There's no way I can do that—it would mean the death of me. And of you, frankly.

"I repeat: lead me to Clara. Now."

The demon paused. *Such a dire predicament. So much risk. I would normally do all I could for you, Mistress—but I can't do this. Unless, well—unless you'd be willing to consider one condition.*

"No conditions, Inverressayte—I'm your mistress."

The one who has her. He's impatient. And deadly.

I bent my will on the connection. "Now."

A thousand realms crisscross each other. It's so difficult to get anywhere at all. Maybe deadly for both of us—but I will do it, if you agree to release me.

"I'm not bargaining with you, Inverressayte."

Then I'm afraid I must suffer your punishment, Mistress. I cannot risk going in there. That poor waif is about to learn why. It's very sad.

"You know where she is?"

Precisely—but, as I said, I can't possibly cross that threshold. Horrifying, all of it.

I leaned into the connection, but the demon pushed back. Not without a cost, for I felt Inverressayte convulsing with pain—yet he remained stubbornly immobile. I relented. "Fine! But you must lead me to her and lead us back before I'll free you. Safely. Quickly. No games."

Let no one say there is a finer witch in this world or any other, Mistress—you will have my eternal gratitude.

"Just take me to her." I slid the rope around my waist and descended into the opening of the demonmere. A faint eldritch glow appeared in front of me, manifested by Inverressayte.

This way, Mistress. With that, the demon led me through a dizzying series of corridors and stairwells, veering quickly off any route Swaine and I had explored. The shifting nature of the demonmere played with scale and dimension, leading me to climb one set of stairs with runners only three inches wide, another down a long hallway tall enough to hide the ceiling well above in the shadows. Strange lanterns burned. Candelabras glimmered with pale flames. Narrow windows let fall slices of moonlight, hints of sunset. As I followed, I spooled out the glamoured rope behind me, unwilling to forgo the safety of finding my way back. The route grew familiar, picking up characteristics of Iris's tavern, of the Whitelocke crypt, of the governor's manse.

"You're leading us back once we find her," I said.

As long as you keep your promise, Mistress.

"You do know where she is, don't you?" I said, passing by a pair of ornate double doors.

Of course, Mistress—she's right down here. Nearby, indeed.

The corridor opened out on one side, and I looked out into an intricate library, stacked high with thousands—millions—of books. Spiral shelves, winding staircases and ladders on wheels, up and up it went, shadows and dim lanterns giving it the appearance of going on forever.

"Where is she?" I said, leaning on the carved railing over-looking the center of the library.

Down below.

There. I spotted Clara, a faint figure leaning with her back against a shelf of folios extending twenty yards overhead.

"How do we get down there?" I said.

Now for your end of the bargain, Mistress—free me.

"Not until we have her safe and you lead me back—I'll free you then."

You'll free me now, I'm sorry to say. Or you'll never reach her. And you'll never find your way back, Mistress—it looks like someone cut your rope.

I twisted, looking at the rope. It extended off into the shadowy corridor we'd come down. "No, it's fine."

Pull it.

I did—and to my horror, the end of it slithered along the floor, sliced clean through.

It seems you have little choice, Mistress. Forgive my bluntness, but you're done for if you don't do as I say.

"Find the rest of the rope, Inverressayte."

It's a little harder to control me in here, isn't it? He made no move to obey my command. My stomach clenched. *Oh, are we alarmed? Mistress, don't trouble yourself so. You've been kind to me, for the most part—though your lack of trust was often hurtful. I will keep my promise to you if you keep your promise to me. There's no need for anything but respect for the worrisome circumstances we each find ourselves in. And if we help each other this one time—why, we can go our separate ways with nothing more than a touch of fondness for our time together. Wouldn't you say?*

"Just do what you promise." I dropped the rope and closed my eye, the ring with Inverressayte resting in my damp palm. After a minute of long, slow breaths, I spoke the words to sunder the binding. As I did, I felt the connection grow tighter and tighter—and then I flinched. The sensation was as dreadful as it was unex-

pected as though I'd reached for a quill only to discover that my hand was missing. I reached into my mind, searching. Nothing. The binding was gone, leaving me with an unnerving mental abscess, an enclosure around a void. No Inverressayte.

"Now take me to her and get us out," I whispered.

Laughter filled the balcony. A hissing voice reflected all around me, no longer in my head, my thoughts. *"No, I don't think so. Honestly, I thought better of you—but you're a pitiful, puny mite. And now you're on your own—I'm not even going to kill you. I will enjoy your suffering, just the same."*

Shadows spun around me, the air frigid.

"And one word of advice—don't let them use you so easily again."

"You promised."

"I lied."

"Who used me?"

"Your master. His new master—an unsavory fiend, that one."

"What do you mean?"

"What do you think I mean? You saw him—not acting like himself, is he? Because he isn't. It's too late for him. You can't pry the thorns loose without taking his sanity with him."

"Are you—are you saying he's possessed?"

"Don't play with our kind, witch—it never ends well. The one who has him—he's not nice, not at all. And his *master is even worse."* His voice grew more distant. *"Don't think I'll ever forget how you imprisoned me, witch. I will* have my revenge. *Until that day, don't trust any shadow, any creak in the night, any stray draught—for I'll be in one of them one day, when you least expect it. That's a promise I intend to keep. Farewell, witch—for now."*

With that, Inverressayte fled. I turned, extending my witchcraft in all directions, terrified and flustered—but I didn't sense him anywhere. I spun this way and that, trying to keep panic from sweeping me away. I turned back to the library, searching the dim spaces between the enormous stacks. With my hands on the railing, I called out for Clara. She disappeared behind a tall row of shelves, book spines of all colors and sizes lining the warped length.

"Wait!" I cried out.

I climbed over the railing, at the edge. Taking hold of wooden shelves, I used them to climb down. By the time I reached the floor, my arms shook from the strain. Not pausing, I sprinted off after Clara. The floor tilted in places. Scraps of paper littered the corners. Teakettles and cups decorated various writing desks. Coming around a corner, I spotted Clara moving into what appeared to be the center of the vast library, a massive domed ceiling extending high overhead. A thousand candles winked and fluttered.

Beneath the dome, a marble floor inlaid with brass glinted in the light. Clara ran into the center of the inlays, an elaborate circular pattern resembling a stylized glamour—and she paused.

"Clara—wait!" I yelled. "Don't run."

I followed her to the center of the floor. She stopped, and turned to face me, a frightened look on her face—and then she vanished. I stumbled. A low rumble shook the floor beneath me and powerful planar energy filled the space. Where Clara had vanished a low column with a flat top stood. On that was a book. I approached it with my pulse galloping. A thick tome, it was closed. Embossed on the cover were words that stopped my breath:

IN, OUT—IT'S A THOUGHTLESS WAY TO THINK

The demon from the infernal vox expander. He'd won. He'd trapped me in the demonmere, on my own, nothing to lead me out.

I reached for the book, but as my fingers were about to touch it, it disappeared, winking out, leaving the column barren. For a moment, nothing happened—until the floor shifted, bucking and turning. I lost my balance. A huge dark energy filled the space. Books tumbled off shelves. The candles overhead shimmied, swinging back and forth.

"Clara!" I yelled. "Where are you?"

"Miss Finch?" A thin voice, high and frightened, came from a space to my left. I rushed over, barely keeping my legs beneath me as though I were on the deck of a ship being tossed by a ferocious Atlantic storm. As I got closer, I spotted a small figure huddled by an intersection of three doorways. In the space around the doors were chests, filled with letters. Coffins. Ravens of stone. Gears. Planar clocks. Maps. More books.

All my secrets.

I pushed past them. When I reached Clara, she looked up at me with a tear-streaked face, pale and stamped with terror—and she appeared to be only ten years old. It was her, all the features hers, but younger. Her clothes—the same ones as I'd last seen her wearing—hung from her like tents, twice as big as she needed.

"Clara?"

She leaped to her feet and threw her hands around my neck, holding on to me with fierce relief. "I'm so scared—thank you, thank you, thank you!"

"What—what happened to you?"

"I don't know," she said, not letting go. "I've been lost and frightened and I only want to get out of here. Please. Get me out, Miss Finch. Don't leave me, don't leave me alone again. Take me home. Please."

"We're going," I said. I took her by the hand. Her grip was iron on my fingers. The library was falling down around us, so I ran with Clara to the sets of doors. Which ones would lead us out? We had to be close to where I'd come in, to the areas of the demonmere that responded to the magic and witchcraft I'd done —I felt it, since it was all my secrets, all about. Where the side of the library met a tall wall, three tall sets of doors stood closed: one of dark wood with iron hinges, one of a rich cherry with no hinges visible, a third of stone.

Which one?

"I need my hand," I said, pulling myself free from Clara's grip.

She clung to my waist instead. Without pause, I extended my witchcraft to the doors, letting it flow and explore the leftmost doorway. As soon as my witchcraft connected, bursts of energy ignited on the floor and walls around us, running over the surfaces like pale lightning, crackling and hissing. Strange patterns appeared in the floor and on the walls—symbols unknown to me. Behind us, the library broke apart, huge slabs of the floor separating, some lifting, others dropping out of sight. It was as if the giant room came alive, abandoning one form to assume another. I watched as new walls appeared, as balconies disappeared, stairs rose from nothing, iron railings racing up into darkness. Shelves folded and vanished, books and tomes transformed into slabs of wood, curving around into the walls of spires. Folios became slate shingles. Ladders became windows.

The floor where we stood shifted, knocking us sideways. Before us, the middle set of doors opened, pried apart by my witchcraft.

"Come!" I yelled, dragging Clara by her wrist through the opening. Planar energy gusted around us, grabbing at our clothes. I felt the nearing presence of demons. "This way."

The corridor beyond the doors was narrow, the ceiling high. As we pounded down across the flagstone floor, the doorway collapsed behind us. A demon rose in front of us, a hulking collection of shadowy scraps—but I yelled Hume's Seventh Ward and watched as it hurtled off, howling in frustration. I pushed my witchcraft to encircle us, even as more demons swarmed in after us. The corridor sloped upward. As I hurried Clara along, I glanced back, only to see the flagstones dropping away into emptiness, the chasm speeding toward us, faster than we could run. At the top, a smaller door stood propped open. I crashed through it, stumbling into a room that looked familiar: a low hearth, tumbled chairs in the corner, their bannister backs cracked and broken.

The Rivers house before it collapsed. Wind chattered around

the eaves, through the missing windows. Cobwebs hung from a warped joist overhead.

I spun, keeping Clara behind me. A vile demon—body segmented like an insect, a dozen appendages covered in barbs—leaped from the doorway. With a yell, I countered with a massive burst of witchcraft, adapted in some fashion from a ward. The demon tore apart, limbs clunking on the floor and walls. Clara yelled, covering her eyes with her hands. I led her to the front entryway, past the spot where Swaine and I had long ago placed the first planar clock. Rumbling filled my ears, along with the curious sounds of material changing from wood to stone, or stone to iron, form and function shifting as the demonmere warped. Strange energies battered us as we struggled to reach the door to the outside. I saw the door itself blow off.

Reaching it, I stopped, holding Clara from falling. Salem extended around us, the ground receding confusingly. It took a moment before I realized we were rising into the air, lifted by the rooms of the Rivers house. Five feet, eight feet.

I wrapped my arms around Clara. "Hold on," I whispered. I jumped from the demonmere, out into the night. We hit the turf hard, both of us grunting. For several moments, the rumbling continued, the ground shaking—and then silence descended and the motion stilled.

"Are you all right?" I said, getting to my hands and knees.

Clara looked up at me, eyes wide, face streaked with tears. She nodded. "Are we out?"

The air smelled fresh, the familiar tinge of the harbor to it. The grass, the earth beneath us, the wind—it was Salem. "I think so."

I looked behind us. Instead of the ruins of the Rivers house, a massive building stood, scribed in shadows and moonlight, blocking out the stars behind it. The wide first floor comprising eight walls of equal length, creating an octagonal base that spanned seventy-five feet at the farthest spots. Narrow windows rose along each wall in pairs, staring blankly out into the night. The second story held four sizeable gables, aligned east, west, north, and south, and larger windows. Atop was the final floor, a circular observatory beneath a dome, with a tall iron spire reaching to the heavens extending from the dome.

I'd only seen it in sketches and plans from the mind of August Swaine and the hand of Robert Twelves.

The sorcerium.

I got to my feet, still clasping Clara's hand.

How was the sorcerium there in front of me, seeming to have risen straight from the demonmere? What had dragged it into existence?

The night around us came alive with spires of intricate magic —the magnificent edifices of witchcraft that marked the lasting handiwork of those who'd survived the ruin of Salem. Brilliant colors sprung from the ground, forming arches, columns, buttresses woven together of finer and finer strands of energy. Ribbons of marigold, of garnet, of cardinal, of flint, of seashell. And where it met the sorcerium, the energies faded and grew dim. Waves of energy crested through the earth, only hinting at their hidden bulk below. Knotted tangles of ember-red strands coiled like vines. Here and there I spotted a lone thread unwind from a larger channel of force. More frayed witchcraft surrounded the edges of the sorcerium.

I stared at the towering building, stunned. As I let my eye take in the complexities of form and magic, my suspicion seemed increasingly correct: a collision of planes, an unexpected tangling of this world and another.

The witches—my distant kin—had built all the energies that rose before me to seal out these planar intrusions, to stitch shut the openings that gaped into unseen planes. I stared at the frayed energy. The sorcerium—the demonmere—had pushed right through the seals, torn them, split them.

I helped Clara to her feet. "You're safe," I whispered. That much was true if only for the moment. "Come—I'll get you away from here. You don't have to worry. I'll keep you safe. We'll find friends."

I led the trembling girl by the hand, away from the strange new building in the heart of Salem. Moonlight glinted off the many windows of the sorcerium. As I comforted Clara, I glanced back over my shoulder toward the manse. A lone light burned, a solitary dab of yellow in the darkness.

Swaine's room.

Is Finch out of time?

This is Finch's finest hour.

Get The Halls of Midnight today!

A WORD FROM KEVAN

Thank you for reading *The Grave Raven*—you're amazing! Finch would approve. I hope you had fun keeping up with her knack for staying one step ahead of mayhem. *Mostly* one step ahead...

Keep up to date on my upcoming books, novellas, and exclusives by joining my private newsletter.

As a welcome, I'll send you a free ebook of *Sorcery of the Stony Heart* (the prequel novella to *The Books of Conjury*), along with *A Spark of Will: The Trans-Atlantic Diary of August Swaine*, an exclusive novelette you can't get anywhere else.

It's easy, just sign up here: **Join Newsletter**

ALSO BY KEVAN DALE

The Books of Conjury Series:

The Magic of Unkindness

The Halls of Midnight

Sorcery of the Stony Heart

The Books of Conjury: The Complete Trilogy

Horror:

Revolutionary Dead

The Devil's Key

Ghost at Dusk

Horror Box Set:

The Demons of New England: A Horror Collection

Find out more at www.kevandale.com